RESPLENDENT

NOËLLE ALEXANDRIA

VANCOUVER INDEPENDENT PUBLISHING

Deluxe Color Hardcover: 978-1-998587-27-8
Standard Hardcover: 978-1-998587-18-6
Deluxe Color Paperback: 978-1-998587-24-7
Standard Paperback: 978-1-998587-30-8
eBook: 978-1-998587-19-3

Library of Congress Control Number:
TBA

Characters and events in this book are fictitious. Any similarity to real persons, living or dead, is coincidental and not intended by the author.

Book design and interior art by Noëlle Alexandria
Editing by Jennifer Long
Cover art by Noëlle Alexandria and Kira Hagen
Cover text by Noëlle Alexandria and Fancy Roberts

This book was made and designed without AI.

Printed and bound in the United States of America

Published by Vancouver Independent Publishing
304 SE Hearthwood Blvd, 872646
Vancouver, Washington 98684
www.VancouverIndependentPublishing.com

Resplendent **is a stand-alone** in the same universe as the House of Sacraments series, six years before the first book, *Benediction.* However, this book spoils nothing in that series, nor does that series spoil this book.

For a list of content warnings,
please see the last page in this book.

I want to thank Alexis M. and Tamara B. for the parts they played in helping this book come to life. *Resplendent* started as a half-crazed idea late one night, just one of those sparks you think will burn out by morning.

But Alexis was all in from the beginning, reading the rough draft literally as I was writing it, chapter by chapter, or even part of a chapter at a time. Her encouragement kept me going when I wasn't sure there was even a full story to be told. To date, she is the *only* person who has read a draft so raw that I did not even reread over before sending them. I just typed and sent. Getting that kind of in the actual moment feedback was just so so helpful, and I am so grateful. (And, Alexis, we've still got to bring your story to life. I won't be forgetting that!)

Months later, Tamara came in with a sharp eye and fresh perspective, helping make sure none of the twists gave themselves away too early. In a story like this, where the "who" matters just as much as the "why," that kind of input is invaluable.

I may have run out of steam without them, and am very, very thankful for their time and dedication!

And I must thank Kira Hagen and Fancy Roberts for their roles. I was close to throwing the towel in since I just did not feel good about the original cover. It felt too lighthearted for the gravity of the things in this book. But I have also not used stock images before. So that was a new thing for me. Kira's expert input and help quite literally saved this book from the scrap heap. Then Fancy came along and helped with the back cover text. To an author, everything on a story seems too important to leave out. So sometimes we say more than we need to rather than focusing on the absolute core of the story, and Fancy helped me do that. Both of them are also authors and I encourage you to check out their work.

And as always, thank you to my dear friend and editor, Jennifer Long. I will be lost in more ways than one without her.

PROLOGUE

Fall 1925, just outside New York City...

The brass key turned in the lock of room 412. He strode into the emptiness of the hotel room one final time, moving at a brisk pace, checking drawers that were already empty, scanning surfaces that held nothing of importance. The business conference had ended as anticipated. Just a bunch of tedious presentations on market trends and industry developments, dinners attended by men thinking too favorably of themselves, and enough professional glad-handing to satisfy his suppliers for another year.

His leather satchel snapped shut. Three days of pretending to care about quarterly projections and supply chain innovations, three days of nodding along to colleagues who believed they were building something meaningful when they all created temporary beauty that was intended to die soon. The irony wasn't lost on him.

The promise of four hours of driving on rutted country roads, leading away from the city's suffocating crowds and toward something far more satisfying, awaited him. But first, a stop at his luxurious apartment to grab a handful of books, some personal effects, and a change or two of clothes. Everything else could wait.

1

His cabin called to him with its isolation and its perfect distance from prying eyes and moral judgments.

He gripped the steering wheel of the black Ford while the urban sprawl gave way to farmland, then to the dense woods that would hide what he really was. The road narrowed with each passing mile, civilization falling away like shed skin. Wooden fences grew sparse, then disappeared entirely. The last farmhouse sat dark and abandoned, its windows staring blindly across overgrown fields. It was perfect. He'd counted on people fleeing to the cities, leaving behind only emptiness and decay. He always got what he wanted, one way or another.

The sedan climbed steadily into the hills, tires crunching over dirt and rocks that hadn't seen another vehicle in weeks. The forest pressed close on both sides, pine branches scraping the car's roof like gnarled fingers. Most people found these woods oppressive, even threatening. They just couldn't appreciate the honesty of a place where pretense held no value, a place where nature stripped away all the comfortable lies of polite society.

The cabin appeared among the pines like something from a fairy tale... at least, if fairy tales told the truth about what happened in remote places where no one could hear you scream.

He sat for a minute in the driver's seat, breathing in the forest's tranquility. No neighbors for miles. No telephones. No possibility of unexpected visitors or unwelcome interruptions. Just him, the woods, and the greatest solitude that money could buy. The previous owner had sold it eagerly, spooked by the isolation and what he'd called "bad energy."

Superstitious fool. Energy came from what you made of it.

Inside, the familiar scents of wood smoke and pine sap welcomed him. He hummed to himself while he moved around the rooms, checking windows, testing locks, ensuring everything remained secure. The basement door stood closed, its heavy oak frame fitted with hardware that would have suited a medieval castle.

Some investments required proper storage.

The kitchen held simple, but functional items: cast iron pans hanging from wooden pegs, shelves lined with preserved goods, a wood-burning stove that heated the entire cabin. He filled the percolator with water from the pump, then measured coffee grounds with the same precision he applied to everything else in his life.

While the coffee brewed, he settled into the leather chair by the window and opened one of the novels he'd grabbed from his apartment. It had been pitched as a mystery, but was actually some romantic drivel about star-crossed lovers and noble sacrifices. The protagonist declared his undying devotion to a woman who'd apparently captured his affection with little more than batting her eyelashes and looking vulnerable. What a waste of perfectly good paper. Love consisted of nothing more than chemical reactions and evolutionary programming, dressed up in poetry by fools who couldn't accept the truth of human nature. The hero's grand gestures and flowery speeches amounted to elaborate mating displays, no different from a peacock's tail or a rooster's crow.

The percolator bubbled on the stove, filling the cabin with a rich coffee aroma. He closed the book with a disgusted shake of his head and poured himself a cup, savoring the bitter warmth. He heard a chain drag over stone. Ah. His investment had awakened. Good. Consciousness made the lessons more effective.

He poured a second cup of coffee, considering the economics of the situation. Every day increased the overhead, but some projects required patience and extended instruction, time for the subject to fully appreciate the generosity of their circumstances and the opportunities he so willingly offered. While most people lived such narrow, purposeless lives, trapped by convention, and limited by their own timidity, he provided them with structure, direction, and the chance to become something greater than they'd ever imagined possible.

He peeked out the window. The forest was darkening as evening approached. The nearest neighbor lived fifteen miles down the road, and the old logging road that led here had washed out during the spring rains. Perfect isolation for the sort of education that required privacy.

The basement stairs waited in the gathering dusk, and somewhere below, his investment learned the true value of the

3

guidance he so willingly offered.

Some lessons just took time to appreciate.

She looked up when he entered, though the movement seemed to cost her considerable effort. Lily had grown thin in the weeks since he'd brought her here, her once-full cheeks now hollow, her dress hanging loose on a frame that had shed too much weight. The iron shackle around her ankle had rubbed the skin raw despite the cloth padding he'd given her.

"Coffee," he said, setting one cup near her. "You ought to keep your strength up."

She followed his movements with the wariness of a trapped animal. "Are you going to let me go today?"

She asked without hope, as if it were a ritual they'd performed so many times it had lost all meaning. He settled into the wooden chair he'd positioned just out of her reach, sipping his coffee and studying her.

"Are you going to try to escape again?" he asked in return.

"No."

The lie came easily to her. They both knew it for what it was.

He nodded anyway. "I could have made your dreams come true, you know. Everything you said you wanted that night at the party, about travel, adventure, a life free from your father's expectations... I could have given you all of it."

"My dream now is just to go home." Her tone was barely above a murmur, all the fight drained out of it.

"Ah, but that's where things have gotten complicated." He took another sip of coffee, savoring both the bitter taste and the way her shoulders tensed. "The price has gone up."

"What price?"

"The price of your discretion. Your cooperation." He set down his cup and leaned forward. "The price of letting you live."

The basement fell quiet except for the drip of water somewhere in the gloom beyond the circle of lamplight. Above them, the cabin settled into its foundations with small creaks and sighs, a house promising to keep its secrets.

"You see, Lily," he continued, as though he were discussing something as mundane as the weather, "you've become quite an investment. And investments are required to pay dividends. You understand now, don't you? How this works? The mathematics of it?" He paused, seemingly curious about her answer. "When someone keeps refusing reasonable requests, in time those requests become... less reasonable."

Lily's lips moved soundlessly, her pallor paper-white.

"But don't worry. I've always been patient. I believe in taking my time with important projects." His grin returned, cold and calculating. "After all, the longer someone makes you wait, the longer you have to plan exactly how they'll pay."

CHAPTER 1

May 1927, New York City...

Blood seeped through the edges of the letter. Sarah's fingers trembled as she unfolded it, the paper crackling under her touch. The ink had smeared into jagged scrawls.

Outside, shadows gathered in the alley. Footsteps clattered against slick cobblestones, closing in like a predator's jaws. *Too close.* Her heart slammed against her ribs. Raw, guttural screams tore through the night, followed by the deafening crack of a warning shot that splintered the air. Sarah spun, her breath hitching, eyes darting to the alley's mouth.

A shadow loomed. Before she could scream, a calloused hand clamped over her mouth, stifling her voice into a choked whimper. His other arm wound around her torso, crushing her until her lungs burned. The killer's breath, rancid and scalding, slithered against her ear.

"You shouldn't have run," he hissed.

Her vision frayed. Her body tensed as terror sank its claws into her soul. The world tilted.

A violent thud shattered the scene.

Footsteps pounded down the hallway outside Serafina's cramped apartment, yanking her from the blood-soaked alley of her new story.

Her hands hovered over the typewriter. Serafina's pulse thundered in her ears, her breath ragged, as if she'd been the one running from the killer's grasp. The footsteps outside faded, swallowed by the hum of the city, but the chill of her own words refused to let go.

She couldn't shake it.

Reality settled over her. Outside, the city stirred to life. A trolley clattered by. A street vendor called out his wares. She rubbed her burning eyes, feeling the strain of another sleepless night. Her coffee sat beside her, long gone cold. She reached over and patted the growing stack of manuscript pages next to her typewriter. Three months of work, nearly finished. If only she could find the courage to send it somewhere.

Serafina moved through her morning routine on instinct: splashing water on her face, pulling on a faded blue dress, pulling her honey waves back with a matching ribbon. It was all as automatic as breathing, and every morning was the same.

By the time she stepped outside, New York buzzed with activity. The scent of fresh bread curled from Mrs. Moreau's bakery, mingling with the damp earthiness of rain on pavement. Newspaper boys barked headlines. Cars honked. Pedestrians bustled past. She moved within it all like a spectator in her own life, watching others live while she remained firmly on the outside.

She sometimes considered being bolder like taking a different route to work, striking up conversations with strangers, or even saying yes to the florist's invitation to have coffee. But the idea of change, of anything that might tether her in place, made her hesitate. She craved adventure but feared what it might cost her.

As she neared the bookshop, Danny stood outside his flower shop, idly twisting a bit of twine. With his sandy hair catching the sun, his sharp jawline, rich brown eyes, and lazy grin, she could see why other women lingered near his shop, giggling over bouquets they didn't need.

She wished she could feel some sort of attraction to him too. It would be so simple.

He looked at her as she approached, straightening a little. "Good morning, Serafina." His pleasant voice carried the same careful hope it always did.

She offered a polite smile. "Good morning, Danny."

He hesitated, but she knew what was coming before he spoke.

"Would you like to get coffee with me sometime?"

Sometime. Never today. Never now. As though leaving it open-ended might make it easier.

Serafina took a breath. "I'm sorry, but I'm really not interested in anything romantic right now. I still don't know whether I ever will be."

The words came out firmer than usual, surprising them both. Danny's fingers stilled on the twine.

"I see," he said in a low tone. "That's... direct."

"You deserve honesty." She felt a pang of guilt at the wounded look in his eyes.

Danny nodded, but his jaw tightened. "I appreciate that."

She bowed her head, then slipped inside the bookshop before the conversation could continue.

The scent of ink and paper greeted her the instant she crossed the threshold and the city's chaos dulled to a hush. Dust motes floated in slants of morning sunlight, and the quiet settled into her bones. Here, in this small world of shelves and stories, she could breathe. Here, she could hide.

Whiskers, the shop's resident tabby, slunk around her ankles. She crouched to scratch his head, his purring a low rumble, then dumped her bag behind the counter and started her day. As she dusted a shelf, she let herself imagine the stories housed within these walls. Did they whisper to each other in the dark? Did the tragedies bleed ink onto the wood? Stupid thoughts, but they were better than facing the emptiness of her own life.

She grabbed a novel from the display, fingers tracing the embossed cover. Inside those pages, someone's heart raced. Someone chased secrets through rain-soaked streets, fell in love, or fought for their life. Serafina cracked it open, letting the words pull her under, away from the monotony of her existence.

The bell above the door jangled, barely pulling her eyes from the page. Clara Randolph burst in, her bright red dress too bright for the shop's muted tones, her blonde curls pinned with precision. She always looked like she belonged somewhere better and grander than this small corner of New York.

"Good morning, darling!" Clara's voice sliced through the peaceful shop like the first notes of a song. She collapsed onto the worn armchair facing Serafina, exhaling in exaggerated relief.

"Rough start?" Serafina asked, closing the book.

Clara's head lolled back. "Mom dragged me to breakfast with some insufferable woman who wouldn't shut up about her son. 'He owns land, Clara,'" she mocked, voice nasal before wiggling her fingers. "As if I care about his stupid horses or where they sleep. Or his mustache! It's like a scrub brush."

Serafina watched her friend for a moment. Clara's leg bounced, her casual sprawl too tense. "What's really going on?"

Clara bit her lip, hesitating. "There's a ball Saturday. I'm stuck going."

"Of course you are."

Clara leaned forward, hands clasped like she was pleading. "Come with me. Please."

Serafina stiffened. "You know I don't do that."

"Don't say no yet." Clara's voice turned urgent. "We'll go shopping, get you a dress—you'd look incredible, I swear. And... Richard Kensington from Kensington Publishing will be there. He's hunting for manuscripts. Mystery, intrigue—your novel's perfect. Meeting him in person could get your work noticed, not just lost in a slush pile."

Serafina's breath caught. Her dream, the one she barely let herself touch, dangled so close she could almost grab it. If she went, if she met him, if he read her work... it could change everything. But the thought of a ballroom, all those eyes, all that noise..."I don't belong in places like that."

Clara's face softened. "You belong with me."

Serafina's throat tightened. Clara had been dragging herself to these events for years, playing the part of the happy socialite despite the accident that stole her fiancé and her future. She smiled, danced, and hid her grief behind perfect curls and bright dresses. Serafina owed her this, didn't she?

"Fine," she said, voice barely above a whisper. "I'll go."

Clara's face lit up. "You won't regret it!"

"I already do."

"It'll be an experience," Clara said, grinning.

"That's what I'm afraid of."

Clara laughed, settling back.

Serafina rolled her eyes. "If you're staying, make yourself useful and help me with this display."

"I hope you're not tossing out Gatsby again," Clara said, smirking.

They spent the morning sorting books. Clara stayed through the trickle of customers. Her chatter was a welcome distraction. She so loved pretending she had a paying job, though her father would never allow it. Poor dear, just wanting to feel useful somehow. By noon, she left for another social obligation, leaving Serafina alone with the silence.

The afternoon dragged, the shop empty until the bell jangled again. The air shifted. Serafina's skin prickled as she looked up.

Two men stood in the doorway. The first was handsome, tall and broad. His suit had been tailored so perfectly that it seemed to have been sewn onto a frame built for breaking things. His dark eyes scanned the shop with a predator's focus, like he was hunting. The second, older, with gray at his temples, lingered behind, his face unreadable but tense.

Her grip tightened on the book in her hands. Something about them felt... off. Too sharp for her sleepy bookshop wedged between a bakery and Danny's flowers.

The taller man's gaze locked onto hers. "I need a book," he said with a clipped Italian accent. "Machiavelli's *Discourses on Livy*. Ricci translation."

Even as he spoke, his shoulders held a fraction too much stiffness. His fingers curled into his palm like he was keeping something in check.

"Of course." Serafina turned to the shelves, her pulse ticking faster. The obscure political memoir wasn't exactly a bestseller. It was more the kind of thing men of influence bought to sound more important.

As she searched, their low voices drifted to her in Italian.

"*Sì, suo marito lo sa,*" the older man murmured. *Yes, her husband knows.*

The younger one, voice taut: "*Come? Ero attento.*"

"*Wrong. You weren't careful enough,*" the older man snapped. "*He'll kill whoever he thinks fucked his wife.*"

Serafina's hand froze on the book's spine. Her Italian was fluent. So she understood every word. An affair. A vengeful husband. A death threat. Her heart thudded, but she kept her face neutral as she pulled the book free.

The younger man's voice shifted, louder now, aimed at her. "Do you usually carry much poetry in Italian?"

She flinched, turning to meet his stare. "Not much," she said, steadying her voice. "Mostly just the classics, like Dante and Petrarch."

Disappointment flashed across his face.

A man who reads love poetry while someone wants to kill him. Fascinating.

"Thank you," he said, holding out exact payment as though he'd known the price in advance.

"You're welcome." Her voice was soft, but her skin burned where their fingers brushed. Not flirtation, not charm... just a fleeting, electric intensity that left her unsteady.

The older man cleared his throat, and they were gone, the door swinging shut with a dull thud. Serafina stared at the empty street, her pulse refusing to slow. He hadn't smiled, hadn't lingered, but something about him clung to her, sharp and unsettling, like the first line of a story she didn't know how to write.

That evening, Serafina sat at her typewriter, fingers poised over the keys, but the words refused to come. Every time she tried to focus on Sarah's escape, her thoughts wandered to the way a simple touch could make her blood race, to hushed conversations about death threats and Italian poetry.

She found herself typing fragments that had nothing to do with her new novel.

His fingers were warm against hers, calloused but gentle. She wondered what those hands might feel like.

She stopped, heat flooding her cheeks. This wasn't what she usually wrote.

She pushed away from her desk, frustration tightening her chest, and began to pace around her apartment. Worry about the ball disrupted her thoughts. *It's just one night*, she reminded herself. *One evening of polite conversation, suffocating fabrics, and trying not to trip over my own feet.*

And yet, her stomach churned.

What if she made a fool of herself? What if she fumbled her words in front of the publisher? What if Clara needed her, really needed her, and she failed?

Serafina let out a slow sigh and sat on the edge of her bed, running her hands down her skirt. An idea crept in...

She could cancel. Yes, cancel and stay home to sink into her writing. Or maybe go out, find a dimly lit speakeasy, and drink something that burn all the way down.

But then she saw Clara's face in her mind, that hopeful, earnest look when she had asked her to come.

Serafina sighed and flopped down onto the pillows.

What's the worst that could happen?

A disaster? Fine. At least it would be something to tell her characters, who seemed closer to being friends than most real people did. A complete humiliation? Nobody at that ball would remember her name. If she was doomed to misery, she might as well embrace the mess.

Two days later, Serafina stood in Clara's bedroom, staring at a stranger in the full-length mirror. The sapphire gown clung to her like a second skin, its beads glinting in the low lamplight. The neckline dipped too low, exposing the sharp line of her collarbone, and she tugged at it, willing it to cover more. Her curls had been pinned to frame her best features.

Behind her, Clara fussed with her own gown, pale champagne silk that shimmered like it belonged in this world. She caught Serafina's eye in the mirror and reached over, nudging a stray curl into place. "There. Perfect."

"I could still fake an illness."

Clara rolled her eyes. "If you were going to fake being sick, you should've done it before I spent a fortune on that gown."

Serafina forced a laugh, but her stomach churned. "Clara, something strange happened at the shop on Thursday."

"Oh?"

"This man came in. He was so sophisticated, and wearing a very expensive suit." Serafina kept her words casual, not mentioning the conversation she'd overheard about death threats. "He asked about Italian poetry. I wouldn't have expected that from someone who was so intimidating."

"Intimidating how? Handsomely intimidating?"

Heat crept up Serafina's neck. "He was striking. Dark hair, deep eyes."

"And Italian poetry? That's practically a love letter." Clara lit up. "He sounds like exactly the type who'd be at tonight's ball."

"You think so?"

"Oh, definitely. If he's there tonight, you'll have to introduce us!" Clara's expression became mischievous. "Unless you'd rather keep the mysterious poetry lover to yourself?"

Serafina's stomach fluttered at the notion. "It was nothing. Just a customer."

"The best stories start that way."

Serafina took one last breath, squared her shoulders, and moved away from the mirror. "I suppose there's no turning back now."

The halls of the Randolph estate were nearly empty when they made their way downstairs, only the quiet voices of the remaining staff. The rest of the Randolphs were already at the ball, leaving them to their own peaceful descent.

Then, far too soon, they arrived.

The ballroom's grand façade rose before them, light spilling from tall windows, jazz music floating into the night air. Everything smelled of fresh flowers and perfume.

The driver opened the door, and Clara stepped out with her usual flourish. Serafina followed, her legs leaden, fighting the urge to run. Clara hooked an arm through hers.

"You've got this, darling," Clara said.

Inside, chandeliers glared overhead, their light bouncing off polished floors and glittering gowns. Couples spun across the dance floor while clusters of guests sipped champagne, their laughter sharp and hollow. Serafina's grip tightened on her clutch, her pulse thudding. She didn't belong here in this sea of silk and wealth. Clara moved like she was born for it, her gown catching the light, her smile effortless despite the grief she carried. This was her world, even if she had never loved it.

Serafina stayed close, unsure where to place herself in the flurry of conversation and passing glances. Her grip tightened on her beaded clutch. Her heart drummed. She had to keep her wits about her. Somewhere in this room was Richard Kensington, the man who could change her life with a nod. And somewhere in the recesses of her mind, she wondered if she might see that tall Italian figure in an expensive suit, dark hair, and darker eyes.

Two young men approached, their attention split between her and Clara.

"May I have a dance?" one asked, addressing Serafina.

Panic coiled tight in her stomach.

"I'd rather not, but thank you," she said at once, offering a small, forced smile.

The man hesitated, then gave a polite nod.

She flushed, feeling foolish.

Clara hesitated, watching her.

"You go ahead," Serafina urged. "I'll just watch."

Clara searched her face for a long moment. "I'll return soon. Try to enjoy yourself, Sera."

She doubted she would, but she smiled anyway.

When the man swept Clara onto the dance floor, Serafina stood off to the side. She should have said no to coming. This wasn't an adventure at all. It was a mistake. The chandeliers burned too bright now. The music swelled too loud. The laughter of elegantly dressed guests grated on her.

She wasn't dancing, wasn't even speaking, yet she felt like she was on display, an outsider to be observed and judged. If the floor beneath her cracked open and swallowed her whole, she would consider it a mercy.

Clara returned, only to be swept into conversation by two women in sleek gowns. Their smiles were sharp, their eyes skimming Serafina before locking onto Clara.

"Miss Randolph, dear!" one of them, a brunette in ice-blue silk, said, sweeping Clara into a brief hug. "I was so hoping you'd be here tonight."

The other, a tall woman in deep burgundy, tilted her head. "We were just talking about the latest exhibition at the Met. Tell me you've seen it."

Clara exhaled, brushing a loose curl behind her ear. "Of course. The new Matisse pieces are absolutely stunning, and—"

"Oh, I knew you'd appreciate them," the brunette gushed. "Your eye for composition is unmatched."

Serafina stood beside Clara, unnoticed and unacknowledged. She might as well have been an extension of Clara's shadow.

Clara, however, turned slightly, her arm still looped around Serafina's. "This is my dearest friend, Serafina Silvano."

The brunette's polite look didn't waver. "Oh, how lovely."

The taller one offered the barest gesture of acknowledgment before her attention flicked once more to Clara. "So tell me, what did you think of that use of color? Quite bold, wasn't it?"

Clara shifted, cutting the conversation short. "Please excuse us." She didn't wait for a response before pulling Serafina aside.

"Sera-darling, are you okay? You don't seem well."

"Neither do you."

Clara let out a quiet huff of laughter. "Yes, well, the night will be over soon."

Serafina swallowed. "Not soon enough."

Then Clara raised her head a little higher. "I agree. But let's find Mr. Kensington. This night's about you and your book. That'll make being here worth it, and I believe in you."

Serafina let Clara lead her away from the group, weaving through the crowd of silk and polished shoes to the quieter end of the room.

"There he is," Clara whispered, gesturing at a distinguished-looking man engaged in conversation with two others who hung on to his every word.

"He looks... powerful," Serafina said, nerves twisting.

"He is. Come on."

Serafina inhaled slowly to calm her nerves and followed. Up close, Mr. Kensington's presence loomed larger. He carried himself with the confidence of a man who knew the value of his authority.

His smile when he turned to them was warm, yet somehow also cold.

"Good evening, Miss Randolph."

"Mr. Kensington, this is my dear friend Serafina Silvano. She's an incredibly talented writer."

Mr. Kensington extended his hand. His grip was firm, his palm smooth. "A pleasure, Miss Silvano. Miss Randolph's father has spoken highly of you."

"Thank you, Mr. Kensington," she said, breathless. "It's an honor to meet you."

"Tell me about your work," he said, shifting his stance ever so slightly, like granting her his full attention was a rare privilege. "What do you write?"

Serafina took a slow breath. This was her moment.

She described her novel, her voice gaining strength as she spoke about her characters and the intricate letters woven throughout the story, her inspirations from *Les Liaisons Dangereuses*, the layered power struggles, the way words could shape destinies, of manipulation and control, of the devastating consequences of temptation and ambition. She skirted calling it romance, knowing men like him often sneered at romance as frivolity.

Mr. Kensington listened, nodding occasionally, but his demeanor unsettled her. He was paying attention... perhaps too much. Then his gaze drifted in a slow, deliberate sweep downward, over her collarbones, the curve of her neck where her pulse hammered visibly, her chest, and down to her hips...

It was so smooth that she almost convinced herself she'd imagined it. But the way his gaze stayed just a fraction too long at the swell of her breasts visible above the gown's neckline made her skin crawl.

Instinct screamed otherwise. Determination kept her where she was.

"Intriguing, Miss Silvano," he said finally, sounding warmer than before. "If you bring it to my office next week... we can discuss it in detail. Privately."

The word "privately" made Serafina's stomach turn. But this was what she wanted, wasn't it? An opportunity? A real chance? But the way he said it, the way his gaze had traveled over her figure like he was pricing merchandise...

She shoved aside the unease coiling in her chest.

"Thank you, Mr. Kensington. I'll do that."

Mr. Kensington then moved off, already slipping into another conversation.

Serafina sighed.

Clara leaned in, speaking quietly, "If he passes on your book, we'll find a way to get you meetings with other publishers. He's interested, Sera. That's a start."

Serafina forced a smile, but her thoughts churned. Had Clara missed that look? Or was it just in her head, her nerves twisting nothing into something?

"Maybe," she said softly. "Thank you for introducing me."

A few other gentlemen approached, asking Clara and Serafina to dance. She declined once more, and again, sent Clara along to waltz.

Serafina wandered around the ballroom, letting the hum of conversation and the lilting notes of the jazz band fade into a blur. Alone, she drifted to the ballroom's edges, where grand paintings stretched high above gilded frames. The crystal and silk and gold leaf were suffocating in their excess. Nearby, two women leaned close, their voices low but sharp enough to carry.

"Did you hear about the Anderson girl?" one whispered. "Disappeared after she turned down that derby horse-breeder. They say she's in Europe now, but no one's seen her."

The other woman's laugh was brittle. "How convenient."

But as Serafina stood there, admiring the peaceful landscape, her thoughts drifted back to the stranger from the bookshop. Kensington's stare had made her skin crawl, but the Italian? His intensity had sparked something else, something reckless. What would it be like to see him here, in this glittering trap, his dark eyes cutting through the crowd?

The thought sent a flush of heat through her that had nothing to do with the warm ballroom air.

As she made her way to the terrace doors, needing air, her heel slipped. Looking down, she saw a dark droplet on the marble floor. Wine, surely, though in the dim light it looked disturbingly like blood.

CHAPTER 2

Their polished shoes struck the stone steps in sharp, relentless rhythms. Francesco Romano's men trailed him, their voices low, thick with cruel amusement as they swapped tales of their latest conquests. They boasted about which senator's wife had begged for mercy, which judge's daughter had screamed until her voice broke.

Francesco tuned out their vile chatter. His focus was a razor, fixed on the task ahead as he led them through the shadows like a wolf hunting in a dying forest. The scent of expensive cologne and cigarettes trailed behind them, marking their territory in the refined air. These gilded rooms, heavy with wealth and lies, were his battlefield. Power here wasn't in titles but in debts that chained men, favors that broke them, lives snuffed out with a whispered order. He wasn't here for the sour champagne or the hollow smiles of high society. He was here to settle a score, one that had festered for years, its weight clawing at his chest like a living thing.

But tonight, his thoughts snagged on a darker thread. Elena Brambilia, beautiful, reckless, and fatally married. The wife of Antonio Brambilia, a rival whose influence matched Francesco's, a man who saw every betrayal before it landed. Elena had called him days ago, her voice cracking over the telephone. "*We need to talk. I think he knows. Please, Francesco. I need to see you.*"

Of course Antonio knew. Men like him didn't rule by being blind.

Touching what was his came with a price, a bullet in the dark, a body in the river. Francesco had cut her off, no room for her panic or her pleas. He didn't waste time on women who mistook good sex for something more meaningful, who turned clingy, who thought a few nights meant he owned them something.

Vito nudged him as they neared the entrance, his voice a low hiss in Italian. "*Capo, they're waiting.*"

Francesco gave a curt nod, his jaw tight as iron. He knew how this would go. The moment he crossed the threshold, the room would choke, conversations would die, eyes would turn. Some would be terrified, some hungry, all scrambling to gauge what his presence meant for their survival. He fed on the way fear bent the air around him, the way power knelt without a word.

"*Remember,*" he said, his voice cold, carrying the heaviness of a death sentence. "*We're here to make an impression. And to remind certain people what happens when they forget their place.*"

His men straightened, their crude banter swallowed by the silence of soldiers bracing for blood. Francesco pushed through the grand double doors, and the reaction was instant.

A hush fell over the ballroom.

"Is that Francesco Romano?" someone near Serafina whispered, the name spoken with dread, as if it might summon a curse. Serafina's curiosity betrayed her. She turned toward the grand staircase, and her breath caught in her throat. It was him, the man from the bookshop, dark hair, darker eyes, but now in a tuxedo. Francesco Romano. The name fit him. She watched him descend the stairs with a predator's calm, the crowd parting like prey before a hunter. Even those pretending not to care stole glances, their eyes pulled to him, unable to resist.

She swallowed hard, the memory of his voice slicing through her. "*He'll kill whoever he thinks fucked his wife.*" A man marked for death, yet here he was, moving through the room like he owned every soul in it, untouched by fear. The contradiction gnawed at her, her writer's mind clawing to pin him into a story she could control.

"Isn't he something?" someone else beside her said, her voice tinged with unease.

Serafina managed a faint nod, though the question hadn't been directed at her. She needed to breathe. Her thoughts moved too fast.

A drink. She needed a drink. Spotting the bar across the room, she pushed through the crush of silk and polished shoes, her gown snagging on her legs, the beads catching the chandeliers' sickly light. She stole another glance at him, unable to stop. He was speaking to the host now, his face a mask of stone, every gesture precise, no trace of weakness. The men around him, powerful in their own right, leaned in, hanging on his words like condemned men awaiting judgment.

The whispers about him swelled, tales of blood, debts, and bodies left in alleys, feeding her dread, deepening the enigma. At the bar, she ordered a merlot, the glass cold against her trembling fingers. She took a slow sip, willing the wine's burn to dull the panic rising in her chest. But her eyes drifted back to the man who read poetry while death stalked him. Who was he, beneath the suit and the menace?

A heavyset man in a tuxedo, looking like a stuffed bird despite the tailoring, scurried toward Francesco, his forehead slick with sweat under the chandeliers' glare. "Ah, Mr. Romano, welcome!" Lorenzo Mancini's voice dripped with forced cheer, his smile too wide, too desperate, the kind of terror you'd expect from a man who'd felt Francesco's gun against his temple and survived.

Francesco fixed him with a stare that could cut glass, his jaw twitching. "Mancini. I trust everything is in order."

"Absolutely," Mancini stammered, his hand shaking as he gestured for Francesco to follow. "Everything is perfect. Come, let me introduce you to some of our esteemed guests."

Francesco followed, his men fanning out like shadows around the room. He paid little attention to the introductions, his attention instead on the fear he stirred. Conversations choked as he passed, laughter died, eyes darted away. Some respected him. Others feared him. He didn't care, as long as they obeyed him.

As he moved through the crowd, Francesco's gaze caught on a man near the bar, middle-aged, nervous, with a nose once broken so badly that it had healed crooked. The man's eyes widened when he saw Francesco, and he turned away, hunching as if he could disappear. Francesco knew him, a thief who'd tried to skim from his shipments six months ago. He'd let him live, but not before breaking his face to ensure he'd never forget. The crooked nose was a warning.

By the windows, two society matrons whispered behind their fans, their voices sharp as knives. "Found him in an alley last week, throat cut ear to ear," one hissed. "Romano's work, they say." The other added, "Crossed him over a shipment. Never stood a chance." They froze when they noticed Francesco's glance, their faces draining of color. He offered a cold smile and moved on. Let them talk. Fear was power, just another form of respect.

"Mr. Romano, this is Governor Harrington," Mancini introduced.

The governor, a balding man in his late sixties with soft, pampered hands, extended a clammy palm. "Mr. Romano, it's an honor to meet you."

Francesco gripped his hand, hard enough to make the man wince. "The pleasure is mine, Governor. I hope the things you've heard have been favorable."

Harrington's smile wavered, his laugh forced. "Oh yes, yes, of course. Your name carries a certain weight, shall we say."

Francesco smiled ever so slightly, relishing the fear behind the politician's words. They moved on, more introductions, more empty words. But he wasn't here for chatter. Mancini's debt demanded repayment, and Francesco had no patience for his groveling longer than necessary.

When they were alone, Francesco turned, his presence a wall of menace. "Mancini. Our arrangement is still secure?"

The banker swallowed, his eyes darting like a trapped animal. "Yes, absolutely. You have my full support."

Francesco held his gaze just long enough to let the man know that, if he was lying, it would be his last.

"Good." He brushed at a nonexistent wrinkle in his cuff. "Then let's enjoy the evening."

He walked away without another word. He despised weak men who begged for mercy, especially for a wife as treacherous as Mancini's. As he scanned the crowd, his gaze caught on a slight figure. The light blue cotton dress from the bookshop was gone, replaced by sapphire silk that clung to her frame, her blonde hair pinned up. For a moment, he thought his eyes were deceiving him. But then she pressed her elbows to her sides, a nervous tic he'd noticed before.

The bookshop girl. What would she be doing at Mancini's ball?

Francesco paused, studying her. What was she doing in this pit of vipers? She moved through the crowd like a ghost, polished but out of place, as if she'd rather be anywhere else. It was her, the one who'd apologized for not having Italian poetry, who'd wrapped his book with trembling hands. The working class didn't belong here, where a gown could cost a month's wages. And yet, there she was.

He pushed the thought aside, turning to business associates who owed him blood and politicians whose careers hung by his strings. Everything proceeded as planned until a woman in emerald approached, her movements bold, her confidence a weapon. Her copper hair spilled over one shoulder, her dress clinging to her curves in defiance of the room's muted elegance. She stepped into his space without hesitation.

He didn't mind.

"Mr. Romano," she purred. "I've been looking forward to meeting you."

Francesco allowed his gaze to rake over her, unhurried, appraising. "Have you now, Miss... ?"

"Isabella Davies, and I've heard much about you," Isabella continued, stepping closer in an understated invitation.

He smirked. "And what have you heard?"

"That you're a man of secrets." Her voice lowered, teasing. "A man like you must have many secrets, Mr. Romano."

"And a woman like you wouldn't be here if she didn't want to know them."

She tilted her head, her smile widening. "Curiosity is a dangerous thing, don't you think?"

He stepped closer, close enough to feel the heat of her breath. "Only if you don't know how to handle the dark."

Her lashes lowered. Her fingers danced up his arm. "And I suppose... you do?"

He brushed a stray curl from her shoulder, letting the strands slip between his fingers before tucking it behind her ear. She didn't pull away. "I live in it." His voice was a low growl. "And what brings you to me, Miss Davies? Are you drawn to the danger?"

Her lips parted, amusement flickering in her gaze. "Perhaps. I find myself drawn to the unknown, to the thrill of discovering what lies beneath the surface."

He leaned in. "Be careful. You may not like what you find. But...would you like to explore it together, *bella*?"

Her gaze locked onto his. "That depends."

Francesco chuckled. "On what?"

"On whether or not you're proposing an alliance," she said quietly, lifting her chin like she was answering a challenge he'd issued.

He smirked. Clever to turn the tables so smoothly. He let a beat of silence stretch before leaning close, his mouth near her ear. "The Waterford Hotel, the grand suite on floor three." His gaze flicked to her lips, then her eyes. "Meet me there at ten."

He left her before she could respond, suddenly far more interested in other matters.

"Just one more, please," Serafina muttered under her breath, signaling the bartender. "Another glass of merlot."

Her nerves had barely settled, dulled by the wine's burn, but her mind churned like a storm. She tried to focus on her breathing, on the weight of the glass in her hand, but her pulse pounded, her fingers drumming restlessly on the bar. She kept catching herself biting her lower lip. She searched for Clara, finding her still deep in conversation with a cluster of young gentlemen. Clara caught her eye and, with an almost imperceptible nod and slow blink, gave Serafina wordless encouragement.

Seize the moment. Do something more than stand there.

The bartender slid the new glass to her. She nodded in thanks, took it carefully, and turned, only to crash into something solid. No, someone solid. The glass slipped from her fingers, and time slowed as a deep red stain bloomed on an impossibly expensive tuxedo.

A tuxedo worn by none other than Francesco Romano.

Serafina's heart plummeted.

"Oh my! Oh no! I'm so sorry!" Her voice rose in panic as she grabbed a napkin, dabbing frantically at the stain. Of all the men in this room, why did it have to be him?

Mr. Romano barely moved, his broad frame utterly unmoved by the collision.

"Please, stop," he said with an unmistakable edge of impatience. "It's just a tuxedo."

But Serafina was too flustered to stop. "I—I didn't see you there! I wasn't paying attention, and I—"

"I said stop."

His tone sharpened, a blade slipping between words, and Serafina's hands froze.

"I really didn't mean to..."

"Stop!"

The word cracked like a whip.

Serafina gasped. Conversations around them hadn't ceased, but the tension had changed. Guests stared openly, their eyes glinting with cruel amusement. Others listened without looking, their careful detachment a mask of high society. A few tittered behind their hands, their laughter sharp enough to slice through her. One woman whispered to her companion, "Clumsy girl, spilling on him," and their giggles cut like shards of glass.

26

She had never felt so exposed, so utterly alone in this pit of vipers. Her cheeks burned with shame, her skin crawling under their gazes. She wanted to sink through the polished floor, to escape the weight of their judgment. Then, a colder sensation prickled her neck, a gaze that felt different, predatory and unseen. She glanced toward the shadows near the terrace doors, but saw nothing, only the lingering chill of being watched. The feeling vanished, leaving her unsteady, her heart racing.

"I..." she stammered, voice barely a whisper.

He exhaled. "Do you ever stop apologizing?"

Serafina's spine straightened. She stepped back, squaring her shoulders. "Excuse me?"

He tilted his head, his eyes narrowing. "You apologize like it's a reflex."

"And you insult strangers like it's a hobby!"

Before he could respond, Clara rushed to her side, slipping an arm around her shoulders. "Serafina, darling," she said with a smile so poised it was nearly lethal, "there you are. I must speak with you for a second. There's another publisher I want you to meet."

He scoffed, his voice dripping with disdain. "A publisher? What do you write? Romance?"

Serafina lifted her chin, defiance flaring. "Why, yes, actually. I do."

He exhaled a short, humorless chuckle and muttered, "*Che perdita di tempo.*"

A waste of time.

Her blood boiled. She glared at him, her voice steady.

"*Non è una perdita di tempo!*"

He stilled. It was the smallest change, but she saw the flicker of surprise and how his eyes narrowed slightly.

"Do you work at a bookshop?" he asked.

"As a matter of fact, I do."

"And you speak Italian?" Mr. Romano continued. "You never mentioned that."

"I'm not generally in the habit of disclosing my languages to strangers, especially ones who call romance pointless." She turned to Clara and repeated, "He called romance pointless."

Clara blinked with a haughty air. "Did he, now?"

"I did," he confirmed. "And it is."

"Then clearly he hasn't read any good ones," Clara said to Serafina.

"No, he hasn't, and I'm not sorry anymore. I hope that stain never comes out."

"Neither do I," he said with an amused grin.

"Come, Clara. Let's find someone who is actually important."

As they walked off, Serafina's pulse thundered in her ears. She wanted to turn back, to storm up to him, to wipe that smug grin off his face, and...

Francesco watched them go, his mind racing. So the bookshop girl spoke fluent Italian, moved in these viperous circles, and had fire beneath that fragile exterior.

Interesting....

The rest of the evening passed in a haze of forced pleasantries and stolen moments where Serafina tried to douse the fire still burning in her chest. She should have let it go. He wasn't worth the energy, and yet, how dare he mock her?

By the time Serafina and Clara went outside, the night air had turned cool. Clara's driver opened the car door, and Serafina sank into the seat with a quiet exhale of relief.

Clara glanced at her. "You're still thinking about him, aren't you?"

Serafina huffed. "No."

Clara arched a perfectly sculpted brow.

"...Maybe a little."

"I thought so. It was a very dramatic exchange."

Serafina pursed her lips. "It was not dramatic. It was—"

"The most dramatic thing I've seen in weeks," Clara supplied.

Serafina huffed. "I just don't like being mocked."

"And yet, you had him off guard for a second." Clara said smugly. "He didn't expect you to snap at him like that."

"Good."

Clara laughed lightly as the car pulled up to Serafina's apartment. "Do try to get some sleep, darling. We'll talk more tomorrow."

The stress of the evening melted once Serafina was in her cramped living room, locking the door against the world. At least she hadn't fallen, though that might have been less humiliating than spilling wine. She caught her reflection in the hallway mirror, her cheeks still flushed, her eyes still sharp with anger.

She changed out of her gown, slipping into a worn cotton nightgown. Her fingers shook as she undid the buttons, her skin prickling with restless energy. She paused before the mirror, trying to mimic the sultry, confident looks she'd seen other women wield. The attempt was clumsy, her reflection mocking her with its awkwardness. She tried again, lowering her eyelids, tilting her chin.

Who was she kidding? She moved to the window and opened it, the distant jazz horns jagged tonight, no longer a lullaby. Her thighs ached with a yearning that pulsed with her heartbeat. She could still feel his gaze raking her neck, the way his eyes had narrowed when she'd snapped at him in Italian. It was as if he could unravel her with a single word in the dark. He'd been a bastard, but bastard or not, she couldn't shake the pull dragging her toward him, awakening a desire she didn't want.

She shut the window and walked over to her bed, determined to handle her needs.

This is madness.

She'd touched herself before, but never with someone specific in mind, not like this, with her body thrumming for a man who'd insulted her. But she needed to imagine it, just once, to banish him from her thoughts.

She climbed into bed, pulling the covers to her waist, the cotton nightgown clinging to her skin. Her nipples hardened, brushing against the fabric, sending a shiver through her. Her hands slid to the hem. She hesitated, then slipped beneath.

The cotton parted easily, and her palm pressed on the soft skin of her belly, lower, lower still, until she found the fine triangle of hair between her thighs.

She was already soaked. She'd never been this aroused, this ready, from nothing other than an argument. She exhaled, her breath unsteady.

Sliding two fingers between her folds, she drew them over the slick heat, biting back a gasp. The pressure was intense, but not enough. She pictured him at the foot of her bed, tuxedo jacket gone, shirt open, watching her with those cold, predatory eyes. Would he mock her still? Or would his voice be darker and commanding?

"Slower," she whispered, imagining his voice instead of her own. "Show me how you like it."

She circled her clit with her fingertips, drawing soft spirals as her hips shifted into the rhythm. The pleasure bloomed and tightened, molten and immediate. She pressed her other hand to her breast, fingers tugging lightly at her nipple through the nightgown, then slipped beneath the fabric to touch her nipple, rolling and squeezing. The ache shot down her spine, connecting directly to the pulsing between her legs.

"Say please," she murmured, picturing him leaning over her, his mouth close to her ear, his hand replacing hers.

Her knees spread wider, thighs trembling as her pace quickened. She slid one finger inside, then a second, her muscles clenching, desperate for more. He'd be bigger. Much bigger, she knew. The stretch would be overwhelming, and his gaze would be intense during the agonizing push inside.

She pumped her fingers deeper, curling them forward, to the spot that made her legs jerk. Her clit throbbed under the pressure of her thumb, and she rubbed harder, panting, her torso flushing with heat. The image of him...towering over her, pushing her over her writing desk, his hands rough and demanding as he lifted her onto it.

"Oh— Oh, God—" she gasped, hips bucking.

She came hard, her palm flying to cover her mouth to muffle the cry that tore from her throat. Her entire body shook with the force, spine arching, her fingers working her through the waves. When the storm finally subsided, she collapsed against the pillow, chest heaving, her skin damp and flushed.

The room was silent, save for her ragged breaths and the city's distant hum. She stared at the ceiling, spent. Francesco Romano had humiliated her, insulted her work, and dismissed her. And now she'd just come harder than she ever had before, thinking about his skin against her body, his whispers in her ear.

She groaned, flinging an arm over her eyes, and muttered, "I hate you."

But her thighs were still slick, and she knew deep down that she didn't hate him at all. What she felt was darker, a hunger that scared her.

Isabella Davies had been what he'd expected. Beautiful. Willing. Utterly forgettable. She'd played her part with sultry glances and breathless moans, but in the black of night, Francesco was already pulling on his clothes. She'd sufficiently satisfied him in the basest sense, but left him cold and empty. She wasn't what he needed.

The sun had nearly begun to rise when Francesco made it home, loosened his tie, and poured himself a glass of bourbon.

His silk tie resisted him, twisting tight around his throat like the evening's restraints. Sometimes he grew tired of the posturing and the proximity to men who feared him while pretending not to, even tired of the women who smiled with their teeth, but watched his every move, calculating what his attention might be worth.

He preferred enemies. At least they were honest.

He dropped into the leather armchair and downed the drink in a single swallow. It burned just enough to cut through the noise in his head, but doing nothing to quiet the thoughts of Serafina Silvano.

He hadn't meant to notice her. Not at all. She'd been almost as forgettable as Miss Davies at first, just a timid little thing. Too pale. Eyes too large. Fingers too fidgety. He'd presumed she was the type of woman who kept her head down and apologized before she'd even made a mistake.

Her trembling hands touched him, not to seduce but in panic. Her lips parted, breaths quick, not to please him. Her eyes flashed with anger, not fear. And then she'd snapped back in Italian, fluent and sharp, spitting the words as easily as if they'd been English to her.

For once, his assumptions were wrong.

He leaned forward, setting the empty glass aside, elbows on his knees. He couldn't shake the way she'd glared up at him with a mix of shame and defiance. Her mouth had been close enough that he could have kissed her right there in front of everyone, and part of him had wanted to. Women like Miss Davies, who threw themselves at his feet for a chance to bed him, were a dime a dozen. He even encountered women like Miss Randolph, the little princess who scoffed, on occasion, but he knew he could coax socialites into submission. But he couldn't recall the last time a woman had stood up to him and made him think he might not win her.

He adjusted in his seat. His slacks had gone uncomfortably tight somewhere between her yelling and her storming off. He should've been insulted. Instead, he was half-hard, frustrated, and aroused by this nobody of a woman. She'd managed to stay at the forefront of his mind.

Not Isabella Davies, with her lipstick games and designer perfume.

Not Elena Brambilia, whose husband might very well try to kill him.

Her.

The bookshop girl. The writer.

Romance, she'd said. As though that word alone was adequate to justify her entire existence.

Goddamn, that spirit in her gave him ideas he knew he shouldn't have.

He shifted again. His cock pressed hard along his thigh.

He looked down.

No.

This was a mistake.

She was no one. She wasn't polished the way his usual women were. But she had backbone and fire and the guts to bite back at him in a room full of people who held their tongues around him.

And now her voice was lodged in his skull. Her beautiful, angry, radiant face kept flickering behind his eyelids every time he closed them.

He let out a long sigh.

Fine. *Fine.* Just this once.

He stood, unbuttoned his stained shirt, and made for the bedroom.

The effect of the one glass of bourbon was already fading, but the fire she'd lit raged on.

He pushed his slacks down, sat at the edge of the mattress, legs spread, already rock-hard.

He could still feel the heat of her palm on his chest, trying to pat his shirt dry, still hear the little gasp she'd made when he'd told her to stop apologizing, still see the way she hadn't averted her gaze when he'd moved closer...

She'd flushed, but not just with shame. Part of her had liked the confrontation, liked him towering over her.

He groaned under his breath. He could imagine what she'd look like with that same passion in her expression, but naked beneath him.

He curled his fingers around himself and stroked, slow and firm. The first stroke made his ass and abdomen tense. The control it took not to lose himself immediately demanded all he had left in him.

He closed his eyes and pictured her in the bookshop, bent over her typewriter, skirt hiked up, looking back at him with that same defiance, daring him to touch her.

He'd push her forward, palms on her back holding her down while he kicked her legs apart. She'd gasp, try to twist around to look at him, but he'd keep her pinned.

"Stay still," he'd rasp close to her ear, and she'd shiver.

He pumped harder, faster. His jaw clenched.

She'd be drenched already. He was certain she was the kind of woman who got wet from being ordered around and being overpowered in matters of sex. He'd slide his fingers between her legs first, testing her, making her squirm while he decided whether she deserved what was coming.

She'd moan when he touched her. She'd push against his hand, whimpering for more of him.

God, he could feel it.

His strokes grew rougher, the sound of his palm loud, matched by his ragged breaths. She'd be tight when he thrust. into her, maybe untouched, the thought of being her first, of teaching her what her body was made for, sent heat racing down his spine.

He'd grip her hips and drive into her, hard and deep, without mercy. She'd cry out, hands scrabbling to steady herself on the desk while he set a brutal pace. But she'd take it. She'd take everything he gave her and beg for him to go faster, for more.

He groaned, the sound guttural, his fingers tightening.

She'd be the sort of woman who couldn't keep quiet when she was being fucked properly. She'd curse him in Italian when she clenched around his cock.

She'd come apart beneath him, still mad at him, still defiant, her body shuddering from the force of her orgasm while he kept taking more of what he wanted.

He was close, too close now.

He leaned back on one elbow, hips thrusting up into his fist. The image of her gasping his name... breathless... wrecked... completely his... driving him to the edge.

"*Cazzo... porca puttana... sì...*" he hissed.

The climax ripped through him, forcing thick seed to spill from him in hard, pulsing spurts, slicking his fingers, flooding his palm, dripping from his grip, onto his stomach and thighs. For a moment, the fantasy felt so real he could almost smell the floral scent that had clung to her hair, and could almost hear her crying out beneath him.

He rested, catching his breath. Romance, she'd said. The biggest fantasy of all. A lie he wanted to believe. He wiped himself with his undershirt, but the release didn't clear his head. She'd gotten under his skin, and that was a problem. The last time a woman haunted him, he'd ended up with Elena and a death threat.

This one was different, a writer who saw through his mask, who didn't flinch when he closed in, who matched his fire with her own. She had no care what he thought of her and no desire to impress him.

And that made her dangerous in a whole new way.

CHAPTER 3

Serafina stared at the empty page. A curl had slipped loose and hung by her cheek. She didn't touch it.

She'd written five different opening sentences in the past hour. Each one died on the page. The words came out hollow, trying to sound clever or literary when they were neither.

She closed her eyes and saw him. That hard stare, the expensive suit, the way he'd looked at her like she was nothing. Or worse, like noticing her at all had been a mistake on his part. But he had noticed. He wouldn't have held her gaze so long otherwise. He wouldn't have let her hand stay pressed to his chest, wouldn't have turned when she spoke Italian, and wouldn't have given her that cold, infuriating grin when she refused to apologize.

She pressed her thighs together. Her nightgown was still crumpled at the foot of the bed. The sheets carried the smell of what she'd done to herself the night before, thinking of him.

Now she was trying to write a short story about a governess falling in love with a French baron to submit to Love Story Magazine.

Serafina leaned back and sighed, staring at the one pathetic line she'd managed.

Miss Catherine smoothed her skirts as she entered the library, where Baron Montclair waited with a leather-bound volume of poetry.

Lifeless.

She ripped the page from the typewriter and crumpled it, hurling it toward the wastepaper basket. It landed on the floor.

What if she wrote something else? Something pulled from real life?

Before she could second-guess herself, her fingers moved again.

He cornered her against the stone wall, his body a cage of heat and menace. She should have been afraid. She should have screamed. Instead, she lifted her chin and met his dark gaze with defiance burning in her own.

"You think you can frighten me," she whispered.

His smile was razor-sharp. "I think you're already frightened. The question is whether you're frightened of me...or of what you want me to do to you."

His hand braced against the wall beside her head, and she could smell his cologne, could feel the warmth radiating from his body. Her heart hammered against her ribs, but not entirely from fear.

"I want nothing from you," she lied.

"Liar." The word was barely a breath against her ear as he leaned closer. "Your pulse is racing. Your lips are parted. Your body knows what it wants, even if your mind won't admit it."

won't admit it."

"Tell me to stop," he murmured. "Tell me to walk away, and I will."

She opened her mouth to say the words, but what came out instead was a breathless whisper: "Don't you dare."

His answering smile was wicked as sin. "That's what I thought."

His mouth crashed down on hers, claiming and demanding. She should have pushed him away. Instead, her hands fisted in his shirt, pulling him closer, drowning in the taste of danger and desire.

Serafina's breath came faster as she typed. Heat pooled low in her belly. She could so clearly see Francesco's broad shoulders, and his hands...quite large.

in the taste of danger and desire.

He pushed her against his desk, scattering papers to the floor. "Is this what you wanted?" he growled against her throat. "Is this the danger you've been craving?"

Serafina jerked away from the typewriter as if it had burned her. Her cheeks were flushed. What was she doing? This wasn't what she set out to write. This was... this was pure fantasy. It was raw and shameless and utterly unpublishable.

She stared at the words, her heart still racing. The little she had written dripped with the kind of passion she'd never dared write before, the kind of desire she'd never let herself acknowledge.

With shaking hands, she reached for the paper, intending to crumple it like the others. But she couldn't bring herself to destroy it. Instead, she read it once more.

She rolled the page back into her typewriter:

She sighed loudly, yanking it free and crumpling it.

She tried one last time to type about Miss Catherine and her baron. But the words wouldn't come. She could hardly even think of them.

With a frustrated sigh, she stormed away from the typewriter. She needed air. She needed to think about anything other than that awful man.

She needed Clara.

An hour later, Serafina stood outside the Randolph estate. The butler showed her to the sun room, where Clara sat in a silk robe, sipping tea and reading the society pages.

"Serafina, darling!" Clara set down her cup and gestured to the butler for another. "What a lovely surprise so early. Though you look rather flustered. Don't tell me you've been up all night writing again."

"Well, I..." Serafina bit her lip.

"Oh, no. What's happening now?"

Serafina hesitated, then shut the parlor doors.

"I must talk to you about last night." She barely paused before lowering her voice. "About Francesco Romano."

At the mention of his name, the teasing light faded from Clara's eyes. "I was hoping you'd have no interest after that exchange."

"I can't stop thinking about him."

"Well. That's troubling." Clara picked up her teacup to sip.

"There's something about him, though. The way people reacted when he walked in, the way the entire room changed. The way he—"

"Mocked you publicly?" Clara's eyebrow arched.

Heat crept up Serafina's neck. "It wasn't just that. It was the way he looked at me. Like he could see right through me, but also like..." She struggled for words. "Like he wanted to...oh, I can't explain it."

Clara was quiet for a moment, studying Serafina's face and waiting for the butler to leave again after bringing a second cup of tea. Then she sighed and moved to the window, her silk robe flowing behind her.

"Sera, do you know he kills people?"

"What?" Serafina shook her head. "How would you know that?"

Clara turned back around, looking grave. "Well, Carlo Romano's death was awfully convenient."

The blood drained from Serafina's face. "Carlo Romano? But he was..." Her mind scrambled to catch up. "Are you saying Francesco—"

"I'm saying the head of the Romano crime family died last month under mysterious circumstances, and Francesco Romano—no relation, *supposedly*—moved up to fill the void with remarkable efficiency." Clara's voice was matter-of-fact. "Some would call that suspicious timing. And the rumors... they say rivals end up with their fingers mailed in envelopes to their families, or poisoned in speakeasies with bad gin."

Serafina sank into the nearest chair, her legs suddenly unsteady. "He's... he's actually..."

"A mob boss. Yes." Clara moved closer, and patted Serafina's shoulder with concern. "He's one of the most dangerous men in the city, if the rumors are true. No one in the mob hasn't killed before. It's what they do."

"Why didn't you tell me last night?"

"Because it was just a brief encounter, and I assumed you'd never see him again." Clara sat facing her, leaning forward. "I certainly didn't expect you to develop an infatuation."

Serafina's hands shook in her lap. "I wouldn't quite call it an infatuation."

"What would you call it then?"

She fell quiet, thinking of the heat in his dark eyes, and the way her own body had responded to his nearness. "It's more like fascination."

Clara groaned. "Oh, God, that's somehow worse."

"Tell me more about him. What kind of man is he, really?"

Clara hesitated, then seemed to make a decision. "Men like him are calculating. He's consolidated power faster than anyone believed could be possible, which means he's either extraordinarily lucky or extraordinarily dangerous."

"Or both."

"Or both," Clara agreed grimly. "The point is, Sera, men like Francesco Romano don't have casual encounters. They don't meet sweet booksellers and develop tender feelings. They use people, and

40

they break them. And when they're done, those people have a tendency to disappear for good."

Serafina's mind turned over every word. So here was a man who lived in the darkness she'd only written about, who embodied the danger she'd only imagined.

"Oh, no you don't," Clara said. "You look far too intrigued by all of this. You need to let it go."

"But I'm intrigued."

"Oh, Sera, Sera, Sera. I adore you, but I do question your survival instincts sometimes, especially in a city that is cruel to dreamers."

A smile tugged at Serafina's lips. "Just promise me something."

Clara exhaled, already looking tired. "Oh, Lord. Here we go."

"If I end up dead, make sure my obituary says I died in the pursuit of knowledge."

Clara squeezed her temples. "Darling, if you end up dead, I'll be too busy grieving to write anything but your name."

Serafina bit her lip. So Francesco Romano wasn't just an enigmatic man with a cruel mouth and an unreadable gaze. He was truly dangerous.

And yet, something about him pulled at her, even when she knew it could destroy her.

Serafina sang to herself as she restocked romance books, but stopped when the bell rang. She took a step back to greet the customer. Instead, Danny entered, looking unusually serious.

"Good afternoon, Serafina," he called, approaching the counter with concern.

"Hello, Danny." She set down the books and headed toward him. "Is everything okay?"

He shook his head, running his fingers through his hair. "I came by because I heard something that troubled me. I was at the Whitmore estate this morning, and I overheard a guest talking about an incident at a ball over the weekend. Something about a young woman who had words with Francesco Romano. Came back as soon as I heard"

Serafina's blood went cold. "Oh?"

"Mentioned it was quite the scene, with wine spilled, harsh words exchanged..." Danny searched her face with growing alarm. "Serafina, please tell me it wasn't you."

She opened her mouth to deny it, but the words wouldn't come.

"It was you, wasn't it? Good God, Serafina, do you have any idea how dangerous that man is?"

"It was just a misunderstanding," she managed, though her voice sounded weak even to her own ears. "I accidentally spilled a glass of wine on him."

Danny stepped closer, gripping the edge of the counter. "You spilled on *Francesco Romano*?" He shook his head. "Serafina, you have to understand that men like him don't forget slights. They hold grudges. You could be in real danger."

His fear made her chest tighten. "I'm sure it's nothing, Danny. It was just a little embarrassment at a party."

"Nothing?" His voice cracked with disbelief. "Listen to me! The most dangerous men are often the ones who seem charming at first. They watch women, and learn their routines and weaknesses. They wait for the right time to strike. You can't tell who's truly dangerous just by looking at them."

"Please calm down. I promise, I have no plans to see him again."

"But I'm still worried about you," Danny said, gentler now. "You're too trusting and too willing to see the best in people. But men like Romano? They prey on intelligent, independent women who think they can handle themselves, like you."

"I appreciate your concern, I really do, but there's no reason for me and Mr. Romano to see each—"

"Let me help you," he interrupted, leaning forward earnestly. "I have connections, people who keep an eye on things and who know how to spot trouble before it finds you. I can make sure you're safe."

"That's generous, but I don't think—"

"Have coffee with me," he said quickly. "Tomorrow morning. We can talk about this properly, somewhere private where we don't have

42

to worry about being overheard."

"I..." She fumbled for an excuse, her mind racing. "I can't. I have to prepare for that publisher meeting I mentioned."

"Kensington?" Danny's expression darkened. "Be careful with him too. Publishers like him... they're not always what they seem either. Trust your instincts, okay? If something feels wrong, it probably is."

Danny glanced over his shoulder at another customer walking in.

"I should let you get back to work. But promise me you'll be careful. The most dangerous predators are the ones who seem harmless until it's too late." He paused at the door. "And if you see Romano again, don't try to handle it alone. Send word to me immediately. Sometimes the people who seem like they're trying to protect you are the ones you need protection from most."

Francesco had been in a foul mood for three days, ever since that clumsy little writer had the audacity to speak to him like he was nothing more than an arrogant bastard at a party.

He'd dealt with far less disrespect and buried the offenders six feet under without losing sleep. Yet he couldn't stop thinking about her, and the way her anger had flashed when she'd snapped at him in Italian, the curve of her mouth when she'd refused to apologize, and how her body had felt pressed against his for those few seconds when she'd steadied herself against his chest.

Christ, he was losing his mind.

He'd tried to solve the problem the way he always did: with other women. But every time he closed his eyes, even with some willing socialite's mouth around his cock, all he could see was Serafina Silvano's defiant stare and that maddening little chin she'd lifted at him.

It was pathetic. He was Francesco Romano, for Christ's sake! He could have any woman in the city with a snap of his fingers, women who knew their place, who wanted the obvious things—his money, his protection, and his body. They were simple, predictable, and controllable.

So why could he not stop thinking about the one woman who clearly wanted none of those things? Why did he give a damn about making her want him?

A soft knock interrupted his brooding. "Come in," he called, not bothering to look up from his glass.

The door opened, and Giulia Moretti slipped inside, her lace robe barely covering her body.

"I thought you might want some company," Giulia purred, slinking toward him.

Francesco's gaze barely lifted from his whiskey. "I'm busy."

She paused, confusion flickering over her face, but she pressed on. "You seemed tense earlier. Let me help you relax." The robe slipped from her shoulders, pooling at her feet.

Francesco finally glanced at her, his gaze raking over her naked form. She was just as stunning as she'd always been, but she felt empty to him now.

"Get dressed," he said flatly, returning to his drink.

Giulia froze mid-step, her confidence cracking. "I'm sorry?"

"You heard me. Get dressed and get out."

Her mouth fell open in shock. "But last night you said—"

"Last night is over. Don't make me repeat myself."

Giulia's face crumpled, anger replacing confusion. "What the hell is wrong with you lately?" She grabbed her robe, clutching it to her chest. "You've been different ever since that stupid ball."

Francesco's jaw tightened. The ball. Of course she'd noticed.

"Nothing's wrong," he said. "I just have more important things on my mind than entertaining you."

Giulia flinched. "Fine. Don't expect me to come running the next time you want someone to warm
your bed."

She fled without another word. The door slammed behind her.

Francesco stared into his glass, disgusted with himself. Giulia had done nothing wrong except be what she'd always been. The problem was that what he wanted had changed, and he hated that it had.

He now wanted fire. He wanted a woman who would stare him in the eye and tell him he was wrong in perfect Italian, then stomp off without a backward glance, who would make him work for her attention instead of offering it freely.

God, he wanted Miss Silvano spread beneath him, to break through her composure and find the passion underneath to prove to himself that she was just like every other woman once you stripped off the pretense.

Francesco drained his glass and set it down. This mild obsession was unacceptable. She was disrupting his ordered world.

When a sharp knock rattled his door, his jaw tightened. Only one person would dare disturb him at this hour without an invitation.

"*Come in,*" he called out in Italian.

Ricci burst through, his usually composed demeanor cracked with tension. "*We've got a problem.*"

Francesco didn't look up. "*It's past midnight.*"

"*Cazzo, Frankie. Elena's pregnant.*"

Francesco's head snapped up. "*Pregnant? How do you know?*"

"*Word gets around. Brambilia's asking questions. Dangerous ones. He knows it's not his.*"

"*Conceived when?*"

"*Who the hell knows? Could be yours. The point is, he's looking for someone to kill, and your name's at the top of his list.*"

Cazzo indeed. Francesco's expression remained controlled, but his fingers drummed once against the chair arm. He couldn't afford to let this bother him. "*So?*"

"*So? Jesus Christ, you need to disappear off his list. Quick, private wedding to Giulia to look settled and domestic, like a man who wouldn't risk everything for another man's wife.*"

Francesco's laugh was sharp and humorless. "*Absolutely not.*"

"*Frankie—*"

"*No.*" He stood, pacing to the window. "*I don't hide. I don't pretend. And I sure as hell won't marry for anyone's benefit. I swore off the idea of marriage after Ginevra, or did you forget?*"

"*No, I didn't forget, but you'd rather die?*"

"*I'd rather Brambilia try.*" The words came out cold. "*Let him*

45

come. I'm not some coward who needs to parade a woman around like a shield."

"This isn't about courage. It's about strategy. You're no good to any of us dead."

"Then I'll handle Brambilia the way I handle every other problem." Francesco's fingers curled into a fist against the window frame. "That's not with theater."

"And when he comes for you in a restaurant? At the opera? In front of witnesses you can't afford to have asking questions?" Ricci stepped closer. "You think this is beneath you, but it's just another weapon. Use it."

"I don't need—"

"So, find a woman to play house and take on some dates for a few weeks," Ricci pressed. "One of the Ziegfeld girls, or—"

"No." The very thought of even pretending domesticity made Francesco's skin crawl. But then he stopped looked down as a face flashed through his mind.

"Frankie?"

"The bookshop girl," he heard himself say.

"Hell no!" Ricci snapped. "There are plenty of women already in our circle. Sophia Dellucci's been angling for attention for months. Or that singer from the Velvet Room. She knows the score, knows how to play the part. Not some innocent girl who—"

"She's perfect," Francesco interrupted.

His mind was already working, but not in the cold, strategic way he'd intended. A different calculation entirely. A month, maybe two of this charade. If he could convince her to play the part, then she would be close enough to touch, close enough to corrupt.

He could take his time with her, and learn what made her blush, and what made her breath catch. Find out if that prim, scholarly composure would crack under his hands, or if she'd bore him within a week and he could move on with the fantasy of her dispelled.

Either way, he'd win. Either she'd end up in his bed for as long as he wanted her, or he'd discover she was as tedious as every other respectable woman and the attraction would die a quick death. No more distracting thoughts. No more wondering.

"She's not wise to what we do," Ricci said, his voice hard. "She doesn't know the rules. The women I mentioned—they understand this world. This girl? She's too innocent. She'll be a liability."

"That's why she's perfect," Francesco said.

For once, someone else's crisis aligned perfectly with his own dark appetites. And Francesco Romano never wasted an opportunity.

CHAPTER 4

Serafina tried to push Mr. Romano from her mind. Even when helping a customer pick out a poetry book, she did not think of him once. The young lady had nearly decided on a purchase when a boy in a Western Union uniform entered, holding a folded telegram in one fist and a crumpled hat in the other.

"Miss Serafina Silvano?" he called from the doorway.

Her heart stuttered. "Yes, I'm Serafina Silvano."

The messenger boy handed her a cream-colored envelope. "For you, miss."

Serafina could count on one hand the number of telegrams she'd received, only holiday greetings from distant relatives in Sicily. She left her customer's side for a moment to fetch a few coins to give him for his trouble. He bobbed a quick bow and hurried out, leaving Serafina holding an envelope she ached to open, but duty held her back.

For the next few minutes, Serafina forced herself to finish assisting the lady, even as her mind whirled. Could it be from a publisher? No, that was foolish. She'd only met Mr. Kensington days ago, and she hadn't even delivered her manuscript to him yet. No one she could recall had business with her.

The young woman finally settled on a slim volume of Keats. Serafina wrapped the book in brown paper.

"Thank you so much for your help. You have such wonderful recommendations."

"Of course," Serafina managed, forcing a smile as she handed over the wrapped book. "I do hope you enjoy it."

The very moment that the young aspiring poet left with her purchase, she yanked the telegram from her apron and tore into it.

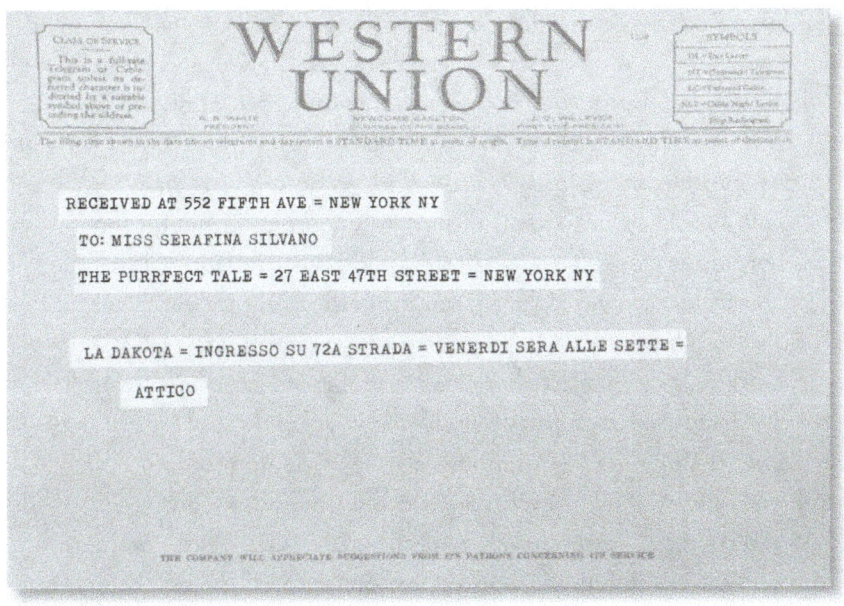

WESTERN UNION

RECEIVED AT 552 FIFTH AVE = NEW YORK NY

TO: MISS SERAFINA SILVANO

THE PURRFECT TALE = 27 EAST 47TH STREET = NEW YORK NY

LA DAKOTA = INGRESSO SU 72A STRADA = VENERDI SERA ALLE SETTE =

ATTICO

It was a summons in Italian, to the most upscale apartment building in the city, that night at seven. There was no name, but only one person she could think of might send her an unsigned telegram in Italian.

Her mouth dried. "...*those people have a tendency to disappear for good.*" Clara's warning echoed like a funeral bell.

But this could be your chance for adventure, her own daring voice whispered in her head. *A chance to see his world, to face its darkness and survive it.*

She didn't have time to decide what to do before the bell jangled again. Serafina shoved the telegram back into her apron pocket while Clara breezed into the shop in a whirl of perfume and enthusiasm.

49

"Serafina, darling!" Clara said, her cheeks pale from the damp fall air outside. "I've been fretting since yesterday. Have you any news? Have you gone to see Mr. Kensington yet?" She gave Serafina's arm a playful nudge, her eyes bright.

Serafina mustered a smile. "Not yet. I plan to go tomorrow, actually."

Clara shared a quiet update on neighborhood matters, her voice lightening briefly as she mentioned a friend's new hat, then softening with concern for a neighbor's illness. Serafina listened and nodded where needed, but talk of courtships and shops felt oddly hollow.

She certainly couldn't tell Clara about the telegram. She'd have a fit and beg her not to go. Or worse, try to accompany her. No, Serafina would have to keep this entirely to herself, though that decision made her uneasy; she rarely hid anything from Clara.

"Earth to Serafina." Clara peered at her with concern, tilting her head with a faint, teasing smile. "Are you all right, darling?"

Serafina hastily shook her head and blinked hard a couple of times. "I'm sorry. I didn't sleep well, and my mind's just on my book." It wasn't a complete lie; if nothing else, the telegram would certainly influence her writing. "Tomorrow is a big day, after all."

Clara's face warmed with a gentle glow. "Oh, yes, sweetheart. I know Mr. Kensington will love your manuscript. Promise to come by after and tell me every detail." She squeezed Serafina's hand.

Serafina promised, though she harbored a twinge of guilt. Clara left soon after, off to another errand, and Serafina finally resumed her duties with thoughts that wouldn't stop racing.

The rest of the day passed in a blur of routine tasks, but beneath it ran an undercurrent of anticipation that made Serafina nearly giddy. Every tick of the clock on the wall felt like a drumbeat urging her onward. By late afternoon, she decided what to do: she would close early, go home to freshen up, leave a note on her counter in case she vanished, and find out what awaited her at The Dakota at seven.

Danny returned to the bookshop when Serafina was just about to turn the sign to "Closed." He carried a particularly lavish arrangement of white roses and baby's breath.

"Good evening, Serafina," he said. "I hope I'm not too late. I wanted to bring you these before you left for the day."

Serafina paused, her fingers still on the sign. "Oh, Danny. They're beautiful, but you really shouldn't—"

"Nonsense." He moved a little closer. "You look... different than you were this morning, like you're excited about something. Did something good happen?"

Heat crept up her neck. "Just eager to get home, I suppose. It's been a long week." She glanced nervously at the clock.

Danny seemed to pick up on her impatience. "Big plans tonight?"

Serafina forced a casual smile. "Nothing special. Just a quiet evening at home, and preparing to meet with Mr. Kensington tomorrow."

"Of course. Certainly." Though he spoke gently, something like disappointment or suspicion flickered in his eyes. "Well, these roses will brighten up your apartment, at least. White roses mean new beginnings, you know."

Serafina accepted the arrangement with a polite thank you, eager to end the conversation. Danny stayed for a moment longer, then sighed.

"Take care of yourself, Serafina," he said finally. "Please stay home tonight. The city can be dangerous for a young woman alone, especially in the dark."

The Dakota Apartments loomed like a storybook castle at the corner of 72nd Street, its ornate gables and turrets black against a purple dusk sky. Gas lamps flickered outside the sprawling German Renaissance-style building. Serafina clutched her coat tighter around herself.

A liveried doorman opened one heavy brass door for her. She walked under the arch. His polite smile changed to subtle surprise when she asked for the penthouse. He directed her to the elevator down the hall. Feeling confident, she strode down to it and went up, but once she stepped off onto Mr. Romano's floor, she faltered.

What am I doing? she asked herself. *I detest him.*

She peered around the small corridor, at rich burgundy damask wallpaper and warm sconces. It smelled like a mix of wood polish, cigar smoke, and expensive cologne. She started to step away, but caught herself and took a deep breath to steady her nerves. She forced herself to inhale, then rapped softly on the only door.

It opened almost instantly, answered by Mr. Romano himself. He must have been waiting. Serafina stared, bottom lip between her teeth. He had traded his formal tuxedo for a somewhat less formal, but still tailored, black velvet smoking jacket. He stared hard at her, like he was trying to read her mind.

Neither of them spoke right away. Serafina's blood whooshed loudly in her ears.

Finally, Mr. Romano stepped aside. "Come in, Miss Silvano."

Serafina's legs were curiously light and numb when she crossed the threshold. She mustered her courage and met his gaze directly. "Good evening, Mr. Romano. I have no idea why you asked me here."

"Follow me."

Serafina trailed him deeper inside, staring at everything she could, at the dark wood paneling on the walls, and the floors adorned with intricate Persian rugs that muffled their footsteps. A crystal chandelier cast warm light over a spacious sitting room where a fire danced in the hearth. She glimpsed an expensive Victrola in one corner, and a telephone on an accent table. Everything was so much darker than the Randolph estate, yet it was every bit as elegant.

Mr. Romano led her through a wide archway into a room much too large for the small mahogany dining table gleaming under soft candlelight. To Serafina's surprise, the table was set for two, complete with fine china, crystal wine glasses, and silver domed platters at each setting.

"Your coat, Miss Silvano?"

She startled. "Oh! Yes." She slipped it off to hand to him to set aside, then settled into the chair he pulled out for her. She eyed the wine. She didn't trust it, didn't trust him, but then he poured some into a second glass and held it up to her in a mock toast before taking a sip.

For several minutes, they ate in near silence. The first sip of wine warmed Serafina's throat and steadied her nerves. The pasta in a savory marinara was divine, but the man opposite her held all her attention. Francesco seemed content not to speak until he'd cleared a bit of his plate. The quiet between them stretched, filled only by the soft clink of silverware on china and the distant crackle of the fireplace in the other room.

When she reached for her wine glass again, Francesco's fingers wrapped around her wrist. Electricity shot up her arm. She gasped. His thumb found her pulse point and pressed lightly.

"You're nervous," he said.

"Somewhat, yes."

"Good. You should be."

Unable to bear the silence, Serafina pulled away and cleared her throat. "I was surprised to receive your message."

"Were you?" Candlelight flickered in his eyes.

"Well, I... I had no reason to believe we'd ever cross paths again. And once more, I apologize if I caused a scene. It was unbecoming."

"Not at all. It was refreshing." He took a slow sip of wine, then added, "Most people only tell me what they assume I want to hear. It isn't every day that someone calls me unimportant."

The way he gazed at her made her feel exposed and want a few minutes alone to handle the pooling heat between her legs. *God, what's wrong with me?*

Mr. Romano tapped his fingertips together. "I have an offer."

Her brows lifted. "Yes?"

"You'd pretend to be my companion. We'd be seen in public, certain hands held, certain... things implied."

Serafina blinked. She'd expected some clandestine courier task, or a warning to keep quiet about overhearing something, or even an attempt at seduction. But this?

"A companion," she repeated, uncertainly. "You mean..."

"Someone to appear as my girlfriend, to be seen on my arm at

53

certain events," he said bluntly. "To play the part of an adoring lover. Strictly a charade."

For a second, Serafina wondered if this was some elaborate joke. But he didn't strike her as a man who joked about business. And his face was utterly serious. She grappled for a response and blurted the first question that surfaced. "Why?"

One dark eyebrow lifted at her question. "Suffice it to say," he answered coldly, "it serves my interests to appear domesticated. The specifics are my concern. All you're required to know is that it will be for a limited time. Four weeks, perhaps five, no longer."

A fake relationship? With him? It was ludicrous! A thousand practical considerations and red flags sprang up. She hardly knew him. He was, by all accounts, a dangerous man. And he expected her to accept with blind faith, no questions asked?

"Does it have to do with the affair you were involved in?"

Mr. Romano raised an eyebrow. "I was involved in no affair, Miss Silvano."

"But I heard—"

"A conversation without context."

Oh.

"Well... then why me?"

"You are presentable, clearly educated, and completely outside the circles of my enemies," he said. "You also have something to gain from such an arrangement. And you've already proven you can hold your own when challenged. That fire you showed at the ball is not something that can be taught."

"Then *why* should I?"

"You'd want for nothing during the arrangement, nor for a long while after, if ever again."

"And what if I don't want your money?"

He tilted his head. "Then what would you want?"

"To understand what kind of man thinks he can arrange people's lives to suit his purposes."

He chuckled once. No humor. "You're not subtle."

"No," she said. "But I'm honest, am I not?"

"I'm not arranging your life," he clarified. "I'm offering you a choice. You're free to say no."

"And what would you expect of me in this arrangement?"

Francesco's eyes darkened. He leaned back in his chair. "I expect you to play the part convincingly. Nothing I wouldn't ask of any woman in your position."

"That's not what I meant—"

"You'll be useful to me, Miss Silvano. That's all you need to be."

The words stung more than they should have. Serafina wondered why. This was supposed to be business, nothing else.

"I see," she said, trying to mask the unexpected hurt.

"Good. This arrangement is temporary and convenient. That is all."

Serafina straightened her spine. The practical part of her knew this was dangerous and reckless. But beneath that, curiosity about this man who moved through the world as if it should bow to him burned.

Imagine the stories I could write, she thought. *The characters I could create from understanding someone like him.* Maybe it was time to step into the arena.

"Then we understand each other perfectly," she said, meeting his challenging stare.

"Good. So. Will you accept my proposition?"

Butterflies beat in Serafina's stomach. "If I agree to this, I have three conditions of my own."

For the first time since she'd arrived, Francesco looked truly surprised. One dark brow arched, and she caught the faintest hint of amusement in his eyes. "Conditions?"

"Yes," she said, lifting her chin. "First, you don't interfere with my job at the bookshop. Whatever this arrangement requires, it can't jeopardize my employment or the shop in any way."

He appeared to consider this, then nodded slowly. "Reasonable. Your work supports the image we want to project."

"Second, I don't want to know details about your business that could put me in danger. The less I know about whatever it is you do, the safer we'll both be."

"I prefer it that way. Agreed."

"And third," she said, her voice steadying, "I want to be able to end this arrangement if I feel unsafe. Not uncomfortable—I expect that. But truly unsafe."

Francesco surveyed her with something that might have been respect. "You believe there's a distinction?"

"I think you're dangerous, but not reckless. There's a difference between being out of my depth and being in actual peril."

A slow smile spread across his lips, forming the first real smile she'd seen from him. "Very well, Miss Silvano. Your conditions are acceptable." He paused. "Anything else?"

"No," she said firmly. "Those are my terms."

"Then we have an agreement." He reached inside his suit jacket and withdrew a leather notepad and a pen. He scribbled something, tore off the page, and held it out to her. Serafina glanced down at a phone number.

"Call that number if you ever need to reach me urgently. It's my private line."

Mr. Romano steepled his fingers, eyes boring into her with renewed intensity. "Now, Miss Silvano, there are rules to our arrangement that you must understand from the outset."

"Rules, now? You should have told me first. I might not agree now."

"We'll have to see, then, won't we?"

"We shall. What are they?"

"First, this arrangement is to remain strictly between us. You will not speak of it to anyone without my explicit permission. That includes Miss Randolph or any friend or family member."

"I agree," she said. "I won't tell a soul."

"Good. Second, when we are out in public, you will call me 'Francesco' and behave like you are a woman in love. The performance must be flawless."

Serafina nodded. "Of... of course. That seems to be the job."

"Third," he continued, tone dropping a notch, "you will comply with my instructions at all times during our outings. If I say we must leave, you do not question. We leave. If I introduce you to someone under a certain context, you play along. And if I touch you, you respond like a woman in love or arousal would respond. I will not needlessly put you in harm's way, but you must trust my judgment."

A prick of unease settled in her stomach. "And if something unexpected happens?"

"Then you follow my lead and remain quiet unless forced to speak."

"But what if I have something to say? What if silence looks more suspicious?"

"Use your best discretion," he allowed. "You proved at the ball that you have a voice and you're not afraid to use it."

Serafina allowed herself a tiny smile at that small concession.

"Finally," he said, reaching into his inner pocket once more. This time he produced a sealed envelope and slid it to her. "Your first stipend."

Serafina stared at the envelope, her jaw tightening. "I said I didn't want your money."

"And yet there will be events that require a certain dress above what your bookseller salary could accommodate," he replied. "Are you planning to ask Miss Randolph to fund your wardrobe?"

Serafina's cheeks flushed. "I..."

"This is a business arrangement, Miss Silvano. Consider it a business expense. You cannot play your part without the proper costume."

Her pride warred with practicality for a second longer. Then she reluctantly picked up the envelope, setting it onto her lap. "Thank you," she said quietly.

Mr. Romano seemed to relax slightly. "That concludes my conditions," he said. "Do you have any questions, Miss Silvano?"

She hesitated. "This arrangement is certainly not something I ever expected."

"Few things in life are," he said dryly. He took a final sip of wine. "You may change your mind at any time before our first outing on Saturday. Call my telephone if you do. But once we begin, I expect your commitment to see it to the end."

"Saturday? That soon?"

His eyes glinted. "Yes. Dress to impress."

Her heart pounded hard again, but this time it was equal parts nerves and a strange exhilaration. Saturday. Two days to prepare for her new role.

"Very well, then."

"Good. Then we're done for this evening." He rose from the table, signaling the meeting's end. "I will see you Saturday at seven, at Il Girasole."

In the foyer, she extended her palm to him. "So, we have a deal, Mr. Romano."

Instead of shaking her hand, Francesco lifted it to his lips. His mouth was soft and warm when he brushed it over her knuckles. The heat of his breath ghosted across her skin as his tongue barely, almost imperceptibly, traced the ridge of her knuckle. But it was his eyes that nearly shattered her composure. His pupils were blown so wide they were nearly black, devouring her with an intensity that made her knees weak and liquid fire race within her veins.

"You may call me 'Francesco,'" he said in a rough whisper against her trembling hand as his thumb tracing a slow circle along her wrist. "We're partners now."

Serafina's breaths came in shallow pants. Her cheeks burned. Her pulse hammered so violently she was certain he could see it.

He released her, a knowing smile playing at his lips. "Perfect," he murmured. "That's the look I want on your face the next time I do that."

The heat in her cheeks became mortification when she realized how transparent her reaction had been, how easily he could read her body's betrayal.

"You're insufferable," she snapped.

"Perhaps," he agreed, unrepentant. "But I'm also right."

Serafina sat in the plush waiting room of Kensington Publishing. Anticipation and unease churned in her gut. This meeting could change the rest of her life. Muted conversation seeped from behind the closed door, making her hands tremble. She ran her fingertips over her manuscript's cover. Months of her life were bound in these pages, and she needed them to see it too.

At least Mr. Kensington valued romance, unlike Mr. Romano, who had dismissed love stories as frivolous wastes of time. But a man like Mr. Kensington, who had built his fortune on tales of passion, should see the work she had put into her own.

The thought of Mr. Romano sparked a wicked little thrill. Once this meeting concluded, she intended to take his generous envelope and spend every delicious penny she could on the most extravagant ensemble she could find. She loved the irony that the man who scorned romance would bankroll her transformation into the perfect false leading lady. If he wanted a fake sophisticated girlfriend to parade around, then she'd give him one that would cost him dearly, and she'd relish every second of it.

When the secretary finally ushered her in, she stopped short. She had expected an agent, not Mr. Kensington himself.

"Miss Silvano," he said, rising from behind a broad oak desk and extending his hand. "A pleasure to see you."

"Thank you for meeting with me, Mr. Kensington," she replied, keeping her voice level.

"Please, call me 'Richard.'" His gaze lingered on her, leering with hunger. "We'll be seeing a great deal of each other."

"Richard," she repeated, softly, as an uneasy prickle climbed the back of her neck.

"May I?" He gestured toward the neatly bound pages she held. She handed them over, and his fingers covered hers, squeezing until she winced. He caressed the cover like it was intimate flesh, his touch possessive and violating. He flipped through the pages very slowly, seeming to savor her discomfort.

"Quite a piece of work." His eyes crawled over her body, lingering on her hips and chest. "A lot of untapped potential."

He slowly rounded the desk, positioning himself between her and the doorway. When he stopped, she could smell the whiskey on his breath.

His palm settled on her shoulder, fingertips digging into her. "You know, Serafina," he said, his tone dropping to a whisper that made her skin prickle, "I have the power to make dreams come true, or to crush them completely."

She tried to step away, but his grip tightened. "What do you mean?"

"Oh, I believe you know what I mean." His free hand traced down her arm. "A bit of cooperation goes such a long way in this business. And you want to succeed, don't you? You want your little stories to see the light of day?"

His lips brushed over her neck. She could taste bile in her throat. His finger slid up to her collarbone, then beneath her collar to touch bare skin. "I could make sure your book gets all the attention it deserves. Every review, every bookshop, every reader who matters."

When the full scope of his proposition became clear, Serafina's heart hammered. She wanted to shove him aside, to scream, to run, but her manuscript lay on his desk. Everything she'd worked for, everything she'd dreamed of, was held captive by this monster.

"What kind of cooperation?" she murmured, though her stomach already knew the answer.

His grin was obscene, lips wet and eyes glittering with cruel anticipation. "You're a smart girl, Serafina. Smart enough to understand how things work in the real world." His thumb traced her collarbone. "Pretty girls who want things sometimes have to give things in return."

The walls closed in. His touch was everywhere, trailing down her throat, gripping her waist, his body pressing her against the desk... Heat radiated from him. The sour hunger on his breath filled the air.

"Think about it," he rasped, his lips grazing her ear. "All your dreams, Serafina. Everything you've ever wanted. All it takes is a little gratitude."

Nausea clawed at her throat. Her vision blurred at the edges as panic set in. This couldn't be happening. This couldn't be the price of her dreams. But his hands were real. His weight was real.

"I don't—" she began, but he cut her off.

"Shh. Don't think so hard. It gets easier once you stop fighting."

60

His fingers found the buttons of her dress, and something inside her snapped. Raw survival instinct flooded her veins, washing away the paralysis of shock.

"No!" She shoved against his chest with both palms, putting all her strength behind it. "Get away from me."

He stumbled back, surprise flashing over his face before it hardened into something ugly and dangerous. "Be careful, little girl. You don't want to make an enemy of me."

"I already have," she said, her voice shaking. She couldn't reach her manuscript. "Keep your hands to yourself and your 'opportunities' for someone else."

"How noble. How naive." He straightened his tie. "But you'll return, Serafina. They always return to me. And when you do, the price will be higher."

CHAPTER 5

Francesco sat in a shadowed corner of Il Girasole's lush dining room, where the air hung heavy with cigar smoke and whispered deals. The clink of crystal and low murmurs masked secrets as much as dinner talk. A lone candle flickered on the white-clothed table, casting jagged shadows across his face.

He tapped his fingers on the table. Sipping a pre-dinner whiskey, his mind was on high alert. This place was chosen for a reason: Antonio Brambilia's men frequented it, sometimes the man himself. Tonight, appearances were everything, and Francesco needed to know who watched.

Yet for all his strategic planning, Francesco's thoughts veered toward Miss Silvano in a carnal way. Despite himself, he'd spent more time than was wise envisioning how she might look beneath that prim exterior, imagining his palms sliding over her skin, pushing her against his apartment door the second they were alone. He wanted her expressive eyes to gaze up at him with desire instead of defiance. She aroused him in ways he hadn't expected.

He drew on his cigarette, exhaling a slow stream of smoke and forcing his attention to concrete matters. Across the room, two of Brambilia's lieutenants had sauntered in. One was marked for death by Francesco's gun. Men with timers never saw it coming.

He took another pull, forcing his shoulders to loosen. His pocket watch read five past seven. Late. A sharp irritation pricked him. Punctuality was respect, and he demanded it. Perhaps she'd reconsidered.

Then the door opened, and there she was.

Miss Silvano walked inside, pausing under the soft glow of the entryway sconce. Francesco's breath hitched. She was a stunning vision in a glittering black dress, high-necked in front, yet scooped daringly low at the back when she turned to look around. The dress skimmed her figure with an elegance that managed to both be fashionable and hint at her figure beneath. A delicate string of pearls graced the throat he longed to graze.

But her face captured him most of all. Her lips were painted a deep rose, curved into a gentle, resolute smile that didn't quite mask the apprehension in her wide eyes. When she saw him, her expression warmed with what looked like relief.

Francesco rose to his feet, setting his whiskey aside. The maître d' stepped forward. Other diners glanced up from their meals, recognizing him, their conversations faltering. He felt their eyes on the striking newcomer and the mobster claiming her. Good. Let them see Francesco Romano with a beautiful woman. Let gossip spread.

"Serafina," he said softly. Up close, she smelled of a subtle floral perfume. He offered her his hand, which she took with a slight tremble.

She looked up at him. "Good evening, Francesco."

Their eyes met, and for a moment, the noise of the restaurant faded.

He guided her to their table, his hand at the small of her back, fingers grazing bare skin where the dress dipped. Leaning close, his breath hot on her ear, he murmured, "You look exquisite. Good enough to fuck right here." His voice was rougher than he intended.

Her cheeks flushed, but she leaned closer, her breath catching. "Thank you," she said, voice shaky. "I hoped you'd approve."

When she settled into her seat, his fingers brushed over her shoulder. The beadwork on her dress caught the candlelight with each subtle movement, and she shivered.

Francesco took his own seat close to her and signaled the sommelier.

"The '19 Barolo," he ordered.

Their waiter appeared right after. Francesco ordered for them both without consulting the menu. When the wine arrived, the sommelier presented it with all the ceremony such a fine bottle deserved, offering Francesco the customary taste. Francesco nodded his approval, and the man filled both their glasses before retreating.

Serafina took a small sip. "This is exceptional," she gasped, taking another.

"You should try rum sometime," Francesco replied, watching her reaction to his casual mention of the illicit drink.

Her eyebrows lifted. A hint of mischief flashed in her eyes. "Who says I haven't? There are speakeasies, you know."

"Well then," he said, leaning forward, "you need to try some from a private collection in Havana. Cuban rum is an entirely different experience."

"You have connections in unusual places," she said.

"I find the warmer climate agreeable for many ventures."

Their appetizers arrived, ending the conversation about his Cuban ties. Serafina tore a piece of crusty bread from the basket, though she only nibbled at it. When she reached for her wine glass again, she glanced at him through her lashes in a gesture that seemed almost practiced, as if she were trying to be alluring.

Francesco recognized the look immediately. He'd seen enough women attempt seduction to know calculated desire from genuine want. Serafina was trying. Badly. It should have amused him. Instead, he found something unexpectedly charming about her clumsy attempts at sophistication. Like watching a kitten try to roar.

"Relax, Serafina." He slid his hand across the table until it covered hers. "Just relax."

Serafina drew a deep breath, but instead of pulling her hand away as he'd expected, she rotated it until her palm faced up, allowing her to interlace her fingers with his. The simple, trusting gesture caught him off guard. His thumb brushed over her knuckles almost without thought.

"It's a beautiful place," she said, loudly enough for any eavesdroppers to hear. "I've never been here before. The chandeliers are quite lovely."

Francesco lifted their joined hands and brushed a soft kiss over her knuckles.

"Anything for you, *amore*."

He allowed himself a small chuckle at the endearment. Serafina's cheeks flushed, and she bit her lip, but instead of seeming overwhelmed, she leaned toward him. Her free hand trailed along his forearm.

"You spoil me," she said with a coy look that didn't quite hide the spark in her eyes.

Francesco nearly laughed at her performance. She was trying so hard, this little scholar playing at seduction. He should have found it tiresome. Instead, his pulse kicked up a notch. Perhaps she'd be more entertaining than he'd anticipated.

Under the table, his hand rested on her knee, feeling her warmth through the beadwork. She gasped softly, her thighs tensing.

Then a shadow fell over their table.

A tall, broad-shouldered man in a pinstripe suit and silk tie stood there with an ingratiating grin. Francesco knew him. Alberto Bartolli was one of Brambilia's mid-level captains.

"*Mr. Romano*," Bartolli greeted in Italian, his gaze flicking toward Serafina. "*What a surprise to see you here. I hope I'm not interrupting.*"

Francesco's fingers tightened on Serafina's knee.

"*Alberto, good evening. Out enjoying la dolce vita?*" he responded in Italian as well. As he spoke, he scooted his chair slightly around the table to drape an arm along the back of Serafina's. His thumb brushed the bare skin of her shoulder.

Serafina went rigid for a second, but then she surprised him again. She leaned into his touch, her body melting against his side.

"Won't you introduce me, dear?" she asked in English.

"Of course." Francesco allowed a faintly indulgent grin to curve his lips. "Alberto Bartolli, meet Sera Silvano...my girlfriend."

Bartolli's eyes narrowed a fraction. Before Francesco could stop him, he bent forward and took Serafina's free hand, brushing a kiss to the back of it.

"A pleasure, Miss Silvano. I don't recall seeing you around here before."

Serafina giggled and pressed slightly closer to Francesco's side.

"The pleasure is mine, sir. I've been rather occupied with my shop until recently, so I'm afraid I haven't attended many social gatherings." She glanced up at Francesco with fondness, though a hint of defiance glimmered beneath it. "But Francesco here convinced me it was time to change that."

"And how did you two meet?" Bartolli asked, his tone edged with suspicion.

"At an art gallery," Francesco replied smoothly. "Serafina was sketching some Italian Renaissance pieces, and I was impressed by her knowledge of the period."

"I was lost in a Botticelli," Serafina added. "Didn't notice this handsome stranger watching me." Her fingers grazed his vest. "He approached after I'd studied it for hours."

"And when, might I ask, was this?"

"Oh, a few months ago," Serafina answered without missing a beat.

Francesco caught the calculation in Bartolli's eyes when they stared at each other.

"Well, I can hardly believe it. Francesco Romano, settling down. But here you are."

Francesco's palm moved higher on Serafina's thigh, his touch becoming more possessive. "What can I say? This beauty caught me by surprise."

He squeezed her shoulder with his other hand, drawing her closer than she already was. He leaned down to whisper near her ear, yet loud enough for Bartolli to hear. "I found myself rather enjoying being surprised by beautiful women who know what they want."

Serafina took a deep breath, but she responded perfectly, glancing up at him with a look that managed to be both shy and inviting. "And here I was, thinking that you hated surprises."

He chuckled and gazed down at her with open desire. "That was true. Only the unpleasant ones, *cara mia*." His tone dropped to a husky whisper. "You, however, are full of delightful surprises." He brushed his lips on her temple.

Watching this display, Bartolli appeared almost disappointed, as if he had hoped to catch them in some sort of facade. "Well, congratulations, I suppose. It does a man good to have an attractive woman by his side, doesn't it?"

"It does," Francesco said, with a subtle edge in his voice.

Serafina glanced past Bartolli.

"Oh, you're married, Signore? How lovely. You must give your wife over there my regards."

As Bartolli walked away, Francesco was impressed. Most women in his world would have frozen under that level of scrutiny, yet she used it to her advantage.

The instant he was out of earshot, Serafina let out a slow breath. Francesco kept his arm snug around her and his palm on her thigh. She started to lean away, but he tightened his hold. "Wait," he murmured at her ear. "He's still watching." Bartolli had already vanished from view, but Francesco found himself reluctant to release her. The warmth of her body against his, the way she fit into the curve of his arm—it satisfied something he hadn't realized he'd been craving. He allowed himself a few more moments, purely for his own satisfaction.

Serafina angled her head toward him. "Who is he?" she asked in a low voice, her breath warm against his neck.

Francesco answered in the same quiet tone, lips barely moving. "No one for you to worry about." His hand traced a slow, steady circle on her thigh, and she shivered at the touch.

When he was sure they were unobserved, he let his arm slip from her shoulders, though his palm stayed on her leg a moment longer. Serafina straightened, her cheeks flushed from more than wine.

Francesco smiled. "You were perfect."

Serafina picked up her fork again, but he noticed the faint tremor in her grip. "I nearly called you Mr. Romano when he appeared."

"But you didn't. You stayed composed, *cara.*"

She gave a small, relieved laugh. "You're not bad at this, Francesco."

"I've had practice at deception," he said wryly. His thumb kept moving in a slow caress across her hand.

Their eyes met for a lingering moment. Then Serafina let out a quiet chuckle. "Well, here's to fooling the world," she said, just loud enough for him to hear.

Francesco lifted the bottle. "More?"

"Yes, please. What variety is this again?"

"A 1919 Barolo from Piemonte, one of the finest vintages," he said, refilling her glass as a smirk tugged at his mouth, before lifting his own glass. "To our charade."

When the silence threatened to settle between them again, Francesco decided to press her in earnest. He kept his tone low. "You seem withdrawn. What's wrong?"

Serafina blinked and finally met his eyes. "I'm fine," she said too quickly. "It's just been a rather overwhelming couple of days. I apologize if I seem out of sorts."

Francesco studied her for a long moment. "Overwhelming? How?"

She bit her lip, then straightened a little. "I had a meeting with Mr. Kensington, the publisher I mentioned at the ball. It didn't go as I hoped."

Francesco's gaze narrowed at the flicker of pain darkening her features. "Trouble with your manuscript?"

Her jaw tightened. "No, but who wants romance, anyway?" She glanced down, twisting the stem of her glass between her fingers.

His hold on her hand tightened without thought. *Focus. Not your business,* he told himself. *She's a distraction, nothing more.* Yet irritation prickled at whoever had put that wounded look in her eyes.

"I see," he said evenly, though an edge crept into his tone that made her glance up sharply. "I'm sorry."

She gave a brittle smile. "It's behind me. I'm trying not to let it ruin tonight."

His pulse jumped when she squeezed his hand. He cleared his throat. "Our *primi*," he said, almost brusque, as a server arrived with their pasta.

Francesco watched Serafina pick at her food, speaking only when prompted. When her glass ran low again, he held up the bottle. She accepted with a nod. The wine helped. By her fourth glass, her shoulders had eased.

"You should have seen it." Her eyes sparkled. "This enormous tabby launched himself through my front window, right into my Jane Austen display." Her hand rested on Francesco's forearm as she spoke, fingers idly brushing the fabric of his jacket. "Books everywhere, glass all over the floor. Poor Mrs. Williams was mortified. It was her cat, you see."

Francesco felt genuine amusement. The image she painted was absurd, and the way she told it, with such earnest animation, caught him off guard. When had he last laughed at something that wasn't dark or cruel?

"What did you do?"

"Well, I couldn't charge her for the window. She's eighty-three and spends half her pension on books. So I told her the cat had excellent literary taste. *Pride and Prejudice* was the only one left unscathed."

When she laughed, really laughed, dimples appeared at the corners of her mouth, and Francesco's chest tightened. He wondered what other sounds he could draw from her, what she might sound like when she wasn't guarded, when she gave herself over completely.

"You're terrible," he said with warmth in his voice that he hadn't intended.

"I prefer 'creative problem-solver,'" she replied, taking another sip. Her hand stayed on his arm as though she'd forgotten it was there.

She slipped once, calling him "Mr. Romano" when thanking him for the refill. Francesco slid his hand over hers, thumb brushing her knuckles. "Francesco," he quietly corrected.

"Tell me something about yourself," she said, her gaze fixed on his face. "Something you haven't told anyone before."

Francesco hesitated. Most of his childhood was too dark for her, but this one he could share.

"When I was twelve, I stole bread from the village baker." He left out the gambling debts, the hunger that had driven him. "Got caught with crumbs on my shirt."

Serafina's expression softened. "She sounds like a kind woman. Were you..." She paused. "Were you not getting enough to eat?"

The gentle question caught him off guard. Most people would have focused on the theft or the punishment; she saw the need behind it. Something in his chest cracked open, just a little. He wasn't sure he liked that.

"A growing boy could never get enough of her pane dolce," he said, steering the thought away. "It was like candy more than bread—sweet, with almonds and honey. Maybe I was just greedy."

"What happened?"

"The baker's wife took pity on me. Made me sweep floors for a week to pay it off." He left out how she'd fed him every day, how she had been the only adult to show him kindness that year, how her death the following winter had been his first real loss... how he'd stood in the snow outside her funeral, too ashamed to go inside.

"She sounds like a kind woman." Serafina's hand settled over his.

The touch shouldn't have affected him. It was just a hand. Just warmth. But something in him responded like a starving dog shown scraps, eager and pathetic, desperate for more

When he turned his palm up this time and closed his fingers around hers, her breathing quickened.

As the evening went on, he grew uneasy with how much he wanted her touches. If they were alone, he would have taken her to bed, but it wouldn't be the quick, detached fuck he'd imagined. He wanted to watch her eyes widen with pleasure, to coax those soft sounds from her throat, to be gentle in ways he'd never bothered with before.

The realization hit him like ice water. Ricci had been right. She was too innocent. Too soft. Too fucking dangerous.

This wasn't supposed to happen. He didn't do vulnerable. He didn't let women see past the mask, didn't share stories about dead bakers' wives who'd shown him mercy he hadn't deserved. Ginevra had taught him that lesson thoroughly, opening him up, making him believe he could be something other than what he was, then... She left him bleeding out emotions he'd thought long dead.

Never again. He wouldn't make that mistake twice. He wouldn't let himself feel anything for the girl sitting across from him with those warm, understanding eyes that saw too fucking much.

Cazzo. This was not what he had planned.

"And then the—"

"Have you ever dated seriously?" he asked suddenly, his voice harder than intended. He needed to know. Needed to understand what he was dealing with.

She blinked. "Well... never seriously, no. I don't know that I want to be married. So why date?" She traced her glass rim. "What about you?"

"Have you ever been with a man?"

"No," she said quietly, turning beet red. "I haven't."

There it was, the confirmation he needed. His suspicion had been right. She was a virgin. Untouched. He pictured her learning from him, opening to his touch for the first time, those wide eyes looking up at him with trust he didn't deserve. Christ, his body wanted it—wanted *her*—with an intensity that made his jaw clench

But something else nagged at him, something that felt uncomfortably like conscience. He didn't touch virgins. Ever. That was a rule he'd established years ago after dealing with the aftermath, the tears, the desperate belief that giving him their innocence meant he owed them something like a future, or love, things he had no interest in providing.

Experienced women understood the transaction. They took their pleasure and left, with no complications.

But this... the thought of taking what she'd never given, of being the one to ruin that innocence, then forcing her to remain close for weeks more because Bartolli had witnessed their relationship" tonight... watching her hope for something real while he counted down the days until he could walk away...

It didn't sit well. He didn't want to hurt her, and that irritated him more than anything else. When had he started caring? What the hell was it about this particular woman that made him give a damn? He'd destroyed plenty of lives without losing sleep. Why should hers matter?

But it did. Goddamn it, it did.

And his body still hadn't gotten the message. Heat still pooled low in his gut every time she moved, every time that fucking perfume reached him, every time her hand brushed his. His cock didn't care about consequences or emotions or the mess this would become. It only knew want.

"We need to go," he said, signaling for the check.

Serafina blinked and drew back. "Did I say something wrong?"

"No. It's getting late."

Outside, she stumbled slightly and caught his arm, laughing under her breath. "I think I had too much wine."

Francesco glanced down the street. The darkness between buildings seemed deeper, and movement in his peripheral vision made him pause. A figure stepped back quickly when his gaze swept the area.

"Antonio will take you home," he said, his voice more distant than before.

"Tonight was nice," she said, leaning against him slightly.

His guard came up fast. "I care about my interests," he said. "Right now, you're aligned with them. It's business, Serafina. Don't mistake it for anything else."

He saw her face cool.

"Of course," she said. "How foolish of me."

"Serafina—"

"No, you've made yourself clear." She pulled away from his hand. "It's business. Nothing more. I understand. I've just—" She hiccuped. "I've just had too much wine."

His driver pulled up. Francesco helped her into the car despite her shrugging off his help.

"Antonio," Francesco told him, "take Miss Silvano home. Walk her to the door and make sure she gets inside."

Antonio nodded. "Yes, sir."

72

Francesco stepped back as the car pulled away, watching the taillights fade. His attention shifted to the dark space where he'd seen movement, his hand going to the gun beneath his jacket.

The street was empty now. Whoever had been watching was gone, likely spooked when they realized he had noticed. He stood there a few minutes longer, scanning, but found nothing.

Probably just a vagrant or some fool considering a robbery. Still, he made a note to have his men watch the area. In his work, caution kept you alive.

As he walked to his own car, Francesco couldn't shake the thought that the evening had gone better than he'd hoped with Bartolli present. But now he had a new problem.

How was he supposed to move forward when every instinct told him to both claim her and protect her from himself?

Outside Il Girasole, he eased out of the darkness between two buildings, watching. The street lamps didn't touch him here. His fists curled tight, nails biting into his palms, as he pictured what had happened inside. He'd shadowed her from the moment she stepped out of her apartment in that black dress. When she crossed the threshold of a place like this, he'd known. She didn't belong in a room like that. Not with a man like him.

When they emerged, she was off-balance, swaying, her laughter slurred. Romano's hands were all over her. She leaned into him like she trusted him.

A slow, hot rage climbed his spine. What had Romano filled her with? Wine? Lies? Both? Men like that only took interest in women like her when they wanted to ruin them. She couldn't see it. She wouldn't. That left it to him. Someone had to keep her safe, even if she fought him for it.

Romano's car slipped away into the dark, carrying her farther from where she was meant to be. He pulled his coat close and turned toward home. The bookshop would be next. She needed him there.

She needed her mind turned away from predators, fixed on something steady. On him. Until she understood, she was exposed. And if she stayed this blind, sooner or later, he would have to make her see.

CHAPTER 6

Serafina wove through the morning crowd, her head throbbing from a restless night and too much wine. Fragments of dark eyes and rough hands clung to her in scraps of memory she could not place. Francesco's words, "It's transactional, don't misunderstand," tightened her stomach. The air was thick with the stench of coal smoke and horse manure, the sidewalks slick from the overnight rain that had turned the gutters into muddy streams. Horns blared from automobiles weaving through horse-drawn carts, and beggars huddled in doorways, their eyes hollow from the war's lingering scars.

Near the bookshop, Danny had been busy setting tin buckets of flowers along the curb, the petals wilting slightly in the damp air. He looked up as she approached, his sandy hair disheveled, his smile steady but tinged with concern.

"Good morning, Serafina." He offered a paper bag that smelled of butter and almonds. "Your favorite. And I chose these flowers thinking of you this morning." He angled the daisies so their yellow faces caught the weak light filtering through the clouds. "I was wondering if you'd like to get coffee with me?"

She paused, a fleeting warmth from the gesture cutting through her fog, even as her thoughts slid to Francesco. Danny had been steady since she started working next door, generous in small ways that felt safe in a city where men like Kensington lurked with their slimy propositions. But the memory of Francesco's hand on her thigh at dinner ran a wet heat between her legs, and the warmth in Danny's offering turned complicated. She said nothing.

"You're not eating," he said, keeping his voice low. "You look worn down. Are you taking care of yourself?"

"I'm fine. Truly."

"Another time, maybe? I could walk you home later. It's on my way."

"That's kind, but no. I am all right."

He accepted the answer with a small breath. "Then take the croissants. They're for you. Have a good day, Serafina."

"You too, Danny." She took the bag and went inside. The bell chimed behind her, and through the glass she saw him still watching, his shoulders a little rounded. The choice was right, but it still stung.

Mr. Thompson, the founder and owner, lifted his head from the ledger. The light struck silver through his hair. Concern gathered near his eyes.

"Morning, Sera. You look tired, my dear."

"Didn't sleep well," she said, tucking her handbag under the counter. "And you're early. How is Mrs. Thompson today?"

His face softened. "About the same. The doctor came yesterday and said the fever is holding steady. Not progress, but not worse. I am sorry I keep leaving you to mind the place. With Prohibition hitting the suppliers and prices up, it's been tough."

"I like running it," Serafina said. "I can manage. You should be with her."

"You're a godsend." He patted her hand. "I don't know what we would do without you." He nodded toward the back room. "A new shipment came in. I'll open the crates and start the catalog before I go."

"I'll handle it," she said, already moving. "I'll see you later, though."

"Thank you." He paused as if remembering a note. "Before I

forget, Richard Kensington called. He said he would stop by later this week to discuss publishing matters with you."

A chill ran down her back, the memory of Kensington's clammy grip and stale breath resurfacing like bile. She kept her face even and nodded, though her stomach churned with revulsion. "I'll be ready."

Mr. Thompson left soon after. The shop fell into a heavy quiet, broken only by the distant rumble of trucks and the occasional shout from vendors outside. Serafina set the typewriter on the counter for the slow hours, and stared at the blank page. The pounding in her head matched the rhythm of the city's pulse.

The bell chimed, and frequent patron Mr. Andrews entered, hat in hand, his cheer forced in the dim light.

"Good morning, Mr. Andrews. Looking for anything in particular today?"

"Miss Silvano, anything new on naval warfare? Something recent, perhaps?"

She led him along the shelves, pulling spines she knew he favored, though part of her drifted. What was Francesco Romano doing at this second? Was he thinking about their arrangement, about the way they'd stood so close in the restaurant, about that moment when his mask had slipped?

Mr. Andrews paid and left. Quiet settled over the shop again. Serafina returned to the counter, fingers hovering above the keys, ready to press the mess in her chest into lines on paper, but the words would not come, blocked by the fear that Mr. Kensington's call had stirred.

The bell chimed again, and this time her heart raced.

Mr. Romano entered alone. They caught each other's eyes from across the room, and a nervous warmth rose under her ribs.

"Good morning, Mr. Romano." She smoothed her skirt with hands that did not quite steady. "Can I help you find something?"

"Your performance last evening was convincing," he said as he reached the counter. "Bartolli believed what he saw."

Heat crept up her neck at the memory of his hand on her thigh. "I am glad it served its purpose."

"You played your part well." His eyes darkened. "Perhaps better than necessary."

The words cut more than they should have. "I thought that was the point."

"It was. It is." He paused, then shifted course. "I would like to browse your poetry."

She came out from behind the counter, grateful for the task. "Any style you prefer?"

"I will trust your judgment."

Between the shelves, the air seemed to tighten. His steps matched hers too closely. The faint trace of cologne threaded through the warmth that bled from his body into the narrow space they shared. The closeness made her aware of every breath. Her nipples hardened under her blouse as she felt his gaze on her back.

She stopped and faced him, finding him much closer than she'd expected. Close enough that she had to tilt her head back to meet his eyes. "You're a contradiction. You say you dislike romance, yet you enjoy poetry. Poetry lives on romance. It relies on the beauty of language, and on the closeness between writer and reader."

"But poetry is honest," he said after a moment. "It strips pretense."

"And you prefer honesty to pretense?"

"In poetry, yes. In life..." He lifted his shoulder, "pretense is often safer."

"Safer for whom?"

Something unguarded touched his gaze, then closed. His hand came up, fingers ghosting along the shelf beside her head, effectively caging her in. Not touching her, but close enough that she could feel the heat radiating from his palm. "For everyone involved."

Her pulse kicked up. She knew she should step away, but she couldn't. "Sometimes real feeling is as fine as any poem, sir."

He considered her, his eyes dropping briefly to her mouth before returning to meet her gaze. "Do you believe that?"

"I must. Otherwise, why write at all?"

"Why do you write romance?" he asked, almost under his breath.

It caught her off balance. "Because love helps people feel less alone."

"Do you write from experience?"

The line of inquiry pressed too close, so she turned, or tried to. His other hand came to rest on the shelf on her opposite side, not quite trapping her, but making it clear she could only leave if he allowed it.

"Answer me."

The command in his voice sent a shiver down her spine. "Well, I..."

"And do you really think that love exists, outside of books?"

She stared up at him, his face inches from hers now. "Of course. Don't you?"

Mr. Romano took long enough to answer that she thought he would refuse. When he spoke, his jaw tightened as if the words scraped coming out. "Some people are not meant for that kind of happiness."

Her chest tightened. She took a small step toward him. "Why would you say that?"

For a moment, something raw flickered across his features. Then his expression shuttered completely, and he dropped his arms, stepping back so abruptly she nearly stumbled forward. "Enough philosophy," he said, brisk again. "Show me what you think I would like."

The sudden shift left her off-balance, as if he'd pulled the ground from beneath her feet. Serafina took a steadying breath, then selected a slim leather-bound volume from the shelf. "This collection might interest you. The poet writes about longing without relying on the usual turns."

She opened to a page she had read many times before. Mr. Romano moved behind her and leaned in to see, but this time he pressed close behind her, his chest nearly touching her back, his breath stirring the fine hairs at her nape. The body heat pressing close sent a fresh wave of wetness between her thighs. She took a breath and read.

> The night leans close, its whispers soft and low.
> Your hands confess what words could never show.
> In silence, heat and tenderness combine.
> The dark itself conspires to make you mine.

"The language is quite beautiful," he said, his voice slightly rougher than before, his mouth so close to her ear that she felt the words as much as heard them.

"Poetry often reveals truths we're afraid to speak plainly." She turned the page with fingers that weren't entirely steady. "This next piece is even more direct."

She continued reading, her voice growing softer.

> Your fingers write in fire upon my skin,
> Each touch a vow that draws me deeper in,
> Our breaths entwine, the world dissolves within,
> Until I know not where you end or I begin.

The words of desire thickened the air between them. Her body yearned for his touch. One step would have closed it.

"Miss Silvano," he said, barely above a whisper.

"Yes?"

His hand came to possessive rest on her hip. She felt the heat of his palm through the fabric of her dress.

For a heartbeat he seemed ready to pull her back against him. Her lips parted. Heat ran along her skin. His attention dipped to her mouth. His fingers flexed, tightening on her hip.

Then he pulled himself back, releasing her so suddenly she felt cold where his hand had been.

"The poetry is... you read that book often."

"Yes. I... I have a copy at home."

"I'll take this one, then."

The spell broke. "All right."

At the counter she wrapped the volume in brown paper. When she passed it to him, their knuckles grazed, and a line of heat ran up her arm. His fingers closed over hers, holding them against the package for a beat too long. His thumb brushed across her knuckles in a slow, deliberate stroke that made her breath catch.

"Wednesday evening," he said, his eyes locked on hers with an intensity that made her feel like prey. "Seven. I'll send a car to your apartment."

"I'll be ready."

"We'll dine somewhere that requires formal dress," he added, businesslike again. "More formal than Il Girasole."

Just like that, the warmth was gone, replaced by cold professionalism. The whiplash left her reeling.

The chime sounded as he left. Serafina held the counter until her pulse eased, the skin of her forearm still alive where they had touched, her body throbbing with unfulfilled need.

She was thoroughly confused by the man who spoke of poetry and love with barely-hidden pain, who claimed to dislike romance, but who leaned close to hear verses about passion and longing. Who touched her like he owned her one moment, then withdrew as if she'd burned him the next. Who looked at her with hunger that made her knees weak, then spoke to her with the cold courtesy of a stranger.

She should be frightened by the control he wielded so effortlessly, by the way he could make her forget to breathe with just his proximity.

Instead, she was counting the hours until Wednesday, and she could not decide which unsettled her more, the thought of nothing happening between them, or the terrifying possibility that something would. That he would touch her again with that same possessive certainty, that she would let him, that she might even beg him to.

Shortly before closing, Serafina totaled the ledger when the bell rang. Clara swept in, radiant with happiness.

"Darling! I have the most wonderful news! George introduced me to his friend, Irving Curtis. Oh, my dear, he's a doctor—an obstetrician! Can you imagine? And such a gentleman! We talked for hours and it felt like mere minutes. He's intelligent, kind, and he has the most delightful sense of humor."

Serafina shook her head and held up her hand. "Clara, please! I'm short of breath listening to you. Slow down and start over. Now, what did your brother do?"

"He introduced me to his friend, Mr. Curtis." Clara's excitement was contagious. Her eyes sparkled as she leaned on the counter. "Oh, I know it's early, but I truly believe there might be something real between us. It's a feeling I haven't had in such a long time, and it's exhilarating."

Serafina's gaze softened. "You deserve every ounce of this happiness. I am so thrilled for you."

Clara beamed and began straightening a few books on a nearby display. "Would you like to have dinner with me tonight? I can fill you in on all the details."

Serafina hesitated. More than anything, she wanted to be alone with her thoughts, to replay every moment of Mr. Romano's visit, every charged glance and heated word. "I'd love to, but I'm rather tired. Could we have lunch tomorrow instead?"

Clara was about to answer when the door opened. Richard Kensington entered. Clara's warmth cooled at once into polite formality.

"Mr. Kensington. How nice to see you."

"Miss Randolph. Miss Silvano." His mouth held a pleasant curve; his gaze did not. "I hope I'm not intruding."

"Not at all," Clara replied. "I was just leaving." She turned to Serafina with a meaningful look. "I'll see you tomorrow for lunch, darling."

The shop seemed to draw in on itself with Clara's departure, the air heavier, the shadows longer.

"Miss Silvano, I believe we have some unfinished business to discuss." A smug smile played on Mr. Kensington's lips. The threat sat in his eyes.

"If you're referring to your publishing offer, Mr. Kensington, I made my position clear."

"Positions can change." He moved closer and she took a half step back. "I'm prepared to be more generous than before."

"My answer is still no."

His smile fell away. Heat lit in his pale gaze. "Unfortunate. I don't take refusals well. Especially not from someone in your situation."

"My situation?"

"A shop girl with literary ambitions. No connections. No independent income." His tone stayed conversational, each word placed with care. "You are not in a position to be selective."

Anger tightened in her chest. "I may lack family money, Mr. Kensington, but I have my job here, and my integrity."

"Integrity does not pay rent. It does not set type. It does not move a book through the press." He closed the gap by an inch, near enough for her to smell the whiskey on his breath. "I can make your life comfortable. Or difficult. You choose."

"Are you threatening me?"

"I am telling you how this world works. Publishing is small. Reputations are brittle. One quiet remark about your character, and doors close across this city."

"You wouldn't," she said, her blood turning to ice.

"Try me. You have until the weekend. After that..." he shrugged. "I expect you can picture the outcomes." He leaned closer. "You have potential. Potential needs guidance."

Fear and anger collided. "I won't be bullied, Mr. Kensington."

His gaze narrowed. He lifted his hand and drew two fingertips along the side of her neck to her collarbone, slow enough to make the meaning plain. She went rigid.

"Such lovely skin," he murmured. "It would be a pity to crease it with worry."

"I doubt you have much fight left," he added, voice pleased. "Good. Remember this: say no and you make an enemy who keeps accounts. I am generous, though. You have until the weekend. Remember that. I will not extend the deadline."

He set his tie straight. "I trust you'll weigh my offer properly, Miss Silvano. Such chances rarely come twice."

"Good evening, Mr. Kensington," she said, keeping her voice steady.

He stayed long enough to make the silence work for him, then left without looking back.

She did not move for several minutes. The threat settled over the shelves like fine grit. Reputation was currency here, and he held the purse strings. She locked up early, checked the bolt twice, and stepped into the evening. The street felt altered, as if his words had dimmed familiar corners. On the walk home she tried not to think of Mr. Romano, yet the memory returned of the poetry aisle and the rough edge in his voice when he spoke of happiness he did not deserve. The truth of it unsettled her.

The stairs to her building felt steeper than usual, her legs heavy with fatigue and worry. She was digging the key from her handbag when she saw the damage to the door. Pry marks scored the lock as if a blade had bitten into it. Gouges marred the brass. Splinters lay across the landing. Her stomach dropped as she took in every scratch.

Her hands shook when she tested the key. The cylinder still turned, though the mechanism had gone loose. She let herself in, threw the deadbolt, and dragged a kitchen chair tight against the frame for good measure.

Mr. Kensington? The timing aligned too neatly to ignore. He had threatened her in the afternoon; by evening someone had worked a blade at her lock. The conclusion chilled her, and no other explanation held up.

Whoever had tried the door had failed, but the harm was done. The sense of safety that belonged to these rooms did not return with the deadbolt.

She sank onto the sofa, wrapping her arms around herself while she tried to think in order. The practical list presented itself: call the landlord, file a report, ask the neighbors if anyone saw a stranger on the stairs.

Another list rose just as quickly. The police would hear "publisher" and "refused advances" and decide she was overwrought. If the complaint found its way back to Mr. Kensington, he would make sure the blame landed on her.

She pulled her spare manuscript from the drawer and ran her fingertips along the stacked pages. Months of work and years of hope suddenly felt fragile.

Maybe he was right about power and connections. He had both. She had this job and a draft. "Shop girl," he had said, as if she and her honest work were beneath the grime of his shoe. Anger burned under the fear as she thought of how many women had been cornered the same way, their work pushed quiet by threats and smiling men. She refused to imagine her name added to that list.

The hours crawled. She washed dishes, the water cold against her skin. She mended a hem, the needle pricking her finger once, drawing a drop of blood. She reorganized her small collection of books, the spines worn from repeated reads, their stories of love and adventure now feeling like mocking illusions in a city where women navigated mafia shadows and Prohibition's hidden vices.

But every creak of the building, every footstep in the hallway made her freeze with terror. The city outside her window hummed jazz spilling from speakeasies and automobiles rumbling past, but inside, the walls closed in.

Night settled in full. Weariness pressed down at last. She changed into her nightgown and tried to read, but the lines would not hold steady. Her eyelids grew heavy even as her thoughts spun, replaying Kensington's greasy touch, Francesco's rough whisper, the pry marks on her door.

She must have dozed, because she came awake to a silence that did not belong to the building. The air seemed to hold itself still, and a prickling at the back of her neck warned her she was not alone.

She rose slowly enough to prevent her mattress spring from creaking, then moved toward the entry, placing each foot where the boards gave least. Cold shot through her when she reached the door.

A dark strip moved under the gap, passing back and forth in measured sweeps. Someone paced in the hallway outside, each footfall soft.

She pressed her shoulder to the wall beside the jamb and kept her breathing shallow. The strip stopped moving. Whoever stood there must have gone motionless on the other side of the thin wood.

A narrow beam of light slid along the threshold, careful and steady, beneath the seam where floor met frame. It traveled from one side to the other and returned, as if the watcher were testing for light or motion inside.

She covered her mouth with her palm to trap the sound rising in her throat. The light held, then blinked out, but the shape outside did not withdraw. Metal touched the lock and lifted away with a faint click. The knob turned a fraction and settled back.

A soft scrape came from outside, of leather on wood, perhaps a shoe shifting. Then nothing again. The tension built until her nerves screamed for release. She wanted to pound on the door, to shout for them to leave, but that would confirm she was awake, alone, and vulnerable.

Instead, she slid down the wall slowly, sitting on the cold floor, her back against the wood. The position brought her eyes closer to the gap under the door. She held her breath and peered through, seeing leather soles and shoes that shone. Suddenly the figure dropped. She sat back upright just in time for the beam of light to return.

She stayed pinned in places. Her pulse hammered hard enough to carry through the panel. Minutes lengthened until she could no longer guess at how long they waited. The strip under the door never moved.

Whoever waited in the hall was not leaving.

They were watching.
Waiting.
And they had all night.

CHAPTER 7

The morning air carried a chill that made Serafina pull her shawl tighter on the way to the bookshop. She walked fast, as if pace alone could outrun the night before. Sleep had barely come after the figure outside her door with a flashlight, poised and listening. The image of a dark shape sliding back and forth under the gap, the measured sweep of that light, had frozen her in place. She spent hours curled in bed, straining for the faintest step in the hall.

"Good morning, beautiful," Danny called behind her.

She flinched, spinning so fast her bag swung wide. Danny stood there, his sandy hair mussed, his smile fading to concern as he saw her panic.

"Serafina? What's wrong?" He quickened his steps to catch up to her.

Her throat tightened, an excuse dying on her tongue. "Someone was outside my apartment last night," she said, voice thin. "They had a flashlight and stood watching my door. I was so afraid. I..."

Danny pulled her against his chest, his arms solid. "Oh, sweetheart," he said into her hair, his words rough with worry. "No wonder you're shaken."

She clung to him, grateful for solid warmth after so many hours of dread, and sobbed into his shoulder, her tears soaking the rough cotton of his shirt.

"It's all right," Danny soothed, tracing slow circles between her shoulders. "You're safe now." He held her until her crying subsided, then gently pulled back to look at her face. "Did you see the person? Anything you can describe?"

"I couldn't. It was too dark, and I was too scared to go closer."

His brow tightened. "Did they try the lock?"

"Yes. And earlier I found fresh gouges near the latch, like someone had worked a tool at it."

"That's awful." His jaw set. Anger flickered in his eyes. "Did you call the police?"

"How? I don't have a telephone. And what would I say if I did? That I saw a pair of polished shoes and a strip of light under my door?" She quickly looked down at his scuffed brown shoes.

"Then let me help. I pass your block every morning. Some evenings I walk to clear my head. If I see anyone hanging around, I'll deal with it. Please be more careful about going out alone at night. This city can be rough for a woman on her own."

She did not have it in her to refuse the offer. "Thank you, Danny. I don't know what I'd do without you."

He squeezed her hands gently, his grip lingering just a heartbeat longer than necessary. "You'll never have to find out. Come on. I'll see you to work. You shouldn't be alone when you're this rattled."

At the shop door, Serafina turned the key with unsteady fingers. Danny waited until she was inside, then gave her an encouraging smile through the pane before turning away, his shoulders slightly hunched.

The morning blurred into small routines that steadied her nerves. Each familiar task put another inch between her and the night before, and her breathing eased. Near noon, the bell chimed and Clara's bright voice filled the doorway.

"Serafina! Perfect timing. I was hoping to steal you away for lunch."

Serafina smiled, glad to see her, and caught the way Clara studied her. "That sounds wonderful." She turned the card in the window to "Closed" and gathered her things.

At their usual café, the air smelled of coffee and fresh bread, but the chatter of patrons felt distant, muffled by Serafina's returning fear.

Clara's eyes narrowed as she set her cup down. "You look tired, darling. Are you all right?"

For a moment Serafina considered confessing about the gouged lock, the watcher's beam, and Mr. Kensington's greasy threats, but Clara's radiance stopped her. She couldn't dim her friend's joy with her own darkness. "Just a poor night of sleep," she said, forcing a smile. "Tell me about Dr. Curtis. You're glowing."

Clara's worry broke into joy. "Oh, Serafina! Last night was absolutely magical. We walked in Central Park and talked for hours about his work at the hospital, my volunteer projects, our hopes for the future..." Her voice softened. "And he spoke so beautifully about his late wife, Margaret. The way he honored her made me think about losing Theodore differently."

Serafina reached across the table and squeezed her friend's hand, setting her own fears aside. "How so?"

Clara's eyes grew misty. "Irving said losing someone you love doesn't mean you stop living. It means you must live and love more fully to honor what you had. Theodore would want me to be happy, and to find love again. I've spent four years feeling guilty for even thinking about another man, but Irving helped me see that guilt dishonors Theodore's memory instead of preserving it."

"Oh, Clara," Serafina said, her own vision blurring. "Teddy was such a good man, but Mr. Irving is right."

"He wants to take me to the theater next weekend," Clara added, dabbing at her lashes with a handkerchief. "Can you imagine? It's been so long since I let myself picture a future with someone."

They talked for another hour about the doctor's kindness, his work delivering babies, and the quiet wisdom that had already lifted Clara's heart. Each word deepened Serafina's resolve to keep her secrets about Mr. Kensington's threats and the watcher locked away. Clara deserved this happiness, untainted by Serafina's shadows.

Back at the bookshop, that lightness held until they reached the door. Two figures waited outside: an elegantly dressed older woman who looked like she could complain about sunshine being too bright, and beside her, the unmistakable figure of Mr. Romano. Serafina's mouth went dry at the sight of him. Clara muttered something under her breath that would have made her mother faint.

They entered together. Mrs. Templeton launched into complaints at once. "The state of this city! All this jazz and bootleg liquor—it's corrupting our youth, I tell you!"

Mr. Romano stood off to the side, posture contained, attention fixed on Serafina.

Serafina turned to Clara. "Would you help Mrs. Templeton find what she needs while I assist this gentleman?"

"Of course, darling," Clara said, cool as she cut Mr. Romano a look before turning to the older woman with a composed smile. "What can I help you find today, ma'am?"

As Clara guided Mrs. Templeton toward the back aisle, Serafina crossed to Mr. Romano. "Good afternoon, sir. How may I help you today?"

He didn't answer immediately. Instead, his eyes traveled over her face. When he finally spoke, his voice was low. "I must apologize, Miss Silvano. Urgent business has come up. I have to leave town for a couple of days, so our dinner must be rescheduled."

Disappointment stabbed her, mingling with a shameful rush of desire... and something else. Relief? Fear that she'd done something to drive him away?. "Of course, Mr. Romano. I hope everything is all right."

He gazed at her for a moment, stepping closer, close enough that she could smell his cologne. A small line formed between his brows. "Are you well? You seem troubled."

"I'm all right. What makes you ask?"

Before he could answer, a loud, imperious call carried from the rear of the shop. "This is absolutely scandalous! Roller coasters and penny arcades—Coney Island is nothing more than a den of iniquity that destroys the innocence of our children and our young ladies!"

Mrs. Templeton gesticulated dramatically while Clara nodded with exasperation she barely bothered to hide. "Yes, yes," Clara said with a sigh.

"The whole place should be shut down before it leads decent

people astray... think of the children, think of the children, won't someone think of the children..."

"She does this every week," Serafina said with a tired half-smile. "Last week it was a film ruining the morals of the young, and the week before it was parents who weren't taking the switch to their children's backsides often enough to suit her."

Mr. Romano's expression grew thoughtful as he listened to the woman's tirade. After a moment, he turned back to Serafina with something almost like amusement in his eyes. But there was something darker beneath it. "Have you ever been to Coney Island, Miss Silvano?"

"No, I haven't."

"What time do you close on Saturday?"

"Usually three o'clock."

He gave a decisive nod. "I'll pick you up at five." He cleared his throat. "And I'll take a book of poetry, whichever you recommend."

Serafina kept her face neutral and reached for the most expensive leather-bound volume on the shelf. Mr. Thompson never expected it to move, and she doubted Mr. Romano would care about the price. At the counter, she wrapped it neatly in brown paper and tied the string.

He accepted the parcel with a slight nod. His dark eyes lingered on her face for a moment, and she found herself unable to look away, caught like a moth in candlelight. She hoped he might say something more, something that might explain the push and pull, the heat and cold, the way he looked at her like he wanted to devour her one moment and couldn't bear to be near her the next. But he turned to take his leave. Serafina watched him stride out, followed by the still-complaining Mrs. Templeton, still pronouncing doom on amusements and seaside boardwalks.

Serafina had barely returned to the counter when Clara came back to her side, mouth set.

"Mr. Romano is nothing but trouble," Clara said, eyes narrowing toward the door. "There's something dangerous about him. Can you not ban him from the shop?"

The warning, layered atop the night she'd had, forced a decision. She needed to cause a distraction, and needed to vent, at least a little. "There's something I should tell you about Mr. Kensington."

"Mr. Kensington?" Clara's brow creased. "What about him?"

Serafina drew a breath. "We met about my manuscript. It went badly. He made it clear I'm not getting signed. We couldn't agree on the terms."

It's not technically a lie, she told herself. It just wasn't the whole horrible truth.

"That ignorant man!" Clara's hands balled into fists. "I'm sure that whatever you asked was reasonable. He passed on a great book. Are you going to be all right? Would you like to come over for dinner tonight? Mom keeps asking when you'll visit again, and it might cheer you up."

Serafina gathered as much confidence as she could. "Tell your mother I'll visit soon. And it stings, but Mr. Kensington doesn't want romance. I'll turn the next one into a thriller. There'll be another chance."

"Are you sure? I was to meet with Irving soon, but I can reschedule. He'll understand. You're more important."

Serafina squeezed her hand. "I'm sure. Enjoy your evening. I'll manage tonight. The payphone is close by if I need anything."

"I only wish you had a telephone of your own so I could ring and check on you," Clara said, lips pressing thin.

"Maybe I'll look into getting a line," Serafina answered, gentler. "I promise I'll think about it."

Some of the tension left Clara's shoulders. She pulled Serafina into a tight hug, tears brightening her eyes. "All right. But promise you'll call if you need anything. I'll be there in an instant."

"I promise," Serafina said, holding on just as firmly.

Once alone, Serafina let out a slow breath, then returned to her typewriter. The words came haltingly at first, her fingers hesitating over the keys as she tried to channel the chaos of the past days into her story. In her mind, the heroine was no longer a damsel waiting for love, but a woman cornered by predators, her courage sharpened by fear. Serafina wrote of shadowed hallways and unseen watchers, of a man whose charm masked a dangerous edge, and another whose kindness felt like a tether she couldn't trust. Yet she couldn't bring herself to type it.

She looked up at the bell, expecting another customer, but Danny appeared with a small bouquet of violets, his smile soft but his eyes still heavy with concern

"I forgot to give you these earlier," he said, setting the flowers on the counter. "Thought they might brighten your day."

Her chest tightened with guilt. "Danny, you're too kind. You don't have to keep doing this."

"It's no trouble." He leaned against the counter. "You sure you're okay?"

She forced a smile, tucking the violets into a glass of water. "Just shaken, but I'll be fine."

He nodded. "If you need anything, day or night, you know where to find me. My shop's open late, and I'm just next door."

"I know. Thank you, Danny." Her voice softened.

He tipped his hat and left, the bell's chime fading into the quiet. Serafina returned to her typewriter, but her thoughts drifted to Francesco's visit, the way his presence had filled the shop with a tension that was both thrilling and unsettling. She wondered what "urgent business" had pulled him away, and whether it was tied to the danger Clara had warned her about.

But that curiosity was dangerous. She was already in too deep, caught between Kensington's threats, the watcher at her door, and her own reckless attraction to a man who admitted he was not meant for love. She pressed her palms to her eyes, willing clarity, but all she saw was Francesco's face, the way his eyes had softened when he'd said, "Coney Island."

Late that night, the city's underbelly stirred. In a narrow service alley, a flickering streetlamp cast a sickly glow across wet brick. The air was thick with the stench of piss and rotting garbage. Francesco crouched behind a rusted dumpster, his pistol steady in a gloved grip, his breath controlled despite the severity of what he was about to do. This wasn't his first kill. It wouldn't be his last.

Up ahead, Salvatore Greco swayed in the sodium glow, unaware that his clock had run down. He fumbled a match to a cigarette. The brief flare licked across a pitted cheek and a brow slick with drink. He leaned on the wall as if it might hold him upright. Don Parisi's stupidity had set this in motion; Greco would carry the loss.

Francesco would stage it as Brambilia's. The rival crew favored cruelty that traveled by rumor: a gut shot to start the screaming, then the mercy round up close. Greco had skimmed from Romano warehouses for months, trusting crates of missing rum to disappear into bookkeeping haze. Pity had no place here, only cold satisfaction at the justice about to be served.

He set the sights on Greco's midline and took up slack on the trigger. A round there would tear through intestines and organs, flooding the bastard's abdominal cavity with acid and bile, and keep a man conscious long enough to contemplate his mistakes before shock or blood loss claimed him.

Pop!

Greco's agonized shriek ripped from his throat as the hollow point bullet punched through his gut. His hands flew to the gaping wound, blood and worse things seeping between his fingers. He slid down the wall and tried to crawl, heels scraping stone. A smear of blood marked his path.

Francesco emerged from the shadows, his patent leather shoes echoing off the brick walls. Greco's pupils blew wide with sheer terror.

"*Per favore. Ti prego. I'll pay it back. Every cent,*" Greco wheezed, words wet in his throat. Blood frothed from his lips. "*Please... I have... I have children...*"

"*You should have thought of them when you started stealing from me,*" Francesco said. The alley carried the copper reek and the sharper stink of a body letting go. "*This is the cost.*"

He raised the pistol and put the second round through the thin bone above Greco's left ear. The impact snapped the man's head sideways. Gray and red spattered the wall. Teeth clicked on stone. The body jolted once and went slack, gaze fixed on nothing.

Francesco surveyed his handiwork with grim satisfaction. The scene was exactly what people would expect from Brambilia's animals. He drove his boot into Greco's ribs and felt something give, then spat on the corpse to finish the signature.

He holstered the weapon and straightened. No triumph warmed him, only the grim certainty of order restored. Men who skimmed, lied, and smiled at the same time made a simple mistake. They assumed they would see the dawn. They were wrong.

Francesco slipped into the maze of backstreets where the darkness embraced him like an old friend as he made his way home, each step carrying him away from the scene of righteous execution.

A couple days later, Francesco sat in his study with a measure of whiskey. Reports had begun to filter back to him. Salvatore Greco lay dead, as planned. The problem lay in the rumor that followed. Police chatter and street talk put the job on a soldier from Cesare Giordano's crew, not on Brambilia.

That complication blew holes in his board. Greco had been a lieutenant for the Constanza family under their new don, Vincenzo Parisi. Removing him had been correct and necessary. But Giordano had been a Romano ally for years, tied by years of loyalty and complicated by family. Worse, Esme Greco, now widowed, was one of Giordano's two half-sisters. The other had been murdered, leaving Parisi himself widowed. If blame settled on Giordano's house, Mrs. Greco would demand blood, flipping alliances into war.

The delicate balance of power that kept the peace in New York's underworld teetered on the edge of collapse. If he failed to steer the story toward Brambilia or another rival, reprisals would hit households as well as soldiers. Families would fracture. Children would vanish. Homes would burn. Francesco refused to let that chaos unfold.

His thoughts flickered to his own sister, Lucia. She was stubborn and soft, herself a lover of stories about grand love. He would not watch her traded as leverage or married into a crew because some man promised the moon. He set a private rule: Lucia would never be used to settle accounts, and he'd be damned if he let her marry any gangster out of some foolish notion of love.

But speed mattered now. A quiet sit-down with Giordano could redirect the narrative to Brambilia, preserving the balance.

His attention shifted to Saturday and Miss Silvano. A different current moved through his chest at the thought of Coney Island. Neutral territory where neither his family nor Brambilia's crew could claim control. Public enough that bloodshed would draw unwanted attention, isolated enough that accidents happened nightly off those piers.

So far, their arrangement fit his needs, covering the meetings he wanted to be seen and blurred the ones he did not. It helped drown talk about Brambilia's wife carrying a child that could be his own. *Cazzo.* But Saturday? Saturday served another purpose. He needed to know if she could handle his world without shattering.

Coney Island would tell him everything he could ask. How would she react when surrounded by potential threats? Would she follow orders without questions? Would she run when she realized the screams from the roller coasters masked other kinds of screams entirely? Would her body betray fear or arousal when she understood exactly how many ways a person could disappear among those crowds and shadows? What would happen to the heat in her eyes when she realized there was no safe exit from his world anymore.

And Christ, he wanted to see that heat again. Wanted to watch her pupils dilate when he got too close, wanted to feel her pulse race under his fingers. His body had been on edge since he'd left the bookshop, half-hard just from the memory of her breathing quickening when he'd stepped into her space.

He could have her. He *should* have her. Work her out of his system in a night or two, prove to himself that she was just another warm body, no different from the rest.

Except she loved poetry. The same dark, honest verses that had sustained him through years when nothing else made sense. She understood the rawness in those words, and saw beauty where others saw only despair. That connection bothered him. It made her dangerous in ways that had nothing to do with Brambilia or business.

Saturday could not arrive fast enough. For a few hours he'd test whether his beautiful little writer could survive being his. The idea drew something dark across his mouth that wasn't quite a smile. He loved it. And he hated it.

Maybe he could keep her. After the charade ended, after Brambilia's suspicions died, maybe he could find a way to...

No.

He cut the thought off with the ruthlessness he'd honed over decades. That path led to weakness. Miss Silvano would eventually try to reshape him into one of the heroes in her fucking romance novels.

Women wanted power over men. They used tears, used their bodies, used whatever weapon they could find to crack a man open and make him vulnerable. He'd spent too long building his armor to let some bookshop girl with wide eyes dismantle it.

No woman would have that power over him. Not again. Never again.

He poured another finger of whiskey. Power was his armor. He'd killed to claim it, and he'd kill to keep it. Morning would bring new choices about who lived, who bled, and who learned. Night placed him where he preferred to be: at the center of the web, issuing orders, answering to no one.

He took stock without romance. He had been shaped for this since boyhood. Blood taught the lessons. He had removed the man who stood between him and command. The result was simple to state: power direct and unquestioned, respect delivered through fear when soft words failed.

Streets, ports, and warehouses answered to him. Order had been reinforced. The weak served. The disloyal paid. And Francesco Romano kept the ledger and closed accounts with a steady hand.

As for Miss Silvano? He would find another woman to fill his needs once this charade ended, someone experienced who understood the rules, who would take what he offered and leave without expectations. He'd work Miss Silvano out of his system by never letting her in at all. Distance. Control. That was the only way this could end.

CHAPTER 8

The days following the stalking incident had passed in a blur of hyper vigilance and sleepless nights. The new lock was a joke. She knew that. Whoever had been in her apartment could get in again whenever they chose. The lock was just something to give her at least some sense of security while she lay awake, counting footsteps in the hallway.

Finally Saturday arrived. With limited wardrobe options, she'd spent too long before the mirror, testing hems and buttons, while imagining Mr. Romano's dark eyes appraising her. In the end, she chose a soft peach skirt that hugged her curves more closely than was wise, paired with a cream-colored silk blouse that she left unbuttoned one button lower than proper to reveal just a hint of the lace chemise beneath and be just a little naughty. The cream cloche hat shadowed her eyes, which she hoped would let him wonder what she was thinking. She dabbed a bit of orange blossom perfume at her wrists.

As the clock neared five, Serafina waited outside her apartment building, heart fluttering. *It's just business*, she reminded herself.

When the sleek black car pulled up to the curb, her body responded with equal parts relief and dread. Francesco stepped out, tall and confident in his expensive suit. She caught the slight bulge of his shoulder holster when he moved. He rounded to open the passenger door, and she noticed one of his knuckles had a large, fresh scab.

"You look beautiful," he murmured as she approached, his voice carrying a rough edge that made her knees weak. His gaze lingered on the exposed hollow of her throat, and heat rushed to her cheeks.

Serafina settled beside him when he got back into the car, shifting unconsciously in her seat as she tried to get comfortable. Her skirt rode up as she shifted, and his eyes dropped to the exposed length of her thigh. His jaw tightened, hands gripping the wheel. He exhaled once, slow.

She glanced at him sidelong, biting her lip. "I have a confession. A couple of weeks ago, I didn't think I'd like you very much," she said lightly, folding her gloved hands in her lap.

Francesco raised an eyebrow, though his attention remained split between her and the mirrors. "Oh? And why is that?"

"Well," Serafina mused, touching her lower lip thoughtfully, "you seemed rather intense and mysterious... and, to be frank, like you hated me when we first met." A small grin tugged at her lips. "Though I suppose that was understandable given the circumstances."

He chuckled softly. "'Hate' is hardly the word I'd use. What do you think now?"

"I'm still not entirely sure," she admitted quietly, her voice growing softer. "But I think that, in another time and place, perhaps we could have been real friends, without any of these temporary arrangements. And..." She paused, gathering courage for her next words. "I think I'm going to miss you when it's over. Business or not, I find myself looking forward to seeing you."

"When we met, 'wanted you dead' might have been more accurate than hate," he said quietly. "You were a complication."

"And now?"

"Now you're a different kind of complication."

"Oh..." She looked down, brushing imaginary lint from her skirt to avoid his gaze. "Well, I still think I'm going to miss you when this ends and you don't need me for anything anymore."

Francesco's knuckles went white on the steering wheel. Surprise, and maybe some regret, flickered across his face. His shoulders tensed like he was fighting the urge to reach for her or push her away.

Silence filled the car as it slipped into motion. Outside, streetcar bells and vendor calls fell away behind them. After a while, city blocks gave way to quieter roads. Streetcars and busy sidewalks yielded to open spaces and the distant sound of crashing surf, until the unmistakable cheerful music of a carnival wafted through the open car window. Serafina's eyes widened with realization and delight.

"Coney Island? Are we going to Coney Island?!"

"It's neutral territory," he said flatly. "Neither my family nor Brambilia's crew controls it."

The implication hit her like ice water. "So we'll be—"

"Listen carefully." His voice dropped. "There will be men there who'd hurt you just to send me a message. You don't leave my side. You don't speak to anyone I don't introduce you to. If I tell you to run, you run. If I tell you to get down, you drop. Is that clear?"

"Francesco—"

"Answer me."

"Yes, sir. It's clear."

"But I do hope you can enjoy yourself."

They parked among dozens of other cars, anonymous in the crowd. Music and screams from the rides created a wall of sound that would mask almost anything happening in the dark. Francesco took her hand as they walked through the entrance. His eyes continuously scanned the crowd.

"Come, Serafina. Let's ride the new roller coaster," he said, loud enough for others to hear. Testing her, she realized. Seeing if she'd play along.

She bit her lip, eyeing the massive structure. The screams from the riders weren't all from joy. She could hear real terror in some of them. "I... I don't know... It looks so much bigger than I expected. All that screaming..."

"Screams of delight," he said, a predatory glint in his smile that should have frightened her and instead sent a thrill through her. His thumb stroked across her knuckles. "Scared already?"

"Of course I'm not afraid," she said a bit too forcefully.

Before she could think better of it, they were in the queue. He pulled her back against his chest, arms holding her. To anyone watching, they were lovers. But she felt the tension in his body, ready to explode into violence. His lips brushed her ear. "Third booth from the left. Two men in gray caps. They've been following us since we arrived."

"What do—"

"Nothing. We're just another couple enjoying the evening." His hand slid to her hip. "But be ready."

Her heart drummed against her ribs by the time they were side by side in the car, with both of their hats safely stored in a small cubby meant for such things. The roller coaster car locked them in place. As the chain lift clanked them skyward, he reached for her hand. Her lips twitched in a nervous smile. When she glanced up at him, she caught him watching her with startling intensity, but the moment their eyes met, he looked away and his jaw clenched.

At the peak, she could see the whole park spread below. Then the bottom dropped out. She screamed as they plummeted, genuinely terrified. The force slammed her against him. His arms came around her, pulling her close against his side. The world became a blur of lights and rushing sound. When the car finally screeched back into the station, her legs trembled; she was plastered to him, breathless.

On the platform, she set her cloche back on with shaking hands.

"Do you want to go again? Or are you afraid now?"

"No!" She managed a breathless laugh. "I'd rather take my chances with Brambilia's men."

"The Ferris wheel will be easier," he said.

Neither of them paid attention to a small sign describing how Coney Island's new Ferris wheel had cars that not only rose high, but also slid and swayed on their own tracks. They learned their mistake soon enough. As their car ascended the wheel, a sudden lurch set it swinging wildly on its rails.

Serafina's eyes went wide with panic as the floor seemed to tilt beneath her. "Oh!" she yelped, throwing her arms around Francesco.

The car swung wildly, and she pressed against him, feeling his heart hammering as hard as hers. Francesco drew in a sharp breath, followed by a low curse. The wheel that was supposed to be gentle had become a pendulum of terror. Francesco's arm tightened around her trembling form.

"Shh, I have you now," he murmured into her hair, his voice possessive. "But there," he said as he pointed, "by the ring toss. Brambilia's men." His hand went to his jacket, resting on his gun. "When we get down, we walk toward the beach. Don't run unless I tell you."

When the Ferris wheel finally ended, Serafina's legs shook so badly she could barely stand. The ground seemed to tilt beneath her feet. Francesco caught her as she stumbled off the platform.

"Steady," he murmured

They wove through the carnival crowds, her body still trembling from more than just the ride. Every few steps, his hand would tighten on her waist, pulling her closer when strangers passed too near.

"Did I say something wrong earlier?" she asked as they moved through a dimmer section between attractions. "In the car?"

"Why would you think that?"

"Your demeanor changed when I said I'd miss you." She studied his profile in the flickering lights. "You went somewhere else in your head."

"Some people aren't worth missing."

Her heart twinged. She could hear in the bitter undertone that he meant himself.

"Well, some people aren't worth fake-dating," she said, trying for lightness despite the tightness in her throat. Her hip brushed against his as they walked. "Yet here I am, being fake-dated by someone who apparently thinks he's worthless."

"You don't know what you're talking about." His voice was flat, controlled.

"Don't I?" She turned to face him while walking backward, a dangerous choice in the uneven ground. "You're so convinced you're some kind of monster that you can't even—"

Her heel caught on a raised board. She pitched forward with a gasp. Francesco moved faster than she could process, catching her hard against his chest. The impact knocked the breath from her lungs.

And then he laughed.

Not a dark chuckle or sardonic sound, but genuine laughter that rumbled through his chest and into hers. Lines appeared beside his eyes. His whole face softened, and for a moment he looked like someone who hadn't a care in the world.

Serafina stared up at him, still pressed against his body, her heart racing for entirely new reasons. "The best thing I've seen you wear is that smile," she said softly. "I like how it makes your eyes crinkle right there."

Her finger traced the air beside his eye, not quite touching.

"Careful," he said, though he still smiled. "Those crinkles show my age."

"They show you're human." The words came out fiercer than intended. "They make you look handsome and distinguished."

His arms tightened around her, and she became more aware of every point of contact between them from the solid wall of his chest to the heat radiating through his expensive shirt to the unmistakable hardness pressing against her hip that made her midsection tighten.

Francesco's eyes darkened. His smile faded into something hungrier. His hand spread across her lower back, his fingers pressing through the thin fabric of her dress. Her body responded without permission, arching slightly into him, and she had to bite her lip to hold back a sound that would have been embarrassing.

"Serafina," he said. But then his entire body went rigid. His head snapped up. His eyes scanned the crowd.

"What is it?" she whispered, though she wasn't sure she wanted to know.

"Nothing you need to worry about." But his hand moved to his jacket. "Come. Let's walk."

He guided her through the crowd, but she could feel the change in him. He steered her away from certain areas, changing direction without explanation and always keeping her close.

"You're scaring me," she admitted quietly.

"Good. Fear keeps you alive." He pulled her against him as a group of men passed. "Do you know what the most dangerous moment is?"

"No."

"When you think you're safe." His eyes tracked something in the shadows between booths. "When you let your guard down. When you forget that every beautiful thing hides teeth."

She swallowed hard. "Is that what you think you are? Something beautiful hiding teeth?"

He looked down at her then, and for a moment his expression was almost vulnerable. "I think I'm the teeth without the beauty."

"You're wrong." The words came out before she could stop them. "You're—"

"Don't." His voice was sharp. "Don't make me into something I'm not. Don't romanticize what I am."

"I'm not romanticizing anything. I see exactly what you are."

"Do you?" He stopped walking, turning to face her fully. "You understand that I've killed men for stealing a few barrels of rum?"

"Yes."

"And you're still here."

"At least with you, I know where the danger is coming from."

He laughed again, but this time it was bitter. "No, *tesora*. You really don't."

Before she could respond, he pulled her toward the game booths. "Come. Let's see if I remember how to use a carnival gun."

The dark humor in his voice made her stomach flip. She was certain Francesco Romano had never forgotten how to use any kind of gun, toy or otherwise.

Behind them, she could have sworn she heard footsteps matching their pace. Francesco's fingers pressed harder against her spine. The games suddenly seemed very far away.

But they arrived at the destination without incident. He gave the barker some money, picked up the rifle, and tested its weight. He adjusted his stance.

"Rigged sight," he muttered, making a subtle correction while taking aim. Shots cracked through the carnival. A target fell with each shot.

"Top prize!" the barker called out, gesturing to a golden-brown teddy bear with a cream satin ribbon around its neck.

Francesco took the bear, turned it in his hands as if assessing its quality, then held it to her with both hands. "It's for you."

"Really? I've never had a teddy bear. Oh, thank you!" She hugged it to her chest. "He's perfect. What should I name him?"

Francesco's eyebrows rose. "You've never had one?"

"Never. My father thought toys were frivolous."

"Your innocence is going to get you killed in my world."

"Then it's fortunate I'm not going to be kept in it," she said lightly. "I think I'll call him Francesco."

Color crept up his neck. "You can't name a teddy bear after me."

"Why not? He's handsome and distinguished, just like—"

His arm hooked around her waist and yanked her closer. His entire body had gone rigid. "Brambilia is here."

The change in atmosphere was immediate and chilling. People nearby began giving them a wide berth without looking directly at them, as if some invisible signal had been given. Conversations quieted. Even the carnival music seemed to fade. A tall, slender, well-dressed man with silver at his temples and cold eyes approached them. She wrapped her arms around Francesco.

"Romano," the man said in accented English, gaze sliding over Serafina. "*Che sorpresa.*"

"Brambilia." Francesco's hand stayed at her waist, but his thumb brushed over her bottom rib.

"And this must be the famous Miss Silvano." Brambilia's gaze traveled over her again, slower. "Even lovelier than the photographs suggest."

Two men flanked him, their hands casually near their jackets.

"I don't believe we've been properly introduced," Brambilia continued, extending his hand to her. "Antonio Brambilia."

She had no choice but to take it. Francesco shifted slightly.

"Protective, aren't we?" Brambilia released her hand slowly. "Tell me, Miss Silvano, how are you finding our Francesco's company? He can be quite intense."

"Mr. Romano has been a perfect gentleman," she said.

"Has he? How refreshing. Tell me, what is it you think Francesco does for a living? He must have told you something about his business interests."

"He owns several properties. Real estate investments." She kept her face neutral, and hoped her made-up answer would suffice.

"Real estate." Brambilia laughed softly. "Is that what he told you? How delightfully vague. And you believed him?"

"Why wouldn't I?"

"Why indeed." He pulled out a cigarette, taking his time lighting it. "Though I imagine a clever girl like you must have noticed things. Maybe the late-night meetings or the men who follow him, the blood on his clothes he can't quite explain..."

Francesco's body tightened beside her.

"I don't know what you mean," Serafina said evenly. "And I'm never with him late enough at night to know about meetings."

"No? You've never wondered why a real estate investor needs armed guards? Never questioned the bruised knuckles?" He blew smoke, watching her face. "Or perhaps you have, and you simply don't care. Some women find danger exciting."

"I find Mr. Romano's company pleasant. That's all."

"Pleasant." Brambilia stepped closer. "Tell me, has he taken you to any of his 'properties'? The warehouse on Pier 47? The club on Mulberry Street? Or perhaps the very special basement beneath his office building?"

He's fishing, she realized. Trying to see if Francesco had brought her into his world and shown her things that would make her dangerous to them.

"We go out to dinner and the museum, usually." She kept her voice steady. "I'm afraid his business dealings aren't particularly interesting to me."

"Aren't they? But surely you must be curious. A woman spending so much time with a man like Francesco... you must wonder what occupies his days... and his nights."

"I assume whatever men of business do."

Brambilia laughed again. "Men of business. Yes, I suppose that's one way to put it. Though Francesco's business is rather more specialized than most. Wouldn't you agree, Romano?"

"She doesn't know anything," Francesco said quietly. "Leave her out of this."

"But she's already in it, isn't she? The moment you chose her, she became part of our world, whether she understands it or not." His eyes returned to Serafina. "Tell me, Miss Silvano, do you speak any languages besides English?"

"A little French," she said. "From school."

"French. How sophisticated. I knew a French girl once," Brambilia continued, "who thought she could play innocent and pretend she didn't see the blood or hear the screams. She lasted almost three months before she broke."

"What happened to her?" Serafina wasn't sure she wanted to know.

"Oh, she's still around. What's left of her. Amazing what the mind does to protect itself when reality becomes too much to bear." He dropped his cigarette and crushed it slowly. "But I'm sure you're made of stronger stuff, Miss Silvano. You'd have to be, to catch Romano's attention. Has he mentioned Paola? Or Maria? No? How remiss of him."

Francesco's hand tightened on her waist.

Brambilia reached out suddenly. His fingers brushed the teddy bear. "Did you name it?"

"Yes. She named it Francesco," Francesco said flatly, a challenge in his voice.

Brambilia laughed. "Did she, now? How precious. Holding onto a stuffed version when the real thing is so much more dangerous." His hand moved from the bear to her arm, fingers trailing down to her hand. "Such delicate bones. So easy to—"

Francesco caught his wrist, hard. "Enough."

The two men stared at each other, violence crackling between them. Brambilia's men shifted, ready for attack.

"Careful, Romano," Brambilia said softly. "You're outnumbered here. Neutral territory, remember? There's no protection."

"She's under mine."

"For now." Brambilia pulled his hand free slowly. "But protection is such a fragile thing. It can be withdrawn, or overwhelmed."

He stepped back. "Enjoy your evening. Do try the beach. The view is spectacular. You can see all the dark corners where interesting things happen, like when people disappear."

He paused, looking at Serafina one more time. "That's a pretty dress, Miss Silvano. Peach suits you, though I'd be careful wearing such light colors. Blood is so difficult to wash out."

With that, he walked away, and his men followed. The crowd began moving again. Conversations resumed. But Serafina could feel the tension left in Brambilia's wake.

"Come." Francesco's hand trembled. "We're walking to the beach."

"Shouldn't we leave?"

"Not yet. We can't look like we're running." He started guiding her away from the games, toward the darker edges of the carnival. "We'll keep walking to let him think he didn't rattle you, but we aren't going toward the beach."

"Did I do something wrong? With what I said?"

"You did fine." His voice was tight. "Better than fine. You didn't give him anything he could use."

"Then why—"

"Because he's right. We're exposed here. And he just declared his interest in you."

"His interest?"

Francesco's laugh was bitter. "He wants to take you, to hurt me and prove he can."

"But you said this was neutral—"

"Neutral doesn't mean safe. It just means the violence has to look like an accident."

As they walked behind booths and rides toward the quieter side of the island, she clutched the teddy bear tight.

"Francesco," she said softly, "what did he mean about your protection being fragile?"

He was quiet for a long moment. The ocean breeze caught his hair.

"It means," he said finally, tipping her chin up, "that I've just painted a target on your back. And every man in New York who wants to hurt me now knows exactly where to aim. This is what it means to be with me. This is what I am."

"What did he mean about Paola and Maria?" she suddenly asked.

His jaw tightened. "Women who got too close. They thought they could handle my world."

"What happened to them?"

"Paola's in a convent in Italy. She decided God was safer than me. Maria..." He paused. "Maria decided the Hudson River was preferable to what was coming for her."

Serafina's blood chilled. "Because of you?"

"Because of what knowing me cost them." His hands dropped. "This is what I've been trying to tell you. Being near me is a death sentence."

"Then why did you ask me to do this?"

"Because I'm selfish." The words came out raw. "I wanted you from the moment you crashed into me at that ball. I thought I could control it, keep you at arm's length, use you for appearances and maybe your body, and let you go to whatever the future held for you."

"And now?"

He backed her against a shuttered booth, his body caging hers. "Now? Do you understand that every man who sees you with me marks you as mine? That some will try to take you to hurt me? That others will hurt you just to watch me burn the city down in response?"

"Yes."

"And you're still here."

"At least with you, I know what the danger is."

"No. You don't." His hand wrapped loosely around the base of her throat. "Listen to me, Serafina. You have no idea what I'm capable of."

Her pulse raced. "Then show me."

Francesco snapped. His mouth crushed against hers. His tongue invaded her mouth as his body pressed her into the wood, letting her feel every hard inch of him.

She made a small sound of surprise. His hand slipped to the back of her neck and tightened. The teddy bear fell as she arched against him. Heat pooled between her legs even as her mind screamed danger.

His free hand yanked her skirt up, fingers digging into her thigh, pulling her leg around his hip. The position left her exposed, vulnerable, and achingly wet. He ground against her. She gasped into his mouth and rolled her hips, meeting his rhythm with desperate, instinctive need.

"This is what you do to me," he rasped against her mouth. "I should end this tonight and put you on a train out of the city."

"Would that keep me safe?"

"No." His laugh was bitter. "They'd find you and use you, then mail you back to me in pieces."

"Then I might as well stay."

"Serafina—"

"I mean it. If I'm marked either way, I'd rather be marked as yours."

Something shifted in his expression. "Tell me to stop," he whispered into her ear.

"If I wanted you to stop, I would have run away already."

His teeth caught her earlobe, tugging hard enough to make her whimper. Her fingers clawed at his shoulders, trying to pull him closer. His hand left her thigh to grip her hip, holding her still as he pressed harder against her.

His mouth moved to her throat, teeth biting just beneath her jaw. When he sucked hard, she cried out. The pain and pleasure mixed until she couldn't separate them.

His other hand slid up her side, thumb brushing dangerously close to her breast. She arched into the almost-touch, shameless.

Her hips rocked against him, seeking friction. He groaned and pressed harder, the wooden booth creaking behind her. His hand fisted in her hair, yanking her head back to expose more of her throat to his mouth.

His knee pushed between her thighs, giving her something to grind against. She took it without shame, riding his thigh with desperate little movements. "Even knowing what I am. What I've done today. I killed a man this morning. Broke his neck with these hands. And you still want me to fuck you."

She should have been horrified. Should have run. Instead, she whispered, "Yes."

Her hands found his face, pulling him back to her mouth. The kiss turned feral. She bit his lower lip hard enough to make him growl. He retaliated by sucking her tongue into his mouth.

His hips jerked against her. Her leg tightened around his hip, trying to get closer, to ease the ache building between her thighs. His hand gripped her ass, lifting her slightly, changing the angle until she was practically climbing him.

"Francesco, please—"

"Please what?" His voice was raw. "Please take you right here where anyone could see?"

"Yes."

For a moment, she thought he would. His whole body tensed, his breathing ragged against her neck. She felt him hard and ready against her, felt his control hanging by a thread.

"Not here," he said roughly, though his body didn't move away. "Somewhere I can make you scream without anyone coming to save you."

The threat-promise made her clench around nothing. He felt her reaction, his smile dark against her skin.

Then he pulled back abruptly, leaving her gasping against the booth. Her skirt was rucked up, her throat marked, her lips swollen.

"Christ," he muttered, running a hand through his hair. His chest heaved. His pupils were blown black with lust. "Come on. I'm taking you home."

The drive back was silent agony. Her body ached, and she could feel his tension. Every time he shifted gears, his hand brushed her knee and she had to bite back a whimper and press her thighs together.

When they reached her building, he came around to open her door.

"Would you..." she began, then gathered courage. "Would you like to come up?"

"You don't know what you're asking."

113

"I'm asking if you want to come up."

"Tell me the truth. Are you a virgin?"

"No," she easily lied. "Is that a problem?"

He held her gaze for several seconds. She could see the war happening behind his eyes, deciding whether or not to trust her response. "No."

The walk up the stairs felt endless. Every step brought them closer to a point of no return. Her hands trembled as she fumbled with her keys.

"Nervous?" His voice came low.

"Should I be?"

"Probably."

The lock finally turned. She pushed the door open and stepped inside, with him close behind.

As if the night were innocent still, she showed him her small apartment. She'd left books stacked beside the couch, and a blue glass mug on the table. She'd forgotten to turn the kitchen light off. She felt exposed, as if inviting him in let him see the quiet corners she kept hidden.

His fingers trailed along the spines of books scattered across every surface. He paused at a particularly worn volume.

"Poetry," he observed, lifting it carefully. The book fell open naturally to a well-read page. His eyes scanned the lines. "When desire burns like fever in the blood, and touch becomes the only..." He trailed off.

When desire burns like fever in the blood,
and touch becomes the only language lovers know,
when shame retreats before the tide of need,
we take what's offered, though we both say no.

Her throat went dry. She had read them alone in her bed more times than she could count. "...and touch becomes the only language lovers know," she continued from where she stood. "When shame retreats before the tide of need..."

"...we take what's offered, though we both say no," he finished, looking up at her. "Show me your room."

She reached for his hand and pulled him toward the door. She nudged it open with her shoulder.

Francesco stared at the sapphire dress hanging on the closet door, the one from the party where they'd met. He stepped closer to it, his hand reaching out to touch the fabric. His fingers rubbed the material between thumb and forefinger.

"You looked beautiful in this." He turned to look at her. "I wanted to tear it off you."

"I thought you hated me that night," she whispered.

"I hated wanting you. I hope I get to see you in it again."

The implication was clear. Before he could say more, she pushed him back gently and shut the door. Changed quickly, her fingers fumbling with the zipper, knowing what she was inviting. Her heart hammered against her ribs. This was madness. This was inevitable.

She stepped back out slowly. "Your wish," she said steadily, "is my command."

The change in him was instant and terrifying. His eyes went black, traveling down her body like he was deciding where to start.

"Turn around."

She obeyed, turning until her back faced him, hearing his footsteps approach. His hands found her waist, yanking her back against him. She felt all of him—the gun under his jacket, the rigid line of his cock, the barely leashed violence in every muscle...

He swept her hair aside roughly, baring her neck. His mouth hovered over the mark he'd left earlier, and she felt his teeth graze it, a promise of more pain and more pleasure.

"Serafina."

"Yes?" Her voice came out breathless, already surrendering.

His hand slid up from her waist, fingers splaying possessively across her ribcage. The other hand gripped her hip, holding her against him. She could feel how much he wanted her, hard and insistent against her lower back.

"You're mine."

CHAPTER 9

Francesco's hand rose over her ribs, until it reached her chest. He closed his fingers around her breasts through the silk. His fingers pinched one of her nipples hard enough to make her gasp. She arched slightly.

He used the scant space between them to find the small metal pull at the top of her dress. The silk slid off Serafina's shoulders as the zipper gave way, bunching at her hips before falling with the soft clatter of beads. Serafina inhaled sharply. She stood in a lavender slip.

He bent to her slowly and brought his mouth to the sensitive spot just behind her ear. He kissed it once, and she gasped again, her hips rocking back into him. The pressure of his thick cock stiffened against the seat of his trousers, pressing firm against the base of her spine.

Her knees weakened. She reached back without thinking, bending her arm until her hand found his head. Her fingers threaded through his hair. Her breath came slower. Her fingers curled in his hair. Her eyes fluttered closed.

Francesco moved a hand between them to undo the buttons of his jacket. "Don't move."

Serafina turned her head slightly, just enough to glance back at him unbuckling his holster before pulling his dress shirt and singlet off. Her eyes moved over his bare, sculpted chest—bare now, sculpted with quiet strength. Her gaze dropped, then rose again, slowly. Her breathing quickened.

He stepped close once more, turning her to face him. His fingertips cradled her jaw, before his thumb brushed her cheek. His lips met hers, gentle at first. Serafina's hands splayed across his chest. She pressed herself against him, and leaned into the kiss.

He reached down between them, his fingers working the buckle of his belt. She broke the kiss just long enough to glance down, then let her hands fall, finding his and helping him.

He groaned softly when his trousers fell.

Hot, bare, and thick, his cock spring free. Her hands stilled, then slid slowly up his sides as her body tipped closer, breath stuttering at the hard length of him pressing into her again.

He took her wrist gently and guided her hand back between them, curling her fingers around the hard length of him. Her breath faltered the instant she felt it in her palm. Her fingers twitched, barely able to close around the thickness of him.

His touch drifted up her back as his lips returned to her neck, kissing her slowly along the line of her jaw, down to the hollow just above her collarbone.

Her knees buckled again.

Before she could fall, his arms closed around her. He lifted her off the floor as though she weighed nothing, turned, and pressed her back against the wall. One of his hands dropped to cradle her ass, fingers spreading to hold her up, keeping her pinned between his body and the wall. Her legs wrapped around his waist, ankles crossing behind him, her silk slip riding high over her hips. Her arms circled his shoulders, fingers knotting in his hair and the back of his neck, desperate to stay close.

He kissed her, quicker this time, deeper. His hips anchored her in place, his cock pressing against the soaked fabric between them as her body trembled in his grasp.

His other slipped between them, gathering the hem of her slip and dragging it up slowly, baring her thighs, her hips, and her softness beneath. The silk bunched at her waist, his palm sliding over the curve of her hip before his thumb moved lower. He found the warm, slick seam of her. His finger traced along the cleft, slow and careful, parting her slightly with the barest pressure, feeling the wetness without entering her. Serafina whimpered.

"You're so wet," Francesco breathed.

His mouth moved hungrily over hers, claiming her lips as her arms tightened around his neck. Her thighs squeezing around his waist.

And then a flicker of fear coursed through her. Would it hurt? Would she know what to do? She didn't have time to worry long before he shifted and guided the thick head through the moisture between her legs. She felt the shape of him pressing.

Then he thrust.

Hard.

He filled her in one deep, brutally stretching stroke.

Her whole body jolted. She cried out as her head fell back against the wall. Her arms locked tighter around him.

A moan scraped up from Francesco's chest. His hips pulled back and slammed forward again, faster and harder. The slap of skin on skin echoed off the walls.

She clung to him, legs locked tight around his waist, fingers gripping his shoulders, her cries muffled against his mouth with every drive deeper.

Then one final thrust sent her arching against the wall. Francesco held her there, their bodies pressed together.

Still inside her, he shifted his grip, arms strong beneath her, and carried her into her bedroom. When he reached the bed, he laid her down on her back and pulled out of her.

Her thighs shook. But then his hands spread her knees. She barely had time to inhale before he moved down her body, trailing open-mouthed kisses between her breasts, and farther still. A shocked gasp tore from her lips.

His fingers parted her, pulling her open, exposing her sensitive flesh still pulsing from being stretched around him. Then his mouth sealed over her clit. Her body reacted before she could make sense of it, and he squealed.

Her hips jolted. Her breath turned frantic, coming in short, uneven bursts as the overwhelming pressure spread through her. Sharp heat rolled across her nerves, too much and not enough. Her head fell against the mattress, eyes squeezed shut, her lips parted.

Her hands moved on instinct, pressing against her stomach, then higher, cupping her own breasts through the silk, trying to hold herself together as everything inside her clenched, twisted, spiraled toward the edge.

She couldn't think. She couldn't breathe. She could only feel was his mouth on her, his fingers keeping her open, and her body answering him faster than she was ready for.

Then he crawled back over her, his hands braced on either side of her waist, his mouth still wet from her. Her breath hitched as his cock pressed back into her. He thrust into her once, twice, filling her in quick, heavy drives that made her gasp aloud. Then he held himself deep. Without pulling out, he smoothly rolled them smoothly, bringing her on top of him, her thighs straddling his hips as she sank down, taking him deeper inside.

Dazed, she blinked. Her hands found his chest for balance. The room was dim, but the light from the moon spilled in through the window, falling over his bare chest, his stomach, the ridges of his arms and shoulders... His hungry eyes stayed on her. With him gorgeously, powerfully exposed beneath her like this, it was the most erotic thing she'd ever seen.

Francesco reached up and pulled her slip up and over her head, baring her completely in the silver moonlight. The cool air rushed over her skin.

Francesco gripped her hips and began to guide her, coaxing her into a slow, rolling rhythm. She followed, her body responding without thought, gyrating against him in tight, desperate circles as he filled her again and again.

She leaned forward, hands planting on his shoulders, her breath breaking into short pants. Her eyes fluttered closed. Her hair fell forward around her face, her body shaking with each upward thrust into her.

His fingers found her again. He slid one hand down and flicked his finger over her clit.

She whimpered as her body edged on seizing in waves. Her walls clenched tight around him.

He pulled her down to him, holding her chest to his, and rolled them again until he was above her, his cock still buried deep, his pace suddenly fast and relentless. His hips slapped into hers as he angled himself to meet the building swell of her orgasm.

Then he reached back and hooked one of her legs over his elbow, lifting it high and pressing it over his shoulder.

"Oh, God!" she cried out. The stretch forced her hips higher. Her body arched under his weight, and the pressure inside her swelled so fast it became unbearable.

Her hands flew up, grabbing for the sheets above her head. But his free hand caught her wrists, fast. He yanked them together and pinned them to the mattress with one firm grip, locking her wide open beneath him.

She screamed out as her entire body clenched, inside and out, every muscle tightening from her fingertips to her calves. Deep inside, her walls fluttered, spasming around him in rhythmic bursts. Her clit throbbed with each over-sensitive contraction, the pulsing so sharp it was almost pain. Her thighs shook, her chest heaved, and her vision whited out at the edges. She gasped and twisted. Her body didn't know how to take it.

But he didn't stop. His hips slammed into her harder, his rhythm ragged. His mouth was open, grunting with every thrust, jaw clenched, his chest heaving. The grip on her wrists tightened as his thrusts grew erratic and rough, throbbing with the pressure of holding it back too long.

Then he buried himself in her one final time, deep and hard, his whole body shaking above hers.

A half growl, half groan broke from him as he pulsed deep inside her as he spilled himself into her. His breath caught. His muscles trembled. He released her leg, then leaned forward, propping himself on his elbows beside her head. He panted against her mouth, against her cheek, until the tremors stopped.

Then he let go of her wrists. He shifted his weight and moved her gently to his side with her leg, the inside of her thigh sticky, still draped over his hip, his body still pressed to hers. She was breathless. He was spent. They were wrapped around each other with nothing between them.

Her cheek rested against his chest, the sound of his heartbeat still uneven beneath her ear. When he shifted, she felt the muscles beneath her move. His hand reached down and touched himself, then shoved his fingers through his hair.

"That was your first time," he said quietly. "Why did you lie tonight?"

"I thought..." Her voice shook. "I thought that you'd think me too naïve, and..."

"Christ, Serafina." His arm around her tightened. "Do you have any idea what you've done?"

Her stomach twisted. "You wouldn't... wouldn't have touched me if you'd known."

"No. I wouldn't have. Virgins bleed. Virgins get attached. Virgins think what happens in bed means something more than it does."

Her throat tightened. "I don't—"

"Don't lie to me again." His hand tangled in her hair, pulling her head back. "You'll think this meant something now. You'll expect things from me I can't give."

"You're wrong."

His jaw clenched. He glared at her. "You should have been nothing but a quick, unexpected fuck to end my night."

"Why do you care that I was a virgin?"

"You had something you could only give once, and you gave it to the wrong man."

Her eyes filled with tears. He closed his, his brow furrowing. His chest rose and fell heavily beneath her. When he opened his eyes again, they were distant. "Don't lie to me again. Just be honest for a few weeks."

She tried to speak past the tightness in her throat, but it would have come out as a cry. So she silently nodded.

His finger traced down her forehead, between her eyes, along her nose, then to her jaw. His touch was almost gentle. "Go to sleep now." His voice dropped lower, quieter. "Innocent blood has a price. And you just made yourself expensive."

The grandfather clock in Francesco's study chimed five times as he paced before the dying fireplace. Dawn was hours away, but sleep was impossible. Every time he closed his eyes, he saw her beneath him, felt the way her body had arched, and heard the sound she'd made when she came apart in his arms. Ash settled in the grate with soft pops, the room smelling of spent wood and leather and the citrus bite of his cologne, and still his nerves would not quiet.

He'd slipped out of her bed while she slept, gathered his clothes from her floor, and dressed in her kitchen while she lay curled beneath the sheets. He had not turned on a single light. Habit kept him in shadows, while a part of him wanted to turn back and kneel beside her just to make sure she was breathing evenly.

What was he becoming? The kind of man who confused business with pleasure? Who mistook good sex for something more? His father had been that way. His father had let emotion cloud judgment, making decisions with his cock instead of his brain. It had gotten him killed. He pressed his thumb to the old scar along his knuckle, a boyhood lesson in pain and restraint, and found neither helped him now.

Francesco's gaze found the silver-framed photograph on his desk. Ginevra smiled back at him, dark hair perfectly arranged, eyes full of promises she'd never intended to keep. She'd taught him that love was worth nothing. Less than nothing, when it left you vulnerable to betrayal. He had built an empire on that lesson, brick by brick, body by body, and tonight he had nearly let it slip for the warmth of a woman's mouth.

Ginevra had taught him to guard against women's lies, yet he still fell for one.

Miss Silvano lied to him, told him at Il Girasole she was a virgin, then inside her door claimed she wasn't. He'd been desperate enough, hard enough, wanting her enough that he'd believed what he wanted to believe. He let himself think it was safe to take her.

He'd known the truth the moment he pushed inside her. The resistance, the way she'd tensed, the sharp gasp that wasn't entirely pleasure—he knew. And he hadn't stopped. Christ, he hadn't even slowed down. He'd taken her like any other woman, fast and hard and rough with need, telling himself her body's response meant it was fine, that the way she'd cried out and clung to him meant he wasn't hurting her.

But he had hurt her. Had to have. And he'd been too far gone to care.

Frustration burned through him, both at her for lying, and at himself for believing the lie when he'd known better. He never touched virgins. Ever. That was one of his few unbreakable rules, learned the hard way. Virgins came with complications, and expectations, with the belief that first times meant something, that giving him that particular gift meant he owed them futures he'd never provide.

But more than that, what made his hands shake, what made shame thick in his throat, was the promise he'd made himself years ago, after what his brother had tried to do to their sister.

The memory flashed before his eyes, of bursting through Lucia's door, seeing Antonio's hands on her, the sick satisfaction on their brother's face, Lucia's desperate, terrified eyes finding his. The rage had been instant and absolute. Francesco hadn't hesitated. He just pulled his gun.

And in that moment, standing over Antonio's body while Lucia sobbed in his arms, Francesco had sworn on everything holy that he would never, *never* be the kind of man who took innocence and hurt someone vulnerable just because he could. Who crossed lines that couldn't be uncrossed.

He'd built his entire code around that. Protected the untouched. Kept his hands clean in at least that one way, even as he stained them with blood in every other.

And he'd broken that oath. Taken what she'd never given before, been rough when he should have been gentle, let his own need override everything he'd promised himself he'd never do again.

He rubbed his hands over his face, shame thick in his throat. *Dio, let me not have hurt her.*

He crossed himself, voice barely audible. *Madonna santissima, abbi cura di lei. If I took too much... forgive me.* He let his hand fall and stared at the crucifix on the far wall until the gilt blurred and resolved again. It did not answer. It never did.

Footsteps in the hallway drew his attention. His consigliere appeared in the doorway, hair disheveled, coat thrown over hastily buttoned clothes.

"*This better be important,*" Ricci muttered, easing into the chair opposite Francesco. "*Maria's having trouble sleeping with the baby coming soon. If I'm not there when she*

wakes—"

"*It's important.*"

Ricci studied him for a moment. "*Let me guess. You fucked the girl.*"

Francesco's hands tightened where they rested on his desk. The memory of her tight heat yielding to him, the way she'd gasped when she..."*She came willingly enough.*"

"*I'm sure she did. Tell me you were careful.*" Ricci rubbed his temples. "*And tell me she's been with another man.*"

Francesco's jaw clenched. The lie burned. "*She told me she had.*"

"*And?*"

"*And she lied.*"

Ricci went very still. "*Cazzo, Frankie—*"

"*I know.*" Francesco's voice came out flat, dead. "*I fucking know.*"

"*One of the few rules you've kept, and you—*"

"*I said I know.*" The words cracked like a whip. Francesco stood and paced to the window. "*She told me she was. Then at her door, she lied and said she wasn't. I wanted to believe her. I let myself believe her.*"

"*Did you hurt her?*"

Francesco's hands fisted against the windowsill. He heard her crying out, felt her nails digging into his shoulders, the way her body had fought to accommodate him…"*I don't know. Christ, I don't know.*"

Ricci was quiet for a long moment. "*After Antonio—*"

"*Don't.*" Francesco's voice was raw. "*Don't say his name. Not now.*"

"*You swore you'd never—*"

"*I said don't.*"

The silence stretched between them. Francesco pressed his forehead against the cool glass, fighting the urge to put his fist through it.

Finally, Ricci spoke again, his voice gentler. "*What's done is done, Frankie. The question is what happens now.*"

Francesco turned from the window. "*Brambilia.*"

"*What about him?*"

"*He as good as accused me last night of getting his wife pregnant. Then he started evaluating Miss Silvano.*" Francesco's voice grew darker. "*After she proved herself, he told her protection is fragile.*"

Ricci stilled. "*That's a direct threat.*"

"*He's letting me know that her safety depends on my behavior. The longer this continues, the more dangerous it becomes for her.*"

"*Look, Frankie,*" Ricci said carefully. "*Maybe you should end this now. Cut it clean before Brambilia decides to act on his suspicions.*"

Francesco didn't answer.

"*You could walk away,*" Ricci continued, "*keep her safe by cutting contact.*"

Francesco moved back to the window. The movement pulled at his shoulders where her nails had scraped him raw. The physical evidence of what they'd done would last a week or two.

The least he could do was to give her a clean ending and let her go back to her quiet life before he dragged her deeper into his world, before Brambilia or someone like him decided she was a weakness worth exploiting.

That's what he owed her: a way out.

"*We have a few more dates,*" he said, voice flat. "*Brambilia will*" expect that much. But then it ends. Two weeks."

Ricci nodded slowly. "When it ends, break it off in a way that protects her name."

Francesco's hand pressed against the cool glass. He could still smell her perfume on his shirt and feel the warmth of her body against his.

Two weeks. If he was going to give her those two weeks anyway, if Brambilia expected to see them together, if the charade had to continue...

Then why not let them both have what they wanted, as long as she understood the terms? As long as she didn't start looking at him like she wanted more than his body. As long as those soft blue eyes didn't start filling with expectations.

Two weeks of pleasure before the inevitable end.

"Maybe you should find someone else," Ricci suggested quietly. "That blonde at the club, or—"

"No." The word came out harder than Francesco intended.

"Francesco—"

"I said no. Not until this is finished."

His voice didn't rise. She was his now, at least for two more weeks. The least he could do was not parade other women in front of her while she still carried his marks on her skin. The least he could do was give her these two weeks of whatever pleasure he could provide before he cut her loose.

Ricci sighed. "Arrange something for this weekend. Somewhere they'll see you. The opera, maybe."

Francesco gave a slow nod.

"And then," Ricci said, voice careful now, "in two weeks, Miss Silvano goes back to her bookshop and her quiet little life."

Francesco met Ricci's eyes. He refused to admit, even to himself, that the thought of her going back to her bookshop, of never seeing those eyes look at him again, of someone else eventually touching what he'd claimed, made something dark and possessive churn in his gut.

No. He wouldn't give any woman that kind of power over him. Not after Ginevra. Not after learning what love could do to a man.

Miss Silvano was his for two weeks. He'd take what they both wanted, keep it physical, keep it simple.

And then she'd be nothing.

That was what he owed her. And it was all he could give.

The morning after her night with Francesco, Serafina woke to sunlight streaming through her bedroom window and the distant sound of church bells. When she reached across the bed, the sheets were cold.

He'd left. Of course he'd left. He probably couldn't get away fast enough once he'd realized what she'd done. For a moment, she lay still, shame flooding through her before memory could even fully form.

She'd looked him in the eyes and lied. What must he think of her now? He would have known the moment he... the moment they... Her cheeks burned. Of course he'd known. There was no hiding something like that, no matter how much she'd tried to seem experienced. A man like him wouldn't have fallen for her attempts to seem like she knew what she was doing.

And he'd said nothing. He just kept going, kept taking, kept—

No. That wasn't fair. She'd wanted it. She'd pulled him closer, wrapped her legs around him, and hoped he wouldn't stop.

He must think her foolish now, the kind of manipulative woman who deceived men to get what she wanted.

She pressed her palms against her eyes, wishing she'd been honest from the start, though even through the guilt, she couldn't quite regret the act itself. Because it had felt...

She let herself remember the weight of his body over hers, the way he'd moved inside her, the pleasure she hadn't known existed... the way he'd made her feel desired...

She forced herself out of bed to try to write, but stared at blank pages for hours. The words wouldn't come. They'd scattered, burned away by the memory of his hands, his mouth, and the way that he'd looked at her.

She'd wished desperately that the store was open, that she could lose herself in the routine of shelving books and helping customers, anything to escape the endless loop of her thoughts.

But what disturbed her most was how different she felt. She was no longer a virgin, and in a society where a woman's virtue was her currency, that should have devastated her. She should have been weeping, wringing her hands, and utterly terrified of being seen as ruined goods.

Instead, she felt awakened, alive in a way she hadn't known was possible. She couldn't bring herself to care about what society demanded she should feel, not when her body still hungered for him, and she wanted *him* again, consequences be damned.

Though how could she deserve it after asking him to believe a lie?

Walking to work on Monday, her thighs still ached with every step, her body still sore from the night before, but the pain didn't slow her. She pressed fingers to her temple, her head throbbing with the sick certainty that he must despise her now for the lie.

She nearly missed the storefront.

Danny stood by the door, arms crossed, shoulders tense.

"You're late." His voice carried an edge. "I was about to start searching."

"I overslept." She fumbled with her keys, avoiding his searching gaze.

"Are you all right? You look..." He paused, studying her face, her rumpled clothes, the careful way she moved. "Different."

"I'm fine."

"You sure?" His gaze drifted to the collar of her coat.

"I said I'm fine."

"You don't look it."

She stopped and turned. "Danny, I'm late. I need to open the shop."

"You've been with him, haven't you? Romano."

Her mouth went dry, but she forced herself to meet his eyes. "He's a customer."

"Listen, Serafina, I know who he is. Everyone does. He's not some charming stranger. He's in the mob."

"You don't know anything about him—"

"I know enough." Danny stepped closer. "Men like Romano don't keep women around for conversation. He's using you." He hesitated. "Look, I had someone. Back in Boston. Her name was Lila."

Serafina stopped to listen. Danny never talked about his background.

"She was smart. Gentle. Not the kind to fall for trouble, but she met a guy who always had the fanciest suits and brought her gifts. He was charming to her, but controlling." He looked down as if the memory pained him. "I thought he was protective until she moved in with him."

"What happened to her?"

His eyes lifted, empty and cold. "When the police found her, she was locked in a soundproof room. Chained up. She'd been there for nearly a month."

Serafina stared at him.

"She died in the hospital from an infection, trying to say his name."

Silence fell between them.

"I'm not saying Romano's like that," Danny said, voice lower now. "But it always starts with secrecy. They make you feel special, like you're the only one who sees them."

She swallowed. "I'm sorry about Lila. But that's not what's happening here. Nothing at all is happening here."

"Promise me you'll be careful," he said. "If anything feels off, you come to me. I don't want to see this happen to you."

His hand hovered in the air like he meant to touch her, fingers twitching slightly, but he didn't.

She stepped back. "Thank you. I need to get to work, now."

His expression tightened. "Mr. Thompson's inside."

That stopped her cold. "What?"

She turned and pushed through the unlocked door.

"Mr. Thompson, I'm sorry I was..."

Mr. Thompson stood behind the counter, a telegram spread before him. His usually neat appearance was disheveled, his tie askew.

"Mr. Thompson?" Serafina approached cautiously. "What's happened?"

"I got a telegram last night. From Kensington House."

Ice water poured into her chest. Her fingers curled against the edge of the counter.

"They said they're reconsidering our partnership and might stop supplying us with books."

She tried to speak, but her voice caught.

"They didn't say why," he added. "But sixty percent of our stock comes from them. If we lose that account..."

"How long do we have?" she asked, surprised by how steady her voice sounded.

"They want a decision by month's end. About 'restructuring our relationship.'" He set the telegram down with careful hands. "Serafina, I may have to close Wednesdays and weekends. Cut our hours until we find new suppliers."

She nodded, mind racing. Kensington was methodical: first the veiled threats, now economic pressure. He was backing her into a corner where saying no would cost everyone around her.

The morning crawled by. She shelved books, helped customers, maintained her professional smile, but underneath, calculations ran through her head. How long before the shop failed entirely? How long before Mr. Thompson lost everything from his livelihood to his wife's security because she'd refused a powerful man's advances?

Each time she looked at Mr. Thompson's kind, worried face, nausea churned through her. This was her fault. All of it. And he had no idea.

By midday, the bell above the door chimed.

She looked up, and froze. Mr. Romano stood in the doorway.

Mr. Thompson straightened behind the counter, his expression hardening as he took in the man filling the doorway. "Can I help you, sir?" His voice stayed polite, but cool.

Serafina stepped forward before the tension could thicken further, her. "Mr. Thompson, this is Mr. Romano." She forced herself to meet the mobster's eyes, to hold that burning gaze even as heat flooded through her. "He purchased that volume you thought wouldn't sell—the Petrarch collection."

"Romano." Mr. Thompson said the name quietly. "Yes, I'm familiar with the face of the Romano family's boss. I've seen it in the papers."

Serafina's nausea kicked up. "He's been in before, Mr. Thompson. He has an appreciation for poetry." She met her employer's worried gaze. "I'll be all right."

Mr. Romano tipped his hat to Mr. Thompson, the gesture almost courtly.

Mr. Thompson hesitated, his hand resting on the counter. His eyes moved from Francesco to Serafina, clearly torn between his meetings and leaving her alone with a man whose reputation preceded him. "Serafina—"

"I'll be fine," she said softly, more gently this time. "Really. Don't you have your meetings to attend?"

He waited another moment. Finally, he nodded slowly. "Lock up when you're done." The words were directed at her, but his eyes remained on Mr. Romano.

She waited, tension winding tighter in her chest, until she heard the bell chime and the shop door shut. Then something inside her snapped. Her hands shook as she hurriedly locked the door, flipped the sign to "Closed," and shut all the curtains. With the flick of a switch, the overhead lights went out.

"I'm sorry." she said, breathless, as she moved to turn on a lamp near the velvet reading sofa. She turned back to face him, and the words tumbled out. "I didn't mean—"

"You look tired," Francesco said, his voice a low rumble as he pulled the chain on another small lamp. Warm light spilled across his face.

"So do you." She glanced at him, then down at her hands. "Look, Saturday night..."

"You lied to me about being with a man before."

Heat flooded her cheeks with shame. She nodded, then forced herself to look back up. "Yes."

"Why?"

"Because I thought..." She swallowed hard against the bile rising in her throat. "I thought you wouldn't want to... that you'd think I was too pathetic for someone like you."

Mr. Romano stayed quiet for a long moment, studying her face as if trying to read something written in a language he didn't quite understand. "Someone like me?"

"Sophisticated and worldly." Her voice dropped. "And dangerous."

"And now?" He stepped closer, close enough that she could feel the heat radiating from his body, and smell the faint scent of his cologne. "Do you still think I'm dangerous?"

"Yes. But I don't care anymore. Saturday night... I've never felt like that before. Never felt so..." She searched for words that could capture the enormity of how he'd made her feel so alive. "So much like a woman. So much like I was burning alive and didn't want it to stop."

His eyes darkened. "You don't know what you're saying."

"Don't say that!" Something fierce and desperate rose up in her, pushing past the guilt, the nausea, and the fear. "I may have been inexperienced, but I'm not stupid. I know what I feel. I know what I want." She took a step toward him, closing the distance he'd been trying to maintain. "I know that every time you look at me, something inside me catches fire. And I know that I'd rather burn than go back to the cold."

"What do you want, Serafina?" His voice was rough, like he was barely holding himself back.

"More of it," she whispered. "I want more."

For a heartbeat, neither of them moved. The air between them crackled. Then, slowly, carefully, Mr. Romano raised his hand to cup her face.

"Are you sure?" he asked, his thumb tracing along her cheekbone with devastating gentleness. "You need to understand, Serafina, that we're only seeing each other for a few weeks at most." His jaw tightened. "Can you accept that? Or do you think you'll end up wanting more?"

She held his gaze steadily, even as her heart hammered against her ribs. "I understand this isn't what you hired me for. And I know what this is, and what it isn't. But if I get nothing else out of any of this than just experiencing what I have with you..." She drew a breath. "It will be worth it."

"You say that now."

"I mean it now." She raised her hand to cover his where it cupped her face. "I'm not asking for forever. I'm just asking for now."

His expression shifted, the careful control slipping for just a moment to reveal something raw beneath. "You're going to make this impossible," he said roughly.

Instead of responding with words, Serafina rose onto her toes. Their lips met softly at first. She exhaled against his mouth, "It's already impossible."

Francesco wrapped his hand around the back of her head. He gently kissed the corner of her mouth, her cheek, a little farther back...

"Tell me to stop," he whispered into her ear.

"If I wanted you to stop, I would have run already."

A low snarl tore from his throat, and the last thread of restraint snapped. His mouth slammed over hers, tongue forcing past her lips to taste her. She kissed him harder, pulling at his coat and trying to get closer. He guided her toward the plush sofa. He seized her hips, spun her, and backed her toward the sofa. Before they dropped, his hands slid under her skirt, bunching the fabric to her waist. Fingers hooked the waistband of her panties; he dragged them down her thighs in one rough tug, the fabric catching on her knees before kicking them aside.

He fell onto the sofa, legs spread, pulling her down to straddle him. Her thighs trembled. His hand snaked down. Two fingers push into her slick heat without warning. She gasped, hips jerking. He curled them, stroking once, twice, dragging a broken moan from her throat.

She worked his belt buckle with shaking fingers, then reached between them, dragging his zipper down. Her hand found him hard and slick with anticipation.

She sank down, guiding him in as he thrust up. The stretch burned, exquisite and overwhelming. She clenched around his thick length, trying to trap him inside. He filled her so completely that her vision blurred. The world shrank to the thick slide of him, the wet heat where they joined, and the slap of skin on skin.

Palms sliding down to cup her ass, his fingers dug into her soft flesh as she rode him fast and shallow with increasing desperation while moans spilled against him. His hands traveled up her back, tangling in her hair with possessive force, mouth scorching the sensitive curve of her neck with teeth and tongue and whispered Italian prayers that made her pulse race faster.

In one rough motion, he lifted and twisted her. The velvet cushions pressed against Serafina's back as Francesco followed her down. She barely had time to catch her breath before he pushed her legs up and over his shoulders. Her hands flew to cushions behind her head as the couch creaked under his force. The deep drive of him stole thought itself.

Her legs trembled. The spiral built too fast, too intense, body threatening to shatter before—

The shift came as release beckoned.

He pulled out long enough to drop back to the sofa. She landed in his lap, back pressed to his chest, cock buried again from this new angle that made coherent words impossible. She began to fall apart as this position drove straight into her sweet spot.

Francesco's grunt vibrated through her, one arm locked around her chest while the other slid around her and down between her thighs. His fingers found her clit, circling fast and tight until she jolted with a sharp gasp.

The crash came like a tidal wave. Hard and tight, clenching, pulsing, body pulling him deeper with every spasm. She bit her lip to keep herself quiet, but a cry escaped anyway.

A hand clamped over her mouth. She grabbed it, pressing harder to muffle her moans as convulsions wracked her frame. Her wet heat contracting around him while he thrust up relentlessly, driving her through every wave.

"Sera..." he growled against her ear as he pulled her down harder, pounding until he finally broke. His release pulsed into her, hips jerking with each pulse. Spent and panting, he let his hand slip to her waist.

Her back rested against his chest, still feeling him throb inside her, his arm wrapped tight around her waist as if he needed to hold her there a moment longer. His breath, warm against her shoulder, began to steady, though his fingers dug into her hip. She could feel his wild heartbeat thundering against her spine.

Her skin hummed. The ache spreading low was warm and intense. He remained inside her, though softening now, and she surrendered, letting herself melt against him.

Her head dropped back onto his shoulder, eyes drifting closed. For one perfect moment, she simply breathed, pretending this meant something more, and that she was his, and he was hers.

Then reality crashed back as quickly as if ice water had been dumped on her.

Her eyes snapped open. She jerked forward with a shuddering gasp as he slipped from her. She nearly stumbled trying to standHer skirt fell crooked around her hips. Her thighs trembled, sticky evidence of him, and her breath came too fast to slow.

What had she done? What had she become?

She caught sight of her crumpled panties beside the couch. With shaking fingers, she bent to retrieve them, then placed them absently on a nearby chair before bracing her hands against the wood to steady herself. The room tilted around her.

Her lungs felt tight. Her belly ached. Down the insides of her legs, thick warmth dripped.

Behind her, she heard the rustle of fabric, the soft metallic slide of a zipper, and then quiet footsteps.

His warm fingers touched her shoulder. She turned, keeping her eyes lowered. She couldn't bear to see indifference on his face, or to see him unmoved while she was unraveling, until his hand cupped her cheek. She flinched, but only for a moment, before leaning into his touch like the fool she was, desperate for whatever scrap of tenderness he'd give.

"I'll pick you up Friday, at eight, for dinner," he said. "Dress to the nines."

Then he stepped back, avoiding her gaze. His head was bowed as he turned away, as if shame or regret had finally caught up to him. He unlocked the door, and then it closed behind him.

For a long moment, Serafina remained frozen. Her heart raced. Her fingers pressed into the back of the sofa. Her skin flushed. Her breath stayed shallow as his scent faded from the air.

She'd given him everything. Her innocence, her body, her trust— and he'd walked away as if it had been nothing to him.

At last, she turned to retrieve her panties.

But they were gone.

.

CHAPTER 10

The morning air bit at Serafina's skin as she approached The Purrfect Tale, but her footsteps slowed when she saw the figure waiting
by the door.

He stood with his back to the shop window, impeccably dressed in a charcoal suit, checking his pocket watch with the casual patience of a man who knew his time was never wasted. When he looked up and saw her, his mouth curved into a smile that made her stomach turn.

Where was Danny? If there was ever a time she wished to see him hovering by the entrance with his too-intense concern and offers of coffee, it was now. But the flower shop next door was still dark, and the street felt too empty and quiet.

She forced herself to keep walking.

"Good morning, Miss Silvano," Mr. Kensington said pleasantly, as if they were old friends meeting by chance.

"Good morning, sir." Her voice came out barely above a whisper. She fumbled with her keys, hands trembling so badly the metal jangled.

"Allow me." He didn't touch her, but he stepped closer.

"I've got it, sir."

She knew he was going to speak with her, and that whatever he wanted, she wouldn't be able to refuse. When she finally got the key into the lock and pushed the door open, she held it for him, unable to meet his eyes.

He followed her inside.

They were barely past the threshold when he spoke.

"I hear Mr. Thompson's been having quite the difficult time finding new suppliers." He walked slowly between the shelves, running his fingers along the spines of books as if he owned them. "Three publishers have declined to work with him this week alone. Quite remarkable, really, how quickly a reputation can be destroyed."

Serafina's throat tightened. "What did you do?"

"Me?" He turned, pressing a hand to his chest in mock innocence. "I simply made a few phone calls. Let certain people know that The Purrfect Tale might not be the most... reliable business partner. That Mr. Thompson has been making poor decisions lately." His smile widened. "Financial troubles, they say. Possible insolvency. You know how these rumors spread."

"You're destroying him," she breathed.

"I'm destroying nothing," Mr. Kensington corrected, his tone sharpening. "You're destroying him, Miss Silvano. Every day you delay, every moment you hesitate, is another nail in this pathetic little shop's coffin." He picked up a book from a nearby display and let it drop carelessly to the floor. "And poor Mrs. Thompson. The medical bills must be astronomical. What will happen to her when he can't afford her care anymore?"

"Why are you doing this?" Her voice cracked.

"Because I can." He stepped close enough that she had to tilt her head back to meet his eyes. "Because you need to understand your position, Miss Silvano. You have no power here, no options, no hope of rescue." He paused, letting the words sink in. "Unless, of course, you do exactly as I say."

She couldn't speak. Could barely breathe.

"You're going to meet me Friday evening. Six o'clock. My apartment on Fifth Avenue." He said it matter-of-factly, as if he were scheduling a business meeting.

"No." The word came out weak, pathetic. "No, I'm not—I can't—"

"You can, and you will." His voice didn't rise, but something in it made her flinch. "Unless you'd prefer to watch this place burn to the ground? Watch Mr. Thompson lose everything? Watch his wife suffer?"

"Please—"

"Friday. Six o'clock." He reached into his jacket pocket and pulled out a card with an address written in elegant script. He set it on the counter. "Fifth Avenue. Don't be late."

"I won't—" She tried again, her voice stronger now, desperate. "I'm not going to—"

"I promise not to touch you," he said smoothly, cutting off her protest. His tone was reassuring, almost gentle, but there was something in his eyes that made the promise ring hollow. "Just a conversation. Just an... understanding between us about how this arrangement will proceed."

The way he said it made her skin crawl. An *understanding*. As if there was anything mutual about this, anything at all that she had agreed to.

"Friday at six," he repeated, turning toward the door. He paused with his hand on the handle, looking back at her over his shoulder. "Oh, and Miss Silvano? Wear something pretty. Not that dreadful brown thing you have on now. I do have standards."

Then he was gone.

Serafina stood frozen in the middle of the shop, staring at the card on the counter. Her whole body trembled. The morning light streaming through the windows felt too bright, too normal, as if the world outside didn't understand that everything had just shifted, that the trap had closed tighter.

Friday at six.

She picked up the card with shaking fingers. The address was written in bold, confident strokes. Fifth Avenue. Where people with money and power lived.

I promise not to touch you.

But she didn't believe him. The way he'd looked at her and smiled was the look of a predator who'd already decided how the hunt would end.

She heard footsteps outside and looked up, hope flaring for just a moment that is might be Mr. Romano. But it was just someone walking past.

She was alone.

And on Friday at six o'clock, she would have to walk into that apartment, into whatever hell he had planned for her, because the alternative was watching everything and everyone she cared about be destroyed.

The card felt like it was burning her fingers. She wanted to tear it up, to throw it away, and to pretend this wasn't happening.

But instead, she slipped it into her pocket, where it sat like a stone against her heart.

Friday at six.

"This is absolutely preposterous!" Clara's voice cut through the elegant sitting room of the Randolph estate, her teacup clattering against its saucer as she set it down hard. "How can Mr. Kensington withdraw his support without explanation? It's unconscionable!"

Serafina sat rigid in the velvet armchair across from her friend, hands clasped tight in her lap to stop their trembling. Every muscle in her body ached from the tension of maintaining this facade, of pretending normalcy when she felt like she was barely holding herself together.

"These things happen in business," she managed, though the words felt like broken glass in her throat.

"But the bookshop has been faithful for years!" Clara's cheeks flushed as she paced, her bright yellow dress swirling around her knees. "And poor Mr. Thompson. What will become of him? The shop's all he has with his wife so ill."

"We'll manage," Serafina said quietly. "Mr. Thompson's closing Wednesdays and weekends. We need to stretch our inventory until we figure out what to do."

Clara stopped short, turning with wide eyes. "Close weekends? But Saturday morning's your busiest time!"

"It's temporary." Serafina forced herself to meet Clara's gaze despite the sick weight in her stomach. "We need to buy time."

"This is wrong, Sera. Dad could speak to someone, or perhaps..."

"No," Serafina snapped. The word came out sharper than intended, making Clara flinch. She couldn't bear the thought of Clara's father getting involved, of questions being asked, of anyone discovering what she'd done. "Please, Clara. Mr. Thompson and I will handle this."

Clara studied her friend's pale face, brow furrowing with concern. "All right, but you look dreadful, darling. When did you last sleep properly? Or eat a full meal?"

The simple question nearly broke through Serafina's defenses. She could feel tears threatening and taste bile rising in her throat. "I'm fine. Just worried about the shop."

"All right for now, but only for now." Clara settled back with the expression she wore when she was trying to fix things and make the world brighter, pretending everything could be wonderful if she just tried hard enough. "Now, Sera, I've been invited to tea Wednesday afternoon, something with the literary society ladies. The hostess said I could bring a guest."

"Clara, I don't think..."

"It'll be perfect for you," Clara continued. "Good conversation, refined company, and a chance to forget your troubles. You need respite. This worry is consuming you. We can't let ourselves be consumed by things we can't control, can we?"

Serafina shook her head, panic rising at the thought of polite conversation when she could barely hold herself together. "I couldn't possibly. With reduced hours, every moment matters."

"Matters for what? Fretting yourself into the grave?" Clara leaned forward. Her eyes showed the same kind of pain Serafina was trying to hide. "Believe me, darling, I know what it's like to let worry eat you alive and to think if you just do the right thing and work hard enough at it, then everything will be fine. But sometimes..." Her voice caught. "Sometimes you need to let people."

"I wouldn't be good company..."

"Nonsense." Clara reached across to take Serafina's hand. The touch made Serafina flinch. Clara's eyes widened slightly. "You'd be my company, and that's enough. I couldn't enjoy myself knowing you're spending the day worrying. Please?"

Serafina felt trapped between Clara's genuine concern and her own churning dread. How could she sit among strangers making pleasant conversation when she felt so dirty, so broken? But Clara's hopeful expression made refusal impossible.

"I suppose, if you truly think it would help."

"Wonderful!" Clara clapped her hands once, face brightening with what looked almost like relief. "You'll see, darling. A change of scene will do wonders. We'll have such a lovely time."

Serafina glanced at the ornate mantelpiece clock. Nearly three o'clock. The sound seemed unnaturally loud. Her stomach clenched as she counted the hours until evening.

"I should go," she said abruptly, rising. "I... I forgot something at the shop."

Clara's smile dimmed at her friend's sudden urgency. "Are you sure you couldn't stay for supper? I feel I hardly see you anymore."

"I'm sorry," Serafina said, gathering her handbag and gloves with unsteady hands. "Things have been chaotic with the shop troubles, and I..."

"I understand." Clara stood, expression troubled. "I worry, you know. You're my best friend, and you seem so..." She paused. Her voice softened. "I know what it's like to feel like you're drowning, Sera. After Theodore..." She didn't finish the sentence, but the pain flickered across her face before she composed herself. "I just don't want you to suffer alone like I did. Promise me you'll tell me if things get too heavy to bear?"

For a moment, Serafina nearly told Clara everything about Mr. Kensington's demand. But the thought of Clara's horror, her pity, and her inability to understand what Serafina would have to endure was unbearable. Clara lived in a world where problems yielded to money and influence, where good intentions fixed things. She couldn't grasp the kind of choice Serafina had faced.

"I'll be fine," Serafina said instead, leaning in to kiss Clara's cheek. "Thank you for the invitation. Next Wednesday afternoon?"

"Two o'clock. I'll collect you myself. No arguments."

"Thank you."

Clara threw her arms around Serafina. "Whatever troubles you, you know you can tell me anything? I may not always know the right thing to say—God knows I've made enough mistakes trying to fix what can't be fixed—but I'll always listen. And we'd all be happy to help you with whatever you need.

Serafina's throat tightened, but she nodded. "Of course. I'll see you then."

Walking down the Randolph estate steps, Serafina felt Clara's worried gaze following her. Her friend meant well, but some burdens couldn't be shared. Some choices had to be made alone. And some pain couldn't be fixed with tea parties and forced brightness, no matter how much Clara wished it could.

The afternoon stretched endlessly before her. She couldn't face going home to her empty apartment where the silence would leave her alone with her thoughts, with the memory of what she'd done. Instead, she found herself walking aimlessly through the city streets, trying to exhaust herself enough that sleep might come without dreams.

By evening, her feet ached and her body was wrung out with exhaustion, but her mind still raced. When she finally climbed the stairs to her apartment, every step felt like a monumental effort.

By the time she reached her building, her hands shook so badly she could barely manage the key. Inside her small apartment, she stood motionless in the entryway, staring at the simple furnishings that suddenly felt precious and fragile. After that night, would she still be the same person who lived here? Would these rooms still be home?

Standing before her mirror, Serafina barely recognized the pale, hollow-eyed woman staring back at her. She looked like a ghost of herself, all the color drained from her face.

"It can't take long," she whispered to her reflection, the words barely audible in the quiet room. "It can't take long."

She took a deep breath, then another, trying to steady the violent trembling in her hands. *Think of Mr. Thompson. Think of the shop. Think of who would suffer if it closed.* This was just one evening, just a few hours of her life in exchange for saving something precious.

The walk to Mr. Kensington's address was like a funeral march. The streets around her seemed strangely muted, the usual sounds of the city fading into a dull background hum.

"It can't take long," she whispered again. "It can't take long. It can't..." She took a deep breath, then another, trying to steady the violent trembling in her hands.

She noticed details during her walk that she usually overlooked. The crack in a sidewalk wasn't there before. The way the lamplight caught the edge of a windowpane made it look like daytime. The smell of coal smoke in the air sickened her. It was as if her mind were desperately grasping for anything to focus on other than her destination. Too soon, she found herself walking up the stairs to his floor.

The door opened almost immediately, as if he had been waiting just behind it. Mr. Kensington stood there with a smug smile, his eyes glittering with malice.

"Serafina," he said, his voice warm and welcoming as if she were a dear friend coming for a social call. "Right on time. Please, come in."

She stepped across the threshold, feeling as though she were crossing into a world where normal rules didn't apply, where decent people didn't dare venture.

"Can I offer you some wine?" he asked pleasantly, gesturing toward the sitting room. "I have a lovely Bordeaux I've been saving for a special occasion."

The casual normalcy of the offer made her stomach churn. "No, thank you."

"Come now, don't be shy. This should be a pleasant evening for both of us." He moved to pour himself a glass from a crystal decanter, the liquid catching the lamplight like blood. "After all, as

145

long as I get what I want, I'll certainly consider resuming our business relationship with the bookshop."

"Consider?" she repeated, her voice stronger now, edged with desperation. "But I thought—you said if I came here—"

"I said I'd consider if the little shop would receive another shipment," he corrected smoothly, taking a sip of his wine. "Surely you understand I need some insurance in place before making any firm commitments."

"Insurance?"

He set down his glass, then crossed to a side table and retrieved a narrow wooden case with brass hinges. When he flipped it open, Serafina saw the gleam of polished glass and ivory objects, leather harnesses, things she didn't recognize, but understood all too quickly.

He held her gaze as he spoke, his tone colder now. "I find it's best to settle certain matters early. A woman may promise discretion, but promises wear thin under pressure. This, however—" he gestured to the contents of the box "—is permanent."

"I don't understand."

"You'll use them on yourself," he said, calm as ever. "While I take photographs."

Serafina stepped back a full pace before she even realized she'd moved. Her breath caught in her throat. "What?"

"I'd rather not," he said. "But I find insurance is prudent in these arrangements. You strike me as clever, Serafina. You understand the position you're in. If you refuse... the shop folds—immediately. No last chances, no rescues, and no one will be surprised when the girl who got too close to me disappears."

Serafina stood frozen, her mind reeling. This was worse than anything she had imagined, more degrading than she had prepared herself for. The room seemed to spin around her as the full horror of her situation became clear.

"Now then, shall we get started? The bedroom is just through there. I suggest you begin by removing that dreadfully plain dress."

"I—I don't understand how this is insurance," she stammered, backing toward the wall.

"Don't be naive, my dear. A few compromising photographs, and

I can be assured of your discretion. Step out of line, and... let's just say your reputation would be quite thoroughly ruined." His patience was clearly wearing thin. "Now stop wasting time and do as I said."

When she still didn't move, his expression darkened. "I won't ask again, Serafina. Either you cooperate willingly, or I'll make this much more unpleasant for both of us."

Mr. Kensington set his wine glass down. The crystal made a soft clink that seemed unnaturally loud in the silence. His eyes traveled over her body.

"You know," he said conversationally, circling closer, "I've done this before. The photographs, I mean. It's remarkable how quickly a woman's spirit breaks once she realizes what she's given away." He paused behind her, close enough that she could feel his breath on her neck. "And you will break, Serafina. They always do."

She couldn't move. Her body had gone rigid with terror.

"The camera doesn't lie," he continued, moving back into her line of sight. "Every moment and all the humiliation will be captured." He smiled. "And the beauty of it? You'll do it all to yourself, with your own hands, while I simply watch and document. No one will believe you didn't want this."

He walked to the bedroom doorway and turned back, his silhouette framed in the dim light.

"When we're done, you'll leave here with nothing more than the knowledge that I own you now. I will own every humiliating image of you doing things you can't even imagine yet." His voice dropped to something almost gentle, which made it worse. "And if you ever defy me, if you ever think about telling anyone what happened here, those photographs will find their way to everyone you know. Your friend Miss Randolph will see them. Mr. Thompson. Your neighbors. Everyone."

"Now." His tone shifted back to businesslike crispness. "The bedroom. Remove your dress. We have a long evening ahead of us, and I do so hate to be rushed."

With shaking hands, Serafina reached for the top button of her dress, her vision blurring with unshed tears. Behind Kensington, she could see the camera already set up on its tripod, waiting. A predator's trap, and she had walked right into it.

His smile widened as her fingers fumbled with the button.

"Good girl," he murmured. "This will all be so much easier if you just do as you're told."

But as the minutes ticked by, that anger twisted into something that felt uncomfortably like fear. Where the hell was she? Had she run? Had she finally come to her senses and disappeared? Miss Silvano was many things, but unreliable had not been one of them.

His fingers drummed against his knee as unwelcome possibilities kept creeping into his mind. Had something happened to her? Was she hurt? The thought sent a violent surge of possessive rage through his chest, which he immediately tried to push down. This was a business arrangement. Her punctuality mattered only insofar as it affected their professional obligations.

He didn't believe that lie any more than he believed the sky was green.

He was about to abandon his vigil when he spotted a familiar figure moving slowly down the street. Even in the dim light, he recognized her walk, though something was devastatingly wrong with it. Her usual graceful stride had been replaced by something broken and defeated.

Francesco rose from the bench and crossed the street, his long legs covering the distance quickly. As he drew closer, he could see her face more clearly in the lamplight, and what he saw there made his chest tighten.

There were shadows under her eyes that hadn't been there before, a hollowness to her cheeks that spoke of more than a missed meal. Her clothes were wrinkled, as if she'd been walking for hours, and there was something in her posture, in the careful way she held herself, that set off every protective instinct he possessed. He wanted to find whoever had hurt her and make them pay in blood.

"Miss Silvano." His voice came out rough, edged with hours of suppressed worry. "Where the hell have you been?"

She looked up, startled, as if she hadn't seen him approaching. Her eyes were red-rimmed, her face pale and drawn, like she'd been crying. "Mr. Romano. I didn't expect..."

"We had an engagement tonight," he said, fighting to keep his tone level when what he wanted to do was shake her until she told him who had done this to her. "I've been waiting for almost three hours."

She stared at him blankly for a moment, as if his words were coming from very far away. "The bookshop is facing some difficulties and may have to close."

Fuck the bookshop.

Francesco studied her face more carefully, taking in details that made his blood run cold. She wouldn't quite meet his eyes. She maintained too much of a distance, as if afraid to get too close. Her hands slightly tremored though she'd clasped them together. "What kind of difficulties?"

"I don't want to discuss it," she said quickly, wrapping her arms around herself. "I needed to walk, and I lost track of time."

Francesco's hands clenched at his sides as he noticed everything she wasn't saying. "Serafina—"

"Please!" She looked up at him with bone-deep exhaustion. "Please, sir, don't ask me about it right now. Everything is still too uncertain. I...I can't discuss it yet."

Francesco's hands formed fists at his sides. He'd seen that look before... on victims... on people who'd been violated in ways that left marks you couldn't see.

And if someone had touched her—

He couldn't finish the thought, because if he did, he'd lose control completely.

"Very well," he said through gritted teeth, forcing himself to step back. The urge to gather her into his arms was almost overwhelming.

But he could see that she was barely holding herself together, and he wouldn't be the one to break her. "But this cannot happen again. Our arrangement requires dependability."

Fuck the arrangement. Fuck dependability. He wanted to know who had hurt her.

She nodded quickly. "Of course. It won't happen again."

They stood there in awkward silence for a moment.

"We'll visit the museum tomorrow," he said finally, his voice carefully controlled. "Ten o'clock. I'll pick you up."

"All right," she said, managing a weak smile that didn't reach her eyes.

"Good." He tipped his hat slightly. "Good night, Miss Silvano."

"Good night, Mr. Romano."

Francesco remained on the sidewalk, watching as she climbed the steps to her building. She moved too carefully. Only when he saw the light come on in her apartment window did he finally turn away.

As he walked back to his car, Francesco found himself analyzing every word and gesture. The pieces were there, scattered but clear enough if he looked. The bookshop. The strain in her voice. The devastation she tried to hide. Someone had broken her, and the thought curdled something deep in his chest.

The possessiveness that surged through him was immediate. *Mine,* something primitive in him snarled. She was his, whether she knew it or not, whether he had any right to think it or not.

But that was exactly the problem.

He needed to put distance between them and end this before he dragged her down into his world, where innocence went to die. She deserved better than what he could give her, better than a life spent looking over her shoulder, wondering which enemy would use her to get to him. Better than loving a man who killed without remorse and would likely die violently long before his time.

He should let her go and end their arrangement before this went any further, before she became a target.

He knew he should. But first, before he could let her go, before he could do the right thing and walk away, he needed to find out who had hurt her.

Whoever it was had made a very serious mistake. A fatal one.

Francesco was going to find out who. And when he did, they were going to learn what happened to people who touched things that belonged to him.

They were going to learn that some men didn't just kill for business.

Some men killed for pleasure.

Serafina's hands fell to her lap as she stared at the blank page in her typewriter. The keys might as well have been foreign objects for all the sense they made. Every time she tried to form a thought, the images from Mr. Kensington's house crashed through her mind. The click of his camera, the satisfied look in his eyes, the way he'd made her pose.

She pressed her hands to her face, trying to block out the memories, but they were seared into her consciousness like a brand she'd carry forever.

It was just photographs, she told herself firmly. That's all. Mr. Kensington hadn't forced himself on her, though what he had demanded made her stomach churn with revulsion even now. The things he'd made her do with those objects, the positions he'd photographed her in...the humiliation was a living thing inside her, eating her alive from the inside out. Worse because she'd done it to herself with her own hands while he watched. She pressed her lips together, trying to block it all out, to forget the taste that lingered despite her desperate attempts to wash it away. She'd scrubbed her mouth until her gums bled. It hadn't helped. He hadn't kept his promise.

Rising on unsteady legs, she went to the kitchen to pour herself a large cup of coffee and wrap her hands around the warm ceramic for comfort. The first sip was too hot, burning her tongue. She welcomed the pain. At least it was clean pain. Pain she could choose.

She jumped at a knock at the door. Coffee sloshed over the rim of her cup. Her heart hammered as she set it down with shaking hands. For a terrifying moment, she forgot who she was waiting for and thought it might be Mr. Kensington, coming to demand more, to collect on whatever sick game he was playing. But then she heard a familiar voice calling her name.

Francesco. God, not now. She couldn't face him like this, couldn't pretend to be whole when she was so thoroughly broken.

He stood there in his perfectly tailored coat, hat in hand, looking every inch the gentleman. For a moment, she was struck by how handsome he was, how safe he made her feel by being there, and how utterly wrong it was that she was standing here covered in invisible filth while he looked at her like she wasn't.

His eyes narrowed the moment he saw her face. "You look unwell."

"I'm fine." The lie came automatically. "Just tired."

He studied her for a long moment, and she could see him analyzing things, like the shadows under her eyes and the way she held herself. "We don't have to go."

"No." She grabbed her coat too quickly. "I want to. I need to get out."

At the museum, they walked through the first galleries in brittle silence. Serafina found herself watching Francesco's hands, as if he might suddenly grab her. When a guard's keys jangled unexpectedly behind them, she startled violently, her hand flying to her chest as panic flooded through her.

Francesco's hand was on her arm instantly. "What happened?"

"Nothing. I'm just—" She couldn't breathe properly. "The sound surprised me."

His eyes were dark. She could see it in the set of his jaw and the way his hand lingered on her arm that he didn't believe her. "Serafina."

"Please." She pulled away. "Can we just look at the art?"

He let her go, but she could feel his attention on her like a physical weight.

They moved into the Italian exhibition, and she saw Francesco's expression change. Something softened in him that she hadn't seen before. For a few moments, he spoke about his childhood in Italy in a thicker accent than usual, but she could barely focus on his words. Her mind kept drifting, kept seeing Mr. Kensington's camera, kept feeling the cold glass—

"Serafina."

She blinked. Francesco was staring at her. "I'm sorry, what?"

"I asked if you were listening."

"Yes. Italy. Your family." She wrapped her arms around herself.

He stepped closer, close enough that she could smell his cologne. "What's wrong?"

"Nothing."

"Don't lie to me." His voice quieted, though his tone sharpened. "Something happened. I can see it."

Fear spiked through her. Could he really see it? Could he tell just by looking at her what she'd become? "I don't know what you mean."

"You're terrified. You can barely stand still. Every sound makes you jump." His hand came up like he was going to touch her face, then stopped. "Did someone hurt you?"

"No." The word came out too fast and high pitched. She jerked her head.

"Serafina—"

"I said no." She stepped back, panic clawing its way out of her. "Can we please just continue?"

His jaw clenched, but he nodded. They moved through more galleries, and she tried desperately to focus, to pretend, to just be normal. But she could feel herself unraveling with every passing minute.

When they stopped before a painting of an Italian village, Francesco spoke again about his family and festivals and music, and all Serafina could think was how wrong it was. How could she stand here listening to stories about innocence and joy when she was so thoroughly tainted? When photographs of her existed doing things that would destroy any chance she had at a normal life?

But then he said something about his mother chasing him and his brother through the streets with a wooden spoon, and despite everything—despite the horror and the shame and the fear—a small, genuine laugh escaped her.

"What?" he asked, his eyes crinkling slightly.

"I just—" She smiled, a real smile for the first time in days. "I can picture you as a little boy, running from your mother."

His expression softened. "We were terrors."

Without thinking, she reached out and touched his arm, her fingers resting lightly on his sleeve. "I think you still are."

He looked down at where she touched him, then back at her face, and smiled, really smiled, in a way that made him look younger, and less dangerous. The moment stretched between them, warm and genuine and so painfully normal it made her chest ache.

Then reality crashed back in. She was barely holding on. Barely breathing. And Francesco kept looking at her like he could see straight through her.

"About last night," she said suddenly. "I need to apologize for—"

"You don't need to apologize."

"But I missed our engagement, and you were counting on me—"

"Serafina." His voice was quiet, careful. "I don't care about the engagement."

"You should care. It was unprofessional of me, and this arrangement requires—"

"Stop." The word came sharper now.

"I can't stop. I need you to understand that I take this seriously, that I'm reliable, that—"

"Tell me what's wrong." Not a request anymore. His eyes had gone dark, intense.

"Nothing's wrong! I was just—"

"Don't." He stepped closer, and she could feel his careful control starting to fray. "Don't lie to me. Something happened, and I want to know what."

"Nothing's wrong! I was just unprofessional, and—"

"This isn't about professionalism." He moved closer, crowding her. "This is about whatever has you looking like you're about to break apart."

She backed up until she hit the wall. "I'm fine."

"You're not fine." He was close now, too close. "You're terrified and trying to hide it, and I want to know why."

"This is business," she said desperately. "Just business. That's all."

"Is it?" His eyes bored into hers.

"Well what do you want from me?" Her voice pitched higher. "You're the one who said this was temporary! You're the one who keeps everything at a distance!"

"Because I have to." The words came out rough. "Because getting attached to you would be—"

"Would be what? A problem?" She laughed bitterly. "Don't worry, Mr. Romano. I'm not getting attached. This is exactly what we agreed to. I play a role, you pay me, and we both walk away clean."

"Clean." He stared at her. "You really think either of us is going to walk away clean from this?"

"I have to." The words broke out of her before she could stop them. "I have to believe that because if I don't—"

She couldn't finish. Couldn't tell him that she was already ruined, already destroyed, already so far from clean she'd never find her way back.

"Serafina." His voice had gentled, but it was worse somehow. The softness hurt more than the anger. "What happened to you?"

"Nothing." She pushed past him. "This was a mistake. I want out of our arrangement."

"What?"

"I'm ending our contract. I'll return the money. I can't do this anymore."

"You can't just—" He grabbed her wrist, not hard, but firm enough to stop her. "Think about what you're saying. Brambilia expects—"

"I don't care what he expects!" She yanked her arm free. "I can't do this. I can't stand here and pretend that—"

"Dear brother!" A bright voice cut through the tension like a knife.

They both turned. A lovely young woman with dark hair and brilliant green eyes stood there, her expression shifting from curious to concerned as she took in the scene. "Frankie, what on earth—"

Francesco's entire demeanor changed in an instant. The dangerous intensity vanished. "Lucia, what are you doing here?"

"Ricci told me where you were." Her eyes moved between them, reading the situation with uncomfortable accuracy. "And who is this?"

Francesco's jaw tightened. "This is Miss Silvano. A business associate."

"A business associate." The woman's eyebrows rose slightly, her gaze taking in Serafina's pale face. "How fascinating. I didn't realize you conducted business in art museums now."

"Lucia—"

"I'm Lucia Romano," she said, turning to Serafina with a slight smile. "Francesco's sister. And apparently the last person to know about his new business ventures."

"It's not—" Francesco started.

"Of course not," Miss Romano agreed mildly. "I'm sure Miss Silvano is here purely for professional reasons." Her eyes sparkled with amusement. "The museum is such a practical place for business discussions."

Serafina could only stare. So this was his sister. The one he'd protected. The one he'd kill for. And she was gently mocking him while reading the situation with uncomfortable accuracy.

"I should go," Serafina managed.

"Before we've been properly introduced?" Miss Romano tilted her head. "How rude that would be. Though I suppose if this is just business, formalities don't matter."

"It is business," Francesco said firmly.

"Then you won't mind if I invite your business associate to my gathering Wednesday afternoon." Miss Romano's smile was innocent, but her eyes were sharp. "It's nothing formal. Just tea and conversation. Unless business associates don't accept social invitations?"

"That's very kind," Serafina said quickly, "but I couldn't possibly impose—"

"Nonsense. It's no imposition at all."

"I have work," Serafina lied, backing away slightly. "The bookshop. I can't just—"

"Surely you can spare a few hours for tea? Unless there's another reason you'd prefer not to come?"

"I'm sorry," Serafina said, wrapping her arms around herself. "I just... I have bills to pay. I can't. But thank you for the invitation."

Understanding, maybe, or concern flickered in Miss Romano's eyes. "Of course. Another time, perhaps."

"Perhaps," Serafina echoed, knowing there would be no other time. "I'm getting tired. I need to go home."

Miss Romano touched her brother's arm lightly. "Take her home. And, Frankie? Whatever business you're conducting—be careful."

Be careful?

But then she was gone, leaving them standing in the gallery with museum visitors pretending not to stare.

Francesco didn't speak as they walked to the car, nor did he touch her. But she could sense the careful distance he maintained. Other visitors moved around them, as if they knew who he was.

The car's leather interior smelled of his expensive cologne and smoke. When he started the engine, the sound seemed too loud. She pressed herself against the passenger door, as far from him as she could get.

They pulled into traffic. His hands gripped the steering wheel, knuckles white. She watched his profile from the corner of her eye, and the way he stared straight ahead like he was holding himself back from something.

The silence was suffocating. Every breath felt too loud. Every block they drove felt like drowning slowly. She wanted him to speak and break this awful tension, but she also dreaded whatever he might say.

When they stopped at a light, he turned to look at her. His eyes were so dark and intense, and she had to look away before she shattered.

"What happened to you?" His voice was deadly quiet.

"Nothing."

"Don't." He turned to face her fully, and the look in his eyes made her chest constrict. "Something did. Someone did. And you're terrified, and I—" He stopped himself. "Tell me who."

"I can't."

"Can't or won't?"

"Does it matter?" She reached for the door handle even though they weren't even close to her building yet, but she needed to escape this car, to escape this conversation, but mostly to escape him.

His hand shot out, catching her wrist—not hard, but firm. "It matters to me."

She looked down at his fingers wrapped around her wrist, and remembered other hands, other touches, the things she'd done to herself while someone else watched. "Why?"

"Because..." He seemed to struggle with the words. "Because you matter to me. More than you should."

The admission should have made her feel something hope, maybe, or happiness. Instead it just made everything worse. The distance between what she was and what he thought she was grew impossibly wide.

"Then let me go," she whispered. "Before this destroys us both."

He released her wrist slowly. His fingers trailed across her skin in a way that felt like goodbye. "I should. But I don't think I can."

The light changed. He drove the rest of the way in silence, but it was heavier now, and more final. When they reached her building, she climbed out before the car fully stopped to make sure he had no chance to speak and break her down.

She didn't look back as she rushed inside and up the stairs. She leaned against the door, breathing hard, listening to his car idle for a long moment before finally pulling away. The sound of the engine fading felt like losing something she'd never really had.

Her hands were shaking. Her whole body was shaking. She slid down the door until she was sitting on the floor, arms wrapped around her knees, trying to hold herself together.

You matter to me.

The words echoed in her head, over and over, until she wanted to scream. How could she matter to him when she was ruined? When photographs of her existed doing things that would make him look at her with disgust instead of whatever that was in his eyes?

She forced herself to stand. Her charcoal pencils were on the table where she'd left them. She grabbed paper and began to draw without thinking, her hand moving in violent strokes.

His face appeared on the page. It wasn't pretty or soft, but raw. She drew the intensity in his eyes, and the way he'd looked at her like she was something he wasted even while calling her a business associate. She drew until her hand cramped and the image staring back at her was so real it hurt to look at.

Even in harsh black lines, he was beautiful.

And she was filthy.

And they could never be anything but broken and impossible.

She set the drawing aside and reached for the teddy bear, pulling it against her chest. The soft fur felt like a mockery of comfort. Nothing could comfort her now. Nothing could fix this. She was so tired of pretending and of holding herself together when everything inside her was screaming.

A soft rasp of paper against wood made her freeze.

An envelope, white against dark floorboards, slid under her door.

Terror flooded through her, so sudden and violent she couldn't breathe. Her heart hammered against her ribs. Her vision narrowed to that single white rectangle.

Her hands shook as she reached for it. She had to try twice to pick it up, her fingers refusing to cooperate. She yanked the door open. The hallway was empty but for the echo of footsteps on the stairs below, already fading into nothing.

Her name was typed across the front with no return address.

She shouldn't open it. She should burn it and run.

But her fingers were already tearing it open and pulling out the single sheet of paper inside. Her blood ran cold.

Miss Silvano,

You have been a very naughty girl. A lady's reputation is
her most precious possession, and yours is in great
danger.

I know where you went. I know what you did. Be more
careful.

Some men prey on innocent young ladies. Fortunately, you
have someone who understands that sometimes a woman
needs guidance to make safe choices. I'm watching over you
now, and I care about your safety.

The city can be so dangerous for pretty young ladies who
don't know their place.

CHAPTER 11

The back room of Berg's Deli reeked of cigars and stale beer. Francesco watched the cards hit the table, one after another, mechanical as breathing.

"Romano, you in?"

He looked at his hand. Kings over eights. Good enough.

He pushed chips forward and tried to focus on the game, on the odds, on anything but the image of Serafina's face that had been haunting him since he dropped her off.

Last night he'd tried to fix it. Went to a bar in the Village, found a pretty French girl who knew exactly what she was doing. She'd taken him to her apartment, dropped to her knees, looked up at him with those practiced bedroom eyes.

And nothing.

His body had refused. Just went dead on him while she worked him over, confusion turning to irritation on her face.

Sixteen years old when he'd lost his virginity. Thirty-eight now. Never had that problem. Not once.

Until last night.

"Vincent's wife caught him with Rosalie," Tommy was saying, dealing out cards. "Came at him with a goddamn rolling pin."

"Jesus." Carlo shook his head. "What'd you tell her?"

Vincent shrugged. "That it didn't mean nothing. Which is true. Rosalie's just—" He made a crude gesture. "You know. A warm hole to put it when I need to."

The other men laughed. Francesco had said the same thing a hundred times about a hundred different women. The words were familiar as his own heartbeat. Now they sounded hollow.

"She buy it?" Tommy asked.

"Hell no. Turns out she's been fucking Rosalie too." Vincent grinned. "Same woman. Can you believe that shit?"

More laughter. Francesco lifted his whiskey, let it burn down his throat.

He'd built his entire life on keeping things simple. Business was business. Sex was release. You didn't mix the two, didn't get attached, didn't let anyone close enough to matter.

Simple rules. They'd kept him alive.

And then little miss Serafina Silvano had walked into his life and broken every single one.

"We worked it out," Vincent was saying. "She gets Rosalie Tuesdays and Thursdays. I get weekends. Fair's fair."

"Modern marriage," Tommy raised his glass. "Here's to it."

Francesco stared at his cards. Three tens had just landed in his hand. Full house.

He couldn't stop seeing the way Serafina had looked at him in the museum, like he'd hurt her. Something had happened to her. He didn't know who, didn't know what, but the not knowing was eating him alive.

"Your bet, Romano."

He looked at his cards again. Full house. Easy money.

"Fold."

He meant to toss them face down.

Silence around the table.

"You fold on a full house?" Vincent stared at him. "The fuck is wrong with you?"

Rookie mistake. The kind that got you labeled distracted and unreliable. Weak. The kind that got you killed in his line of work.

"Wasn't feeling it," Francesco said.

Tommy was looking at him now, with an expression that Francesco knew meant he was filing this information away for later. "You feeling all right?"

"Fine."

But he wasn't. He'd forgotten how to play poker, forgotten how to fuck, forgotten how to be the man he'd spent twenty goddamned years becoming, all because of one woman who looked at him like he might be something other than a monster.

The next hand was worse. And the one after that. He was hemorrhaging money and didn't care, couldn't make himself care, because all he could think about was the way her hands had shaken when she'd tried to explain why she'd missed their engagement, and the shadows under her eyes, and the way she'd flinched at unexpected sounds. But the careful, careful way she held herself... someone had hurt her.

And Francesco was going to find out who.

"Maybe we should call it," Vincent said finally. "Early day tomorrow."

The other men filtered out. Francesco stayed, finishing his whiskey, staring at the cracked felt on the table.

He should end this, like she wanted. Pay Serafina what he owed her—she didn't owe him anything—and walk away before this thing between them got him killed, before he forgot how to function without her.

He should.

But he kept thinking about her face, her eyes, the soft sounds she'd made when he'd touched her. He kept thinking about the fact that he'd kill anyone who tried to hurt her, and he didn't even care that it made him weak.

The glass cracked in his hand. He looked down at the spider-web fracture spreading through the crystal, at the blood welling from his palm.

He was losing control.

And he didn't know how to get it back without letting go.

Francesco walked through the lobby of his building, nodding to the doorman who tipped his cap. The elevator carried him up toward his penthouse, but when the doors opened on the top floor, he didn't step out. Instead, he went back down one floor, to where he'd set Lucia up in her own place, close enough to keep her safe, but far enough to keep her away from anything that might happen in his world. It was their compromise, the way they'd found to let her live her own life while still giving him the peace of mind that came with knowing she was protected.

The knock echoed in the quiet hallway, and then he waited. He heard the sound of multiple locks turning, the chain sliding free, the deadbolt clicking back.

"Francesco?" She opened the door wearing a silk robe over her nightgown, her dark hair loose around her shoulders. Her face was flushed with anger. "Do you know what time it is?"

"I know it's late—"

"It's past midnight. And you missed dinner again." She stepped aside, letting him into her apartment. "That's three Sundays in a row without so much as a phone call to let me know you won't be here."

"I'm sorry," he said, hanging his coat on the hook by the door. "I lost track of time."

"You lost track of time," she repeated, walking toward the kitchen. "At a poker game that goes until midnight."

"How did you—"

"Know where you were? Same way I knew where you were yesterday at the museum." She pulled out a jar of coffee, her movements precise and angry. "I called Ricci because apparently that's the only way I can find out what my brother is doing with his life."

Francesco watched her measure coffee beans, recognizing the stubborn set of her shoulders. His mind kept drifting to the curve of Miss Silvano's hip under his palm, the sound she'd made when he'd—

"Are you even listening to me?"

164

He forced his attention back to Lucia. "You never told me why you missed last Sunday either. No call, no explanation, *niente!*" She filled the percolator with water, her back to him. "I waited until ten o'clock. Gloriana had your favorite meal sitting on the table getting cold, and I waited."

"I'm sorry."

"'Sorry' doesn't tell me why you disappeared. 'Sorry' doesn't explain why you've been avoiding me for weeks. Until yesterday, I thought something had happened to you. I thought—"

"Nothing happened to me."

"Then what? What's going on that's so important you can't even let me know you'll miss dinner?"

Francesco ran his hands through his hair, suddenly feeling exhausted. "I've been dealing with some business complications."

"And you can't pick up a telephone?"

"You could have called. You could have come upstairs. You didn't need to track me down at the museum."

"You're right," she said, her voice getting sharper. "I should have called. But then I wouldn't have met your girlfriend, would I?"

Francesco's stomach clenched. "She's not my girlfriend."

"No? Because you looked like you were having a pretty intimate argument for two people who are business associates."

"We are only business associates."

"Business associates who look at each other like they're about to tear each other's clothes off?"

Francesco's jaw clenched. His hands curled into fists at his sides, remembering how she'd looked beneath him, how tight she'd been, how she'd gasped..."Drop it, Lucia."

"Don't 'Lucia' me." She turned to face him fully, her hands on her hips. "I saw the way you looked at her, Francesco. I saw the way she looked at you. That wasn't business."

"It has to be," he said, harshly. "That's all I can let it be."

"Why?"

"Because Brambilia's already made her a target. Because keeping her close is a risk I can't afford."

"Complicated how?"

165

"Lucia, I said drop it."

"No." She crossed her arms over her chest. "I won't drop it. You've been miserable for months, Frankie. Months! And yesterday was the first time I've seen you look alive in I-don't-know-how-long."

"I'm not miserable."

"You're not living."

He couldn't argue with that. The truth of it sat in his chest like a stone. He poured himself a glass of wine from the bottle she had left open on the counter, buying time to figure out how to explain something he didn't understand himself.

"She's different," he said finally.

"Different how?"

"She believes in love and happy endings and all that fairy tale bullshit."

"And that's bad because?"

"Because I'll ruin her. I'm already ruining her." His voice came out rough. "And I'm selfish enough to keep doing it anyway."

Lucia studied his face, her expression softening. "Do you care about her?"

He took a sip of wine to buy a moment before answering. "I don't want to."

"But you do."

"Yes," he admitted. "I want her. I want to keep her. And that's why I can't."

"Well, what's the problem?"

He swirled the wine in his glass. "The problem is I'm not going to stop. I'm going to take what I want from her for as long as I can get away with it, and then I'm going to walk away before Brambilia decides she's worth killing to hurt me. That's the problem."

Lucia turned off the burner under the percolator and went to stand in front of him. "Does this have to do with Ginevra?"

"I don't want to talk about Ginevra." He set down his wine glass, his hands trembling slightly.

"Maybe you need to."

"Do I?" Francesco snapped. "She told me she loved me. For three years, she told me she loved me. She let me believe—" He stopped

166

and took a shaking breath. "She let me believe we had a future. I was going to marry her. I had the ring, I had plans for us." His voice broke slightly. "When she got pregnant I thought we were going to have a family, but the whole fucking time, she was married to a banker I'd had deals with for years."

Lucia's face crumpled. "I know, Frankie. It—"

"I was going to kill him," he said, the words coming out in a rush. "Mancini. I was going to kill him so I could have her, marry her, and claim the baby as mine. I had my gun pressed to his head, and he was begging me to spare him, telling me he had a wife and a baby on the way."

The memory was as vivid as if it had happened yesterday. The banker's terrified face, the way his hands had shaken as he'd pleaded for his life. And Ginevra, standing in the corner of that hotel room, watching the whole scene with cold amusement.

"He looked at her like she was the sun and the moon and all the stars combined. And she didn't even care. And sometimes I still think about going back," Francesco said, his voice becoming cold. "Finishing what I started with Mancini. Not for her. Fuck her. But because he got to keep his pretty lies while I choked on the truth. He gets to go home every night to his wife, believing she loves him, while I—" He stopped himself.

"She wasn't worth killing for."

"She wasn't worth killing for," he echoed. "But Christ, some days I wish I had anyway."

"Francesco—"

"Don't look at me like that. You wanted the truth, there it is. I'm not a good man, Lucia. I never have been."

"But you didn't kill them," she said quietly. "That counts for something."

"Does it?" He laughed, the sound bitter. "Love is a weapon, Lucia. The best one there is. It makes you believe in things that don't exist, makes you vulnerable, makes you—" He stopped, his jaw working. "It turns you into someone you despise. I can't let myself love anyone."

"You love me, don't you?" she asked quietly.

"That's different."

"How?"

"You're my sister."

"Family is supposed to be safe." Lucia's voice was soft, understanding. "But it's not always, is it?"

Francesco pulled a couple coffee mugs from the cabinet, knowing where this was going.

"That's not the same thing."

"Isn't it? Family didn't mean anything to Antonio." Her voice was calm, but he could see the old pain flickering in her eyes. "You think that blood makes you safe or someone will love you?"

"Lucia—"

"You put a bullet in our brother's head because he tried to violate me. Being family didn't stop him from being a monster." She stepped closer, her hand coming up to touch his arm. "And being a monster didn't stop you from being my protector either."

Francesco's throat closed up. The memory of that night, of finding Antonio in Lucia's room, the sick satisfaction on his face, the way Lucia had looked at Francesco with such desperate relief when he'd burst through the door... He would never forget any detail of that moment.

"What you did for me, Frankie, that's real love." She reached out and covered his shaking hands with hers. "So yes, maybe you're capable of it. The question is whether you'll let yourself have it, or if you'll destroy it first just to prove Ginevra was right."

Francesco pulled his hands away. "I'm going to hurt her, Lucia. It's inevitable. The only question is how much damage I do before I walk away."

"Then why not walk away now?"

"Because I can't. I've already taken too much to give her back. She's mine now, at least for a little while longer, and I'm too fucking selfish to let go until I have to."

Lucia sighed. "You're going to ruin her, aren't you? Just like Ginevra ruined you."

"Yes."

They stood there in silence for a moment. Francesco felt raw, his old wounds torn open and he didn't know how to stop the bleeding.

"You can't, Frankie. You just can't." Lucia said finally, her voice soft. "You can't hurt her like that. Ginevra knew exactly what she was doing to you. But this girl? She looked at you in such a desperate way, like, like she didn't want to leave you."

"Then she's a fool."

"Maybe. Or maybe she sees something in you that you've forgotten exists." Lucia picked up her coffee cup. "Just promise me one thing."

"What?"

"When you do walk away—and you will, because you're too scared not to—make it clean. Don't drag it out. Don't give her hope that you might come back." Her eyes held his. "If you're going to be a monster, at least be a merciful one."

Francesco stared at her. His hands clenched, remembering how Miss Silvano had told him he was worth missing. "In the time we have left, I'll take what I want. And then I'll let her go before Brambilia uses her to destroy me."

"Or before you fall in love with her."

"That won't happen."

"You're already halfway there, Frankie. I can see it."

"Then I'll claw my way back." He met her eyes again. "I won't be that weak again. Not for anyone."

Lucia sighed, setting down her coffee cup. "Do you know what I think?"

"That I'm damned?"

"I think you're terrified. Not of Brambilia, and not of getting hurt again. You're terrified that maybe this time it could be the real thing, and you'd rather destroy it yourself than give it a chance to destroy you."

Francesco stared at her. The possibility terrified him more than any gun pressed to his head ever had.

"And if I'm right? If I let myself believe and it all falls apart?"

"Then at least you won't spend the rest of your life wondering what if."

"I'd rather wonder than bleed."

"You're already bleeding. You've been bleeding since Ginevra.

The question is whether you're going to let yourself heal, or if you're going to make sure no one else ever gets close enough to hurt you again, even if it means cutting yourself off from anything good."

Maybe Lucia was right. Maybe he was scared. But being scared had kept him alive this long. But the question was whether Miss Silvano would even see him again. But maybe not would be better. Cleaner. Let her hate him now, before he dragged her any deeper.

So if she let him back in, he'd have to be the one to push her away, hard enough that she wouldn't come back, and cold enough that she'd believe it was always just business, nothing more.

If she gave him the chance, he'd make sure she understood exactly what he was. He'd make sure she saw the monster clearly enough that she'd run before Brambilia made her a target, and before Francesco's selfishness got her killed.

Two weeks. If she'd even give him that. Two weeks to push her away so thoroughly she'd never look back.

The bag shuddered. Again. Again.

Francesco's knuckles had split through the tape an hour ago. Blood made the leather slick under his fists. He didn't stop.

Left hook. Right cross. Pivot. Again.

Serafina's face. That hurt look in her eyes at the museum. The way she'd flinched when the guard's keys jangled. Something had happened to her. Someone had—

The bag exploded under his fist, sand pouring out onto the gym floor.

"Jesus Christ, Frankie."

He turned. Ricci stood in the doorway, newspaper in hand.

"What?" Francesco's voice came out rough.

"We've got a situation." Ricci crossed to the bench, dropped the paper. "Page three."

Francesco's hands were shaking as he unwrapped the tape. Blood and sweat made the fabric stick to his skin. He picked up *Fuck*.

It was from the museum. Yesterday, in that moment before everything went to hell. Her hand was on his arm, his hand possessively on her waist. She was smiling like an angel. And he was looking down at her like she was his whole goddamn world.

Mystery woman captures the heart of notorious mob boss Francesco Romano. Our sources say the lucky lady is a local bookstore employee, but her identity remains unknown. Is New York's most dangerous bachelor finally ready to settle down?

"*Fuck*," he snarled. His hand crushed the newspaper, crumpling the image.

"*It's not that bad,*" Ricci said carefully.

"*Not that bad?*" Francesco's voice was deadly quiet. "*Look at my face in that picture. Look at it and tell me I don't look like a man who'd burn down the world for her.*"

Ricci was silent.

"This puts a target on her back," Francesco said. "Every two-bit enforcer and beat cop looking to make a name for himself just got handed a roadmap to destroying me."

"Then end it." Ricci's voice was flat. "Clean break. Walk away now while you still can."

The words hung in the air between them.

Francesco looked at the crumpled newspaper in his fist.

"That's the plan, ain't it?" Ricci pressed. "You use her to make Brambilia think you're serious about settling down, then you end it. She goes back to her bookshop, you go back to business as usual."

"Yeah." Francesco's throat felt tight. "That's the plan."

"So do it now. Before this gets worse."

Francesco smoothed out the newspaper and stared at the photo again, and though of that genuine laugh that had surprised them both, and the way she'd said "I think you still are" with teasing warmth in her voice.

"We can't," he said finally.

"What?"

"If I end it now, it looks suspicious. We've only been seen with each other a few weeks. A relationship right after a looking like this photo surfaces? Brambilia's not stupid. He'll know it was fake."

"Frankie—"

"We need to give it a little more time to make it look real." He was still staring at the photo.

Ricci studied him for a long moment. "You sure that's why you want to keep seeing her?"

"What the hell is that supposed to mean?"

"It means you just destroyed a heavy bag because you can't stop thinking about whatever's wrong with her. It means you're standing here making excuses instead of doing what you know you should do."

"I said we need to maintain the appearance—"

"Bullshit." Ricci's voice cut sharp. "You don't want to let her go."

Francesco's jaw clenched. "It's not about what I want."

"Isn't it?"

The silence stretched. Francesco looked down at the photo again. "I'll handle it. We'll see it through to the end of the month. Long enough that ending it looks natural. Then she goes back to her life and I go back to mine."

"And in the meantime?"

"In the meantime, this photo is everywhere. Everyone knows her face now. Everyone who wants to hurt me knows exactly where to find my weakness." Francesco's hands curled into fists. "So we better hope nobody tries anything stupid."

Ricci shook his head slowly. "You're playing a dangerous game."

"I know."

Ricci held his gaze for a moment, then turned to leave. At the door, he paused. "For what it's worth? That photo? You look happy."

The door closed behind him.

Francesco stood alone in the ruined gym, staring at Serafina's smile, and at his own face, showing everything he'd been trying to hide.

He smoothed the paper out carefully, pressing the wrinkles flat with the heat of his hands. Then he folded it, tucked it into his gym bag.

He should throw it away or burn it, forget what it felt like to look at someone that way, to let his guard down even for a moment. But he had work to do. A shipment coming in at the docks that he'd nearly forgotten about. Too busy thinking about her face. Not now. Not when one mistake could cost him everything. He needed to hope to God he hadn't already fucked that up, too, by letting his mind wander for the past three days.

CHAPTER 12

Clara's voice filled the small reading nook like music. The morning had been slow, with only a handful of customers browsing the shelves, leaving them time to talk.

"Not that I was beautiful that night, or that I looked beautiful in that dress," Clara continued, her cheeks flushed pink with the memory. "But that I was beautiful. Present tense. Permanent. Do you see the difference?"

Serafina nodded from her chair, forcing a smile that felt like broken glass. "He sounds wonderful."

"He is. Oh, Sera, he really is." Clara clasped her hands together. "I never thought I could feel this way again. After Theodore died, I was so certain that kind of love only happened once in a lifetime."

The words twisted something in Serafina's chest. She gripped the arms of her chair, trying to focus on Clara's happiness instead of her own spiraling thoughts. Maybe love did come twice for some people. Maybe Clara was proof that hearts could heal and trust could be rebuilt.

But Serafina's heart wasn't just broken. It was being systematically destroyed, piece by piece, by men who saw her as nothing more than a means to an end.

"Irving's already talking about children," Clara continued, her voice dreamy. "Can you imagine? Little ones running through the house. He wants a spring wedding—orange blossoms in my hair and silk that catches the light." She paused, her expression softening further. "I can already picture walking down the aisle to him, seeing that look in his eyes like I'm his whole world."

"You'll make a beautiful bride," Serafina managed, though her voice came out hollow.

Clara's smile faded slightly. She leaned forward, studying Serafina's face with growing concern. "You've been so strange lately, darling. One day you're practically glowing, humming while you shelve books, and the next you look like you haven't slept in a week. And you keep canceling our Tuesday lunches. It's not like you." She reached out and touched Serafina's hand. "You're not even really listening to me right now, are you? A month ago you would have been planning my entire wedding, squealing over dress patterns. But lately, it's like your mind is always somewhere else. With someone else, maybe?"

But before Serafina could figure out what lie might satisfy her friend's concern, the bell above the shop door chimed.

Both women looked up to see Mr. Kensington stepping inside. His eyes swept the shop with interest before settling on Serafina with that familiar focus that made her want to crawl out of her own skin.

Serafina's gaze darted to Mr. Thompson's office. The door was closed. She could hear the murmur of his voice, on the telephone, maybe. But too far away to help, and too occupied to notice.

She was alone with Kensington, and he knew it.

"Clara," Serafina said quickly, her voice tight, "we'll finish talking later."

Clara's gaze shifted to Mr. Kensington, and her warm expression cooled to polite professionalism. She gathered her coat and purse, but not before squeezing Serafina's shoulder, her fingers lingering in a way that said *I know something's wrong.*

"I'll see you Wednesday, darling."

Serafina watched her leave, wishing desperately that she could follow. But Mr. Kensington was already approaching the reading nook, his footsteps unhurried.

"Miss Silvano." Her name rolled off his tongue like an obscenity. "You look lovely today. Blue suits you."

"Thank you." She forced herself to stand, though her legs trembled. "What can I help you find?"

"I'm not here for books." He moved closer. Too close. Close enough that she could feel the heat radiating off of his body. "I wanted to confirm our next appointment."

Her stomach dropped. "Sir?"

"Friday. Six o'clock." His eyes traveled down her body slowly studying her throat, her collarbone, down the modest neckline of her dress. "The Waterford Hotel. Room four-twelve."

A hotel room. Not his house this time. Somewhere public, where she'd have to walk through a lobby, past a desk clerk, knowing exactly what she was there for. Somewhere she couldn't pretend was anything other than what it was.

"I remember the arrangement," she whispered.

"Good." He reached out, his fingers hovering near her shoulder, not quite touching, but close enough to make her flinch. "Wear something that doesn't require much effort to remove. I do so hate wasting time with complicated fastenings."

The bile rose in her throat. She managed a nod.

"I've been thinking," he continued, his tone shifting to something almost conversational, "about how beneficial our relationship could be for this little shop. I know people, Miss Silvano. Publishers, collectors, auction houses. The kind of connections that could transform this place from a struggling second-hand store into something quite profitable. First editions, rare volumes, the inventory that serious collectors seek." He paused, letting the implication sink in. "Of course, such generosity requires... ongoing cooperation."

"I understand."

"I thought you might." His smile was predatory. "And I do hope Mr. Thompson appreciates your dedication. Loyalty is such an admirable quality, don't you think?"

The threat was clear. *Keep servicing me, or I'll destroy this place and everyone who depends on it.*

176

"Yes, sir."

"Six o'clock sharp, Serafina. Don't disappoint me." He adjusted his cufflinks. "I have such plans for Friday evening."

The bell chimed again as he left. Serafina gripped the back of her chair to keep from collapsing. Her hands shook. Her breathing came in shallow gasps that didn't seem to bring enough air. She barely had time to collect herself before the door opened again.

Danny stepped inside, his usual quiet demeanor replaced by something harder. His hair was disheveled, as if he'd been running his hands through it. His eyes found her immediately, scanning her face with an intensity that made her want to step back.

"Serafina." His voice was tight. "What did Kensington want?"

"Just business." The lie came automatically now, worn smooth from repetition.

"Business." He moved closer, and there was something in his expression she'd never seen before, something almost angry. "I saw him leaving. I saw the way you looked after he left. That wasn't business."

"Danny, please—"

He reached into his jacket and pulled out a folded newspaper clipping. The paper was worn at the creases, as if it had been opened and refolded many times. "We need to talk about this."

Serafina's heart sank as she stared at it, at Mr. Romano's hand on her arm, both of them smiling at each other with unmistakable warmth. In black and white, frozen in that single moment, their connection was undeniable. "Where did you get that?"

"Everyone has it. The flower vendors, the other shop owners, people at the market." His voice carried an edge she'd never heard before. "They're all talking about Francesco Romano's mystery woman, and some of them recognize you."

"We were just talking—"

"Don't." The word came out sharp enough to make her flinch. "Don't lie to me, Serafina. Not you."

"I'm not lying. We ran into each other at the museum. He's Italian, and so was my father. We were talking about Italy, about art, and someone must have taken that photo when we were laughing about something." The words tumbled out too quickly, too desperate. "It doesn't mean anything."

Danny's expression darkened. "You're sleeping with him."

"No—"

"I can see it in your face." He stepped closer, and she found herself backing up until her hip hit the counter. "That's why you've been so different. So distracted. Francesco Romano has his hooks in you."

"You don't understand—"

"I understand perfectly." His voice dropped lower, more intense. "Do you know what he is? What he does?" He thrust the clipping toward her. "This man kills people, Serafina. Not in some abstract way. He does it himself. With his own hands. He's murdered more men than either of us could count, and you're what? Playing at being his girlfriend?"

"It's not like that—"

"Then what is it like?" His hand shot out and caught her wrist—not hard enough to hurt, but firm enough to stop her from moving away. "Explain it to me. Because from where I'm standing, you're caught between two monsters. Kensington circling you like a shark, and now Romano? Do you think either of them sees you as anything more than something to use?"

"Let go of me." She tried to pull away, but his grip tightened.

"Not until you listen." His other hand came up to cup her face, his thumb brushing across her cheekbone in a gesture that might have been tender if not for the desperation in his eyes. "You don't see the danger you're in. You never do. You think everyone has good intentions, that people can be trusted." His voice softened slightly. "But they can't. Not men like Kensington and Romano. They'll destroy you."

"Danny, you're scaring me—"

"Good. You should be scared." But his grip on her wrist loosened fractionally. "Someone needs to protect you from yourself. Someone who actually cares about you, not just what you can give them."

"I appreciate your concern, but—"

"We're having coffee on Friday, after the shop closes."

"I can't—"

"Six o'clock. We'll talk about this properly, away from here." His grip tightened again. "You need someone looking out for you, Serafina. I'm not going to stand by and watch them hurt you."

"Danny, please—"

"Six o'clock." He released her wrist and stepped back, his eyes still fixed on her face. "Don't make me worry more than I already am."

Then he was gone, and she was alone with the crumpled newspaper clipping on the counter and the marks his fingers had left on her wrist.

Six o'clock Friday. The same time Kensington expected her at the Waterford Hotel.

She stared at the photograph, at Francesco's face, and felt her chest tighten with longing and terror.

"Serafina?" Mr. Thompson's voice made her jump. He stood in the doorway of his office, his kind face creased with concern. "I'm afraid I have some troubling news."

She looked up, trying to compose herself. "What is it?"

"I spoke with Blackwood Publishing this morning. They're pulling their accounts. Citing 'strategic business decisions,' whatever that means." He studied her more closely, taking in her pale complexion and the dark circles under her eyes that no amount of powder could hide. "Are you feeling all right, my dear? You look quite unwell."

"I'm fine. Just tired." She tried to force a smile, but it came out strained. "Blackwood is our second largest wholesale account. Perhaps I should work extra hours to help compensate—"

"Absolutely not." His voice was firm but gentle. "You already work harder than anyone should have to." He paused, watching as she swayed slightly. "Why don't you take tomorrow off? You need proper rest."

"I couldn't. You should spend the day with Mrs. Thompson. I'll come in so you can be with her—"

"Actually," he interrupted, his expression brightening slightly, "the doctor says she's making wonderful progress. She'll be able to go outside again soon." The smile faded as he looked at her exhausted

179

face. "But I think we'll both take the day off. I'll close the shop tomorrow. When's the last time you took a proper holiday?"

She wanted to protest. The shop needed to stay open. They couldn't afford to lose a day's sales, especially not now with Blackwood pulling out. But she couldn't form the words. Her throat felt tight, her eyes burned with unshed tears.

"That sounds nice," she managed.

"It's settled then." He patted her shoulder gently. "You go home and rest. Perhaps things will look better in the morning."

If only that were true. But she nodded and gathered her things, grateful for his kindness even as she wondered if anything would ever look better again.

When closing time finally arrived, she locked the door with trembling hands. The street was busy with people heading home from work, couples meeting for dinner, the normal rhythm of city life that felt increasingly foreign to her. She walked slowly toward her building, in no hurry to reach the emptiness waiting there.

By evening, restlessness had settled into her bones like a fever.

Things are returning to normal, she told herself, pacing her small living room. *This is what you wanted. Professional distance. The end of whatever foolishness you thought was happening.*

But her heart ached with the lie. She wanted to hear Mr. Romano's voice and to feel his hands on her face again. She wanted to believe that what she'd seen in his eyes for that moment at the museum had been real.

She threw on her coat and decided to walk. The night air might clear her head and help her think. There had to be a way out of Friday at six o'clock. There had to be.

The streets were busier than usual for a weeknight. Couples strolled arm in arm, their laughter floating on the cool air. Groups of friends headed to restaurants or theaters, their voices bright with anticipation. Serafina walked aimlessly through it all, a ghost moving through the living.

The first crack split the night like thunder. For a heartbeat, she didn't understand what it was. Then came the second shot. The third.

Rapid succession, close enough that she smelled gunpowder on the air. Close enough that her ears rang with the aftershock.

A woman screamed, high and shrill, the kind of sound that bypassed thought and went straight to instinct. Men shouted. Serafina couldn't process the words, just the panic in their voices. All around her, people scattered like startled birds. Some dropped to the ground, arms over their heads. Others ran for doorways, alleyways, anywhere that offered cover. A man in a business suit stumbled past her, his briefcase clutched to his chest like a shield, his face drained of color.

Serafina's legs wouldn't move. She stood frozen in the middle of the sidewalk, her breath caught somewhere between her lungs and her throat.

Then someone crashed into her shoulder and the impact broke whatever spell held her. Serafina stumbled backward into a recessed doorway, pressing herself against the cold stone, her heart hammering so hard she could feel it in her skull.

Through the chaos of running figures and panicked voices, she could see a dark shape in the street.

A man lay on his back, his body twisted at an unnatural angle, one arm flung out as if he'd been reaching for something when he fell. His coat had fallen open. His shirt was darkening. The streetlight caught the gleam of blood spreading beneath him, a widening pool that seeped between the cobblestones.

"Someone call the police!" A man's voice, ragged with fear.

"Oh God—oh God, Johnny? Johnny, can you hear me?"

More gunshots echoed from somewhere down the block—fainter now, moving away. Serafina pressed herself harder against the door, her hands flat against the stone, trying to make herself smaller. Her breath came in short, sharp gasps that didn't seem to bring enough air.

This was happening. This was real. A man was dying in the street and she was watching it happen.

When she opened her eyes—she didn't even remember closing them—a young woman had appeared beside the fallen man. She couldn't have been more than Serafina herself, her dark hair falling loose from its pins. She dropped to her knees in the spreading blood, her dress soaking it up like a sponge.

"Johnny, please—stay with me, please—"

Her hands pressed against his chest, trying to stop the bleeding. But there was so much blood. It welled between her fingers. Her hands were shaking so badly she could barely keep pressure on the wound.

"Someone help him! Please, someone—"

But no one moved. The few people who hadn't fled watched from doorways and windows, faces pale with shock or morbid curiosity. No one wanted to get involved. No one wanted to be next.

Serafina's stomach lurched. She tasted bile.

This was Mr. Romano's world. Violence and death and people broken in the street while others watched from the shadows. This was what it meant to be close to him and to live in a world where men shot each other over debts or insults or territory, where women knelt in their lovers' blood and begged them not to die.

This was what Danny had tried to warn her about.

The young woman was sobbing now, her whole body shaking as she pressed down on Johnny's chest. "Please don't leave me—please, I can't—Johnny, please—the baby—"

The man's chest rose. Once. A wet, rattling sound came from his throat. His arm twitched, fingers grasping at air.

Then... nothing.

The woman's sobs turned to screams, raw, animal sounds that scraped against Serafina's ears. The woman collapsed forward onto the man's chest, her blood-soaked hands clawing at his shirt, as if she could pull him back by sheer force of will.

"No, no, no—Johnny, wake up—please wake up—"

Sirens wailed in the distance. Growing closer. The machinery of law and order responding to another night of violence in a city that bred it faster than it could be contained.

Serafina couldn't breathe. Couldn't think. All she could see was the blood. The woman's shaking hands. The man's empty stare.

This could have been Francesco lying in that street. Or it could have been her, caught in the crossfire of someone else's war. One wrong moment, one wrong place, and she could be the one dying while strangers watched from doorways.

The sirens were closer now. Shouts of "Police!" echoed down the block.

Serafina moved. She didn't remember deciding to move. Her body just did it. Some animal part of her brain took over while the rest of her was still frozen in that doorway watching a man die.

Her legs felt wrong, like they belonged to someone else. She walked fast. Her heels clicked against the pavement in a rhythm that didn't match her racing heart. Then faster. Then she was nearly running, her breath coming in short, sharp gasps that burned in her chest.

She needed to get home. Get inside. Get somewhere with a door she could lock.

She turned down a side street, not her usual route, but she couldn't walk past that blood, couldn't make herself go anywhere near where the body still lay. Another turn. Then another. The streets blurred together. She kept checking over her shoulder, certain she'd see someone following. But there was no one, just shadows and the distant wail of sirens and her own footsteps echoing off brick walls.

Her lungs burned. When had she started running? She couldn't remember. Couldn't remember turning this corner or passing that shop. The city felt alien around her, full of dark windows and narrow alleys where anything could be hiding.

By the time her building came into view, sweat had soaked through her dress despite the cold. Her hands trembled as she fumbled in her purse for her keys. They slipped through her fingers once, twice, the metal clattering against the sidewalk. She snatched them up, her vision tunneling.

Every shadow looked like a man with a gun. Every sound—a door closing somewhere above, footsteps on a distant street, the rustle of wind through newspapers—made her flinch.

She got the building door open. The stairwell smelled like cabbage and old plaster, familiar and nauseating now. She took the steps too fast, her hand gripping the railing to keep from stumbling. Second floor. Down the hall. Her door was just ahead.

When she reached it, she stopped.

Another copy of the newspaper article was stabbed to the wood. But this one had Mr. Romano's face pierced through with dozens of holes, and her own face similarly mutilated. The paper was torn where something sharp had gone through again and again and again.

A small ice pick protruded from the center, driven deep enough into the wood that she was certain it pierced the other side.

Serafina's hands shook so badly she dropped her keys twice before managing to get the door unlocked. She tore the article down and shoved it in her pocket. She yanked the ice pick loose, but dropped it. It clattered to the floor and she kicked it away like it might bite her.

Inside, she locked the door, slid the chain, and checked the lock again.

Then she sank to the floor, her back against the door, and something broke inside her.

She pulled the crumpled articles from her pocket with shaking hands, both of them. The one Danny had shown her and this new one, mutilated beyond recognition. She smoothed them out on the floor beside her, staring at the holes piercing through their faces.

This was what happened to people in Francesco's world. They became targets. Collateral damage.

A sob caught in her throat. Then another. Then she was cried for the first time since this nightmare began. For the bookshop that was failing. For Mr. Thompson's kindness that she didn't deserve. For Clara's happiness that she'd never have. For the man dying in the street. For Francesco's face in the photograph, smiling at her like she might have cared about her for a moment. For Friday at six o'clock in a hotel room. For Danny's grip on her wrist. For the ice pick in her door.

For everything she'd lost and everything she was about to lose.

She didn't know how long she sat there, but it was long enough that her legs went numb and the tears stopped and left her hollow.

Finally, she stood and folded the articles carefully. She put them in her desk drawer with all the other evidence of her unraveling life.

She moved through her apartment like a sleepwalker, checking the windows, the lock on the door, the chain. She left lights on in every room. She pulled the teddy bear from the shelf and clutched it against her chest.

When she finally lay down in bed, still fully clothed, she couldn't close her eyes. Every time she did, she saw the man in the street. The blood. The holes in the photograph. Kensington's smile. Danny's grip. Francesco's face.

The ice pick.

She stared at the ceiling and listened to every sound in the building. Footsteps in the hall. Doors closing. The creak of old pipes. Any of them could be someone coming for her. Someone who'd seen that photograph and decided she needed to pay for standing too close to Francesco Romano.

Dawn was starting to gray the windows when exhaustion finally pulled her under.

Her last conscious thought was that she had two days until Friday at six o'clock.

Two days to figure out how to survive this.

Two days that already felt like not enough time at all.

Late that night, after the storefronts had gone dark and the streetcars stopped running, he moved through the streets with the confidence that came with being a man such as himself when he had a job to do.

The air stank of coal smoke and stale beer, gutters running black with rainwater and old refuse. The smell didn't bother him. If anything, it suited his mood. It was raw and honest... stripped of pretense. This part of the city wore its ugliness openly, unlike the facades people maintained in daylight.

Her name pulsed in his head with every step.

Serafina.

Serafina.

His Serafina.

The girl who was supposed to know better!

Instead, she had opened herself to another man. She was supposed to recognize what he had, and what she owed. Instead, she'd let another man touch her. He'd seen that damned museum photograph that everyone was passing around like cheap gossip. Her hand on Romano's arm. That smile on her face with the kind of expression she should have reserved for *him* alone. But she'd smiled for Romano, probably undressed and spread her thighs and made sounds that he himself planned to force from her.

The thought brought a slow burn to his chest, a burn that needed tending to. She needed to understand her mistake. Needed to learn what happened when you gave yourself to the wrong man. Tonight, she would learn.

He turned onto her street, keeping his pace unhurried. He was just a man with legitimate business. Nothing to see here. Nothing to see. His lifted his eyes to the second-floor windows, adjusting his fedora as he did. Her building was a shabby affair with peeling paint and crooked shutters, the kind of place that housed shop girls and seamstresses and other women scraping by on too little money. She deserved better. He could give her better. He *would* give her better, once she understood.

Her window was dark. Good. She was home, probably sleeping, unaware of what was coming.

The building's front door gave easily. No lock. No security. These places never had proper protection. He stepped into the stairwell and climbed to the second floor, his footfalls soft on the worn runner. At the landing, something metallic caught his eye. He stopped, bent, and retrieved his ice pick from where it had been kicked aside.

He rolled it once between his fingers, appreciating the familiar weight, then slipped it into his coat pocket. Everything had its place. Everything returned to where it belonged. She belonged to him.

At her door, he crouched and pressed his ear to the frame. Silence. No movement. Just the quiet stillness of sleep.

He set down his leather bag. Quality craftsmanship, the kind that didn't advertise itself but spoke to those who knew. Then he drew out the small crowbar. The tool was old but maintained, pitted with use but perfectly functional. He'd used it before for similar purposes. It never failed him.

He positioned the wedge against the doorjamb, braced himself—

Footsteps echoed from the stairwell below.

He took his sweet, sweet time slipping the crowbar back into the bag. He felt no panic, no need for rushed movements. Just smooth efficiency as he stood and adjusted his coat.

A young woman emerged onto the landing. Twenty, perhaps, or twenty-one. Red hair pinned loosely, falling out on one side. Her house robe was thin, belted carelessly, and her cheeks were flushed the way women looked after they'd been thoroughly used. Coming home from a lover's bed, no doubt. The cheap perfume confirmed it.

She saw him and smiled. Not wary. Not cautious. Just friendly and perhaps a bit drunk.

He touched the brim of his hat in acknowledgment but said nothing.

She moved past him, humming something under her breath, fishing in her robe pocket for her key. Two steps past. Three.

He moved.

The garrote came out of his pocket in one smooth motion— braided wire, thin and strong, with wooden handles worn smooth from use. One hand looped it over her head before she could process what was happening. The other yanked it tight.

Her body jerked backward into his chest. Her heels skidded on the runner, hands flying up instinctively. The key clattered to the floor.

He held steady. No need to rush.

She made a high and breathless sound, more surprise than pain at first. Her fingers clawed at the wire, nails scraping her own neck as she tried to find purchase between the garrote and her windpipe. It was always the same. They always went for the wire first, as if their soft hands could do anything against braided steel.

He adjusted his grip, casually pulling tighter, steadily increasing the inexorable pressure.

Her body bucked against his. She tried to scream, but the sound came out as a wet, strangled gurgle. Her robe slipped off one shoulder. Her feet kicked against the floor, heels drumming uselessly against the baseboard. The sound echoed in the narrow hallway, desperate and increasingly weak. *Thump, thump, scrape... scrap...*

He leaned back slightly, bracing with one foot against the wall, using his weight to maintain pressure. Her spine twisted as she fought. Her whole body convulsed, that final animal panic when the brain realized it wasn't getting oxygen. The thrashing was violent but brief.

Her fingernails had torn her own skin. Blood welled in thin lines where she'd clawed herself. Her face had gone from pink to red to a deep, mottled purple. The capillaries in her eyes burst. He could see them rupturing as tiny red threads spread across the whites.

Then came the smell, acrid and unmistakable. Her bladder let go. Warm urine soaked through her robe and dripping onto the floor. It always happened. The body's final indignity.

He kept the garrote tight for another fifteen seconds. No point in being careless. Her body had gone slack against his, all the fight drained out with her last breath, but he'd learned not to trust that. Better to be thorough.

When he finally eased the pressure, her body sagged like a puppet with cut strings. He lowered her carefully to the floor. No need to let her head crack against the boards and make unnecessary noise.

He crouched beside her, pressing two fingers to her throat out of habit more than necessity. No pulse. Her eyes stared at nothing, still wide with that last moment of understanding.

He retrieved her key from where it had fallen, glanced at the number, then gathered her up, one arm under her knees, the other cradling her back. She weighed almost nothing. Women like her usually didn't. All that nervous energy, all that running around, left them insubstantial.

He carried her up one more flight, moving carefully to avoid bumping her limbs against the walls. At the door at the end of the hall, he used her key to let himself in.

Her apartment was what he expected—small and cluttered, clothes draped over furniture. The scent of her poverty perfume was stronger here. He laid her on the sofa, arranging her carefully. He smoothed her hair back from her face, fixed her robe so she looked almost peaceful.

Wrong place. Wrong time. Too bad for her. If she'd been home in her own bed where she belonged, she'd have lived through the night.

He locked her door on the way out, leaving the key on her mat where someone would find it, sooner or later. No need to make this look like anything other than what it would appear to be—just a woman strangled in her own home. The police would investigate, question neighbors, then eventually file it away with all the other unsolved murders in a city full of them.

In the hallway outside Serafina's door, he retrieved his bag and ice pick. He stood there for a moment, looking at her door, imagining what lay beyond it. Her sleeping form. Unaware. Vulnerable...

He'd been planning to use the crowbar, force the lock, let himself in quietly. She'd wake up with his hand over her mouth, his weight on top of her. He'd take his time. Make her understand what she'd done. Make her feel every consequence.

But not tonight. The interruption had been... inconvenient. But it wasn't insurmountable. He was a patient man. He'd waited this long. He could wait a little longer.

Besides, anticipation had its own pleasures.

He descended the stairs, moving with the same measured pace as when he'd arrived. Outside, the street was still empty, the windows still dark. No one had heard anything. No one ever did in neighborhoods like this.

He walked back the way he'd come, hands in his pockets, breathing easy.

Soon. Very soon.

She'd understand exactly who she belonged to.

CHAPTER 13

Serafina's hands trembled as she adjusted her hat in the back seat of Clara's car. She did her best to conceal the dark circles under her eyes and to brighten up her cheeks. Every time she'd closed her eyes, she'd seen that man's body twisted in the street, blood pooling beneath him, and heard the woman's desperate sobs echoing off the building.

"Darling, you look even more dreadful in daylight," Clara said, settling beside her as the driver pulled away from the curb. "Please, won't you tell me what happened?"

Serafina stared out the window, watching the city roll past in a blur of motion and color. Her hands lay outwardly motionless in her lap, but she could feel them shaking underneath. She knew Clara wouldn't let this matter go.

"There was a shooting, near my building. A man was killed. He looked at me when he died. And a woman was screaming for him."

Clara's hand flew to her throat. "My God, Serafina. You were there when it happened? Were you hurt?"

"I was out for a walk. I heard the gunshots, and I saw..." Serafina's voice caught. "I'd never seen someone die before. I've never watched the light go out of someone's eyes while they tried to speak and couldn't."

"Oh, darling." Clara reached over and squeezed her hand. "How awful. No wonder you look so shaken."

Serafina closed her eyes, trying to push the terrible images from her mind and to steady her breathing as they continued through the city. Clara seemed to sense her need for quiet, resting her hand over Serafina's.

After several minutes of silence, the motorcar drew up in front of an elegant restaurant, its windows gleaming in the afternoon sun. A small sign announced a private function, and well-dressed guests were already entering, the kind of people who moved through the world as if they hadn't a care in it.

Clara and Serafina walked side by side into the restaurant. Crystal chandeliers cast dancing light across the room, where at least fifty guests mingled with champagne glasses.

"I expected a small tea party," Serafina said, her voice weak.

Clara bit her lip. "Me too. This was supposed to be the literary society."

As they moved deeper into the crowd, Serafina fought an urge to turn and run. The room felt too bright. She felt too exposed, like she was standing naked in a spotlight.

"Clara! How wonderful that you could come." Lucia Romano embraced Clara warmly before turning to Serafina with a bright smile of recognition. "And Miss Silvano! What a delightful surprise to see you again so soon. I'm so pleased you could attend after all."

Clara's brow furrowed slightly. "Again? Do you two know each other?"

"We met at the Metropolitan Museum this past weekend," Serafina said quickly, giving Miss Romano a meaningful look. "I went by myself since I had a rough night. Miss Romano and I were both admiring the same painting in the Italian collection."

"Yes, that's right," Miss Romano said a little too brightly with a meaningful nod to Serafina. "A passing conversation about art. I'm afraid I barely remember the details."

Clara's expression smoothed. "How lovely that you've crossed paths before. Sera has such an appreciation for art."

"Indeed," Miss Romano said graciously, her smile now perfectly polite rather than warmly familiar. "Miss Silvano struck me as quite knowledgeable about Italian Renaissance works, especially the Caravaggio we were viewing."

Serafina felt a surge of gratitude for the quick cover-up, but hurried to correct her. "Oh no, I don't really know that much about any of it, but Miss Romano was very kind to share her insights about that piece."

"Well, isn't this wonderful," Clara said, clearly pleased by this coincidence.

As they chatted about inconsequential matters, Serafina scanned the crowd with growing dread. Where was Mr. Romano. The not-knowing made her stomach clench with anxiety. Perhaps he hadn't come after all. The tension began to ease.

But then she saw him.

Mr. Romano stood near the far wall, elegant. His attention was focused on an older gentleman who was speaking animatedly about something, but even from across the room, Serafina was drawn to him. Several women had positioned themselves nearby, circling like moths drawn to a flame that would burn them alive. They didn't seem to care. They were rich. The rich never suffered.

So he was here, in the same room, and she had to pretend he was nothing more than a stranger. She had to pretend his hands hadn't skimmed every inch of her skin, and that his mouth hadn't drawn sounds from her that she hadn't known she could make.

"Well," Miss Romano said, "since you're all here, why don't we find your seats for our luncheon? I believe we're about to be called to the table."

She led them toward the dining room, where elegantly set tables waited. Serafina noticed her place card read "Miss C. Randolph, Guest" in gold ink. Miss Romano quickly and discreetly switched Serafina's card with another guest's.

"I'm sorry I couldn't move you farther away from my brother without drawing notice," Miss Romano whispered close to Serafina's ear as they approached the table. Then, even more quietly, she asked, "So Miss Randolph doesn't know about you and Frankie?"

"There's nothing to know," Serafina whispered back urgently. "It was business. We aren't together."

Miss Romano's eyebrows rose slightly, but she nodded with a knowing look that made Serafina's cheeks burn. "I see."

"Thank you," Serafina murmured.

Still, Serafina found herself placed almost directly across from Mr. Romano. Her heart hammered against her ribs as she took her seat, doing everything in her power to avoid meeting his eyes. She focused on her napkin, the silverware, the centerpiece—anything other than the man whose presence seemed to fill the entire room.

A striking blonde woman in a pink dress sat to his left. She introduced herself as Vivian Ashworth, daughter of some railroad magnate. Her smile was calculating as she sized up Mr. Romano. Her gaze raking over him with undisguised and unashamed hunger.

Something dark and ugly twisted in Serafina's chest. *Mine*, some primitive part of her wanted to snarl. *He's mine*. But he wasn't. He'd never been. This was business. Just business. She was disturbed at her own possessiveness.

As the first course was served, Miss Ashworth turned her considerable charm on Mr. Romano, leaning to give him an admirable view of her breasts.

"Mr. Romano, I've heard so much about your business ventures." Her tongue darted out to wet her lips. "Such an impressive operation you run. My father says you control half the distribution in the city. The kind of business that requires a certain... ruthlessness."

Mr. Romano chuckled one. "Your father talks too much."

Miss Ashworth laughed back. "Oh, I can be very discreet. Daddy also says the most interesting business happens after dark. That's the kind that requires real courage and strength and power." Her fingers traced the stem of her wine glass as she spoke, the gesture obscene in its suggestiveness. "I do so admire a man who isn't afraid to take what he wants, consequences be damned."

Mr. Romano's eyes sparked with dark amusement. "Be. careful, Miss Ashworth. That sounds like an invitation."

The woman laid her hand on his sleeve.

Serafina's fork clattered against her plate. Her chest felt tight, as if someone had wrapped iron bands around her ribs and was slowly crushing her lungs. *That* hand. On *his* arm. Where Serafina's hands had been just days ago, touching him in ways this woman could only imagine. She glanced around. Those seated adjacent seemed to be trying to ignore the overly-flirty behavior happening right beside them.

"A woman can tell when a man has real power," Miss Ashworth continued, her voice dropping to an intimate purr. "There's something about the way you carry yourself." She leaned even closer, her lips nearly brushing his ear. "Tell me, Mr. Romano, is it true what they say? That you can make problems disappear with just a word?"

Francesco's smile turned cold, amused. "What do they say, exactly?"

"That men who cross you tend to have unfortunate accidents. That the police look the other way when your name comes up." Her fingers traced patterns on his sleeve. "That you own this city."

"You shouldn't believe everything you hear, Miss Ashworth."

"I don't," she breathed. "I believe what I see. And I see a man who's accustomed to getting exactly what he wants, when he wants it."

"Usually," Mr. Romano agreed, his voice a low rumble that made Serafina's stomach clench with unwanted heat and rage. "Though sometimes the chase is half the pleasure. The taking is always sweeter when they fight first."

Miss Ashworth's breath caught. "How deliciously wicked."

The pain in Serafina's chest intensified, spreading outward like poison through her veins. She bit her lips together hard to keep from making a sound. Her throat felt raw, scraped clean by unshed tears and swallowed sobs. She wanted to reach across the table and claw that woman's hand off his arm, to stand up and scream that he was hers.

But she had no claim.

This was it, wasn't it? This was the "something more" he'd warned her about. And he'd been right.

"Tell me," Miss Ashworth purred, her fingers now tracing circles on the back of his hand, "do you ever mix business with pleasure?"

"I've found," he said slowly, his words clearly meant for Serafina even as Miss Ashworth leaned closer, "that some pleasures are best kept temporary. Before anyone gets the wrong idea about what they mean." His gaze finally lifted and landed directly on Serafina. The impact of his eyes meeting hers stole her breath. His expression was cold and unreadable. "Expectations can be so... disappointing."

Serafina's hands clenched in her lap, nails biting into her palms. He knew. He knew exactly what he was doing to her.

"But that depends on the pleasure," Mr. Romano said, his his eyes on Miss Ashworth once more, gleaming with dark promise. "And whether the woman can handle what I offer."

"I assure you, Mr. Romano, I can handle anything you give me." The innuendo was so blatant it made Serafina's stomach turn.

"Bold words," he murmured, his thumb stroking over Miss Ashworth's knuckles in a gesture that made Serafina want to vomit. Or scream. Or both.

"Most women claim they want danger until they're faced with the reality of it."

"Then they're weak," Miss Ashworth said dismissively. "I'm not most women."

"No," Francesco agreed. "I can see that."

"Perhaps we should continue this conversation somewhere more private," Miss Ashworth suggested, her voice honey-sweet. "I'd love to hear more about your business interests. All of them."

"You flatter me, Miss Ashworth," Mr. Romano said, but his tone suggested he was anything but displeased by her attention. In fact, he looked like a cat toying with a mouse and enjoying every moment of the game.

Serafina reached for her water glass with trembling fingers. The heat of familiar tears built up behind her eyes, threatening to spill over into humiliation she absolutely could not show, not here in front of all these people. Especially not in front of him. She would not give him the satisfaction of seeing how thoroughly he'd hurt her.

"I doubt that's possible," Miss Ashworth said. "A man in your position must be used to getting exactly what he desires, when he desires it."

"Usually," Mr. Romano agreed, taking a slow sip of wine. "Though sometimes anticipation makes the eventual satisfaction more... intense."

The conversation continued, each word a fresh cut across Serafina's already bleeding heart. She wanted to look away, to focus on anything else, but she couldn't. She was trapped, forced to watch this woman stake her claim and to witness Francesco's clear enjoyment of the attention.

Was this what he wanted? Some society princess who understood his world and could move in his circles without shame? Someone who wouldn't tremble with fear and want in equal measure?

The jealousy was a living thing inside her chest, yet she had no right to it. She'd agreed to this, to the limited time and the inevitable end. But knowing that didn't make it hurt any less.

"And what do you do, Miss Silvano?" asked the gentleman seated on Serafina's other side, a thin man with wire-rimmed spectacles. Mr. Hartwell, she thought his name was.

"I work at a bookshop," Serafina forced herself to say, her voice barely steady. "The Purrfect Tale."

"How charming," Mr. Hartwell said. He lowered his voice. "I know I recognized you from somewhere. The Society Pages, wasn't it? There was a rather interesting photograph."

Serafina's blood turned to ice. Her heart stuttered in her chest, missing several beats before racing to catch up. "I... I don't..."

"Don't worry," Mr. Hartwell said quietly, his tone almost kind but with an edge of warning. "I'm quite discreet. Though I must say, you make a striking couple."

He winked, then turned away then, engaging the woman on his other side in conversation about something mundane, leaving Serafina sitting there with panic clawing up her throat. Clara. If Mr. Hartwell recognized her, who else had? How long before Clara saw the photograph, before she asked questions Serafina couldn't answer?

The rest of the meal passed in a blur of forced smiles and mechanical responses. Serafina barely tasted the food, barely heard the conversations happening around her. All she could focus on was

196

the sound of Miss Ashworth's laughter, the way Francesco smiled at something she said, the casual intimacy of their body language.

By the time dessert was served, Serafina felt like she might shatter if one more person spoke to her.

As the guests began to rise from their tables and return to socializing, Serafina saw Clara excuse herself and walk purposefully toward Mr. Hartwell, who was standing near the windows. Their conversation looked intense, and Clara's expression grew more troubled with each word. Mr. Hartwell kept his voice low, glancing toward Serafina once with an apologetic expression before continuing whatever he was saying.

No. No, no, no.

Serafina made her way through the crowd to where Mr. Romano stood with Miss Ashworth and another woman, both of them hanging on his every word. "Excuse me," she said. "Mr. Romano, might I have a word? It's rather urgent."

Miss Ashworth's expression cooled. "We're in the middle of a conversation."

"It's business," Serafina said flatly, meeting the other woman's eyes with a directness that surprised even herself. "Unless you'd like to discuss it here?"

Mr. Romano's eyes narrowed slightly. "If you'll excuse me, ladies."

They moved to a quieter corner of the room, away from prying ears. Mr. Romano leaned against the wall with casual arrogance, looking entirely unbothered by the urgency in her voice. "This better be good, Miss Silvano. Miss Ashworth was just about to invite me to her family's estate in the Hamptons."

The casual cruelty of it stole her breath. "Clara knows," she managed to say. "That man, Mr. Hartwell—there was a photo in the Sun's gossip section. He recognized me. He told her."

Mr. Romano's expression didn't change. "I saw it."

"You saw it?" Her voice rose despite her efforts to control it. "You saw it and you didn't think to warn me?"

"I assumed you could handle the situation," he said coldly. "Was I wrong?"

Before she could respond, Clara appeared at their sides, her face a mask of controlled emotion and barely suppressed fury. "I think we need to have a conversation. All three of us. *Now.*"

The blood drained from Serafina's face so quickly she felt dizzy. The elegant restaurant seemed to tilt around her, the chandeliers blurring into streaks of light like tears. Her delicate world was about to shatter. The friendship that meant everything to her would crumble, and she'd be left with nothing but the wreckage of her own deception. And Mr. Romano would walk away unscathed, probably back to Miss Ashworth's eager arms.

Mr. Romano nodded toward a small alcove off the main room. "Privacy would be advisable."

His calm voice made her panic worse. How could he be so controlled when her entire life was about to implode? Serafina's throat closed up.

The walk to the alcove felt endless. Her legs wobbled, like the floor might give way beneath her at any moment. The walls of the restaurant seemed to close in as the beautiful room transformed into a trap with no escape.

She was drowning in plain sight, suffocating on her own lies while surrounded by the glittering remnants of the life she was about to lose. She should have run earlier. She should have never agreed to any of this.

Once they were alone in the alcove, Clara turned to Serafina with hurt blazing in her eyes. "That photograph in the newspaper— that was you, wasn't it? With him?"

"Clara—" Serafina gasped, but the word came out broken.

"Mr. Hartwell was quite thorough in his explanation. He apologized profusely for bringing it up, said he thought I already knew. How could you not tell me you were involved with Francesco Romano? With *him?*"

"I'm not," Serafina said, her voice shaking so badly the words came out as barely more than a whisper. "I'm not involved with him, Clara. I'm not."

A single tear escaped despite her desperate efforts to hold it back. She quickly wiped it away with the back of her trembling hand.

"Then why are you crying?" Clara's voice softened slightly, confusion mixing with her anger. "Sera, if there's nothing between you, then why do you look like your heart is breaking?"

"She's not involved with me," Mr. Romano said calmly, stepping forward. "Miss Randolph, I understand your concern for your friend, but you're misinterpreting the situation."

Clara's eyes flashed. "Then explain it to me. Explain why my best friend has been lying to me for weeks."

"I hired Miss Silvano to catalog a private collection of rare books. The work required discretion, which is why she couldn't discuss it with you." Mr. Romano's lie came easily. "The collection belonged to my late uncle. Many of the volumes are sensitive in nature—banned socialist texts from the old country, underground publications that could cause difficulties if their existence became public knowledge. Books that certain government officials would prefer remained forgotten. Books... that could be dangerous in the wrong hands." #

"And the photograph?" Clara demanded.

"We ran into each other at the museum. It was taken while we were discussing a particular volume that related to the collection." Francesco's expression was sincere. "Miss Silvano's expertise in literature made her invaluable for the project. The intimacy you perceived was merely the intensity of our shared interest in rare books. Nothing more."

Clara looked between them, her anger slowly giving way to uncertainty. "Then why didn't you tell me, Sera? Even if it was confidential, you could have said you had a temporary job. You could have trusted me."

"I wanted to," Serafina said quietly, the words true even if nothing else was. "But Mr. Romano insisted on complete secrecy. And I didn't want you to worry when you're so happy with Mr. Curtis. I didn't want to burden you with my problems."

"Miss Randolph," Francesco said, his voice taking on an edge of finality, "your friend has conducted herself with complete professionalism throughout our business relationship. She is nothing more than a temporary employee, and her work concludes this

Saturday. After that, you won't have to worry about her association with me or my family."

Saturday? *Saturday?*

Clara studied their faces for a long moment. Finally, she sighed. "I suppose that makes sense. But Sera, I wish you'd trusted me enough to say something, even if you couldn't give details. You know I would have understood."

"I'm sorry," Serafina whispered, and she meant it. "I should have."

"We'll discuss this later, when we're alone," Clara said, her tone making it clear this conversation was far from over.

Mr. Romano turned to Clara with formal politeness that somehow felt like mockery. "Miss Randolph, might I have a moment alone with Miss Silvano? There's a business matter we need to conclude regarding her final payment and the terms of her discretion agreement."

Clara's eyes narrowed slightly, but she nodded. "Of course. I'll wait outside. But Sera, we really do need to talk after this."

Once Clara had stepped away, Mr. Romano's expression became unreadable again. "I'll pick you up Saturday evening, at six. We'll have dinner and discuss the formal conclusion of your employment, your compensation, as well as any attention you might expect now that people have seen us together. There may be some lingering curiosity about our association that you'll need to manage."

"Of course," she managed, her voice barely steady. "Business."

He nodded curtly and turned to leave. Serafina followed on unsteady legs, her heart heavy with the knowledge that Saturday would truly be the end. The end of the pretense, the end of the lies, the end of whatever this thing between them had been. Now that the end was so near, her heart began to feel a strange pull.

As they emerged from the privacy of the alcove, Mr. Romano paused. In full view of the party guests, including Miss Ashworth, who was watching, he reached for Serafina's hand.

The gesture was so unexpected it stole her breath.

He raised her fingers to his lips, but instead of the chaste kiss she expected, his mouth opened slightly against her knuckles. His tongue swept across her skin in a slow stroke that sent heat flooding through her body. His eyes gleamed with something that looked like possession.

"Until Saturday," he murmured, his voice low enough that only she could hear. "Take care of yourself, Serafina. Try not to get too attached to things that were never yours to keep."

The words were a knife between her ribs, but then his cold mask slipped for just a heartbeat, and she saw something raw sadness and regress beneath it. Or perhaps loss. His jaw tightened, before the coldness returned. He released her hand and walked away, leaving Serafina standing there, her fingers tingling. She watched him go and return to Miss Ashworth's side. The other woman's hand slid around his arm.

And Serafina hated herself for the jealousy that consumed her. She hated him for making her feel it. She hated that even knowing it was ending, even knowing she was nothing to him, she still wanted him.

Clara appeared at her side immediately, her eyes searching Serafina's face. "Business?"

Serafina looked down at her hand, still feeling the warmth of his mouth. "Yes," she lied, because what else could she say? "Business."

As they moved back toward the main party, Miss Romano approached them, her face both knowing and sad. "I hope everything was resolved satisfactorily," she said, glancing between Serafina and Clara.

"Everything's fine," Clara replied, though her tone suggested otherwise. "Isn't it, Sera?"

"Yes," Serafina managed. "It was a misunderstanding."

Miss Romano nodded. She looked at Serafina with sympathy. Then she looked toward the main room where several guests were gathering around someone telling an animated story. "Miss Randolph, I believe Mrs. Pemberton is asking for you. Something about the charity committee?"

Clara looked in that direction and sighed. "I suppose I should go see what she wants. Sera, will you be all right for a moment?"

As Clara moved away to speak with the other guests, Miss Romano stepped closer to Serafina, her voice dropping to a whisper.

"My brother told me this morning that your arrangement would be ending soon. He seemed..." She paused, choosing her words carefully. "Affected by the prospect. More than I expected."

Serafina's heart clenched. "Did he?"

"Francesco doesn't show his emotions easily. He's learned to bury them so deep I'm not sure even he knows they're there anymore." Miss Romano's eyes were kind but honest. "But I've seen the way he looks at you. It's like he's drowning and you're air. It shouldn't have to end this way. I hope he realizes that before it's too late."

Serafina wanted to laugh at the absurdity of it. "Your brother was just flirting with Miss Ashworth for the entire meal. I don't think he's drowning over me."

"My brother is an idiot," Miss Romano said bluntly. "And a coward. He's spent so long protecting himself from feeling anything real that now, when faced with something genuine, he doesn't know what to do except push it away." She touched Serafina's arm gently. "Give him time. Or don't. You don't owe him anything. But know that what I saw between you isn't as one-sided as he wants you to believe."

Before Serafina could respond, Miss Romano smiled and moved away, leaving her standing alone in a room full of people, more isolated than she'd ever felt in her life.

Across the room, Mr. Romano laughed at something Miss Ashworth said with his hand resting casually on the small of her back. And Serafina understood with crushing clarity that even if everything Miss Romano said was true, it didn't matter.

Francesco Romano was a man who took what he wanted and discarded what he didn't. And come Saturday, she would be the latter.

The Church of the Most Precious Blood was empty except for Francesco and the flickering candles that cast dancing shadows across the ancient stones. At midnight, it was a different place than during the day. Quieter. Heavier, as if the weight of countless confessions had soaked into the walls.

Francesco dipped his fingers in the holy water font near the entrance. The coolness was familiar against his skin. He crossed himself—forehead, chest, left shoulder, right—the gesture automatic after decades of habit. *In nomine Patris, et Filii, et Spiritus Sancti.*

He couldn't stop seeing her face. The way she'd looked at him when he'd said Saturday. When he'd told her it was ending. That devastation in her eyes—he'd put it there. He'd done that to her on purpose.

He slipped into the confessional booth. The wood creaked. The scent of old incense and something musty filled the cramped space. He knelt, staring at the mesh screen that separated him from whoever sat on the other side.

If anyone sat there at all. Surely the attempt would count to something, anyway.

"*Bless me, Father, for I have sinned.*"

The words came in Italian. He couldn't remember the Latin. How long had it been? Years. Maybe longer.

"*It's been... I don't know. A long time.*"

Silence from the other side. He couldn't tell if the priest was even there, but it didn't matter. The words needed to come out.

"*I killed a man Tuesday night. Shot him in an alley off Mulberry Street. He owed money he wouldn't pay. He could have, but he wouldn't.*" Francesco's hands gripped his knees. "*I put two bullets in his chest. He was twenty-three. Had a wife. I didn't realize she was nearby.*"

His voice was flat. This was familiar territory, all the violence, the blood, and the bodies. He'd confessed these sins before, years ago when he still thought absolution meant something.

"*Thursday, another one. This one I beat to death with my hands. He'd been skimming from shipments. I made it last so the others would see and understand what happens when you steal from me.*"

The booth seemed to shrink and heat up.

"*I've lost count of how many, Father. A dozen. Maybe more. I tell myself it's business, and it's necessary. It's the only way to survive in my world.*" He paused. "*But I don't know if I believe that anymore.*"

His breathing began to come unevenly.

"*There's... there's a woman.*"

The words came out strangled. He hadn't meant to say it like that, to sound like he was drowning.

"*An innocent woman. She has nothing to do with my world, with any of this. She works in a bookshop. She writes stories. She...*" He stopped, trying to find words that didn't exist. "*She's good, Father. Pure. And I've—*"

His throat closed.

"*I've defiled her. I knew I would. I knew from the beginning, but I did it anyway.*"

Silence. The priest, if there was a priest, said nothing.

"*I took her to bed.*" The confession came out raw. "*She was innocent in every way, Father. In every way. And I took that from her. I had no right to touch her. But I did it anyway because I wanted her and I've never denied myself anything I wanted.*"

His hands were shaking now. When had they started shaking?

"*And now I can't—I can't stop thinking about her. Every night I wake up and she's not there and I—*" He pressed his palms against his eyes. "*I don't know what's wrong with me.*"

The words started coming faster, getting harder to control.

"*Today there was a luncheon. Her friend was there, so I couldn't even talk to her without making it obvious. So I sat there, and there was this woman next to me, flirting, touching my arm, and I just... I let her.*"

His voice cracked.

"*I let this woman hang on me while Miss Silvano sat across the table watching. I flirted back with the woman. I laughed at her damned jokes. I said things... cruel things about temporary pleasures and how people expect too much. And the whole time I was looking at Miss Silvano's face, watching her break.*"

He felt he was suffocating. The air in the booth wasn't enough.

"I don't know why I did it. I was hurting, and I wanted her to hurt too, maybe. Wanted to push her away before she got too close. But she's already—" The realization hit him mid-sentence. "She's already fallen for me. I saw it in her eyes today. She loves me."

The confession booth pressed in around him.

"And I—Christ, I think I love her too."

Saying it out loud made it real, made it impossible to deny anymore.

"But I can't. I can't love her, Father. Men like me don't get to love women like her. I'll destroy her. Everyone who gets close to me dies or gets destroyed, and she's so... she's so breakable."

His hands were fists now, pressed against his thighs.

"Before she left the luncheon, I kissed her hand. Right there in front of everyone. I couldn't let her walk away without touching her one more time. I didn't care who saw. I didn't care that it made everything worse."

The tears surprised him. He hadn't cried since he was a child, since before he learned that crying made you weak. But they came anyway, hot and shameful against his palms.

"I told her it ends Saturday. I looked her in the eyes and told her our arrangement is over, and I watched her—I watched something break inside her. And I wanted to take it back. I wanted to tell her I was lying and that I can't let her go, that she's mine and I'll never let her go."

His voice dropped to a whisper.

"But I can't keep her. Can I, Father? A man like me can't keep something that pure. I'll drag her down into my world. She'll become a target. Someone will use her to get to me. Someone will hurt her or kill her, and it'll be my fault for being too selfish to walk away."

Silence. Endless, suffocating silence.

"I don't know what to do." The admission came out broken. "My whole life, I've always known what to do. Kill or be killed. Protect what's mine. Take what I want. But with her, I'm—I'm lost."

He pressed his forehead against the mesh screen.

"I'm supposed to end it Saturday. Sit across from her and tell her it's over. Watch her walk away. Never see her again." His breath came in gasps. *"But I don't think I can. I don't think I have the strength to let her go."*

The candles outside the booth flickered. Their light danced through the gaps.

"I'm asking for a sign, Father." His voice was barely audible. *"Some guidance. Something to tell me if I should save her from myself, or if maybe... if maybe even a man like me gets to keep something good. Just this once."*

He waited. The silence stretched on, broken only by his own ragged breathing.

No answer came.

Finally, Francesco rose from the kneeler, his legs stiff. *"Thank you for listening, Father,"* he said quietly, though he wasn't sure anyone had been listening at all.

He stepped out of the confessional into the main church. The altar waited beneath its crucifix, Christ's face serene in death. Even here, in this sacred place, Francesco felt the weight of his choices pressing down on him.

He walked to the front pew and knelt, his hands clasped before him. The prayer came slowly, words he hadn't spoken since childhood.

"Padre nostro che sei nei cieli..."

Our Father, who art in heaven.

His mother's voice echoed in his memory, teaching him this prayer when he was barely tall enough to see over the pew. She'd clutched her rosary, whispering these same words, praying for her sons' souls even as they slipped deeper into darkness.

"Sia santificato il tuo nome..."

Hallowed be thy name.

But what was Francesco's name worth now? What was left of the boy his mother had prayed for? He'd become exactly what his father wanted—ruthless, efficient, and feared. And then he'd become worse when he'd killed his own brother.

"Venga il tuo regno..."

Thy kingdom come.

Would there be a place for him in any kingdom? He'd

206

committed every sin, broken every commandment. Killed without remorse. Taken what wasn't his. Coveted. Lied. Destroyed.

"*Sia fatta la tua volontà, come in cielo così in terra...*"

Thy will be done, on earth as it is in heaven.

But what was God's will for a man like him? Francesco had stopped believing in divine providence the day he'd put a bullet in Antonio's head. If God existed, if He cared, He wouldn't have let his brother become the monster he'd been.

And yet Serafina made him want to believe again. Made him want to think that maybe there was a reason she'd walked into his life. That maybe even men who'd done what he'd done could be offered something good.

"*Dacci oggi il nostro pane quotidiano...*"

Give us this day our daily bread.

He thought of her small apartment, her coat that was slightly threadbare at her shoulder, the way she worried about if the bookshop could make enough to stay open. He could give her everything and keep her safe and warm and fed. He could protect her from the world.

Except he couldn't protect her from himself.

"*Rimetti a noi i nostri debiti come noi li rimettiamo a coloro che ci hanno offeso...*"

Forgive us our trespasses as we forgive those who trespass against us.

Could she ever forgive him for what he'd done to her today? For the cruelty at the luncheon? For touching her when he had no right? For making her fall in love with him and then telling her it was ending?

Could he forgive himself?

"*Non ci indurre in tentazione...*"

Lead us not into temptation.

But he was already deep in temptation. Already drowning in it. She was the temptation. Her smile. Her laugh. The way she looked at him like he was something more than a killer. Like he could be good somewhere in his soul.

"*Ma liberaci dal male...*"

But deliver us from evil.

He was the evil. He was what she needed deliverance from. And yet he was the one praying for salvation, for some sign that keeping her wouldn't destroy them both.

"Amen."

The word hung in the empty church.

Francesco waited, his head bowed, hoping for something. A voice. A feeling. Some sense of what he should do.

But God, as always for a man like him, remained silent.

He rose slowly, his knees protesting. At the altar, he paused, looking up at the crucified Christ.

"*Per questo ti chiedo, Signore*," he whispered. *For this I ask you, Lord.* "Give me a sign. *Tell me what to do. Tell me if I should let her go or if I'm allowed to keep her.*"

The candles flickered. Nothing else.

Francesco turned and walked toward the door. His hand was on the handle when he stopped and looked back one more time.

"*If you won't give me a sign,*" he said softly, "*then I'll have to make this choice myself. And God help us both if I choose wrong.*"

He crossed himself one final time before pushing open the heavy door. It closed behind him with a sound like heaven locking him out.

Outside, the night air was cold against his face. Francesco walked to his car, his footsteps echoing in the empty street.

In less than seventy-two hours, he would sit across from Serafina and tell her their arrangement was over. He would watch her walk out of his life forever. He would tell himself it was for the best.

But as he drove, Francesco couldn't shake the feeling that he was about to make the biggest mistake of his life.

And there would be no taking it back.

CHAPTER 14

Serafina arrived at the bookshop earlier than usual, hoping the familiar routine of organizing shelves and helping customers would settle her nerves. But the moment she stepped inside, she knew something was wrong.

Mr. Thompson was already there, sitting at his desk with papers spread before him. His face was etched with worry. He looked older than she'd ever seen him.

"Good morning, Mr. Thompson," she called softly, not wanting to startle him.

He looked up with red-rimmed, exhausted eyes. "Oh, Serafina. I'm glad you're here early. We need to talk."

Her stomach dropped. The coffee she'd forced down that morning threatened to come back up. "Is it Mrs. Thompson? Is she—"

"No, no, she's doing well." He gestured to the chair across from his desk. "This is about the shop. About our suppliers."

Serafina sank into the chair, her hands gripping the armrests hard enough that her knuckles went white. "What's happened?"

"Three more publishers contacted me yesterday afternoon. Meridian Press and Henderson & Associates. They're both... hesitating to continue our relationship."

"What..." Serafina blinked hard.

"They cited concerns about maintaining their partnerships with larger distributors." He picked up one of the letters, his jaw tightening as he read. "Distributors who also carry works from other publishing houses. They were quite apologetic about it, actually. Very sorry. Very understanding. Complete nonsense, of course."

"Which other publishers?" Serafina asked, though she already knew.

"Kensington Publishing, primarily." Mr. Thompson set the letter down. "It seems they've been told—quite clearly, I imagine—that continuing to supply us might jeopardize their more lucrative contracts."

The blood drained from Serafina's face. Her vision tunneled slightly, and she had to focus on breathing. In. Out. In. Out.

This was her fault. All of it. Mr. Kensington was destroying the shop because of her. Because she'd said no.

"Mr. Thompson, I—"

"There's more." He held up a hand to stop her, and she saw that his fingers. "Mr. Kensington's company has made us an offer. Very generous, actually. They'll provide exclusive distribution rights, guaranteed inventory, and favorable terms. They'll even help with our rent arrears."

"Which means?" She fought back tears.

"Which means we become entirely dependent on what Kensington Publishing decides to provide. No other publishers. No independent suppliers. No ability to choose our own inventory or set our own terms." Mr. Thompson leaned back in his chair, suddenly looking every one of his sixty-plus years. The fight seemed to drain out of him. "It would save the shop, Serafina. It would keep the doors open, keep you employed, keep everything afloat. But it would also mean surrendering everything that makes this place special, everything my father built, and everything I've tried to maintain."

Serafina's throat felt tight. She couldn't swallow. Couldn't speak.

"What will you do?" she finally managed.

"I don't know yet. The offer stands until next Saturday. One week to decide whether to sell my soul or close my doors." He looked at her closely then, really looked at her. "Serafina, you look terrible. Are you sleeping? You're pale as a ghost."

"I'm fine. Just worried about the shop."

"This isn't just worry. You look like you've been through something." His voice gentled. "Is there something you're not telling me? This feels personal, not business. The way Mr. Kensington's been... the timing of it all."

She couldn't meet his eyes. Her hands were shaking in her lap, and she pressed them together to hide it. "I don't know what you mean."

"Serafina." Mr. Thompson's voice was gentle but insistent. "If there's something I should know. If someone is threatening you, or pressuring you, or—"

The bell above the door chimed.

Serafina's head snapped up, and her heart stopped.

Mr. Kensington stepped inside, immaculate as always in his expensive coat and perfect hat. His eyes swept the shop with proprietary interest, taking in Mr. Thompson at his desk, Serafina frozen in her chair.

"Mr. Thompson, Miss Silvano." His smile was coldly pleasant. "I hope I'm not interrupting anything important."

Mr. Thompson rose from his chair, his manner professionally courteous but noticeably cooler than usual. "Good morning, Mr. Kensington. How can we help you?"

Serafina had never heard that edge in his voice before.

"I wanted to follow up on our conversation yesterday. Have you had time to consider my offer?" Mr. Kensington moved deeper into the shop.

"I'm still reviewing the terms."

"Of course, of course. These decisions shouldn't be rushed. One must be thorough." Mr. Kensington's gaze shifted to Serafina, and his smile became more intimate. Warmer. The kind of warmth that made her skin crawl. "Miss Silvano, you look lovely this morning. That color suits you."

She couldn't respond. Her throat had closed completely.

"I trust you haven't forgotten our appointment this evening?" His tone was casual, conversational. As if they were discussing something perfectly innocent. "Six o'clock?"

Serafina's eyes went wide. Tonight? Her mouth opened, but no sound came out at first. "Tonight?" The word came out strangled. "I thought—I thought we were meeting tomorrow night. I wasn't—"

"Change of plans, I'm afraid. Business matters require I adjust my schedule." His smile didn't waver. "You can make it, can't you? I do hope this won't be inconvenient."

It wasn't a question.

"Yes, sir," she whispered.

"Excellent." Mr. Kensington's satisfaction was evident. "I'll expect you at six sharp, then. Don't keep me waiting." He tipped his hat to both of them. "Mr. Thompson, do give my offer serious consideration. It really is quite generous, all things considered. Good day."

The bell chimed again as he left, the cheerful sound mocking the heavy silence he'd left behind.

Serafina couldn't move. Her hands were shaking so badly now that she had to grip the armrests to hide it. Tonight.

"Serafina."

Mr. Thompson's voice cut through her panic. She looked up at him, and saw him watching her with a concerned expression that made her want to cry.

"What was that about?" His voice was careful. Too careful.

"Nothing important."

"An appointment at six o'clock?" He moved around the desk, closer to her. "What kind of appointment?"

She had to say something. Had to give him something that would make him stop looking at her like that. "He's... he's expressed interest in my novel. In publishing it. He wants to discuss terms."

Mr. Thompson stared at her. The silence stretched between them, heavy and terrible.

"Your novel," he repeated, his voice flat.

"Yes. He re-read some pages and he thought—he said there was potential, and—" The words tumbled out too fast, tripping over each other. "I thought we were meeting tomorrow to discuss it, but apparently he needs to move it to tonight, and I—"

"Serafina." He said her name quietly. "Look at me."

She forced herself to meet his eyes.

"Is that the truth?"

The question hung between them. She could see in his face that he knew she was lying and that something terrible was happening. But he was giving her a chance to tell him, to let him help.

"Yes," she whispered, and watched something in his expression crack.

He held her gaze for another long moment. Then he nodded slowly, his jaw tight. "I see."

They both knew she was lying. They both knew he didn't believe her. But he was letting it go anyway, and that somehow made it worse.

"Serafina." His voice was gentle now, almost breaking. "If you need help with anything... anything at all... you can come to me. You know that, don't you?"

The kindness in his voice was unbearable. Tears burned in her eyes, but she blinked them back furiously.

"I know," she managed. "Thank you."

But they both knew she wouldn't. She couldn't.

"I should—" She stood abruptly, nearly knocking the chair over. "I should open the shop. Get ready for customers."

"Of course." Mr. Thompson stepped back, giving her space. But his eyes stayed on her face. "Take your time."

She fled to the front of the shop, her legs unsteady. Behind her, she heard Mr. Thompson return to his desk and the rustle of papers.

Her hands hardly felt like hers as she unlocked the front door and flipped the sign to "Open." The morning light streamed in, bright and ordinary, as if this were just another day and her world wasn't crumbling. As if she wasn't trapped in a nightmare with no way out.

Six o'clock. Tonight.

She pressed her hand against her stomach, fighting nausea. And after tonight, there would be another appointment. And another.

And another. Until Mr. Kensington got tired of her, or until she found a way to escape.

She glanced back at Mr. Thompson's office. He was sitting at his desk, but he wasn't looking at his papers. He was staring at nothing, his face gray with worry. He knew. Maybe not the details, but he knew enough. And she'd lied to his face.

Serafina turned back to the empty shop and tried to breathe through the tightness in her chest.

Tonight. Six o'clock.

She had no choice but to go.

Serafina stood before her open wardrobe, staring at the dresses hanging there. Her hands trembled as she reached for her favorite skirt with buttons down the front, and a button-front silk blouse. If he wanted easy access, this might help him. She hated herself for already thinking as his accomplice.

She lifted the skirt and laid it on her bed, then the blouse. Tomorrow she could burn them. After tonight, they would be tainted beyond redemption.

She had a plan, though. She wouldn't be the reluctant victim that Mr. Kensington expected. She would be aggressive, confident, and act like she wanted him. She'd even create a character in a similar situation, and try to see tonight as research. She'd laugh at his jokes, be coy and flirtatious, pay attention to how everything felt. She could use that later when writing a new story.

And maybe if he thought she was willing, eager even, he'd be gentler. Maybe he'd be satisfied with less. Maybe she could maintain some sliver of control in a situation where she had none.

She'd spent time rehearsing in front of her mirror, practicing sultry smiles and confident gestures. Every movement felt false, but the expressions were the only armor she had.

As she dressed, she said goodbye to the body that would no longer be entirely hers. The next time she felt air on her skin, it would be for Mr. Kensington's pleasure.

She applied rouge to her cheeks with a heavy hand, trying to mimic the flush of excitement rather than the pallor of fear, and a touch of red lipstick. In the mirror, she looked beautiful and terrified. Her reflection stared back at her with wide, frightened eyes that no amount of powder could disguise.

On her way to the door, she paused at her typewriter. When had she last had time to write?

The machine sat waiting for her return. She ran her fingers over the keys, thinking of the satisfying click-clack of words flowing onto paper, the magic of creating worlds where love conquered all and happy endings were guaranteed. Those days felt distant now.

She picked up a page from the single copy of her manuscript that remained and read a passage about her heroine's first kiss, written in what now seemed like naive optimism about love and romance. Mr. Kensington would make sure it could never be published. She was certain of it now.

Looking at the words she'd written, she felt a flicker of pride despite it all. The story was good. The characters lived and breathed on the page. Maybe she could bind it somehow and give it to Clara as a gift. At least then someone would read her story. Someone would know she'd created something beautiful.

She set the page down gently and walked toward whatever hell awaited her.

Too soon, the Waterford Hotel loomed before her. She'd passed this building countless times without a second thought, never imagining she'd one day climb its stairs as a sacrifice to save the bookshop she loved.

The lobby was all marble and crystal. The clerk behind the desk didn't look up as she passed. She wondered how many other women had walked these same halls toward their own destruction. How many others had climbed these stairs with fear clawing at their throats?

Room 412. Fourth floor, at the end of a long corridor carpeted in deep red. Each step down that hallway felt like descending into Hell. Her heart hammered against her ribs so hard she was certain it would burst from her chest.

At exactly six o'clock, she knocked lightly on the door. Her knuckles barely made a sound against the wood.

"Come in," Mr. Kensington's voice called from inside.

Serafina pasted on the brightest smile she could manage and pushed open the door. "Good evening, Mr. Kensington. I hope I'm not late."

He stood by the window, already in his shirtsleeves with a glass of whiskey in his hand. The room was expensively furnished with dark wood, rich fabrics, a bed with a high canopy and velvet curtains.

And on the bedside table, coiled neatly, was a length of rope.

Her smile faltered. Just for a second, but she saw his eyes catch the moment, the satisfaction that flickered across his face before he smoothed it away. Her gaze darted away from the rope, back to him, trying to recover. Trying to pretend she hadn't seen it.

But she had seen it. And he knew she had.

Another length of rope lay on the dresser. Longer than the first. And was that? Leather straps? Metal? Her stomach lurched. Her carefully rehearsed confidence crumbled at the edges.

He'd prepared, not just the room, but tools and implements. He'd planned every detail. Before she'd even left her apartment thinking she had a plan, thinking she could control this, he'd been here arranging everything. The rope. The restraints. Whatever else she couldn't bring herself to identify.

Her plan had never mattered. She'd never had any control at all.

"Right on time." His voice was warm, almost kind. "And my, don't you look lovely tonight."

"Thank you." Her voice came out higher than intended. She forced it lower, sultrier. "I wanted to look my best for you. I've been looking forward to this."

Mr. Kensington's eyebrows rose slightly. A slow smile spread across his face. "Have you now? How delightful." He took a slow sip of his whiskey, watching her over the rim of the glass. "Come here, my dear."

Serafina sauntered toward him, swaying her hips. She tried not to look at the rope again

"You have excellent taste in hotels," she said, letting her voice drop to what she hoped was a seductive purr. "This room is beautiful."

"Not as beautiful as you." His hands found her waist, pulling her closer until she could smell the whiskey on his breath and the pomade in his hair. "You seem different tonight. More... willing."

His touch made her skin crawl. Goosebumps rose on her arms despite the warmth of the room. She forced herself to lean into him, to place her hands on his chest as if she found him attractive. If he weren't so cruel, he might have been handsome.

"Maybe I've realized what I was missing," she said, letting her fingers trail down his shirtfront. The lie came easier than she'd expected, desperation making her a better actress than she'd known she could be.

"And what might that be?" His thumb traced her collarbone, and she felt her pulse jump beneath his touch. Could he feel it? Could he tell?

"A man who knows what he wants and takes it."

"Hmm." The sound was almost approving, but his eyes were calculating. "You've been practicing this, haven't you?"

Her breath caught. "I don't know what you—"

"The way you walk. The way you're talking. It's very good, Serafina. Very convincing." He stepped back slightly, still holding her waist. "Almost convinced me for a moment."

Ice flooded her veins. "I meant every word."

"Did you?" He released her, moving to pour himself another whiskey. He was enjoying this. "Would you like a drink? You look like you might need one."

"I'm fine." But her voice shook.

He handed her one anyway. "To new beginnings," he said, raising his.

"To getting what we both want," she replied, forcing herself to meet his toast. Every instinct screamed at her to run, to flee this room and never look back, bookshop be damned. She locked her knees to keep from swaying.

The whiskey burned, but she smiled through it. Her stomach churned, bile rising, but she swallowed it down and maintained her bright expression.

Mr. Kensington stepped closer. When he reached out to touch her cheek, her skin crawled, but she forced herself to lean into the caress. The contact made her want to scrub her face raw.

"You're trembling," he observed, his voice mild.

"Am I?" She tried to laugh. "Must be excitement."

"Must be." His fingers trailed down her neck to rest at her collarbone. Her pulse hammered wildly there, too fast, too hard. "Your heart is racing."

"Like I said. Excitement."

"Of course." But his smile said he knew better. "You're full of surprises tonight."

He set down his glass and moved behind her, his hands settling on her shoulders. She could feel his breath against her ear as he spoke, hot and alcohol-laden.

"Tell me what you want, Serafina."

Her mind went blank with terror. The rope on the nightstand seemed to pulse in her peripheral vision. But she managed to turn in his arms to face him, fixing her smile back in place. "I want you to stop treating me like a frightened child. I'm a woman. I know what I'm doing."

"Do you indeed?"

She answered by reaching up to touch his face, her hand trembling so badly she couldn't hide it. "Show me what you've been imagining all week."

"What an excellent idea." He caught her wrist, gently, but firmly. "But first, let me tell you what I've been imagining."

Her breath stopped.

"I've been imagining you walking in here with that brave little smile." His thumb stroked the inside of her wrist, right where her pulse betrayed her. "Pretending you're not terrified and that you want this, and putting on a performance for me."

"I'm not—"

"And then," he continued as if she hadn't spoken, "I've been imagining the moment when you realize your little performance won't save you and you understand that I see right through you... that I've always seen through you."

The room tilted. "Mr. Kensington—"

"When you realize," his voice dropped lower, intimate and terrible, "that your fear is exactly what I wanted all along."

Her mask crumbled. Just for a second, pure terror showed on her face before she tried to reconstruct it. But it was too late.

"There, there," he said softly.

When he began unbuttoning her blouse, she forced herself to help him. She had to keep trying. Maybe if she just—

She let the garment slip from her shoulders, standing in her chemise, trying to breathe, trying with all her might to maintain some fragment of her plan even as it disintegrated around her.

But then his hands were on her wrists, pulling them behind her back with sudden, brutal force. She felt the rope before she understood what was happening.

"What—" she began, still trying somehow to maintain her façade even as panic exploded in her chest. "Are we playing games? How exciting."

The rope tightened around her wrists, cutting into flesh and cutting off circulation. Her fingers began to tingle, then go numb. This wasn't part of the plan. This wasn't—

"Oh, we're playing games, my dear," Mr. Kensington said. His voice had lost all pretense of warmth. What remained was cold, clinical. "But not the kind you're pretending to enjoy."

Another loop of rope, pulled tighter. Pain shot through her shoulders as he wrenched her arms back further. Serafina forced another laugh, high and brittle and desperate. "I don't know what you mean. I'm having a wonderful time."

"Drop the act, Serafina." His fingers gripped her chin, forcing her to meet his eyes. They were flat, emotionless. "We both know you don't want this. We both know you're terrified."

She tried to hold onto the smile. Tried to keep her voice steady. "That's not—"

"Your pupils are dilated." His thumb brushed across her trembling lips. "Your breathing is shallow. You have goosebumps all over your arms. Your pulse is racing so fast I can see it in your throat. Every inch of your body is screaming that you want to run."

Tears burned in her eyes. She blinked them back furiously.

"And that," he continued, his voice dropping to something almost gentle, something that made her stomach turn, "is what makes it so much more interesting."

The mask finally slipped from her face completely, leaving only raw, undisguised fear. Her breath came in gasps now. The rope cut into her wrists. The room felt too small, too hot, closing in around her.

"Please—" The word broke out of her. "Please, I'll do whatever you want. I'll be good. I'll—"

"Oh, Serafina." He released her chin, letting his hand trail down her throat. She could feel her pulse hammering against his palm. "You already are doing exactly what I want."

She was shaking now, her whole body trembling. The performance was over. The plan had failed. She had nothing left but the truth of her terror.

"Please," she whispered again, hating herself for begging, unable to stop. "Please don't—"

"There she is," Kensington said with satisfaction, his thumb brushing across her trembling lips. "There's the frightened little girl I've been waiting to meet."

The bathwater had long gone cold, but Serafina remained in the tub, scrubbing at skin that would never feel clean again. This was her third bath since returning home in the early hours of the morning, and still she felt his hands on her, still tasted his whiskey-soaked breath, still heard the sound of her own voice begging him to stop....

The sponge was rough against her skin, but she couldn't stop scrubbing. Her wrists were raw from the rope. A few purple bruises formed around her throat where his fingers had pressed. No amount of hot water could wash it all away, but she kept trying, hoping that if she scrubbed hard enough, she could somehow return to the person she'd been before.

Twenty-four hours. It had been twenty-four hours since Mr. Kensington's hotel room, and she still couldn't close her eyes without seeing him or hearing his voice.

Soon, Francesco would come to take her to their "breakup" dinner to conclude their arrangement. She had to try to piece herself back together and find some way to face him without falling apart.

She forced herself to stand. Water sluiced off her reddened skin. She wrapped a towel around herself and walked to her bedroom on unsteady legs.

Her favorite blue dress hung in the wardrobe. She'd worn it to tea with Clara, to walks in the park, to dozens of ordinary moments that now seemed impossibly precious. She needed those memories tonight, memories that felt like her.

By the time she'd finished applying makeup, she looked almost like herself. Anyone looking closely would see the cracks, but from a distance, in dim light, she might pass.

When Francesco knocked, she was as ready as she could be.

But the moment she saw his somber, distant, face, looking as if he was already saying goodbye, her careful composure nearly cracked.

"You look beautiful," he said quietly, offering his arm with the formal courtesy of a stranger.

"Thank you."

His eyes lingered on her face. A slight frown creased his brow as he studied her.

"Are you feeling well?" he asked, his voice gentler. "You seem—"

"I'm fine," she said quickly, forcing a brighter smile. "Just tired."

They walked to his car in silence. She was grateful he didn't try to fill it with conversation. She wasn't sure her voice would remain steady.

She settled into the passenger seat, making sure her scarf hid her throat and her sleeve covered her wrists. Through the window, she watched normal people living normal lives, unaware that her world had ended in a hotel room the night before.

He'd chosen a small, intimate restaurant tucked away from

prying eyes. They were seated at a corner table where they could speak without being overheard.

Wine arrived. As Francesco poured, she noticed the slight tremor in his hands.

"The arrangement worked better than we'd hoped," he said carefully, his voice professionally neutral. "Brambilia is convinced we were genuine."

Serafina picked up her fork and cut a small piece of veal. She lifted it to her mouth, chewed, and swallowed. It could have been cardboard. Her hands shook slightly as she set the fork down. She pulled them into her lap quickly.

"Good. That's... good."

Francesco's eyes sharpened. "The photograph, Miss Randolph's reaction, our argument... all of it worked. He believes we were lovers who had a falling out."

She flinched at the word "lovers," then pushed the veal around her plate, cutting it smaller and smaller without eating. When she reached for her water glass, the purple marks on her wrists extended past her sleeve.

Francesco's professional mask dropped away immediately. What replaced it was cold and deadly.

"What happened to your wrist?"

Serafina tugged her sleeve down. "Nothing. I bumped into something."

"Serafina."

The way he said her name made her look up. What she saw in his eyes made her stomach clench, but not with fear. At least, not for herself.

"Who did this to you?"

"Francesco, please—"

"Was it Kensington?"

She couldn't lie when he was looking at her like that. Her silence was answer enough.

His hands clenched into fists on the table. For a moment, she thought he might leave to find Mr. Kensington right then. Instead, he leaned forward, his voice dropping to barely above a whisper.

"Tell me what he did."

"I can't." Her eyes filled with tears. "Please don't make me say it. I chose to go. I thought I could handle it."

His jaw worked as he fought for control. "You need to eat something."

"I'm not hungry."

"Serafina—"

"Please!" The word came out sharper than she intended. "I'm fine."

But even as she said it, her fork clattered against her plate. Her hands shook too violently to maintain the pretense. "I'm fine."

They sat in silence. Francesco made a valiant effort with his own meal, but she could see he was struggling too.

Finally, he reached into his jacket and withdrew an envelope and slid it across the table.

"You'll receive one of these every month. It's the least I can do."

Serafina stared at it. Money. Payment for services rendered.

"No." She pushed it back with more force than necessary. "I don't want it."

"Serafina—"

"Donate it. Build something. I don't care. But I can't—I won't take money for this. I'm not your whore."

Francesco's knuckles went white on his wine glass, but he pocketed the envelope without argument.

"I'm sorry," she whispered. "I didn't mean—"

"You have nothing to apologize for."

When they reached his car, he sat behind the wheel for a long moment without starting the engine. His hands gripped the steering wheel.

Serafina watched his profile in the dim light, memorizing it. The strong line of his jaw... the way his hair curled at his collar... the small scar above his eyebrow she'd never noticed before.

Finally, he turned to her. Something in his expression had changed, and he seemed vulnerable and uncertain.

"Would you like to go to Coney Island?" he asked quietly.

The question surprised her. She let out a soft, broken laugh.

She needed this, needed to feel like a person again instead of a

223

victim. She needed to pretend, even for an hour, that she was still whole. That last night hadn't happened. That she could still have one good memory with him before everything ended.

"I would like that."

He started the car and drove toward the boardwalk, where the night air was cooler and carried the scent of the ocean. Most families had gone home, leaving the space to couples and thrill-seekers stealing moments they shouldn't have.

Francesco headed straight to the cotton candy vendor.

"Thank you," she said, pulling off a piece and letting it melt on her tongue. "Francesco."

His name felt strange in her mouth. Too intimate. But also right.

"Try some," she said, pulling off another piece and holding it toward him.

When his lips brushed against her fingers as he took it, she jerked her hand back. The touch, so gentle, so different from last night, made her eyes well with tears.

Francesco froze. "Serafina..."

"I'm sorry." She wrapped her arms around herself. "I don't know why I... it's not you. It's not your fault."

"Look at me." He didn't move closer. Didn't back away. "You're safe. I won't hurt you."

She nodded, wiping her eyes. "I know. I know you won't."

But her body didn't know. Her body remembered other hands. Rough rope. The pain.

She took his arm as he led her toward the games, positioning herself so she could see his hands at all times. When he moved, she startled slightly before catching herself.

He noticed. She could see him noticing. He started moving slower, telegraphing his movements.

At the shooting gallery, his shots were perfect. The vendor offered them their choice of prizes. Francesco pointed to a bear with golden fur and a blue ribbon. He handed it to her.

She looked at the bear, then at him. "This one should be yours. Then we'll have a pair." She tried to smile. "His and hers. So you'll have something to remember me by."

The words came out wrong and desperate.

Francesco took the bear carefully. "I'd like that."

They moved to the skee-ball lanes. Serafina stared at the curved ramp.

"I've never played before," she admitted. Her voice sounded thin to her own ears. "What do I do?"

"It's simple." He demonstrated, the ball landing with a satisfying thunk in the fifty-point ring. "Now you try."

She picked up a ball. It was heavier than expected. She rolled it tentatively, then watched it miss entirely.

"Like this." Francesco moved as if to step behind her, then stopped when he felt her tense. "May I?"

She nodded, wanting to be normal.

But when he moved behind her, her whole body locked up. She couldn't breathe. The enclosed space—him behind her—it was too much like—

Francesco stepped back immediately.

"I'm sorry," she whispered, shame burning her cheeks. "I didn't mean—"

"Don't apologize." His voice was firm. Gentle. "Not for that. Never for that."

He moved to stand beside her instead, close enough to guide her arm, but not touching. "Feel the weight of the ball. Let it roll naturally."

This time, the ball landed in the thirty-point ring.

She tried to smile. Tried to feel proud. But all she felt was nothing.

"Do you want to try the Ferris wheel?" he asked.

She looked up at the towering wheel. Thought about being enclosed in that small car, trapped with no way out.

Her chest tightened. But she nodded anyway. "I think I'd like that."

She needed to try to prove to herself she could still do normal things.

As they walked, she slipped her hand into his. Their fingers laced together. Francesco glanced down but didn't comment.

The operator smiled in recognition. "Back again? Sometimes the best things are worth doing twice."

The got into the same car for the same gentle sway as they rose into the night sky. But as they climbed higher, Serafina's breathing became shallow. The car suddenly felt too small. She gripped the edge of the seat, knuckles white.

"Serafina?" Francesco's voice seemed distant. "Look at me. Just look at me."

She forced herself to meet his eyes, to focus on his face instead of the enclosed space. The trapped feeling.

"Breathe," he said quietly. "You're safe. I've got you."

When he put his arm around her, she tried to nestle close and lean into his warmth. But her body was rigid, yet trembling, fighting between the need to be held and the terror of being touched. At the top, with the lights spread below them, she let out a shaky laugh that sounded more like a sob.

"Better this time?" he asked, but she could hear the concern in his voice.

"Much better," she lied, turning in his arms to face him. Her hands came up to frame his face, memorizing the sharp angles, the darkness in his eyes. "You were wrong, you know."

"About?"

"You're worth missing." The words came out broken with a suppressed sob. "You're worth everything it costs to love you."

For a moment, his control slipped, and she saw straight through to the damaged soul beneath. His hands tightened on her waist.

By the time they climbed out, her whole body shook. He kept her hand in his, fingers interlaced, his thumb stroking over her knuckles. As they walked toward the beach, the moon cast everything in silver and shadow.

"I owe you an apology," Serafina said as they reached the water's edge. "At the museum, when I got angry... I didn't mean to fall for you, and I'm sorry. This was never supposed to become..."

"Real?" His fingers came up to trace her cheek and to brush a strand of hair behind her ear. "Do you think I meant for this? Do you think I wanted to need you like I need air?"

226

She pressed her face into his touch, closed her eyes, and tried to seer this moment into her memory before it was taken away. "I'm broken, Francesco. Not by you, but I'm broken now, and I don't know how to be whole again."

"Look at me." When she did, his eyes were fierce, burning. "You're not broken. You're mine."

She pressed her face against his hand, wanted to feel safe, to feel anything other than ruined.

"I don't want to say goodbye. Please. Not yet." Her breaths came in sharp gasps through her teeth.

He pulled her against him with sudden desperate force, crushing her to his chest, each breath shuddering. She pressed her face against him, listening to his heartbeat, willing her to beat in time with his. His hand cradled the back of her head, fingers tangled in her hair.

"Would you like to go dancing with me next Saturday?" he asked quietly.

Her heart leaped even as her stomach clenched with dread. The thought of strange men, crowded spaces, hands that might touch her... but this was Francesco offering her time beyond tonight.

"If you mean it, then yes." She pulled back to search his face. "But Francesco, I... I don't know how to dance, and I don't know how feel normal anymore."

"Saturday." His thumb traced her bottom lip. "I'll take you somewhere beautiful and safe. It'll just be us."

"So we're not saying goodbye?"

"No," he said roughly. "You're in my blood now, Serafina. I couldn't cut you out without bleeding to death."

Then he kissed her.

For one perfect moment, she wasn't the girl who'd been violated, and he wasn't the man with blood on his hands. She gripped his coat lapels, pulling him closer. One of his hands slid into her hair while the other pressed pulled against her back.

Then his hand pressed against the bruises on her ribs, the ones Mr. Kensington had left when he'd—

Sharp pain coursed through her. She gasped against his mouth.

Francesco pulled back immediately. "Did I hurt you?"

227

"No. I just—" She couldn't tell him about all the places that hurt. "I'm sorry."

"Serafina." His forehead rested against hers. ""Tell me who did this to you."

She shook her head, unable to speak it.

"I'll make him wish he was dead for hurting you."

A sharp gust of wind swept off the water. She shivered, but not from cold.

"Come on," he murmured, pressing his lips to her forehead. "Let me take you home before you freeze."

In the car, his hand rested on her knee. She covered it with both of hers, holding tight. But she couldn't stop trembling, couldn't stop waiting for his gentleness to turn to violence. She forced herself to breathe. This was Francesco, not Mr. Kensington. Francesco, who moved slowly now, who asked permission, who pulled back when she tensed. But her body didn't know the difference. Her body was still in that hotel room.

When they reached her building, he turned off the engine but made no move to leave.

"I should go up," she said, though the thought of being alone in her apartment, surrounded by shadows and memories, made her want to scream.

"You should," he agreed, but his hand turned beneath hers and held on. "Will you be all right?"

"I... I don't want tonight to end though."

She couldn't tell him that she didn't want to go back to her apartment, to be alone with the memories, to face another night of scrubbing herself raw and still feeling dirty.

"Neither do I. Let me walk you up."

As they climbed the stairs, his posture changed. He became more rigid and alert. His eyes darted to corners and shadows. She wanted to ask what was wrong, but the words stuck in her throat.

As they reached her floor, Serafina's unease built. The hallway stretched before them, dimly lit. Then she saw it. Her apartment door stood wide open.

She gasped. Francesco shoved her behind him. He cocked his gun.

"Stay behind me," he whispered.

They crept forward, Serafina's heart hammering.

At the threshold, she caught her first glimpse inside of the destruction. It was complete and utter destruction.

When Francesco finally led her in, her knees nearly buckled.

Broken dishes scattered across the floor. Her precious books lay broken and bent, spines cracked, pages torn. Her bed had been stripped, the mattress slashed open. Papers were everywhere. Her stories lay torn to pieces.

Some of her things still smoldered from a fire set in the middle of the room. She knelt, picking up a torn piece of paper, part of a story about a girl who believed in happy endings.

Her typewriter lay overturned on the floor, broken, with keys scattered.

She looked up at Francesco through her tears. He still held the gun, eyes sweeping the room.

"Why would someone do this?" she whispered.

He holstered his gun and placed his hands on her shoulders to draw her close. She collapsed against him. The solid warmth of his chest was the only real thing in this nightmare. His arms wrapped around her and she buried her face in his coat.

As the shock began to fade, she pulled away and began collecting papers. These pages had contained her hopes and dreams. Now they were just paper and ink, as easily destroyed as everything else.

"Serafina." Francesco's voice seemed distant. "I'm so sorry."

"It was just a story," she muttered, dropping torn pages onto burned clothes. "A stupid romance story that meant nothing."

"It's not stupid," Francesco said quietly.

All the fear and violation and helplessness transformed into rage. She whirled to face him, tears streaming.

"What do you know about romance or love?" Her voice cracked. "You don't even believe in it!" She gestured at the destruction. "This was my dream, and all my hope for a happy ending. And look at it now. Look at it!"

Her gaze fell on her sapphire gown, the one from the ball, that she'd word when... Not it lay slashed to ribbons.

"I never felt so pretty in all my life as I did in that."

She went to the broken door latch and knelt, fingers tracing the splintered wood. "I'm not sure how to fix this," she said, her voice becoming tight, breathless. "But I need to lock it. I have to lock it so no one can get in." Her fingers kept tracing the same broken piece. "How am I supposed to fix this? I don't know how. But I need to... I need to lock the door..."

She grabbed at her hair, wanting to tear something apart, when suddenly Francesco's arms were around her, pulling her back against his chest.

She clung to him, to this man who claimed not to believe in romance, but who, in the wreckage of everything she'd built, was the only solid thing left standing.

"I can't—" she sobbed against him. "I can't do this anymore. I can't—"

"I know," he murmured into her hair. "I know."

"Everything's destroyed. Everything. And I tried—at Coney Island, I tried so hard to be okay, to be normal, but I'm not okay. I'm not—"

"You don't have to be okay." His arms tightened around her. "You don't have to be anything right now. Just mine."

She shook in his arms as all of the past twenty-four hours finally broke through. She'd tried to hold it together, tried to give him one good evening, tried to pretend she could still be the woman she'd been before, but she couldn't. That woman was gone.

CHAPTER 15

Francesco paced the length of his study, his eyelids growing heavy despite the adrenaline still coursing through him. The combination of sleeping pills and brandy had finally helped Serafina fall asleep in his guest room, but for him, the night stretched on, and he was far from ready for rest.

"What do you want to do about Giordano stealing babies to send to Tennessee?" Ricci asked, leaning against the desk. "Goddamn, having one myself now... I'd do something worse than murder."

"What's worse than murder?"

"Make him disappear piece by piece. Start with his fingers, work up to bigger parts. Let him think about what he's done to those families while he watches himself come apart."

Francesco's jaw clenched. "We'll deal with him. But not tonight." He resumed his pacing. "Right now, I want every man we have looking for whoever destroyed Serafina's apartment. Someone saw something. Someone knows something."

"You think it was Kensington?"

The name sent a wave of cold fury through Francesco's chest. His hands curled into fists. "Kensington is mine. No one else touches him until I decide what to do with him. When I'm done, he'll wish he'd never been born."

Ricci nodded grimly. "The boys won't like waiting."

"They'll wait because I'm telling them to wait." Francesco's voice dropped to something deadly quiet. "I want this done right. I want him to understand exactly what he's done. I want him to suffer for every mark he left on her."

As the sky began to lighten outside the study windows, the door opened. Paulie, one of his street bosses, walked in carrying a typewriter, a stack of papers, and a teddy bear.

"Sir," Paulie said, setting the items carefully on the desk. "I grabbed all the papers I could find that weren't too burned or torn up." He paused, a hint of a smile touching his lips. "And the teddy bear. My little girl has one that makes her feel better when she's scared. Couldn't leave it behind. Thought maybe it makes Miss Silvano feel better too."

Francesco's chest tightened. He looked at the teddy bear he'd won for her, then back at Paulie. "Thank you. I'm sure it will."

"Can the typewriter be fixed?" Ricci asked, examining the broken keys.

Paulie shrugged. "Not sure. But I know a guy who works on them. I'll take it to him first thing."

Before Francesco could respond, two more of his men entered. Their faces were grim. One of them, Marco, held a key between his thumb and forefinger.

"Boss," Marco said. "We searched the whole building like you asked."

"And?"

"Third floor. Apartment 3A." Marco set the key on the desk. "There's a smell coming from under the door. Bad smell."

"What kind of smell?"

"Death." Marco's expression was stone. "We found this key on the welcome mat right outside the door. Used it to get in."

The room went still. Francesco stopped pacing.

"There's a body," the other man, Sal, said quietly. "Woman. Red hair. Looks like she was strangled. Been dead a few days. Starting to decompose."

Third floor. One floor up from Serafina. The killer had been in

232

her building, had murdered someone in her building, had left the body there.

"*Miss Silvano lives on the second floor,*" Ricci said, voicing what Francesco was already thinking.

"*I know.*" Francesco said, roughly.

"*Could have been her,*" Marco added. "*Could have been Miss Silvano we found up there instead.*"

The thought made Francesco's vision narrow. His hands gripped the edge of his desk hard. Serafina could have encountered the killer in the stairwell. She could have been the one strangled and left to rot. She could have been the body his men found.

Or she could have gone upstairs for some reason, to borrow something from a neighbor, to investigate a sound, and found the corpse herself. Another trauma layered on top of everything else Kensington had done to her.

"*The door's open now,*" Sal continued. "*We left it that way. Let the smell out. Someone will find her soon and call the cops.*"

"*The woman have a name?*" Francesco asked.

"*Don't know. Didn't go through her things. But she's young. Maybe twenty. Looks like she was coming home when it happened. Still wearing a robe.*"

Francesco's mind raced. A young woman in a robe. Probably coming home late at night. Wrong place, wrong time. Or—

"*Was she the target?*" he asked. "*Or was she just in the way?*"

Marco and Sal exchanged glances.

"*Hard to say, boss,*" Marco admitted. "*But the way it was done... professional and clean. The kind of kill that's practiced.*"

Francesco closed his eyes, pressing his fingers against his temples. When he opened them again, his gaze went to the hallway that led to his guest room.

"*The apartment was destroyed when we found it,*" Ricci said slowly, following Francesco's thought process. "*Someone broke in and tore it apart. But they didn't wait for her to come home. Didn't ambush her.*"

"*Because she wasn't the primary target,*" Francesco said, the pieces falling into place. "*The destruction was a message. A threat. But the woman upstairs—*"

"*Wrong place, wrong time,*" Paulie finished. "*Maybe she came home while he was in Miss Silvano's apartment. Maybe she heard something. Maybe she just had the bad luck of being there.*"

Or maybe, Francesco thought darkly, *the killer had been waiting outside Serafina's door and the redhead had interrupted him.* Maybe she had saved Serafina's life without knowing it, and paid for it with her own.

"*I want to know everything about apartment 3A,*" Francesco said, his voice sharp with command. "*Who she was, who she knew, if she had any connection to Miss Silvano. I want to know if anyone saw anything unusual in that building. And I want to know—*" He paused, his jaw working. "*I want to know if Miss Silvano knew her.*"

If she did, if they'd been friendly, if they'd chatted in the hallway or borrowed sugar from each other, then Serafina would have another death on her conscience. The victim might be another person destroyed by her proximity to Francesco's world.

"*On it, boss,*" Marco said.

"*And get the typewriter fixed,*" Francesco added, looking at Paulie. "*I don't care what it costs. Get it fixed.*"

The men filed out, leaving Francesco alone with Ricci.

"*You can't tell her,*" Ricci said after a moment. "*About the body.*"

Francesco didn't answer. He stared at the key on his desk, the key that had been left outside a dead woman's door.

"*She's been through enough,*" Ricci pressed. "*You tell her there's a corpse one floor up from where she lives, and she'll never sleep again.*"

"*I know.*" Francesco's voice was barely above a whisper.

"*So?*"

"*So I don't tell her.*" He picked up the key, rolling it between his fingers. "*Not yet. Not until I know more. Not until I know who did this and why.*"

But even as he said it, Francesco knew the truth. Someone had been in Serafina's building. Someone dangerous enough to kill without hesitation. That someone who might come back.

Serafina sat on the sitting room sofa, so close to Francesco that their legs touched. She wore one of Lucia's borrowed dresses. Her hands were folded in her lap, trembling slightly despite her attempts to still them. Every sudden sound from the tick of the clock to Mr. Ricci's footsteps in another room made her flinch.

Francesco's arm rested along the back of the sofa, his fingers occasionally brushing her shoulder. Each time, she leaned into the touch like it was the only thing keeping her calm.

"Serafina," Lucia said gently from the armchair across from them, "can I get you anything? Tea? Something to eat?"

Serafina shook her head. The thought of food made her stomach turn.

"She needs to rest," Francesco said, his voice low. "She barely slept for what she's gone through."

"The pills helped," Serafina whispered, though her voice sounded hollow even to her own ears. "Thank you for those."

"Of course. I just wish..." Lucia trailed off.

The silence stretched. Serafina stared at her hands, trying to ignore the faint marks visible on her wrists where the rope had been. She'd tried to position her sleeves to cover them, but they kept sliding up.

"Serafina," Lucia began carefully, "You're safe here, and you can stay as long as you need. I have plenty of dresses you can borrow, and—"

"Thank you. You're very kind."

Lucia glanced at her brother. "Frankie, it... it looks like your arrangement has changed, that you're not just..."

She didn't finish, but Serafina understood what she was asking.

"We're not pretending anymore," Francesco said quietly, his hand settling on Serafina's shoulder. "If that's what you're asking."

"I can see that." Lucia said gently. "I'm glad. I thought—well, I hoped something might develop between you. But Serafina, are you—"

A sharp knock at the door interrupted her. Francesco's posture shifted immediately, his hand moving fully to Serafina's shoulder. Ricci appeared from the kitchen, already moving toward the door.

"That should be Miss Randolph," Francesco said.

Serafina's stomach tightened. When she'd called Clara that morning and told her about the apartment, Clara had said she was coming immediately and that Serafina would stay with her family. But Serafina wasn't ready to leave Francesco. He was the only thing that felt safe.

Mr, Ricci opened the door. Clara stepped inside, her face pale with worry, her usual composure cracking at the edges.

"Serafina!" Clara rushed toward her, then stopped short when she took in the sight of Serafina sitting so close to Francesco, wearing borrowed clothes, looking exhausted and broken. "Oh my God, what happened to you?"

Serafina stood on unsteady legs. "Clara, I—"

Clara pulled her into a tight embrace. Serafina stiffened at first, then collapsed into her friend's arms. The familiar scent of Clara's perfume was too much. Tears spilled down her cheeks.

"Sera, you look terrible. What happened?" Clara murmured into her hair. She pulled back, searching Serafina's face. "This looks like more than a break-in."

"I'm fine."

"You're not fine." Clara's eyes were fierce now, protective. Then her gaze shifted to Francesco, who had risen to his feet. "What did you do to her?"

"Clara," Serafina said weakly. "It's not—"

"I didn't hurt her," Francesco said. "I would never hurt her."

"Then why does she look like she's been through hell?" Clara's voice rose. "Why is she here in your house, wearing someone else's clothes, looking like she hasn't slept in days?"

"Because her apartment was destroyed," Lucia interjected, standing as well. "And she had nowhere else to go."

"She has somewhere to go." Clara's chin lifted. "She's staying with my family. We insisted when I told them what happened."

"She's safer here," Francesco said.

"Safer?" Clara's laugh was sharp, bitter. "With you? A man who—" She stopped herself.

"Say it," Francesco said quietly, dangerously quiet. "A man who what?"

"A man who kills people." Clara's voice didn't waver despite the threat in his tone. "I know exactly who you are, Mr. Romano. Everyone in New York knows the Romano family, and everyone knows what that means violence and danger and death."

"Clara, please," Serafina whispered.

"And yet you brought her into your world anyway." Clara's eyes blazed. "Whatever arrangement you had with her—and I'm starting to understand it was never about cataloging books, was it?—you made her a target. Someone destroyed her apartment because of you."

Francesco's jaw clenched, but he didn't argue.

"That's not fair," Serafina said, her voice breaking. "It's not his fault."

"Isn't it?" Clara turned to her. "Sera, look at yourself. You're terrified. You're exhausted. And you're sitting here in a mobster's house like you have nowhere else to turn."

"I don't!" The words burst out of Serafina. "I don't have anywhere else. My apartment is destroyed. Everything I own is—" Her voice cracked. "Everything's gone."

"So you live with us," Clara said firmly. "My family sees you as family, and you'll be somewhere safe and respectable and—"

"She won't be safe." Francesco's voice cut through. "Whoever did this knows where she lives. He could find out where your family lives just as easily."

"And he certainly knows where you live," Clara shot back. "She's in more danger here than anywhere."

"I have men and resources. I can protect her."

"From what? From the enemies you've made? From the violence that your family condones and initiates?" Clara's voice softened

237

slightly. "Mr. Romano, I understand you care about her. I can see that. But don't you see? The best way to protect her is to let her go. End whatever this is between you before she gets hurt worse than she already has been."

Serafina looked at Francesco.

"Is that what you want?" he asked Serafina quietly. "To leave?"

"I don't—" She couldn't finish. Didn't know what she wanted. "I don't want to be a burden."

"You're not a burden."

"But Clara's right." The admission hurt. "I'm not safe near you. I'm not..." She wrapped her arms around herself. "I don't belong in your world."

"Serafina—"

"I'll go with Clara." She couldn't meet his eyes. "Her family is expecting me. It would be rude to refuse."

The silence that followed was suffocating.

"Fine," Francesco said finally, his voice flat. "If that's what you want."

The finality in his words made her chest ache.

"I'll pack some dresses for you," Lucia said quietly, breaking the painful silence. "You can't go in just what you're wearing."

"I should—" Serafina looked around the room helplessly. "I should get my things. But I don't have anything. Everything was—"

Clara waited by the door, giving her space but ready to leave.

"Thank you," Serafina whispered to Francesco. "For everything."

He nodded but didn't speak. Couldn't, maybe. His jaw was clenched so tight she could see the muscle working.

She took a step toward the door. Then another.

Then she stopped.

She couldn't leave like this. Couldn't walk away without—

She turned and ran back to him, throwing her arms around his neck. He caught her immediately, his arms wrapping around her waist, pulling her close. She buried her face in his chest, breathing in his scent, memorizing the feel of his heartbeat against her cheek.

"I'm sorry," she whispered against his shirt. "I'm so sorry."

His arms tightened around her. "You're still mine. That's not changing."

She pulled back just enough to look at his face. Her hand came up, trembling, to touch his cheek. Her fingers traced the line of his jaw, the scar above his eyebrow she'd memorized. His eyes closed at her touch, something like pain crossing his features.

Neither of them spoke. There were no words.

Finally, she dropped her hand and stepped back. His arms released her slowly, reluctantly.

She turned and walked to Clara on unsteady legs before she could change her mind.

As Clara led her out into the cold morning air, the world suddenly felt too big, too dangerous, too empty. And now she was walking away from the only person who made her feel safe, because staying would destroy them both.

Serafina had barely stepped through the door of the Randolph mansion before Mrs. Randolph pulled her into a hug. For a moment, Serafina's spine stiffened. Trapped. Then she forced herself to relax, to lean into it. Normal. She had to be normal.

"My dear girl," Mrs. Randolph said, pulling back to look at her. The concern in her eyes deepened. "Clara told us what happened. How are you—" She stopped mid-sentence, her hand coming up to cup Serafina's cheek. "Oh, sweetheart. You look exhausted."

"I'm fine. Just tired. I didn't sleep well."

She had to be fine. Had to prove she could handle this.

Mrs. Randolph exchanged a look with her husband.

Clara's older brother George stepped forward, his face grave. "Serafina, do you have any idea who might have done this? Any enemies? Anyone who might wish you harm?"

She shook her head.

"George," Mrs. Randolph said firmly, "give the poor girl a moment to breathe before you interrogate her."

"I'm not interrogating, I'm—"

"It's all right," Serafina said. "I appreciate the concern, but I really don't know who did it."

Mr. Randolph studied her for a long moment, his eyes sharp. "You're wearing borrowed clothes."

Serafina looked down at Lucia's dress. Heat rose in her cheeks. "Yes. Everything I owned was destroyed. I don't have anything left."

"Then we'll remedy that immediately," Mrs. Randolph said. "Clara and I will take you shopping this afternoon. You'll need clothes, toiletries, everything."

"Oh, I couldn't," Serafina protested, her voice coming out too high. "The expense—I can't ask you to—"

"You're not asking. We're offering." Mrs. Randolph's tone left no room for argument. "Consider it settled."

"But I have savings, I can—" She stopped. Did she? Her bank book had been in her apartment. Was it destroyed? She didn't even know. "I can manage."

"Serafina," Clara said gently, taking her hand. "Let us help you."

Serafina wanted to argue, but being just a broken thing being passed from house to house because she couldn't take care of herself drained the fight from her.

"Thank you. You're very kind."

"Nonsense," Mrs. Randolph said, though her eyes were suspiciously bright. "You're family, dear. Now, let's get you settled. The housekeeper has prepared the blue room. You remember it, don't you?"

Serafina nodded. The blue room. Pretty and pristine and nothing like her small apartment had been.

"I'll need to go to the bookshop tomorrow," she said suddenly. "Mr. Thompson will be expecting me."

Everyone stared at her.

"Serafina," Mr. Randolph said carefully, "surely Mr. Thompson would understand if you took a few days—"

"No. I need to work. I can't just—I need to be useful. I need to..." Need to pretend this didn't happen.

"Dear, you've been through a terrible ordeal," Mrs. Randolph said gently. "No one would blame you for taking time to recover."

"I'm fine. Really. I slept last night, and I'll sleep tonight. By tomorrow I'll be perfectly capable of working."

Clara squeezed her hand. "If you're sure..."

"I'm sure. Besides, staying busy will help. Give me something to focus on besides..." She gestured vaguely. "Besides everything."

George frowned. "Is it safe? If someone targeted your apartment, they know where you live. They might know where you work."

"The bookshop is public. Lots of people around. I'll be fine."

"Well," Mrs. Randolph said after a moment, "if you're determined to work tomorrow, then you should rest this afternoon. Clara, show her to the blue room. We'll have lunch sent up. You look like you haven't eaten in days."

"That would be lovely. Thank you."

As Clara led her up the grand staircase, Serafina kept her back straight and her face composed. One foot in front of the other. That's all she had to do. Keep moving. Keep functioning. Keep pretending.

At the door to the blue room, Clara paused. "Are you really all right?"

"Yes." The lie came easier each time she did it. "I'm just tired."

"You know you can tell me anything, right? Whatever happened—"

"Nothing happened." Serafina's voice came out flat. "My apartment was destroyed. That's all."

"That's not all." Clara's voice was soft but insistent. "I saw how you looked at Mr. Romano's house. I saw how you looked at him, and I saw how hard it was for you to leave."

Serafina's chest tightened. "Clara, please—"

"I won't push. But when you're ready to talk about it, I'm here." She squeezed Serafina's hand. "Whatever it is. I'm here."

Serafina nodded, not trusting herself to speak. Clara opened the door to the blue room, and Serafina stepped inside.

The room was beautiful. Pale blue walls, white furniture, a canopy bed with pristine linens. So clean. So perfect. So utterly

241

wrong. The door closed softly behind Clara. Serafina stood in the middle of the perfect blue room and tried to breathe.

She was fine. She had to be fine. Tomorrow she'd go to work. She'd smile at customers and shelve books and prove that she was still capable of living a normal life.

She just had to make it through tonight first.

She sat on the edge of the bed, her hands folded in her lap. They were shaking again. She pressed them together harder, trying to make them stop.

Fine. She was fine. She'd be fine.

She just had to keep telling herself that until it was true.

Francesco's fingers ached. He'd been sitting on his study floor for hours, surrounded by scraps of paper. Some pieces were no bigger than his thumbnail. Others had burned edges that crumbled when he touched them. All of them had to be sorted, matched, aligned, and carefully taped back together.

The work was tedious. His back hurt from hunching over, his eyes strained in the lamplight, and his hands cramped from the precise movements required to match torn edges without obscuring the words.

Another piece. He held it up to the light, squinting at the partial words. *...loved him despite...* He set it aside, then searched through the scattered pieces for its match.

The whiskey glass beside him had been empty for over an hour. He'd stopped drinking around three. He needed steady hands for this. The study was silent except for the soft sound of tape being pulled from the roll, the rustle of paper, and his own breathing.

Four hours ago, Paulie had brought him a box of hundreds of torn and burned pieces of her manuscript, collected from the destruction. Francesco had looked at the box and known immediately what he was going to do.

He picked up another scrap. *...dangerous man...* He matched it to another piece, aligned the edges, and taped them together.

Someone had torn these pages. Ripped them apart. Burned them. Destroyed what she'd created with her own hands.

His jaw clenched so hard it ached.

Another piece. *...she knew better than to want...* He matched it, aligned it, and taped it. Her words. Her story. Someone had tried to erase.

Francesco smoothed another piece of tape across a mended tear, his fingers more forceful than necessary. These pages were hers, which meant they were his to protect. His to restore.

He stopped, a piece held between his fingers.

When had he started thinking of her things as his?

Francesco set the piece down carefully and reached for another. His hands began to shake slightly.

The front door opened.

"*Frankie,*" Ricci's voice. "*Any word from—*" He stopped in the doorway. "*Christ. What are you doing?*"

Francesco didn't look up. "*What does it look like?*"

"*It looks like you've been sitting on the floor for hours taping together scraps of paper.*"

"*Then you answered your own question.*"

After a long pause, Francesco found a match for the piece in his hand, aligned the edges, pulled off a strip of tape.

"*How long have you been at this?*" Ricci asked.

"*What time is it?*"

"*Almost five.*"

Five hours. Francesco had started around midnight, after Serafina had finally fallen asleep in his guest room with the help of sleeping pills. Five hours of this while she slept down the hall, drugged and fighting a nervous breakdown.

Because of Kensington.

Francesco's hands stilled. The piece in his fingers crumpled slightly before he forced himself to smooth it out.

"*Any word from the boys?*"

"Nothing solid. We're still canvassing the building."

"Someone saw something." Francesco set down the page, picked up another. "Keep looking."

"You still think it's Kensington?"

"I know it's Kensington."

Francesco's hands clenched, crumpling the piece he was holding. He forced his fingers open, tried to smooth out the damage. His hands were shaking harder now.

"And when we confirm it?" Ricci asked.

"Then I kill him."

Ricci watched him for another moment. "Boss, you should sleep."

"Close the door on your way out."

After Ricci had been dismissed, Francesco sat alone in the silence.

He stared at the paper in his hands. *...never felt so safe...*

She'd felt safe with him.

And he loved her. He loved her laugh and her stories and the way she looked at him like he could be good. He loved her innocence and her hope and the way she'd touched his face before leaving this morning. He loved her so much that sitting here taping together the shreds of her destroyed manuscript felt like the only thing keeping him in his right mind.

She was his. And someone had hurt her. They were going to die for that. Slowly. Painfully.

But first, this. First he had to put her words back together. Had to restore what they'd tried to destroy.

Another fragment in his hands. *...belonged together...*

By the time the sun rose, Francesco had finished another dozen pages. His fingers were cramping badly now, his back screaming when he finally shifted position.

He didn't care.

He picked up another fragment and searched for its match. Hours of work still ahead. He'd finish every single page if it took him days.

Because Serafina was his. And Francesco Romano protected what belonged to him.

He sat alone in the darkness of his study, avoiding the electric lights. The glow of the streetlamp cut through the blinds, painting long bars of light across the table. Just enough to see.

Twelve photos, printed matte. Gloss made the skin too plastic. He wanted to feel like he could touch her.

Serafina smiled in three of the photos. She walked alone in nine. Her skirts were always modest. Her gaze turned down or to the side. Never at him.

She never looked at him.

He picked up the one where her fingers brushed her collarbone, caught mid-motion. That mouth, parted slightly, as if she might speak his name if he watched long enough. His thumb traced the edge of the photograph.

Everything had changed since Clara had brought Serafina into his path. Suddenly all his careful plans for the socialite seemed foolish. Why settle for Clara's brittle sophistication when he could have Serafina's genuine sweetness? Clara was beautiful, yes, but she was also sharp-tongued and willful. Serafina was soft, vulnerable, everything a woman should be.

He'd been watching Clara for months, learning her routines, planning his approach. He'd even broken into the Randolph house— through the kitchen window when the staff was out, through Clara's own bedroom window on a night when the family was at the opera... He'd memorized every room, every hallway, every creak in the floorboards. He'd stood in Clara's bedroom, touched her things, and imagined how she'd look tied to her four-poster bed.

Serafina staying with the Randolphs now was fortuitous. She was no longer alone, no longer vulnerable, but much easier to reach. And Romano...

Romano had claimed her. The newspapers had made that clear. And she'd thrown herself at the first dangerous man who'd shown her attention. But that didn't matter. Mr. Randolph wouldn't trust the mobster.

He sat there, fingering one of the photographs. He could have done this differently. Would have, if she'd just come along quietly and willingly.

She'd been given every opportunity. The notes. The waiting. He didn't want to frighten her. He wanted her to understand. He could take care of her. Give her everything she needs. His resources were more than adequate.

But she had to make it difficult.

He reached for the whiskey. The glass clinked as he poured it. He downed it in one swallow, chasing the bitterness that rose from his gut. He didn't want to hurt her. That was never the plan. But some women only understand force. Some women have to be reminded. She wasn't leaving him a choice. Whatever happened now...her fault. All hers.

Goddammit, she had no right to ignore him! No right to act like his eyes hadn't followed her. Like she didn't know exactly what she was doing in that skirt, brushing past him without apology. She knew. Girls like her always knew.

She was asking for it. He knew what to do now. Peace washed over him. Soon...*soon*.

And so the Randolph house wouldn't be challenging at all. The blue guest room, where Serafina would likely be staying, had a window that faced the alley. Same side of the house as Clara's room, same floor, just three rooms down the hall.

He still had the ladder he'd made for Clara. All he needed to do was shift targets, shift rooms. His plans could proceed almost exactly as before, just with a much more deserving prize at the end.

He opened the drawer. The fabrics were folded just like delicate treasure. Her bras curled inward. Her panties, some from her hamper, lay nestled between slips and stockings. He pulled out the lilac pair, silk with a little lace. They were worn.

He pressed them to his face. The scent was faint now, barely there, but his cock stirred anyway. He closed his eyes and inhaled again. There. A trace of her. Soap, a little powder, something sweet that lived in the fibers that had touched her.

He unzipped, pulled himself free. It was already half-hard, thickening with every heartbeat. He wrapped the panties around it.

Slow at first. A twist of fabric, a hint of pressure. His fist stroked in time with a thought he hadn't said aloud yet.

Don't make me hurt you.

He didn't want to.

But she was forcing his hand.

In his mind, she was spread out on her own mattress, tied open with those useless little arms stretched above her head. Her mouth gagged, of course. Couldn't have her ruining the moment with her shrieking. She'd be crying, of course. Fighting. The way they always did at first.

But eventually she'd stop.

They all did.

He squeezed hard, just below the head, and hissed through his teeth. The lace dragged against the tip. His other hand dropped to his balls, cupping them, rolling them with firm pressure.

He imagined the moment he pushed inside her. Her legs kicking...her hips squirming...that tight little voice begging behind the gag.

"You made me do this," he murmured, stroking harder now. "You made me."

His breath came ragged, his body jerking as he edged closer. The room swam in silence except for the slick sounds of his fist moving and the low rasp of his breath. He thought of her hair stuck to her cheeks, her mascara streaked down to her jaw. Thought of her trying to turn her face away as he forced her to see him.

He came with a grunt and a pulse that spilled across his hand, the lace, his lap. His hips bucked up once more, then went still. His heart thudded in his ears.

He wiped himself off with the panties and held them for a long moment, then folded them gently and set them back in the drawer, on top of the clean ones.

Soon, she'd be his. One way or another.

And if she was a good little girl...he'd give her everything she ever dreamed of.

But if she was a bad little girl...

CHAPTER 16

Serafina stood at the window of her blue room at the Randolph estate, watching the gardeners rake the fallen maple leaves into neat piles on the manicured lawn. The October sky threatened rain as pedestrians hurried along the sidewalk beyond the estate walls with their collars turned up against the autumn chill.

George knocked softly before entering, already dressed in his dark wool coat and carrying his leather briefcase.

"Ready?" he asked.

"Yes, but you really don't need to stay all day. Surely you've got important things to do."

"Dad and I discussed it last night. We think it's best if I'm there with you this week, just in case." His expression was serious. "If the break-in at your apartment was personal rather than random, I want to make sure you're safe."

"But what about your work?"

George held up the briefcase. "It's a week of legal briefs. I can read those at the shop and take the notes I need there just as easily as at the office."

Serafina felt a wave of gratitude wash over her. "Thank you, George. I'll feel a bit better with you there."

The automobile ride passed in comfortable silence, George occasionally pointing out changes in the neighborhood as they drove.

When they arrived, he parked along the curb and came around to open her door. The morning air was crisp, carrying the scent of autumn leaves and the distant smell of fresh bread from the bakery down the street. Serafina stepped onto the sidewalk, adjusting her burgundy dress and gathering her courage for whatever the day might bring.

They had barely taken three steps toward the bookshop when Danny appeared, seemingly from nowhere. His usual friendly smile was replaced with something wounded, hurt.

"Good morning, Serafina." His voice was soft, careful. "I waited for you Friday evening."

She stopped walking, confusion creasing her brow. "Friday evening?"

"At six o'clock. I told you I'd meet you." Danny's eyes searched hers as if looking for some explanation that would make sense of her absence. "When you didn't come, I thought maybe you'd misunderstood which day. So I came back Saturday evening, just in case."

Serafina's stomach dropped. Had she agreed to meet him? She couldn't remember. Everything from the past week was a blur of fear and exhaustion. "Danny, I'm so sorry. I don't think I—I must have misunderstood. I'm so sorry you waited."

George stepped closer, his posture shifting. "Where exactly were you planning to meet her?"

Danny's attention moved to George, and something flickered in his expression before smoothing away. "At her apartment. She'd given me her address a few weeks ago when I helped her home after an evening out. I'm a gentleman. When I tell a lady I'll meet her, I don't stand her up."

"And you went to her apartment? Both nights?" George's voice carried an edge Serafina had never heard before.

"Of course I did." Danny's tone grew more defensive. "I waited outside her door Friday. When she didn't come down, I thought perhaps I'd gotten the day wrong. So I returned Saturday evening. Before I went into the building, for nearly an hour I could see shadows moving behind her curtains, so I knew someone was home, but she never came to the door."

Serafina felt guilt wash over her. He'd come back a second night looking for her, and she hadn't even known. "Danny, I'm so sorry. I should have—I don't remember anything. Everything's been so confusing lately."

George moved slightly, positioning himself between them. "You saw movement in her apartment Saturday night and didn't think to check if something was wrong when she didn't meet you?"

"I didn't want to appear pushy." Danny's jaw tightened. "I respect Serafina's privacy."

"Funny kind of respect," George muttered. "Watching someone's windows for an hour."

"I don't appreciate your implications." Danny's voice dropped lower, harder. "I've never been anything but respectful toward Serafina. We have a relationship—"

"A relationship?" George's free hand curled into a loose fist at his side. "Based on what? Lurking around her apartment?"

The hostility between them crackled like electricity before a storm. Both men moved closer to each other, their shoulders squared, their stances aggressive in a way that made Serafina's heart pound in fear.

"Stop." Her voice came out small, breathless. "Please, both of you."

Neither man seemed to hear her. They had moved close enough that she could see the tension in George's jaw, the vein pulsing in Danny's temple.

"Maybe you should mind your own business," Danny said quietly, dangerously. "You don't know anything about what Serafina and I—"

"Stop!" Serafina pushed between them, her hands pressing against their chests. Her whole body was shaking. "Please stop, you're scaring me!"

A few passersby had stopped to watch. The public attention seemed to break whatever had overtaken both men.

Danny immediately stepped back, his entire demeanor shifting. When he looked at her, his eyes held nothing but gentle concern. "Serafina, I'm so sorry. I never meant to frighten you. That was

250

inexcusable." He reached out slowly, carefully, and when she didn't pull away, he drew her into a hug.

She let herself lean into the warm embrace and mindlessly wrapped her arms around his waist.

"I think I know who might be responsible." Danny's said, his chest rumbling slightly under Serafina's ear. "Richard Kensington has been pressuring you about business matters. And Francesco Romano—" He paused. "I've seen him around the neighborhood. Both men have reputations for getting what they want, regardless of who gets hurt."

George's eyebrows drew together sharply. "Francesco Romano? The mobster?"

Serafina raised her head from Danny's shoulder, but didn't step away from the embrace. Her heart dropped into her stomach. "He just buys books sometimes. Poetry. That's all."

"Poetry?" George echoed.

Then something in the window of the florist shop caught her eyes. "Danny," she said, "what's that sign?"

He followed her gaze to the "For Sale" sign propped in the display. His expression shifted to something almost apologetic. "I've been a florist for so long I can hardly remember how to be anything else. I suppose I decided it's time to pick up and try new adventures."

"But where will you go?" Serafina asked. Sudden alarm rose within her at the thought of losing a friend. "What will you do?"

Danny shrugged, his eyes drifting toward the bustling street, then back to her. "Somewhere with horses. I've always loved them. Besides, the flower business isn't what it used to be anyway." He paused, then added quietly, "A man has to do what he thinks is right to protect the people he cares about, even if they don't understand it at the time."

"I'll miss you when you're gone," Serafina said softly. "You've been a cheerful part of the mornings."

Danny's expression grew more earnest, almost hopeful. "This will probably be the last time I ask, but are you sure you don't want to get some coffee with me? To talk, as friends? Maybe this evening, after you finish at the bookshop?"

Serafina hesitated, but there was nothing more than friendship in her heart for him, and it wouldn't be fair to let him hope otherwise.

"I'm sorry, Danny, but no," she said gently but firmly. "I can't."

"Just coffee," he pressed, his voice still friendly but carrying a note of disappointment. "I'd really like to—"

"She said no," George interrupted, his tone firm.

Danny's jaw tightened as he looked at George, then back to Serafina. After a long moment, he nodded. "I see. Well, I suppose that's that, then." He stepped back, hurt flickering across his features before he masked it. "Good luck with everything, Serafina."

As they walked toward the bookshop, Serafina said quietly, "You didn't have to be so rude to him. He was just worried about me."

George's expression was unreadable. "Was he." It was a statement, not a question.

The familiar jingle of the shop's bell provided a small comfort as they stepped inside. The scent of old paper and leather bindings wrapped around her. At least the bookshop still felt like home.

Mr. Thompson stood behind the counter, but instead of his usual neat appearance, he looked harried and stressed. His tie was askew, his hair mussed as if he'd been running his hands through it.

"Good morning, Mr. Thompson," Serafina said softly.

He looked up with a distracted expression. "Oh, Serafina. Good morning." His gaze skimmed over George without really registering him. "I'll be in my office most of the morning. Some matters to attend to."

George settled himself in the comfortable reading chair near the front window, pulling out his newspaper and a folder of legal documents.

The morning passed slowly. Few customers came in, and Serafina found herself unable to focus on even simple tasks. She kept thinking about Danny's hurt expression, about the way he'd waited for her two nights in a row. The guilt sat heavy in her heart.

She was shelving books when the shop's bell chimed with unusual force. Serafina's hands froze on the book she was holding. The room tilted.

"Miss Silvano." Mr. Kensington's voice was gentle, soothing, like someone trying to calm a frightened animal. "Please don't distress yourself. I'm here on purely business matters today."

His gaze shifted to George, who had set aside his newspaper and was watching with sharp attention. "I don't believe we've been introduced. Richard Kensington, of Kensington Publishing."

George rose from his chair. "George Randolph. I'm here as a friend of Miss Silvano's."

"Ah, the Randolph family." Mr. Kensington smiled. "Your father's reputation precedes him."

Serafina couldn't move. She couldn't breathe. The book in her hands felt too heavy.

"I need to speak with Mr. Thompson about some business arrangements," Kensington continued, still in that unnaturally gentle tone. "Now, if you'll excuse me." He stepped back with theatrical courtesy. "Where might I find Mr. Thompson?"

Serafina had to force her legs to move. She led him to the office door, knocked softly, and waited for Mr. Thompson's distracted "Come in" before stepping aside.

As the office door closed behind Mr. Kensington, George moved closer to her. "That's Richard Kensington? The publisher?"

She nodded, unable to speak.

"There's something about him..." George's frown deepened. "Something that doesn't sit right."

They waited. Serafina tried to focus on straightening shelves, but her hands shook too badly. She kept glancing at the closed office door, straining to hear what was being discussed, but the voices were too low and muffled.

The meeting stretched on. Ten minutes. Twenty. Thirty. An hour. Two.

When the door finally opened, Kensington emerged with an expression of deep satisfaction. Mr. Thompson followed, his face pale and drawn.

"A pleasure doing business with you, Mr. Thompson." Kensington's smile didn't reach his eyes. He turned to Serafina, his gaze holding hers for a beat too long. "Miss Silvano, I look forward to our continued collaboration this week."

The words were spoken loud enough for Mr. Thompson to hear, casual as if he were confirming a simple business appointment. George's attention sharpened slightly, but he didn't seem to pick up on any deeper meaning.

After Mr. Kensington left, Serafina wanted to scream to break the silence.

"Serafina," Mr. Thompson said, his voice strained. "Could you come to my office, please? We need to discuss some changes."

George stood. "Should I—"

"Please," Mr. Thompson said. "This concerns Serafina directly. You should hear it as well."

In the office, Mr. Thompson gestured for them to sit. He remained standing, pacing behind his desk like a caged animal.

"Before we get to business matters," Mr. Thompson said, pausing in his pacing to look at her, "what was Mr. Kensington referring to? A collaboration?"

"Oh, that." Serafina waved her hand dismissively, forcing her voice to stay light. "Just some follow-up about my manuscript. Nothing important."

Mr. Thompson's brow furrowed slightly, but he nodded and continued pacing. "There have been some changes to our business arrangement with Kensington Publishing." The words came out rushed, like he wanted to get through them as quickly as possible. "The bookshop will be closed for the rest of this week. All of our current stock that isn't from Kensington Publishing will be packed up and removed."

Serafina's stomach dropped. "What? But why?"

"The Purrfect Tale will now carry exclusively Kensington Publishing titles." Mr. Thompson couldn't meet her eyes. "It's part of the new arrangement."

"But our other publishers—the poetry collections, the classics—"

"Gone." Mr. Thompson's hands trembled as he gripped the back of his chair. "And there's more. There's a lien being placed on the bookshop. The title will be held by Kensington's company."

"A lien?" George's voice was sharp. "On what grounds?"

"Business security, he called it." Mr. Thompson finally looked at Serafina, and she saw desperation in his eyes. "If we can successfully sell five thousand Kensington Publishing books by the end of the year, the lien will be removed."

"Five thousand?" Serafina's voice came out as a whisper. "That's impossible. We've never sold anywhere near that many books in two months."

"I know." Mr. Thompson sank into his chair. "But it was this or lose everything immediately. He's already had three of our other publishers pull their contracts. Without inventory, we can't operate."

The room spun. Serafina gripped the arms of her chair.

"I want you to know," Mr. Thompson continued, "you don't have to come in this week. I'll pay you for the full week regardless. This isn't your burden to—"

"It's not about the week." Her voice sounded strange, hollow. "Mr. Thompson, has Mr. Kensington been... has he said anything else? Made any other demands?"

Mr. Thompson's brow furrowed with confusion. "No. Just the business arrangements. Why would he—" His expression shifted to concern. "Serafina, is there something you need to tell me?"

"No." The lie came automatically. "No, it's nothing."

"You can tell me if—"

"I said it's nothing!" The words came out sharper, louder than she'd intended. Harsher.

Mr. Thompson recoiled slightly.

George stood, moved closer to her. "Serafina—"

"I'm sorry." She pressed her hands over her face. "I'm sorry, Mr. Thompson. I didn't mean to—it's just everything with the apartment, and now this, and I can't—"

"It's all right." But Mr. Thompson looked hurt and confused. "I understand you're under a great deal of stress. Perhaps you should take some time—"

"May I use the back room?" The words tumbled out. "Just for a moment. I need a moment."

"Of course. Take all the time you need."

Serafina fled to the back room before either man could say anything else. She closed the door behind her and leaned against it, her whole body shaking. She sank down onto an overturned crate, wrapped her arms around herself, and tried to breathe.

But she couldn't.

The sobs came suddenly, violently, tearing out of her chest. She pressed her hand over her mouth to muffle the sounds, but they kept coming.

She was trapped. Completely, utterly trapped.

If she refused Mr. Kensington, the shop would be destroyed. Mr. Thompson would lose everything his father had built. It would be her fault. All because she'd made Mr. Kensington angry, because she'd attracted the wrong kind of attention, because she'd been stupid enough to—

But if she went to that hotel, if she let him—

Francesco's face filled her mind. Oh, the way he'd looked at her before she left his house, and when he'd held her at Coney Island. So careful, and gentle. And the way his hand had rested on her knee in the car, that simple touch meaning everything.

He'd want to know why she went back. He would see it as betrayal. Or worse, he'd see how dirty she was, how used, how broken. Why would he want her after that?

She loved Francesco Romano, and going back to Kensington would destroy any chance she and Francesco had.

But not going would destroy Mr. Thompson.

There was no good choice. No right answer. Either option guaranteed pain and loss.

Eventually, the sobs quieted to ragged breathing. She wiped at her face, then tried to compose herself enough to go back out. When she finally emerged from the back room, her eyes were red-rimmed, but dry.

Clara stood near the shelves with a tall, distinguished gentleman with kind eyes and an unmistakably fond expression as he looked at her. George was by the counter, and Mr. Thompson was explaining something about the book removal process.

"Serafina!" Clara rushed over immediately, pulling her into a hug. "George told me what happened. The lien—I can't believe it. And it's all my fault. I'm the one who introduced you to Kensington in the first place. If I hadn't—"

"No," Serafina said, fighting to keep her voice steady. "It's not your fault. Please don't blame yourself."

The gentleman approached with Clara, his expression gentle and concerned. "You must be Miss Silvano. I'm Dr. Irving Curtis. Clara's told me so much about you."

Serafina shook his hand, immediately struck by his warmth and the way his attention kept drifting back to Clara with such obvious affection. Despite the stress churning in her gut, she found herself managing a small smile. "I can see why Clara's so taken with you, Dr. Curtis."

A faint blush colored Clara's cheeks, and Irving's expression softened even further as he glanced at her.

"I'm terribly sorry about the circumstances," he said. "This seems rather heavy-handed for a business arrangement."

"It is," George replied, his voice carrying a note of determination.

Mr. Thompson looked up from where he'd been sorting through a stack of invoices. "I'm going to start pulling books this afternoon. Get a head start on what needs to be done."

"I'll stay and help," Clara said immediately. "I know the inventory almost as well as you do, Mr. Thompson."

Dr. Curtis smiled at her. "Then I suppose I'll stay as well. I need to discuss a few things with your brother."

George and Dr. Curtis moved toward the front of the shop, their voices dropping to a quiet conversation. Serafina caught fragments about legal precedents and business law, but she was too drained to focus.

She tried to act normal and help Mr. Thompson identify which books needed to go, but nothing felt normal. They were supposed to add books, not take them away! Her movements were stiff, and her fingers kept twitching. Clara kept glancing at her with concern.

The afternoon dragged on. They worked mostly in silence, the only sounds the rustle of pages and the soft thud of books being stacked.

It was nearly closing time when the Western Union boy pushed through the door. "Telegraph for Miss Silvano," he announced, consulting the address written in careful script.

"That's me," Serafina said. As soon as the boy was out the door, she tore open the envelope and unfolded the paper. The message was brief, almost the same as the one Francesco has sent before, but this time, he wanted to see her on Thursday.

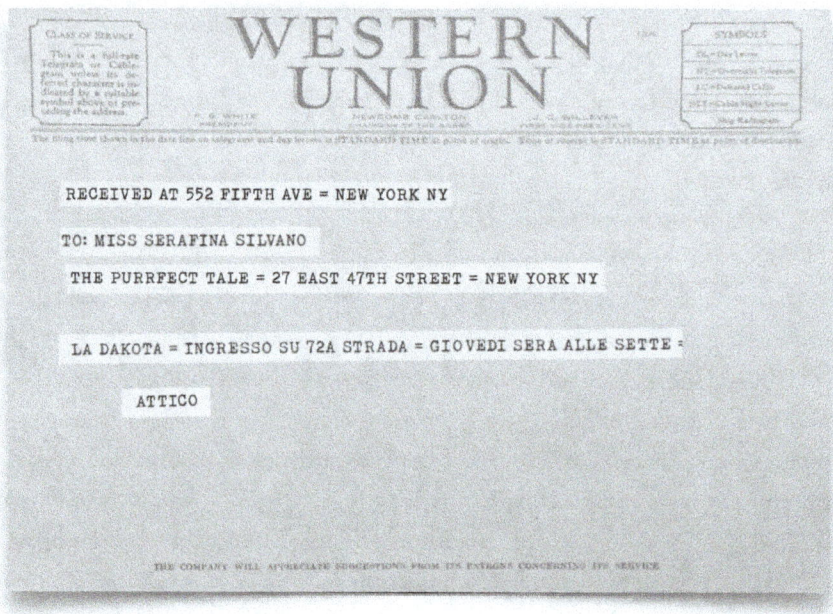

Part of her wanted to smile. He still wanted to see her, and now she had a chance to see him, to be near him and to feel safe for a few hours. But it would be the last time before Mr. Kensington expected her at the hotel. She felt a tear slip down her cheek and quickly wiped it away.

"Bad news?" George asked, rising from his chair.

Serafina quickly refolded the telegram, forcing her expression into one of disappointment. "Another rejection letter for my manuscript.

Publishers can be so cold in their responses."

"I'm sorry to hear that," Mr. Thompson said gently. "But don't lose heart. The right publisher will recognize your talent eventually."

George's eyes narrowed slightly. "Why are you getting your telegrams here instead of at home?"

Serafina met his gaze, keeping her voice steady, relieved to get to tell the truth about something. "Because this is where I usually am when telegrams are delivered. It makes more sense than using any other address when I'm here all day."

He seemed to accept the explanation, though something in his expression suggested he wasn't entirely convinced.

But Serafina could hardly care too much just then. What did it matter? What did any of it hatter then all good things get taken away?

That evening at the Randolph house, Serafina sat quietly in Mr. Randolph's study while he and George pored over documents spread across the desk.

"Under New York law, a lien obtained through fraud or duress can be voided," George said, flipping through a thick legal volume. "But we'd need to prove Kensington threatened Thompson's business relationships unless he agreed."

Mr. Randolph gave a low whistle. "I've seen men ruined by less. The Court of Appeals called it straight in Adams v. Irving National Bank, back in eighteen-ninety. Remember that one? Threaten to destroy a man's trade and the contract is void for business compulsion. No ifs, no appeal."

George nodded sharply. "Exactly. And the United States Supreme Court doubled down in Dean v. Davis, just a decade ago. Brandeis writing: a mortgage given to crush a borrower or to compound a crime is void ab initio. Public policy wipes it off the books the moment the threat is proved."

He pulled another volume from the shelf. "I'll also cite our own

Court of Appeals in Eadie v. Slimmon. 'A contract obtained by duress is void.' And if Kensington claims the lien was voluntary, we hit him with Clements v. Moore."

Serafina's hands tightened on the arms of her chair as she watched them work.

Mr. Randolph tapped the lien document. "So Thompson swears Kensington threatened to blacklist him with every paper mill from Holyoke to Niagara unless he signed. Two other shop owners give affidavits they got the same shakedown. You file in Supreme Court, New York County, tomorrow morning—verified complaint, order to show cause, prayer for preliminary injunction."

George nodded. "Right. But first we need Thompson's affidavit. Then we need to track down at least two other shop owners willing to testify they received similar threats. That's a week of interviews, minimum. Then drafting the complaint, filing the motion, waiting for a hearing date—we're looking at three weeks, possibly four, before we're even in front of a judge. And if Kensington gets wind of what we're doing, he could foreclose immediately and claim Thompson defaulted. We'd have to move very quietly. Very carefully."

Serafina's chest tightened. Three weeks. Four weeks. She had four days. Her breathing grew shallow. The voices continued, but she stopped listening. It was all pointless. By the time they built their case, it would be too late.

"Miss Silvano?"

She opened her eyes to find both men looking at her with concern.

Mr. Randolph's expression softened. "I know this is difficult to hear. But I want you to know that we will fight this. What Kensington is doing is extortion, plain and simple, and we will do everything in our power to help."

"Thank you, Mr. Randolph."

Clara appeared in the doorway. "Dad, Mom wanted to know if —" She stopped, taking in the scene, her gaze moving to Serafina. "Is everything all right?"

"Just discussing the legal situation," Mr. Randolph said. "Come in, Clara."

Clara entered slowly, taking a seat near Serafina. Her expression clouded with guilt. "I still can't believe I introduced you to Mr. Kensington. If I'd known—"

"But you. couldn't have," Serafina said quickly. "Please don't blame yourself."

Mr. Randolph leaned forward. "Now, is there anything else you need to tell us? Anything at all that might help us understand the full scope of what we're dealing with?"

"No," she said. "It's just the business arrangements. The lien."

"Are you certain?" Mr. Randolph pressed gently. "Because if there's more to this, if Mr. Kensington has made any inappropriate advances or threats—"

"There's nothing like that. He's just... a businessman trying to expand his influence."

George exchanged a look with his father, then paused. "There's something else that's been bothering me since this morning. Danny mentioned that Francesco Romano has been around the neighborhood, and stopping in the bookshop."

Serafina's heart stuttered. She kept her face carefully neutral. "He's come in a couple times to buy books. Poetry, mostly. That's all."

"Is that really all?" George's tone suggested he didn't quite believe her. "Francesco Romano, boss of one of the five families, just happens to shop at The Purrfect Tale?"

"Lots of people shop there," Serafina said, forcing her voice to stay steady. "I can't control who walks through the door."

The silence stretched. Clara's gaze burned into the side of Serafina's face, and she didn't need to look to know her friend was glaring.

"Poetry," Clara said softly, and there was something sharp in her tone. "How literary of him."

Serafina's cheeks warmed. She didn't dare look at Clara.

George pressed forward. "Serafina, I need to ask you something, and I need you to be honest with me. Are you in danger? Not just the bookshop—you personally. Is someone threatening you?"

The room went silent. All three Randolphs watched her, waiting.

Serafina's heart pounded. "I... I don't think so. Not directly."

261

"But you're not certain," George said.

"I'm not certain of anything anymore." It was the truth, at least partially. "Everything feels dangerous. Everyone feels like a potential threat."

Clara leaned forward slightly, her voice quiet but intense. "Serafina, we can't keep you safe if you're not honest with us."

Their eyes met, and Serafina saw the plea in her friend's expression, and beneath it, the hurt on betrayal.

"Is there anyone else who might be involved in this situation?" George asked. "Anyone who could help? Or who might be making things worse?"

Serafina glanced at Clara, just for a heartbeat.

"No," Serafina said, looking back at George. "There's no one else."

Clara's posture went rigid. She stood abruptly, her face carefully neutral. "I should go help Mom with dinner preparations."

"Clara—" Serafina started.

But Clara was already moving toward the door. "Excuse me."

"We'll continue this discussion tomorrow," Mr. Randolph said, his eyes following his daughter with concern. "Miss Silvano, you should rest. You've had a difficult day."

Serafina nodded and left the study, her heart heavy. She found Clara in the hallway, standing by a window and staring out at the darkening grounds, her arms crossed tightly over her chest.

"Clara—"

"Not here." Clara's voice was tight. She glanced around, then pulled Serafina into the nearest room, a small sitting room rarely used. She closed the door behind them with more force than necessary.

Clara crossed her arms again. The air between them felt charged, dangerous.

"You lied to them," Clara said finally, her voice low and hurt. "You lied to my father and to George, and even to me."

"I didn't—"

"Don't." Clara's eyes flashed. "Don't lie to me again, Serafina. My family opened their doors to you. They're trying to help you, to protect you, and you're lying to their faces."

"I'm trying to protect all of you!" The words burst out before Serafina could stop them. "You don't understand what's at stake—"

"Then tell me! Make me understand!" Clara stepped closer, her voice rising slightly before she caught herself and lowered it again. "We can't keep you safe if you won't be honest with us."

"Francesco would keep me safe," Serafina said quietly.

Clara's expression hardened. "Francesco Romano. The mobster. That's who you're counting on? That's who you looked at me about when George asked if there was someone else?"

"He's not—it's not what you think—"

"Isn't it?" Clara's voice was sharp. "Because it looks to me like you're caught between a predator like Kensington and a dangerous criminal like Romano, and you're lying to the people who actually care about you and can actually help you legally."

"You don't know him," Serafina said, feeling tears sting her eyes. "You don't know what he's—"

"I know he's dangerous. I know he's involved in things that could get you killed. And I know you're so blinded by whatever you feel for him that you can't see it." Clara's voice cracked. "I thought we were friends. I thought you trusted me."

"I do trust you—"

"Then tell me the truth!" Clara turned away, pressing her hand to her mouth. When she turned back, her eyes were bright with unshed tears. "Tell me what Kensington did to you. Tell me what Romano's involvement is. Tell me why you're so terrified that you're lying to everyone who's trying to help you!"

Serafina opened her mouth, but no words came. How could she explain the photographs, the hotel room, the way Kensington had touched her? How could she explain that Francesco was the only person who made her feel safe? How could she admit that she was in love with a man who lived in a world of violence and death?

"I can't," she whispered. "I'm sorry, but I can't."

Clara stared at her for a long moment, hurt and frustration warring on her face. "Then I can't help you." She moved toward the door, then paused with her hand on the handle. "And neither can my family. We're throwing open doors, offering you every resource we have, and you're shutting us out in favor of a criminal who will only drag you further into darkness."

"Clara, please—"

"I love you, Serafina. You're like a sister to me. But I can't watch you—" Her voice broke. "I can't watch you destroy yourself like this. Not when you won't even let us try to save you."

Clara left, closing the door quietly behind her.

Serafina sank into a chair, arms wrapped tight around herself. The day had stripped her bare. Danny's departure. George's suspicion. Kensington's threats. The telegram that should have been joy but couldn't be. And now Clara, her best friend, her sister, was gone too.

The sobs came again, but this time she didn't try to muffle them. There was no one left to hear.

CHAPTER 17

Later that evening, Serafina waited in the hallway outside Clara's room, pacing nervously as she listened for Clara to return from her date with Irving. When she finally heard Clara's soft footsteps on the stairs, Serafina quickly intercepted her at her bedroom door.

"Clara," she whispered urgently, her eyes red-rimmed from crying, "I need your help."

Clara paused, her hand on the doorknob, the glow from her evening out fading as she took in Serafina's appearance. Her expression cooled. "What's wrong?"

"I need to get out on Thursday night, and back in, without anyone knowing."

Clara's jaw tightened. She stepped into her room, leaving the door open. "No."

Serafina followed her inside, closing the door behind them. "Please. I wouldn't ask if it wasn't important."

"Important." Clara turned to face her, arms crossed. "This is about Romano, isn't it?"

Serafina's silence was answer enough.

"Of course it is." Clara's laugh was bitter. "You stood in the sitting room not four hours ago and lied to my face about him. And now you want my help sneaking out to see him?"

"Clara, I need—"

"What? What do you need from him that you can't get from my family?" Clara's voice rose slightly before she caught herself and lowered it again. "My brother is building a legal case to protect you. He's working day and night to find a way to challenge that lien. We've opened our home to you, taken you as one of us. But it's not enough, is it? You'd rather run to a mobster."

"You don't understand," Serafina said, her voice breaking. "I just need to see him. Just once. Before—" She stopped herself.

"Before what?" Clara stepped closer, her eyes searching Serafina's face. "What aren't you telling me?"

Serafina looked away. "Nothing. I just need to see him."

"Then go during the day. Walk out the front door like a person with nothing to hide."

"I can't. Your parents would—George would—"

"Would what? Stop you from making a terrible mistake?" Clara's voice cracked. "Serafina, he's dangerous. The Romano name means violence. It means people disappearing in the night. And you want to sneak out to meet him in the dark?"

"He's not what you think he is."

"Then what is he?" Clara demanded. "Tell me. Make me understand why you're willing to betray my family's trust for him."

Serafina's hands clenched into fists at her sides. "He makes me feel safe."

"Safe?" Clara stared at her in disbelief. "Safe? Serafina, listen to yourself. A crime boss makes you feel safe?"

"More safe than I feel anywhere else. More safe than I've felt since—" She stopped, tears spilling down her cheeks.

Clara's expression softened slightly, hurt mixing with concern. "Since what? Since Mr. Kensington?" She took a step closer. "Sera, please. Tell me what happened. Let us help you properly, through the law and proper channels."

"The law takes too long," Serafina whispered. "I don't have long to wait."

"What does that mean? Long to wait until what?"

Serafina shook her head, unable to answer.

Clara was quiet for a long moment. When she spoke again, her voice was soft with resignation. "You're going to go anyway, aren't you? Whether I help you or not."

"Yes."

Clara's eyes filled with tears. "Then I can't stop you. But I won't help you either." She turned away and moved toward her dressing table. "If you're determined to destroy yourself, you'll have to find your own way to do it."

"Clara—"

"Please go." Clara's voice broke. "I can't look at you right now."

Serafina stood there for a moment, wanting to say something, anything, that would bridge the widening chasm between them. But there were no words. She left quietly.

Alone in the hallway, Serafina leaned against the wall and closed her eyes. She'd have to find another way out. And she would. She had no choice if she wanted the strength to get through another Friday night.

Frost settled between Serafina and Clara over the next two days. They exchanged pleasantries at meals, but nothing more. Serafina caught Clara watching her sometimes, her eyes troubled, but neither of them broke the silence that had formed between them. If anyone else noticed, they didn't comment.

Thursday afternoon found them in the parlor after lunch, Clara reading while Serafina sat by the window, staring out at nothing. She didn't see the manicured gardens or the gray November sky. She was seeing the hotel room and feeling Mr. Kensington's hands.

The silence stretched until Clara finally set down her book and sighed.

"Are you planning to stay home tonight?" Clara asked quietly, though her tone suggested she already knew the answer.

Serafina looked up, meeting Clara's eyes for the first time in days.

"No."

Clara's jaw tightened. "Serafina..."

"I'm going, Clara, with or without your help."

"I know." Clara closed her eyes and pressed her fingers to her temples. "That's what terrifies me. You'll climb out a window if you have to. You'll find a way, and you'll get yourself killed doing it."

"Then help me do it safely."

Clara looked at her. "You're not just going to see him, are you?" Clara's voice dropped to barely a whisper. "There's something else."

Serafina stayed silent.

Clara stood abruptly and moved to the window, staring out with her arms wrapped tight around herself. "I keep thinking about what you said. That the law takes too long and you don't have time, not that the shop doesn't have time." She turned back, her eyes bright with unshed tears. "What is that about?"

"Nothing that concerns you."

"Everything about you concerns me!" Clara's composure cracked. "You're my best friend, and you're walking into something terrible, and you won't let anyone help you except a man who kills people for a living."

"He's never hurt me."

"Yet." Clara's voice broke. "But what about everyone around him? What about the people who cross the Romano family? They disappear, Serafina. They're found in the river or they're never found at all."

"I know what he is."

"Do you?" Clara stepped closer. "Because from where I'm standing, it looks like you're so desperate to feel safe that you can't see you're running toward a different kind of danger."

"Maybe." Serafina's voice was hollow. "But at least with him, I choose it. I..."

Clara stared at her, horror dawning in her expression. "Oh God. Mr. Kensington. That's what this is about, isn't it? He's..."

Serafina looked away.

Clara sank into her chair, her face pale. For a long moment, neither of them spoke. Then Clara stood again, her movements jerky, determined. "Come upstairs. If you're going to do this, we're doing it right. You're not getting yourself killed on my watch."

Serafina followed her up to her room. Clara shut the door behind them and leaned against it, closing her eyes.

"If anything happens to you tonight," Clara said, her voice shaking, "I'll never forgive myself. But I'll also never forgive him. If Mr. Romano hurts you, if something happens to you out there, my family will know exactly who to blame. Do you understand me?"

"Yes."

Clara moved to the wardrobe and began pulling out dresses. "The blue one. It brings out your eyes, and—" Her voice caught. "And I want you to look beautiful. Just in case—" She stopped, pressing her hand to her mouth.

"Just in case what?" Serafina asked quietly.

"Just in case this is the last time I see you alive."

Serafina took the blue dress from Clara's trembling hands. As she held it up, her own hands shook badly enough that the fabric rustled.

Clara noticed. "When did you last eat?"

"I don't remember."

"Jesus, Sera." Clara sat heavily on the bed. She reached into her pocket and pulled out a small brass key, staring at it for a long moment before holding it out. "This is to the servants' entrance at the back of the house. It's how I used to sneak out to meet Theodore before we were courting properly."

Serafina took the key, the metal cold against her palm. "Clara, you never told me—"

"Promise me you'll be safe," Clara interrupted, her eyes bright with tears. "Promise me you'll come back home alive. Promise me I won't lose your like I lost Theodore. I can't lose you, too. And promise me that whatever is happening with Mr. Kensington, that you'll be all right."

"I promise I'll try."

"That's not good enough."

"It's all I have."

Clara stood and pulled Serafina into a fierce hug. "Then make it through tonight. And tomorrow we'll figure out how to make you survive another night, and another."

They held each other for a long moment. Serafina's chest tightened as she felt Clara's shoulders tremble.

"Before dinner," Clara said finally, pulling back and wiping her eyes, "I'll mention that you're feeling poorly with female troubles. Mom will insist you not be disturbed, and the men won't ask questions about such matters."

"And if someone checks on me?"

"I'll tell them you're sleeping and don't want to be bothered." Clara walked to the window, her back to Serafina. "But you must be back before dawn. The servants rise early, and if you're caught... if my parents discover I helped you..."

"They won't," Serafina promised. "I'll be careful."

"Will you?" Clara turned back, her expression grave. "Because it seems to me that you stopped being careful the moment you decided Francesco Romano was your salvation instead of your damnation."

Serafina had no answer for that. The words struck too close to the truth. Maybe Clara was right that she was trading one form of captivity for another. But at least Francesco's cage felt like it had been specially built for her alone.

As the family gathered for dinner that evening, Serafina waited upstairs. She tried to eat the tray Clara had brought up to her, but managed only a few bites before pushing it away. Her hands wouldn't stop shaking.

She paced the room, going over all the ways the evening could go wrong. What if Francesco had changed his mind about her? What if he saw her desperation and found it pathetic? What if Mr. Kensington was having her watched and followed her? What if this was the last time she'd feel Francesco's arms around her before Mr. Kensington destroyed whatever was left of her?

What if she told Francesco the truth about the next night, and he walked away?

What if this was her last moment of feeling anything but fear?

An hour later, Clara slipped into the room. "It's time," she said quietly. "Everyone's in the drawing room. Dad's reading the newspaper, Mom's embroidering, George is reviewing case files. We have maybe twenty minutes before they start wondering where I am."

She helped Serafina into a dark cloak and led her down the servants' stairs. The narrow passage was dimly lit, and Serafina's heart pounded. They reached the kitchen entrance, and Clara paused with her hand on the door.

"I ordered a cab, and it should be waiting at the corner," Clara whispered.

"Clara, thank—"

"Don't." Clara's voice was tight. "Don't thank me. I'm not doing this because I approve. I don't approve, at all. But I love you, and I'd rather you be with a mobster who just might protect you than you sneaking out alone and getting yourself killed."

She opened the door. The cold November night hit them both.

"Please be careful," Clara whispered, pressing Serafina's hand one final time. "And remember—before dawn. If you're not back by then, I won't be able to cover for you."

Serafina nodded, then slipped out into the darkness.

Serafina didn't know what to expect when she stepped through the door. Francesco led her inside to a small table set for two near a crackling fireplace. A pair of tall candles burned low in crystal holders. As she moved closer, a middle-aged woman in a crisp black uniform entered from a side door and set a silver-domed plate on the table. Another followed with glasses of red wine.

The woman nodded to Francesco, and disappeared without a word.

Serafina's gaze lingered on the flickering shadows, the careful attention to detail. "I never would have thought you'd be so romantic," she said, almost to herself.

Francesco pulled out her chair, his fingers brushing her shoulder as she sat. "Don't tell anyone," he said with a faint smile that reached his eyes. "I have a reputation to uphold."

She laughed softly, biting her lip as her eyes sparkled. When Francesco lifted the silver dome, steam rose from a delicate plate of veal scallopini, potatoes roasted in duck fat, and green beans glistening with butter. Her stomach grumbled. She hadn't realized how hungry she was until now. She waited for him to pick up his fork before she picked up her own.

"You know," Serafina said, sipping her wine, "the last time I ate anything this good, I had to pretend I spoke French."

Francesco's laugh was warm and genuine. "How'd you get through it?"

"Smiled a lot. Nodded when I hoped it made sense. And prayed I didn't accidentally agree to marry someone."

"You would've made a very charming bride."

"And a terribly confused one."

When she finished the last of her potatoes, Francesco refilled their glasses and settled back in his chair, watching her with obvious contentment. The candlelight played across his features as they talked, about books, about a few years early in her childhood in Sicily that she barely remembered, about his sister's latest endeavors...

"She's threatening to take up painting now," Francesco said with fond exasperation.

"You adore her. I can tell."

"She's the only family I have left." His expression grew thoughtful. "The only person whose mattered to me." He paused. His dark eyes finding hers. "Until now."

Serafina found herself fully relaxing for the first time in weeks. Laughter began coming naturally as Francesco shared stories of his early, less successful attempts at intimidation.

"You're telling me the great Francesco Romano once got chased down an alley by a baker's wife with a rolling pin?" she teased.

"I was fifteen and thought I was much tougher than I was," he admitted, his eyes crinkling with amusement. "Mrs. Castellano set me straight fast enough."

But even as she laughed, part of her mind remained fixed on tomorrow night. Friday at six. Kensington's hands. The hotel room. She forced the thoughts away. Not tonight. Tonight was hers.

As the evening wore on and the candles burned lower, Francesco's expression grew more serious. He stood and crossed to a side table in the shadows. When he returned, he carried a thick bundle of pages bound with strips of tape.

Serafina's breath caught as recognition dawned. "My manuscript..."

"Every page," he said softly. "I put it back together the best I could."

She stared at it for several seconds before reaching out with shaking hands. Her chest tightened as she realized the hours upon hours this must have taken him.

"Francesco..." she breathed.

"I know how much it means to you," he said.

A cry of gratitude escaped her. She held the pages to her heart. "This meant everything to me. And Mr. Kensington has the other copy, and he's using it to—"

The words broke loose. She couldn't hold them anymore. "Kensington, he... he made me..." The touching, the threats against the shop, the photographs, last Friday, the bruises, the shame, the way he'd forced himself on her and left her feeling gutted and dirty, all of it tumbled out. And tomorrow night, she had to go back and had to let him—

Francesco's hands curled into fists. For a moment, Serafina glimpsed the lethal, merciless man who had built an empire on fear. Then he breathed out through his nose. "Tell me his address" he said, his voice terrifyingly calm.

"Francesco—"

"Tell me." The words came out soft, but deadly. "And I'll make sure he never touches you again."

"Are you going to... to kill him?"

"I won't tell you," Francesco said sternly "But the shop will be safe. And you are never, never going back to Kensington's home. And you are not to speak of this to anyone. Not the Randolphs, not Clara, not a soul. Do you understand?"

"Yes, yes, I..." Relief crashed over her so suddenly she became dizzy. "The shop is..."

"Safe."

Silently, Francesco guided her into his bedroom to the sofa near the hearth. He gathered a handful of kindling and a couple logs, and in what seemed like no time, he'd built a roaring blaze. Serafina sniffled. Francesco sat beside her and pulled her into his arms.

Serafina had curled against Francesco's side. Her head came to a rest on his shoulder, and her body could finally release the last of its tension. His hand moved in slow, soothing circles on her back, while his other hand covered hers where it rested on his chest. In the warm glow, with his strength surrounding her, Serafina felt something she thought she couldn't experience again: peace.

"I'm sorry," she eventually murmured. "I'm sure a distraught woman wasn't what you intended for tonight."

"I planned time with you, without an audience." His thumb traced along her cheekbone. "There's nowhere I'd rather be than here, holding you."

"I feel so safe with you," she whispered. "More than anywhere else. Does that make me crazy? That a man who—" She stopped.

"Who kills people makes you feel safe?" he finished quietly. "Maybe. Or maybe you understand that the world isn't divided into good and evil, and that sometimes the monster is the only one who can protect you from worse monsters."

Serafina shifted slightly against him, tilting her head back to look up at his face. "What started all of this? Why did you ever need someone to act as your girlfriend in the first place?"

Francesco's gaze moved from her face to the flames, and stared off for a moment. "I was involved in an affair with a married woman." He paused, his hand stilling on her back. "Brambilia's wife."

Serafina's eyes widened.

"I needed to convince him that I was devoted to someone else, and that his wife meant nothing to me."

"Why were you..."

"Why? Because before that, there was someone I loved for three years. I was ready to marry her. Then I found out she had a husband the whole time. I swore I'd never consider marriage again. I'd never let anyone have that kind of power over me again."

"Do you think..." she hesitated. "Do you think you'll ever get married now?"

Then his hand moved to cup her face. Their eyes met in the flickering light, and for an intense moment, everything else faded away. "You're mine, Serafina. *Capisci?*"

"*Capisco.* I love you," she whispered, the words escaping before she could stop them. "Even knowing what you are. Especially knowing what you are."

"*Ti amo anch'io,*" he murmured back. His voice dropped lower, rougher. "I mean it. You're mine now, Serafina. Not just tonight, but always. No one else will ever touch you like this. No one."

He leaned in, and their lips met in a kiss that was soft, tentative, and everything she'd been hoping for. He cradled the back of her head as he pulled her closer. His thumb stroked a sensitive spot behind her ear that made her melt. The kiss grew hungrier. All the tension they'd buried, the nights they'd lain awake aching for each other's touch, and all the longing they denied bled out of them.

Without breaking the kiss, Serafina pulled herself up until she straddled his lap. Her arms wrapped around his neck and tugged hard enough to draw a low groan from his throat. She kissed him harder, her tongue dancing with his. Francesco's hands found her waist and pressed her down against the growing hardness in his trousers, making them both gasp into each other's mouths.

One of Serafina's hands clutched his shirt while the other traced the strong line of his jaw. His stubble lightly scraped against her fingertips. Francesco's hand slid beneath the hem of her dress, his palm warm and slightly calloused against the silk on her thigh. Her skin prickled.

His mouth dropped to her neck, beneath her jaw. His teeth lightly scraped her skin She gasped, her fingers tightening in his shirt, her hips rolling involuntarily against him.

"*Mia bellissima Serafina,*" he murmured into her ear. "I dream of you, every night. I dream of touching you, and tasting you, and showing you you're mine."

His hand slipped higher, fingers trailing along her inner thigh. The backs of his fingers brushed the edge of her already damp panties, drawing a shiver that rolled up her spine. She gasped a few times.

"Francesco..."

He paused for a minute, then pulled back just enough to look into her eyes "Do you want this?" His breath was warm on her lips, his voice tender despite the fire burning in his gaze. "Not just tonight, but forever. I want you to be mine until death. Do you understand what that means? What it would cost?"

"Yes," she whispered, her hands framing his face. "I want you, all of you. Despite everything you are, or maybe in spite of it. And I'm yours."

"*Ti amo*," he whispered.

Her heart soared as desire pooled between her legs. She tried to unbutton his shirt. Her fingers trembled enough that she struggled with the top one.

"Damned button," she muttered.

Francesco's laugh was low and warm. "Let me."

He quick took care of them, then pulled his shirt and undershirt both off over his head. Serafina's breath caught. She'd seen him undressed, but not like this, not with the chance to really look at him. Shadowed caused by the firelight defined every muscle by shadow and bronze.

And the scars... so many scars.

Her fingers traced the puckered bullet wound near his shoulder, and the knife marks across his ribs.

"Those should frighten you," he said.

"They're what you've survived." She looked up at him. "So they don't scare me. You're a survivor."

"Then you see me for the life I lead." His hand covered hers, pressing her palm flat against a particularly ugly scar over his heart. "I've killed, Serafina. I've broken bones and done terrible things. I'll touch you with nothing but gentleness, but you need to know what I am."

276

"I know." She leaned forward and pressed her lips to the old bullet wound. "I still want you anyway."

She shrugged her blouse off her shoulders and let it fall, then reached for the zipper at her waist. She stood slowly, her hands trailing down his chest as she rose, and eased the skirt past her hips, watching his eyes follow every movement. The fabric fell to the floor, leaving her in new blue silk lingerie and stockings.

Francesco sharply inhaled. Then he stood too, quickly removing the rest of his clothing with her help. When his trousers hit the floor, she bit her lip at the sight of him. He was large and fully aroused, his foreskin drawn back to reveal the flushed head. Though she'd had him before, the sight made her nervous. He settled on the sheep's wool rug and held his hand up to her.

She looked him over as she sank to her knees beside him. His legs stretched long. The corded muscle of his calves led up to his powerful thighs, dusted with dark hair. His hipbones jutted sharp beneath his skin. His well-defined abdomen led up to the broad span of his chest and shoulders. She glance back down. The thick length of him rested hard against his stomach, already glistening at the tip.

Her mouth parted, tongue darting out to wet her lips as she stared. "Francesco, you're..."

"Yours."

He rolled to his side. His hand slid behind her back, pulling her close until their skin touched everywhere, chest to chest, hip to hip, heartbeat to heartbeat. His mouth found hers again. She melted.

When they broke apart, both breathing hard, Francesco's eyes searched hers in the firelight. "Show me," he whispered, his voice tender. "Show me what you like. What makes you feel good?"

For a moment, she heard his words, but then something in her mind fractured. The thought of her own hand moving lower collided with the memory of cold leather and the click-click of Mr. Kensington's camera, his cruel voice directing her like she was a mechanical doll he was posing. She drew in a panicked breath, and she pulled away from Francesco's warmth as if burned.

"I—" The word died in her throat.

Francesco's expression shifted immediately. He lifted his hands away from her body, seeming to understand. "I'm sorry," he said quickly. "Serafina, I'm sorry. We don't have to—"

"It's nothing." But her voice shook. She forced herself to meet his eyes, to push past the shame. "Could you... could you show me first? What you like?"

Francesco's searched her eyes for a moment. He brought her hand to his chest. "Start here," he whispered, guiding her palm over his heart. He moved her hand across his skin, showing her the places that made him shiver. The sensitive spot at the base of his throat, the hollow of his collarbone, the trail of hair that led down his stomach... Her nerves melted away.

When he finally wrapped her hand around his cock, he pulsed against her palm. He was thick and heavy in her grasp, Her thumb brushed over the tip, slip with his arousal. Francesco groaned deep in his throat. It rumbled through his chest and vibrated against her body where they touched. His head fell back against the rug, fully exposing his throat, and she watched his Adam's apple bob when he swallowed.

"Like this," he rasped. His hand wrapped over hers to tighten her grip almost painfully. He guided her into a slow, twisting motion that made his hips buck off the rug. "Tighter at the base... *Dio*—" His words broke off into a moan as she obeyed.

She experimented with different pressures, different speeds, watching his face with an intensity that bordered on her own possession. She wanted to learn every reaction, every sound, learn exactly how to unmake him. When she swept her thumb over the sensitive head, collecting the moisture there and using it to ease her strokes, his breath hissed between his teeth. When she varied her quick, light touches with firm strokes, his muscles tensed and a flush spread across his chest.

"Tell me," she whispered, her voice darker now, hungrier. "What else do you like? What do you think about when you touch yourself?"

His eyes opened, pupils blown so wide they looked black. "Your mouth," he admitted. "I dream about your mouth on me. About you on your knees, looking up at me while you—" He swallowed hard.

"But not tonight. Tonight I need to be inside you when I come."

Serafina's cheeks burned, but the heat pooling low in her belly was stronger than any shyness. She bit her lip, eyes flicking up to meet his.

"I... I want to," she whispered, the words trembling yet sure. Her fingers traced the rigid length of him. "I want... I want to taste you the way you taste me. Please. Let me have this. Let me have *you*."

His breath hitched, a low, broken sound that made her belly clench and fresh slickness gather between her legs. His cock throbbed against her palm, fierce and alive, and it sent a rush of need through her so intense she had to press her thighs together.

She shifted down his body. Her lips brushed the taut skin of his chest, tongue darting out to taste the salt of his skin. She traced the ridges of his abdomen. The muscles jumped and flexed.

When she settled between his thighs, she looked up again, her eyes wide, darkened with want. Her tongue darted out, wetting her lips, and she saw the exact moment his control began to fray. His jaw clenched. His hands fisted in the rug like he was trying to steady himself.

"Serafina... *Tesora*, you don't have to—"

She didn't wait any longer. She leaned in, breath ghosting hot over the flushed, weeping head, and then her mouth closed around him.

"*Ah—cazzo—*" The Italian curse punched out of him.

The musky salt taste of him flooded her senses and she moaned low in her throat, the vibration traveling through his shaft. He jerked against her tongue. His hips rose before he forced them back down with what looked like monumental effort. His thighs trembled beneath her palms.

She took him deeper, cheeks hollowing, and watched him, eyes locked on his face, drinking in every twitch of his jaw, and every shudder that rolled through his big frame. The tendons in his neck stood out. His chest heaved. He looked like he was losing himself, and the power of reducing this experienced, controlled man to trembling need sent a fresh rush of arousal through her.

Her hand wrapped around what her mouth couldn't, and God,

there was so *much* of him, thick and hot and pulsing in her grip. She stroked in time with the slide of her lips, twisting slightly at the base. She traced the thick vein underneath with the flat of her tongue. His whole body shuddered. "*Mmm,*" she hummed, feeling him swell impossibly harder.

"*Cristo,* Sera—" Suddenly his fingers were tangling in her hair. "*Amore mia,* you're *perfetta,* you're perfect, I can't—"

His breathing had gone ragged. His cock twitched and leaked some of that sweet saltiness onto her tongue. She took him deeper still, relaxing her throat. Her eyes watered slightly but she didn't care. She was too focused on the stretched-full feeling of him in her mouth, the obscene wet sounds filling the room, and his abs flexing and rippling above her.

"Nnh—no, *bella,* stop—" His voice cracked. "*Fermati,* you have to—"

His hands tightened in her hair pulling her gently, almost frantically up. His cock slipped from her mouth with an obscenely wet *pop,* glistening with her saliva, flushed dark and twitching wildly in the cool air between them. A string of saliva still connected her bottom lip to the swollen head, and she watched it break as he pulled her higher.

She made a sound of protest in the back of her throat, reaching for him, wanting him back in her mouth, wanting to finish what she'd started. But he was already moving, sitting up and hauling her into his lap.

"Then touch me?" Her words barely made it past her lips. Her hand trembled as she brought his palm to her breast, the heat of his skin burning through the thin silk of her brassiere.

Francesco let her guide him. He cupped her breast exactly how she positioned it, and when she tugged the silk aside to expose her nipple, already peaked and aching, her fingers covered Francesco's, showing him the circling motion that made her breath catch. When he repeated it without her guiding him, desperation unfurled low in her belly.

280

"Like this, *bellissima?*" He alternated between gentle teasing and firmer pressure, watching her face with the same intensity she'd watched him. "Or this?"

She gasped, then his mouth replaced his fingers. Her breaths quickened. With shaking hands, she guided his other hand down her body, over her waist to the curve of her hip. She glanced at him, at the man who'd killed for her.

When she slipped his hand beneath the silk of her panties, between her thighs where she was already slick and swollen, a whimper escaped her that she couldn't control.

"*Cristo.*" His curse was nearly inaudible. She covered his hand with hers, guiding him to part her folds.

"Here." She placed his fingertip against her clit. Electricity shot through her entire body. "Gentle circles, like—*oh—*"

Her eyes closed. Her toes curled.

"*Più,*" she gasped. *More.* The Italian slipped out without thought. "More, Francesco, please—"

He added another finger. She stretched to accommodate him. His thumb continued those maddening circles against her clit. Then his control slipped, just for a heartbeat, and his fingers curled roughly inside of her, hitting some spot even she didn't know existed.

Stars exploded behind her eyes. She choked out a groan.

"*Cazzo.* Did I hurt you?"

"No." She could barely form words. "Don't stop. Please, God, don't stop. I need you. Please, Francesco. I need you inside of me."

When he pulled back, his hand lingered on her cheek. His other hand traced the fading bruises on her wrist. His jaw clenched. Murder flashed through his eyes.

"He'll suffer for every mark he left on you," he said quietly.

Dark satisfaction curled hot and vicious in her belly. "Good."

Francesco's gaze held hers for a long moment. His expression softened at the edges while somehow growing more intense.

"Are you certain about this?" Francesco's voice gentled, but still had a possessive edge. "This isn't like before. Once we do this tonight, you're mine. *Completamente*. Forever. No matter what happens tomorrow or the next day or any day after. You'll always be mine. Do you understand?"

"I've never been more sure of anything." She pressed the words against his lips.

He kissed her once more, soft and sweet, then his fingers found the thin blue straps of her brassiere. He slid them down her arms slowly, then kissed her shoulder as she arched so he could reach the hooks and bare her breasts to the firelight.

His breath deepened. He lowered his head and kissed between her breasts, his mouth warm and soft, then let his lips find one hard nipple while his hand cupped the other. His fingers stroked the soft underside, thumb circling the tip until she was squirming beneath him, making desperate little sounds she'd never made before.

Her spine curved, pressing herself more firmly into his mouth, and his hand slid down her ribs, over her belly, hooking at the waistband of her panties. She lifted her hips. He dragged them down.

One stocking had slipped, the garter loose at the top, and he paused to look at her with her legs spread, silk stockings still clinging to her thighs, completely exposed.

When she moved to remove them, he caught her wrist.

"Let me."

Then he unclasped each garter, rolling the stockings down inch by inch. He took his time, kissing every bit of skin he uncovered. The inside of her knee, her ankle, the arch of her foot...

His hand trailed back up her inner thigh, leaving goosebumps in its wake, until he reached the wet heat between her legs. His fingers parted her again and She whimpered, already so sensitive she could barely stand it.

"I need..." she breathed, her hips moving restlessly against his hand. "I need all of you."

He shifted over her, covering her body with his. Her legs fell apart. Her hips lifted.

He shifted over me, covering her body with his. The weight of him, the heat, the hard length of his cock pressing against her thigh—it was overwhelmingly perfect.

282

Her legs fell open, her hips lifting instinctively. She reached for his shoulders.

"*Guardami,*" Francesco commanded, voice low and rough.

She did, eyes wide and trusting, trained on his, her lips parting as she inhaled deeply. He positioned himself at her entrance and she could feel him there, thick and hard and ready.

"*Ti amo,*" he whispered, eyes locked on her as he pushed inside.

She let out a soft cry at the exquisite stretch. Her eyes fluttered, but stayed locked on his, letting him see everything she felt. Her hands gripped his arms, nails pressing into his skin as he moved, inch by inch, until the full length of him was inside her, stretching her open, filling every place she'd ever felt empty.

This. *This* was what it should be. Not Mr. Kensington's brutal taking, not being held down and used, but *this.*

When he was fully inside her, he stayed still, buried to the hilt, and for a breathless moment they lost themselves in each other. His guard was gone. His carefully constructed walls he kept between himself and the world had crumbled. She saw everything in his dark eyes: the violence he was capable of, the tenderness he showed only to her, the possessive need that would never let her go, and beneath it all, something raw and almost frightened. Love, but the dangerous kind, the kind that destroyed as easily as it protected.

A tear slipped from the corner of her eye, trailing down her temple.

His thumb caught the tear. "Why are you crying, *amore?*"

"Because I get to be yours," she whispered. "Completely and utterly yours."

Her legs came up around his hips, ankles locking at the small of his back. "Please?."

He kissed her cheek, her jaw, the corner of her mouth, then began to move—slowly at first, a gentle roll of his hips that made her breath catch. He withdrew almost entirely before filling her again, and she whimpered at the loss, at the return. His lips found her throat, the hollow beneath her ear where her pulse hammered wild.

Almost at once, something seemed to break something loose inside him. His pace increased. Serafina met him instinctively, her body finding the rhythm of his. Her fingers traced the ridges of his spine, the flex and tension of muscle beneath sweat-slicked skin. Her heart swelled impossibly full, so full she thought it might burst. This had to be a dream. This man, this moment, this love was somehow surviving things that should have destroyed it.

"More," she gasped against his mouth. Her nails dug into his shoulders as he drove deeper, and she arched beneath him. "Harder. I need—"

He groaned and complied, driving into her with more force, the sound of their joining filling the room along with their breathless moans. His control was slipping. His movements grew erratic.

"You have no idea what you do to me," he growled against her throat, his hips snapping harder. The civilized mob boss facade cracked, showing her the real violent, possessive man beneath. "How much I want you. How much I need you. Mine, Serafina. You're *mine*." His teeth grazed her pulse point.

His hands caught her wrists and wrenched them above her head, pinning them to the rug with one hand while he thrusted harder into her. "Say it. Tell me who you belong to."

"You," she gasped, helpless beneath him, loving the weight of his control. "Only you."

"You," she gasped, helpless beneath him, loving his control over her. The image flashed through her mind, of Francesco tying her wrists, spreading and tying her legs apart, keeping her open, taking his time... She wanted things with him she'd never imagined she coul want after... Yet she did, with him. "Only you, Francesco."

He kissed her again, slow and tender despite the brutal pace of his hips. As his thrusts quickened, waves of heat surge through Serafina's body, each movement increasing in intensity. Pulses of pleasure radiated from her core, tightening her muscles around him, drawing him further in. A fluttering sensation danced in her stomach, escalating with every powerful push. Her skin tingled, heightened by urgency in his kisses.

Francesco's rhythm sent electric shocks through her. She needed release. Each thrust sent her spiraling closer, closer, a crescendo of sensation building within her. Tears spill from her eyes from the overwhelming connection.

"Please... I'm so close," she whispered.

"*Aspetta.*" Wait. "*Aspettami.*"

She managed a nod, vision swimming, drunk on the stretch of him inside her. He shifted, hips angling deeper, and his fingers slipped between their joined bodies to find her swollen clit.

The first touch against that bundle of nerves punched a gasp from her lungs. Her spine went rigid. A whimper tore from her throat while his fingers worked her clit in maddening circles. Pleasure built like a storm surge within her.

Her heels dug into the rug. Her thighs quivered against his hips, trembling with the effort of holding back the tidal wave threatening to crash through her. The pressure coiled tighter, tighter, a spring compressed past its limit. Her back arched until only her shoulder blades pressed the floor, her body a drawn bow.

"Now." His lips brushed her ear, and his fingers pressed firmer, circling faster. "Come for me."

The spring snapped.

Her body bowed up into his, every muscle locking in a seizure of pure sensation. The climax ripped through her like white-hot lightning. She clamped down on his cock in rhythmic pulses she couldn't control, each contraction wringing a sharp cry from her throat. Her cries came out broken, raw, soaked in love and lust and surrender.

Above her, Francesco groaned from deep in his chest. His hips snapped forward, driving deep, and his whole body went rigid. She could feel him pulsing inside her, and the tremor that wracked through him as his release poured into her.

His arms shook where they her head. Another shudder rolled through him, his hips jerking in short, desperate thrusts as the last waves of his orgasm crashed through him.

Aftershocks rippled through her core, little earthquakes triggered by each twitch of his cock. Her hands smoothed up his sweat-slicked back, palms mapping the rigid tension of muscles still locked tight, the racing thump of his heartbeat against her breasts.

For a minute, there was only the sound of their harsh breathing and the fire crackling, their hearts gradually slowing from their frantic pace. Francesco collapsed beside her, gathering her against his chest. Serafina curled into him.

"*Anch'io ti amo,*" she whispered. "I love you so much it frightens me."

His arms tightened around her until she could barely breathe, and somehow even that felt right. "Good," he murmured into her hair, his voice dark and possessive. "You should be frightened. I would do terrible things to keep you. Already have."

His fingers drew slow patterns along the curve of her hip. She pressed closer to the warmth of his body, knowing she was addicted now, that she'd never be able to walk away even if she wanted to.

She tilted her face up to look at him. "This is the happiest I've ever been."

He kissed her forehead, the tip of her nose, then her lips. "You're mine now, Serafina. Forever. There's no going back from this."

"I don't want to go back."

The firelight continued to dance in the hearth. Wrapped in each other's arms, she had his love, and he had hers. A love built on blood and secrets, on protection and possession, on the kind of devotion that would burn anyone who tried to come between them.

And love, like fire, warms what it touches, but in the shadows outside The Dakota, someone waited for her with months of patient planning, knowing that all flames must eventually burn out.

CHAPTER 18

Serafina woke to soft knocking on her door. Her body ached in the most wonderful way, but she didn't mind, not when it was Francesco's hands and his mouth and the rest of his body that caused so much pleasure. Her heart felt lighter than it had in weeks.

"Come in," she called softly, sitting up and wrapping her bed jacket around herself.

Clara slipped inside, still in her dressing gown. "Thank God. I was so worried that something had happened, and you wouldn't be here, and you look exhausted."

"I'm fine." Serafina couldn't stop the smile that spread across her face. "I'm better than fine."

Clara's eyes narrowed. Then they went wide. "What happened last night?"

Serafina cheeks hate. She looked down at her hands, still smiling like a fool. "Well... um..."

"Oh my God." Clara crossed the room and sat on the edge of the bed. "Did you and he—" She stopped, unable to say it explicitly, her voice dropping to a whisper. "Did you?"

Serafina nodded, biting her lip.

Clara's mouth fell open. Then she let out a soft breath, reaching for Serafina's hands. "Was he... was he good to you? Did he hurt you?"

"It was perfect," Serafina whispered, her eyes shining. "Clara, it was so different from— He was gentle and patient. And he made me feel..." She struggled for words.

Clara's shoulders relaxed. "Irving and I... we haven't been able to wait." The admission came out quietly, her face turning slightly pink. "I know it's wrong, and that we should wait until we're married, but he's so gentle and patient, and I love him so much already."

Serafina squeezed her hand. "It's like that for me too, with Francesco."

"But you care for him?"

"More than I should."

Clara's expression turned more serious. "We both need to be careful, Sera. Neither of us can afford to get pregnant before we're married. I have a diaphragm. I got one months ago. But we should get you one too."

Serafina brows knit together. "Where would I...?"

"I have a doctor. No, not Irving. She's someone discreet. Her name is Dr. Brennan. I'm sure she can fit you for one this afternoon." Clara squeezed her hand. "We can go together. I'll tell her you need to be safe."

"Thank you," Serafina whispered. "I don't know what I'd do without you."

"You'd be considerably worse off, for one thing." Clara stood, smoothing her dressing gown. "Get dressed. We'll go to the bookshop first, check on Mr. Thompson, then to Dr. Brennan's office."

The Purrfect Tale looked smaller than usual when they arrived in Clara's Rolls Royce mid-morning. The "Closed" sign still hung in the window, but Serafina saw movement inside. She tried the door. It opened.

Mr. Thompson stood behind the counter surrounded by stacks of books, his face drawn and tired. He glanced up when they entered, forcing a smile that didn't reach his eyes.

"Serafina. Miss Randolph. I wasn't expecting visitors today."

"When will you call me 'Clara'?" Clara asked gently. "We wanted to check on you. How are you managing?"

"As well as can be expected." He gestured at the books. "Pulling everything that isn't Kensington inventory. Cutting down to only what he owns." His voice cracked slightly on the last word. "At least I'll have more room once it's done."

"Mr. Thompson, please don't lose heart," Serafina said, stepping closer, certain things would improve as Francesco had promised. "Things will get better. I'm sure of it."

He studied her for a long moment. "You sound very certain of that."

She offered a small smile. "I just have faith."

Mr. Thompson nodded slowly, though he didn't look entirely convinced. "Well. Faith is something, I suppose." He turned back to his books with a sigh. "Thank you for stopping by, girls."

Outside, they walked down the street toward where Clara's driver had parked the Rolls Royce. They'd only gone a few steps when they nearly collided with Danny, who was locking up his flower shop early. He turned at the sound of their voices, his eyes brightening when he saw Serafina before quickly replacing it with concern.

"Serafina." He sounded cautious. "I haven't seen you all week."

"I've been... busy."

"I can see that." He looked her over from head to toe and back again. "Miss Bradley and I are going to dinner tonight. She's a sweet girl. Uncomplicated."

Serafina felt her throat tighten. "I'm happy for you, Danny. She's lucky, and so are you."

"Am I lucky?" He took a step closer, his voice dropping. "Or am I the fool who's settling for second best because the woman I actually care about has thrown herself at a monster?"

"Danny—"

"It's Romano, isn't it?"

Serafina's blood turned to ice, but she didn't deny it. Couldn't, really, not when Danny was looking at her with hurt in his eyes, and he deserved to know the truth.

Clara shifted beside her but said nothing.

"You've been such a good friend," Serafina said quietly, reaching out to touch his arm. "I'm sorry I couldn't give you what you wanted. But I hope things work out with Miss Bradley. You deserve to be happy."

Danny's expression softened, though pain still lingered in his eyes. "And what about you, Serafina? Do you deserve to be happy? Or do you deserve whatever it is that man is going to do to you?"

"I know what I'm doing."

"Do you?" Danny's jaw tightened. "I've heard things about what he does to people who get in his way, and I've seen the way he looks at you." His voice remained gentle, but there was hardness underneath. "Men like him don't love. They own people before they destroy them. And when they're done, there's nothing left."

The words should have frightened her. And part of her knew they were true. Francesco Romano was dangerous in ways that went beyond the violence he inflicted on others. He was dangerous to her heart, her soul, even her sense of who she was.

But she'd already given herself to him and loved him. She let him promise to protect her.

"I appreciate your concern," she said quietly. "Truly. But my choices are my own."

But after a moment, Danny simply shook his head. "I hope you're right, Serafina. I really do." He glanced down the street. "I should go. Miss Bradley is meeting me at the restaurant at six, and I still need to pick up the flowers I'm bringing her."

"From your own shop?" Clara asked, trying to lighten the mood. "The shop you just locked up?"

"Where else?" A ghost of Danny's usual smile appeared. "The florist business treats me well enough. Better than most people think, anyway."

He gestured toward an extraordinarily expensive automobile

parked just beyond where they stood. A gleaming black Packard with chrome fixtures that caught the afternoon sun.

"That's yours?" Clara couldn't hide her surprise.

Danny shrugged, almost defensive. "High society pays well for the right arrangements. Weddings, balls, and funerals are my bread and butter. Mrs. Vanderbilt alone spends more on flowers in a month than most men make in a year. The right connections make all the difference."

Something about his tone struck Serafina as odd, but before she could prod, Danny had walked toward his automobile.

He paused with his hand on the door handle and turned back. "The shop closes for good on Sunday. Kensington's buying my shop, too. Guess he wants the whole block." His voice carried bitterness. "Good luck with everything, Serafina. You're going to need it."

Then he climbed into his Packard and drove away, leaving Serafina standing on the sidewalk with an uncomfortable knot forming in her stomach despite her earlier confidence.

Clara's Rolls Royce waited another twenty feet down the street, her driver standing beside it. Clara squeezed Serafina's shoulder. "Come on. We still need to get to Dr. Brennan's office."

When Serafina and Clara returned to the Randolph estate in the late afternoon, George's automobile was already parked in the drive. Voices drifted from Mr. Randolph's study, his own and his son's.

Clara started toward the parlor, but Serafina was drawn toward those voices. Something in George's tone made her pause in the hallway.

"Sera?" Clara whispered. "What are you doing?"

"Shh." Serafina pressed closer to the study door, which stood slightly ajar. Clara hesitated, then joined her.

"—moving money through shell companies for years," George was saying. "Hiding assets, payments to city officials, judges, police captains... This is bigger than simple extortion. Kensington's been bribing public servants across the city."

There was a rustle of papers. "Where did you get these documents?"

"A clerk at the county recorder's office. They're authentic. I've verified the signatures, cross-referenced the dates."

"If this is all true, Kensington could face serious criminal charges. Racketeering, bribery, conspiracy..."

"He could go to prison," George said. "For a long time. It'll take time to build properly, We'll need affidavits, corroborating evidence, expert testimony on the financial transactions..."

Serafina's heart pounded.

"But by George, George, this is solid work. We have enough to start. How long?"

"Two, maybe three weeks to file. Then the investigation, the trial... it could be months before he's actually behind bars."

Serafina's heart dropped. Weeks. Months. And in all that time, those photographs would hang over her head like a guillotine.

"There's something else, though," George said, his voice dropping. "One of these shell companies—Consolidated Maritime Holdings—has been moving significant amounts through your bank."

Silence. Then: "My bank?"

"Yes. I didn't think you knew. The transactions are buried deep, routed through multiple accounts. But if I prosecute this case, if I bring charges against Kensington, all of this will come to light. The public will know that Randolph National has been facilitating some of these transfers."

"We didn't know—"

"I know that. But it doesn't matter. The press will have a field day. 'Prosecutor's Dad's Bank Implicated in Corruption Scandal.' Even if the bank did nothing wrong, even if you had no knowledge of what Kensington was doing, the association alone could be devastating."

Another long silence.

"What are you saying, George?"

"I'm saying that if I move forward with this prosecution, it could destroy your bank's reputation, our family name, and everything you've built. Mom's standing in society, Clara's engagement—you know how Dr. Curtis's family is about scandal."

Serafina's stomach twisted. She pressed closer to the door.

"But if I don't prosecute," George continued, "Kensington walks free. He continues to hurt people like Serafina and Mr. Thompson. He keeps destroying lives. And I become complicit in that."

"George..." Mr. Randolph's voice was heavy. "This is an impossible position."

"I know. But Dad, I didn't become a prosecutor to protect my family's reputation. I did it to seek justice. And if that means our name suffers, then perhaps that's the price we pay for letting men like Kensington operate unchecked for so long."

Serafina pulled back from the door, her stomach churning. Clara stared at her, face pale.

They walked quietly down the hall, not speaking until they reached the garden.

"Did you hear that?" Clara whispered. "If George prosecutes Mr. Kensington, it could ruin Dad's bank and our family."

Serafina wrapped her arms around herself. The afternoon sun felt cold suddenly.

"But that's not your fault," Clara continued. "None of this is your fault, Sera. Mr. Kensington did this. Not you."

But it felt like her fault. Even if George went forward, it would take weeks to file the charges. Months for a trial. And if—no, when—Mr. Kensington realized what was happening, he would strike first. He'd release those photos to destroy her credibility, to humiliate her, and to punish everyone who'd tried to help her.

She imagined George's face when he saw them. Mr. Randolph's disappointment. Clara's horror. Irving looking at Clara differently, knowing her best friend was...

No. She couldn't let that happen.

Francesco's way would be different. It would be quiet and swift. Whatever he did to Richard Kensington, it wouldn't involve courts or evidence or public trials. The photographs would disappear along with their owner. No one would ever have to know what she'd endured. Mr. Thompson's shop would be safe. The Randolphs would be spared both the scandal of the photographs and the scandal of their bank's unwitting involvement.

And she...

She would have to live with knowing she'd chosen violence over justice, and that she'd let Francesco Romano handle her problems the way he handled all his problems—with methods she didn't want to think about too much.

...Men like him don't love. They own people before they destroy them.

But Francesco had been gentle with her last night, and so tender. He'd made her feel safe and wanted. Was that owning her? Or was it love?

Did it matter?

She pressed her hands against the cold stone balustrade. The truth was, she'd already made her own choice, last night, when she'd given herself to Francesco and let him promise to protect her. She'd fallen in love with a man who solved problems with violence.

This was just the consequence of that choice.

"Sera?" Clara said softly. "What are you thinking?"

Serafina turned to her friend, forcing a smile. "I'm thinking that your family has done so much for me already. And I won't let you sacrifice everything because of my problems."

"That's not—"

"Clara." Serafina took her hands. "Whatever happens with Mr. Kensington, it won't touch your family. I promise you that."

Clara narrowed her eyes. "How can you promise that?"

Serafina just squeezed Clara's hands and looked out at the garden, at the careful order of it all, knowing that Francesco Romano was probably already moving to act and handling things the only way he knew how.

She'd chosen his protection. And she would have to live with what that meant. Another consequence.

She's have to let George agonize over whether to prosecute and let Mr. Randolph worry about his bank's reputation. It wouldn't matter in the end. By the time they were ready to act, Francesco would have already solved the problem, and no one would ever know what she'd chosen.

Standing there in the fading afternoon sun, with the memory of Francesco's touch still alive on her skin and Danny's warning still echoing in her mind, Serafina found she could live with it.

Whatever Francesco was planning, she hoped he did it soon.

He glanced at the book on her nightstand. *Wuthering Heights.* He'd moved the bookmark last night, to the page where Heathcliff talks about wanting to absorb Catherine into himself and make her part of his flesh. But he knew she wouldn't see it. He knew she was out with Romano. He crossed to her dresser, silent as a phantom. His fingers trailed over the surface to her hairbrush. He'd counted the strands caught in its bristles. Twenty-three. He wrapped them carefully in tissue paper to add to his collection.

His gaze moved to the bed.

There she was. Serafina. *His* Serafina, even if she didn't know it yet.

She lay on her side, one hand tucked under the pillow, her hair spilling across the white linen like gold. She looked every bit the angel that her name meant. Her new nightgown had ridden up slightly, exposing the curve of her calf and the delicate delicate arch of her foot.

He moved closer, each step careful. He knew which ones creaked. The week she'd been here on its own hadn't been long enough for him to learn, but he'd first had his eye on Clara, and he practiced coming in through this room. Then Serafina caught his eye. She saved Clara's life without knowing it.

Standing over Serafina now, he watched the vulnerable curve of her neck. His fingers ached to press against her pulse and to feel her heart rate spike with fear and confusion. Her lips were slightly parted in sleep, and he wondered what she was dreaming about. The first night be came here, he'd whispered to her while she slept, letting his voice become part of her dreams.

You're mine, he'd told her, his mouth so close to her ear that his lips nearly brushed her skin. *You've always been mine. You just don't accept it yet.*

But tonight was different. Tonight, rehearsal ended. Tonight, Serafina slept, unaware that her last moments of ignorant peace were ticking away.

But first, he had to make sure the escape route was clear. He moved through the darkened halls, making sure the quiet floorboards were still quiet. He cracked open the door to the servants' stairs and left it ajar just enough. Thank God the hinges were always oiled. They never made noise. Then to the side entrance near the kitchen. The lock clicked softly as he turned it. He eased the door open half an inch, just enough that he could push through it quickly when the time came.

Back through the halls, up the main staircase this time. Everything would be perfect. No delays, no obstacles, no chance for her to scream and wake the house. He'd have perhaps three minutes from the moment he applied the chloroform until he was clear of the property. That meant a scant three minutes to carry her unconscious body down two flights of stairs, through the prepared doors, and across the garden to where his car waited three blocks away.

At her door, he paused, hand on the knob. This was the moment. Eight months of preparation distilled into this single action. Once he crossed this threshold, everything would change.

His heart hammered against his ribs, but his hands were steady. He pushed the door open and stepped back inside.

She was still sleeping, exactly as he'd left her. Perfect.

He reached into his pocket and pulled out the cloth and the small bottle. The chloroform had cost him a small fortune. Obtaining it had required careful planning to acquire without arousing suspicion. But it was worth it, and overall, it was pocket change. No one knew who he was or what he did a few times a year at the races.

He soaked the cloth carefully, the sweet hay smell filling his nostrils even through his shallow breathing. Too much and he could kill her without meaning to. Too little and she'd wake during transport. He'd practiced the dosage on random whores no one would ever miss. He'd calculated weight and lung capacity, and tested until he'd determine the optimal amount to keep her under without ending her life.

Padding to the bedside, he looked down at her one last time as she was now. Such a sweet, unaware angel, still believing herself safe in the Randolph house, still believing Romano could ever care.

You're mine, he thought. *Finally, completely, mine.*

In one smooth motion, he pressed the cloth over her mouth and nose.

Serafina eyes flew open instantly, wide with shock and confusion. Her hands came up, grabbing at his wrist, her body bucking. He pressed down harder, using a leg to pin her down, keeping the cloth sealed against her face even as she thrashed beneath him.

He leaned close, his mouth near her ear. "Shh. Don't fight it. This is meant to be. Just breathe deep now."

She tried to scream against the cloth. Her nails dug into his skin through the glove, and for a moment her strength surprised him. But the chemical was already working. He could feel the moment her struggles began to weaken and her movements became sluggish.

Her eyes were still open, still terrified, staring up at him as consciousness slipped away and her lashes fluttered to her cheeks. He watched every second of it.

"There," he whispered as her eyes finally fluttered closed. "That's my good girl."

He kept the cloth pressed for another thirty seconds, counting in his head, making sure she was fully under. When he finally pulled it away, her breathing was shallow but steady.

Working quickly now, he wrapped her in the blanket from her bed to contain any involuntary movements she might make. She was small enough that he could manage her weight easily, but she could always lash out and make noise in her sleep.

He lifted her, cradling her against his chest. Her head lolled against his shoulder. He pressed his face briefly into her hair, inhaling deeply. Finally his.

The escape went exactly as he'd practiced. Through her door, down the hallway, careful to keep her head from hitting the doorframe. Down the servants' stairs, through the door already open, through the kitchen, past the side entrance he'd unlocked, out into the garden.

He carried her around to the garden gate that he'd oiled three weeks ago. Through the gate, across the neighboring property's lawn, and finally to the street where his car waited.

By the time anyone discovered her missing tomorrow morning, he'd be long gone. *They'd* be long gone.

Serafina stirred slightly as he settled her on the back seat. He loosely draped the cloth over her face to make sure she didn't wake. He arranged her carefully, positioning her body so she wouldn't slide. Then he allowed himself one moment, just one, to cup her face in his hand.

"Shouldn't have said no, Serafina," he whispered. "Shouldn't have said no."

He closed the door and moved to the driver's side. As he started the engine and pulled away from the curb, he couldn't stop the smile that spread across his face.

Eight months of watching. Eight months of waiting. Eight months of patience.

And now, she was his. It had all paid off. All of it. All.

Romano would rage when he discovered the theft. He'd probably tear the city apart looking for her, promising all the violence and revenge and all the impotent fury of a man who'd lost what never belonged to him in the first place.

But it wouldn't matter because Serafina was already gone, in transit to the secret place he'd prepared for her.

The city lights blurred past as he drove, and in the passenger seat, Serafina slept on, unaware that her life as she knew it had just ended, and the life she was always meant to live was about to begin.

It was like swimming up from the bottom of a deep, dark pool. Serafina's head throbbed with each heartbeat. Her mouth tasted of something metallic, like licking copper pennies. The surface beneath her was cold and unforgiving. Cold stone, not the soft, warm mattress.

For a moment, she couldn't move. Her limbs had become both heavy and disconnected from her body, as if she were still half-submerged in whatever darkness she had just come from. Her thoughts moved sluggishly, trying to piece together fragments that didn't quite fit.

She'd been in bed, at the Randolph house. She'd been sleeping, dreaming about—

Eyes above her in the darkness. A cloth pressed over her mouth and nose. The sharp, overwhelming smell. Panic flooding through her as she'd tried to scream, tried to fight, her hands clawing at wrists she couldn't see properly in the dark, and then... nothing but a void where time should have been.

Serafina's eyes flew open.

Nothing but more darkness. She blinked hard, trying to force her vision to adjust, but there was only an oppressive blackness. She took a deep breath. The air smelled damp and stale, with an underlying scent of soil and mildew.

She tried to sit up, then immediately regretted it. The world tilted violently. Nausea churned. She fell back against the stone, gasping, her heart hammering so hard she could feel it in her temples.

Breathe. Just breathe.

But breathing was difficult when panic was closing her throat, when her mind was screaming questions she couldn't answer. Where was she? How long had she been unconscious? Who had taken her?

She forced herself to focus her physical sensations. The stone beneath her was rough, unfinished. Cold seeped through the thin fabric of her nightgown that she still wore. Her feet were bare. She could feel the cold stone against her soles when she tried to move them. The damp mildew smell. But nothing to see. Nothing to hear. She could still taste copper.

Moving slower this time, she managed to sit up and reached out with trembling hands, feeling all around her. More stone. A wall, perhaps three feet to her right. She turned, extending her other hand. Another wall on the left. Behind her, more stone, this one damp to the touch. She crawled forward. *Bars.*

The realization that she was in a cell sent a fresh wave of terror through her. She scrambled back, then turned herself around and inched forward on her hands and knees, ignoring the rough stone scraping her palms and tops of her feet. Her fingers wrapped back around icy cold iron, pulling herself up to standing on legs that shook so badly she nearly fell.

"Hello?" Her voice came out as a croak. "Is anyone there?"

Silence, not even an echo. The darkness seemed to absorb sound. Wherever she was felt both vast and suffocatingly small.

She shook the bars, but they didn't budge. How long had someone been planning this? How long had she been watched? Studied? Targeted? Why her?

Francesco. The thought came suddenly. Francesco would find her. He'd promised to protect her. He'd—

But Francesco didn't know where she was. No one did. She'd been taken from the Randolph house in the middle of the night. By the time anyone realized she was missing, she could be anywhere. Miles away. States away, even. Buried so deep that—

No! She couldn't think like that. She couldn't let panic take over.

Serafina sank down, still gripping the bars, her forehead pressed against the metal. She needed to think, needed to remember everything she could about what had happened. The more information she had, the better chance she had of... of what? Escaping? Surviving? Understanding who had done this and why?

The face. She'd seen a face above her, just for a moment before the cloth covered her mouth. But it had been dark, and her eyes had been blurry with sleep and then with tears as she'd struggled. She couldn't remember features, couldn't conjure the image clearly enough to—

Wait.

The voice. He'd spoken to her. What had he said?

"Shh. Don't fight it. This is meant to be. Just breathe deep now."

That voice had been low and intimate, almost tender, as if he were comforting a child rather than kidnapping her, as if this was somehow an act of love.

Her stomach heaved, and she turned toward from the bars just in time to violently vomit through them. Nothing came up nothing but bile. When it finally subsided, she shook so hard her teeth chattered.

She wiped her mouth with the back of her hand and crawled away from the mess, back toward what she thought might be a corner. The cold stone wall pressed against her back. She pulled her knees up to her chest, wrapped her arms around them, and tried to make herself as small as possible.

This can't be happening. This can't be real.

She was supposed to be safe at the Randolph house. She was supposed to see Francesco tomorrow. Today? How long had she been unconscious? Hours? A day? More?

The darkness made it impossible to tell. There was no way to mark time, no way to know if it was day or night, if she'd been here for hours or days. The disorientation was almost worse

The sound of faint, distant footsteps cut through the silence. Serafina's head snapped up, her heart suddenly racing so fast she felt lightheaded though she hadn't risen from the ground. The footsteps grew closer.

Then light spilled through a doorway. She squinted and shielded her face. The faint illumination hurt her eyes after so long in complete darkness.

"You're awake. Good. I was beginning to worry I'd used too much chloroform. I'd hate to have damaged you."

Serafina's eyes were still adjusting. She could make out a silhouette in the doorway. Just a shape.

"Who are you?" Her voice came out steadier than she felt. "What do you want?"

The man chuckled. "What do I want? Serafina, I want what's always been mine. I want you to finally understand what you are and who you belong to."

"I don't belong to anyone I don't want to belong to!" she snapped.

"Oh, but you do." He moved slightly, still silhouetted against the light from beyond. "You always have. You just forgot. But that's all right. I'm going to help you remember."

"You're insane."

He laughed again. "Insane? No, Serafina. I'm the only sane one in this entire situation. They're the ones who've been lying to you, misleading you, trying to take what isn't theirs. Your Mr. Kensington with his threats, and your precious Francesco Romano with his *protection.*" The last word dripped with contempt. "They're the insane ones, thinking they could have you when you were always meant for me."

"How long have you been watching me?"

"Watching?" The silhouette shifted. "Oh, Serafina. I haven't just been watching. I've been with you outside your apartment, in your room at the Randolphs', standing over your bed. I've touched your things, learned your routines, become part of your life. You just didn't know it yet."

The easy admission of invading her privacy, the nights she'd slept thinking herself safe while he'd been there, touching her things, standing over her... it was too much. Too much! Serafina pressed herself harder against the wall, trying to disappear into the stone.

"You're afraid." The voice sounded pleased. "Good. Fear is honest and real. It's better than all those pretty lies everyone's been telling you. You thought Romano could keep you safe?" The voice paused. "He couldn't, because I'm the threat he doesn't know exists. He can't protect you from because he doesn't even know he should be looking."

"He'll find me." Serafina forced herself to say. "Francesco will find me, and when he does—"

"When he does what?" The voice turned cold and hard. "When he does, I'll be long gone. And you'll be here, or somewhere else, or nowhere at all. Do you understand, Serafina? Do you? You breathe because I allow it. You breathe because I permit it. Everything about your life right now is my choice." The silhouette leaned closer to the bars. "Romano is nothing. He's a child playing at being dangerous. I'm the real thing."

Then he stepped closer and crouched down near the bars, and the light from behind finally caught his features.

Serafina's breath stopped.

The recognition that slammed into her was so shocking, so impossible, that for a moment she couldn't process it. Couldn't breathe. Couldn't think.

"No," she whispered. "You? Why?"

"Hello, Serafina." His expression turned gentle and tender. "Would you like some coffee, now?"

CHAPTER 19

Clara knocked on Serafina's door the next morning, her knuckles rapping lightly at first, then more insistently. It wasn't like Serafina to sleep so late.

"Serafina, darling, are you awake?"

There was only silence.

Clara frowned and knocked again, harder this time.

"Serafina?"

Still no response.

Clara turned the handle. Taking a shaky breath, she slowly pushed the door open.

The room was in disarray. Serafina's bed was empty. The sheet and a blanket lay strewn across the floor. Clara's heart skipped a beat. Maybe... maybe Serafina had left early? But something just felt wrong. She quickly made her way downstairs.

She approached the first maid she saw. "Have you seen Serafina this morning?" Clara asked, trying to keep her voice calm.

The maid shook her head. "No, Miss Clara, I haven't seen her at all."

Clara's anxiety spiked. She asked several other staff members, but none had seen Serafina. Then she heard the gardener's voice at the back door, speaking urgently to one of the cooks.

"What's going on?" Clara asked, her voice tight with worry.

The gardener looked at her. "I need to speak to Mr. Randolph immediately."

"Why? What's happened?"

"There's a ladder," he said.

"A ladder? What do you mean? Where?" Clara's pulse quickened.

"Outside, going up to Miss Silvano's window," the gardener explained.

Clara's eyes widened in horror. Without another word, she bolted through the door and around the side of the house. Her breath caught in her throat when she saw the ladder leaning against the wall, reaching up to Serafina's window. Panic surged through her as she started screaming, "Dad! Dad!"

She sprinted back inside, her heart racing madly as she frantically searching for her father. "Dad! Where are you? Dad! *Dad!*"

Her screams echoed through the house, piercing the morning calm. "Dad! Help!" She tore through the hallways when finally her father rushed down the hall toward her, his face etched with concern.

"Clara, what's wrong?" he asked.

Clara couldn't get the words out. Her father grabbed her by the upper arms, trying to steady her.

"Clara, breathe. What happened? Take a deep breath."

"Serafina... there's a ladder... to her room and... someone's taken her..." Clara stammered, her words coming out in a rush before she burst into tears.

Her mother came up behind them and pulled Clara into a tight hug. Clara clung to her mother, hardly able to stand.

Her father didn't waste a second. He turned and darted up the stairs, taking them two at a time. He was back quickly. Without a word, he strode to the phone and grabbed the receiver. "Operator, connect me to the police. It's an emergency... Yes, it's an emergency! One of my girls is missing. We found a ladder up to her window— No, we don't know where she is. Please send someone quickly."

Clara had never been so scared in her life. The news about

Theodore had come quickly. But who knew about Serafina?"

Her father hung up the phone and turned to face his wife and daughter. "The police are on their way, and I'm going to find George. We'll find her, Clara."

Clara nodded, trying to hold onto his words, but the dread drowned her. She held onto her mother, sobbing, as the minutes stretched into an eternity.

The police officers took the ladder down and started going through Serafina's room searching for any clue that might give them a lead. Clara sat on a chair in the parlor, her eyes red and swollen from crying, with her mother by her side. An officer, kind-faced, but serious, sat across from her, a notebook in hand.

"Miss Randolph, I need you to try and talk to me," he said. "Anything you can remember might help us."

Clara nodded, but when she tried to speak, the words got caught in her throat. Her head hurt. Her face hurt. Her chest hurt. "I'm sorry," she whispered, her voice breaking. "It's so hard..."

"I understand," the officer said softly. "Take your time. Do you know anyone who might have wanted to take her? Anyone she's had trouble with?"

Clara's throat tightened. "Mr. Richard Kensington, of Kensington Publishing. He's been... there's been trouble there. And Danny—I don't know his last name, but he owns the florist shop next to the bookshop where she works."

The officer's pen scratched across paper. "Anyone else?"

Clara's hands twisted in her lap and quickly glanced at her mother, then up at her father, and back to the officer. "She's been seeing Francesco Romano."

The officer's pen stopped. "The gangster?"

Mr. Randolph's face had gone white, then flushed deep red. "What?"

"Yes." Clara's voice grew stronger, more insistent. "It was the mob. It has to be them. His world—the mob—they did this. I know they did!"

Mrs. Randolph's arms went rigid around Clara. "Clara, are you certain?"

"Yes." Clara's voice was fierce despite her tears. "I warned her this would happen. I told her nothing good comes from getting involved with men like that."

The officer sighed, rubbing his temples. "Miss Randolph, we can question Mr. Kensington and the florist, but approaching the mob... they don't cooperate with police. Even if they know something, they won't say."

"Then what's the point?" Clara's voice broke. "If they took her and you can't even ask—"

"We'll do what we can," the officer said gently. "But you need to understand the limitations we're working with."

Mr. Randolph's jaw was clenched so tight Clara could see the muscle jumping. She'd never seen her father this angry.

Mrs. Randolph stroked her daughter's hair. "Come on, dear. Let's get you upstairs. You need rest." She led Clara up the stairs.

"Mom, please... call Irving for me," Clara managed to say, her voice barely above a whisper.

"Of course, sweetheart. I'll call him right away," her mother promised, guiding her into her room. She helped Clara into bed and handed her a small pill to help her nerves. "Try to sleep, dear."

Clara took the pill and lay down. The exhaustion and fear pulled at her. Her mother stayed by her side, continuing to stroke her hair until the pill began to take effect. Clara's eyes fluttered shut, and despite the turmoil inside her, she began to drift off.

As she lay there, her mother's gentle presence a small comfort, Clara's mind swirled with thoughts of Serafina. This was the mob's doing. It had to be. Tears slipped down her cheeks as she whispered a silent prayer for her friend's safety. In a short while, the sleeping pill took hold, and Clara finally cried herself to sleep.

307

Clara woke to Irving sitting beside her bed, elbows on his knees, lost in thought.

"Darling?" she said softly, her voice still hoarse from crying.

Irving broke from his thoughts and turned to her, his face grave. "How are you doing?"

"Serafina's missing," Clara said, her voice trembling. "They took her. The mob took her."

"Your father told me." Irving's jaw tightened. "The officers plan to question Kensington and the florist."

"But not Mr. Romano. Because the mob is untouchable. Even when they do this, no one can touch then."

"Clara, listen to me. If gangsters took her, then Romano needs to know."

Clara gawked at him. "What?"

"Think about it. If another gangster took her—maybe trying to get leverage over Romano—he'd want to know. He has resources the police don't. Connections. and ways of finding information."

"But it's his fault." Clara's voice cracked. "His world did this to her."

"Maybe. Or maybe someone's trying to hurt him by taking her." Irving took her hands. "Either way, if she means something to him, he'll tear the city apart to find her. Isn't that what we want?"

"You really think we should tell him?"

"I do," he answered firmly, already rising from his chair. "Do you know where he lives?"

"At The Dakota."

"Let's go."

Clara jumped up, quickly checking herself in the mirror. She grabbed a hat and rushed out the door. As she passed the parlor, she saw George had arrived, but didn't stop. She only yelled, "I'll be back shortly!"

Irving drove almost fast enough to be reckless. "What did you tell the police?"

"About Mr. Kensington, and Danny, and..." She swallowed hard. "And Mr. Romano."

"And your father?"

"He's furious. I've never seen him that angry."

When they arrived at The Dakota, Clara's steps slowed as they approached the building. For once, she was overwhelmed at the thought of approaching someone. This wasn't a ball with formalities. This was heading into a mobster's home to ask for his help.

"I don't know which apartment. I know which one is his sister's, though."

"A man like him would have the penthouse," Irving said after a moment.

The elevator operator's eyes widened when Irving made his request, but he pulled the brass gate closed and threw the lever. Rising to the top seemed to take an eternity. Clara's hands were still shaking. She clasped them together. but it didn't help.

The hallway of the top floor was carpeted in deep burgundy, muffling their footsteps. Wall sconces cast warm light on cream-colored walls. Everything was hushed and elegant, he kind of place where violence seemed impossible, except Clara knew better now. Clara raised a trembling hand to knock.

"Let me," Irving said, stepping forward.

He pounded on the door with the side of his fist, three solid hits that echoed down the hallway like gunshots. The sound made Clara flinch.

They waited. Irving raised his fist again.

The door opened.

Mr. Romano stood in the doorway, perfectly dressed despite the early hour. His expression shifted from mild irritation to sharp concern the moment he saw Clara's face.

"Miss Randolph." His voice was controlled, but Clara could see something dark moving behind his eyes. "What's happened?"

"Serafina." Clara's voice broke. "Someone took her. Last night. There was a ladder to her window and she's gone and—"

She didn't get to finish. Mr. Romano's expression turned cold, his eyes looking murderous.

"Inside. Now." He turned toward the telephone. "Tell me everything."

Within minutes of telling him everything she knew, Mr. Romano's penthouse transformed into something that reminded her of a military command center. Men appeared from nowhere. To her surprise, she recognized a few from seeing around the neighborhood. She understood very little of what was happening.

Mr. Romano stood by his telephone giving clipped, cold orders. A pause. More orders. He hung up and immediately dialed again. More orders. He and his men came together and worked like a well-oiled machine primed to start working.

"Mr. Romano," Irving said quietly. "What can we do?"

Mr. Romano's eyes snapped to him. "You're a doctor?"

"Yes."

"When we find her, she may need medical attention. Be ready."

"Mr. Romano," Clara timidly began, "do you think the mob took her?"

"No." His response was firm, and he did not elaborate.

Finally, leaving one of his men—Ricci, Clara gathered—to coordinate from the penthouse, Francesco grabbed his coat and headed toward the door.

"Where are you going?" Clara asked, realizing now what a small comfort she had in seeing him in control of the search.

"To your estate to get answers." His expression was terrifying in its cold certainty. "Someone took what's mine. They're going to learn what that costs."

Clara and Irving followed him. When they pulled up to the Randolph estate, the place was crawling with police. Mr. Romano's jaw tightened, but he calmly walked toward the open front door with the confidence of a man who had every right to be there.

He knocked once on the doorframe.

"Come on in, Mr. Romano." Clara stepped through the door before him.

George appeared in the foyer. His face went from surprise to fury in an instant.

"You." The word came out as a snarl. George moved forward fast, his fist already coming up.

Mr. Romano didn't flinch. He simply stood there, hands at his sides, watching George come at him.

Two police officers suddenly stepped between them, grabbing George's arms.

"Mr. Randolph, please," one of them said. "This isn't helping."

"George!" Clara pressed on his chest. "George, listen—"

George struggled against them and ignored his sister, his face red. "Get your hands off me! That bastard—his people did this!"

"No," Francesco said quietly, his voice cutting through George's rage like a blade through silk. "They didn't."

"How would you know?" George spat. "How do we know you didn't—"

"If any of the families had taken her, they'd have called me by now to gloat and to make demands." Francesco's voice remained eerily calm His eyes were cold as winter.

"Then who?" George demanded, still straining against the officers' hold.

"That's what I intend to find out." Francesco's gaze moved past George. "Has anyone spoken with Richard Kensington?"

"We're planning to question him this afternoon, sir," one of the officers replied.

"I'll handle Kensington."

"Now wait just a minute—" the officer started.

Mr. Romano turned to look at him. The officer stop talking.

"I said I'll handle him." Mr Romano's word was final.

Mr. Randolph stood in the doorway to his study, his face drawn. "Mr. Romano, I appreciate your concern, but we have the police investigating. Your help isn't needed."

The temperature in the room seemed to drop ten degrees.

Mr. Romano turned slowly to face Mr. Randolph. When he spoke, his voice was quiet, but it carried through the foyer like thunder.

"With all due respect, Mr. Randolph, you don't get a say in this."

Mr. Randolph's eyes widened. "I beg your pardon?"

"Miss Silvano is mine, not yours. She's mine." Mr. Romano took a step forward. "So help me God, when I find out who did this, when I find out who put their hands on what belongs to me, there won't be enough of them left to question."

"I have men searching every inch of this city," Mr. Romano continued, his voice never rising above that deadly quiet. "I have contacts the police don't have. I have methods the police can't use. And I have motivation that makes your concern look like a passing thought." His eyes locked with Mr. Randolph's. "So no, sir. My help isn't optional. It's inevitable. You can either work with me or stay out of my way, but you will not tell me what I can and cannot do to find her."

Mr. Randolph stared at Francesco for a long moment. Then, slowly, he nodded. "Find her, Mr. Romano."

"I will." Francesco's voice carried absolute certainty. "And God have mercy on whoever took her because I won't."

He turned and walked out, leaving a room full of stunned officers and a family that suddenly understood exactly what kind of man Serafina had gotten involved with.

Clara watched him go, and for the first time since finding Serafina's empty room, she felt something other than despair. She felt something very closer to hope.

Francesco loomed over Mr. Kensington in the man's lavish living room. He stood with his hands clasped behind his back, relaxed in as if watching a couple kittens play only those. about to play weren't so harmless.

Lamp cord bound Kensington velvet armchair. It had already begun cutting into his skin. Blood welled where he'd struggled. Such a pitiful sight. His once-proud face sagged beneath fear and fury, his cheek split open from Francesco's earlier knuckles to his bone. Sweat and blood soaked through his fine suit.

"I told you, I know nothing," he said, voice trembling despite the effort to sound defiant. His eyes flicked desperately between

Francesco and the pistol aimed steady at his skull. Bruno, massive and mute, stood with his finger resting against the trigger, his expression carved from stone. The gun barrel was close enough that Kensington could probably smell the oil on it.

The silence thickened. Francesco let it stretch until the publisher's breathing turned ragged.

"I'll ask one last time," Francesco murmured, voice soft. He crouched down, bringing himself eye-level with his prey. "Where is she?"

Kensington's bravado collapsed. His eyes widened. "I swear to God, I don't know where she is. She ran, I don't—please, I'm telling the truth!"

Francesco studied him a moment longer, then gave the faintest nod. Bruno slid the gun back into its holster.

The relief on Kensington's face a scant two seconds. Francesco stepped closer. His shadow swallowed the publisher. When he spoke again, his voice carried the gravity of a death sentence.

"Now. The other matter."

At his gesture, Carlo produced a stack of pages bound with string. He dropped Serafina's manuscript onto Kensington's lap.

"You've read this?"

"Yes," Kensington rasped. His chest rose and fell too fast. "It's brilliant. One of the best I've seen."

"If she were a stranger—no connection to me—would you have published it?" Francesco tilted his head slightly. "Answer honestly. Was she rejected on her merit, or because she didn't want your advances? Answering no won't cost you."

Kensington hesitated, then nodded. "Yes. I would have, on its merit alone."

"Then she earned it." Francesco's expression remained flat and unreadable. "I am now her agent. We will discuss terms when Serafina is found, safe, and ready to move forward."

Relief flickered across Kensington's face.

Then Francesco smiles.

"Now," he whispered, leaning closer, "about those photographs you took. The ones you used to ensure her...compliance."

Every drop of color drained from Kensington's face. "I—I don't know what you mean."

"Don't insult me." Francesco's smile widened. "You posed her and arranged her like a toy. Told her what those pictures were for. Insurance, you called it. Leverage."

"That was different, it was just business, it was—"

"Something she deserved?" Francesco's voice dripped with venom. "For daring to want her words in print? For believing you when you said you'd help her?"

"I gave her a chance—"

Francesco's hand shot out, gripping Kensington's neck. The publisher's words died in a choked gasp.

"You took something from her." Francesco's eyes were black pits, endless and pitiless. "You took her dignity and sense of safety. You humiliated her." He released Kensington's neck with a shove. "Bruno. Carlo."

The two men stepped forward.

"Whatever Mr. Kensington thought fit for Miss Silvano," Francesco continued, voice light now, almost conversational, "is now fitting for him. Every pose." He straightened his cuffs. "Be creative. Document everything on film."

Terror dawned in Kensington's eyes. "But—I don't have a—"

"Use whatever holes he does have," Francesco said, examining his nails. "His mouth will do for a start. Then get creative with the rest."

Bruno cracked his knuckles. Carlo reached for Kensington's jaw, forcing his head back as the man thrashed against the chair. The lamp cords cut deeper. Blood ran down his wrists. Pleas spilled from him in broken sobs, rising higher as their shadows closed in and Bruno began unbuckling his belt.

"Please—God—please don't—"

Francesco paused at the threshold, one hand on the doorframe, listening to the panic unravel behind him. The first real scream tore through the air. He closed his eyes briefly, savoring it the way another man might savor fine wine.

"Art imitates life, Mr. Kensington," he said, voice calm, almost gentle beneath the sounds of violence. "And you are about to learn the value of a good performance. Make it convincing. My men have all night."

Francesco moved through Danny's flower shop like a shadow given form, his eyes dragging over every detail eyes trained to find secrets. The air was thick with the cloying sweetness of roses and lilies.

Funeral flowers, he noted. *How fitting.*

Danny stood at the counter, trimming rose stems. His hands trembled just slightly. Francesco had spent his life stripping masks from men, peeling back layers of lies until only raw truth remained. Shy, nervous, soft-spoken—that was the florist Serafina had known. Beneath this one, something darker shifted. Francesco knew it.

His gaze traveled to the tall shelves at the back. Vases in ceramic and glass, some heavy enough to crack a skull, lined the them, with with books on floristry worn from use, their spines creased and faded. He noted everything: the pruning shears within arm's reach, the door opposite the bookshop that opened into an alley, the loose floorboard near the register that gave slightly under his weight... every potential weapon...

"So you know..." Francesco began.

"Absolutely nothing. Serafina's a good girl. Sweet, you know? She must be so scared right now, wherever she is." Danny looked up, eyes wide and earnest. "I like her a lot. I just hope she's safe."

Francesco's eyes narrowed to slits. The concern in Danny's tone was real enough, but it felt rehearsed. Too smooth, too ready.

"Can you think of anyone who might want to hurt her?" he asked.

Danny hesitated for a fraction of a second. Quick, but not too quick for Francesco to catch.

"Well, yes," Danny said. "There are a few regulars who come around." His hands moved faster over the roses as he arranged them.

"Mr. Kensington, definitely. He is really intense about her, you know? And some others too, always hanging around, chatting, staying too long."

Francesco's man Bruno wrote names down in a small notebook. He murmured something to Carlo beside him. Carlo slipped out the door.

Francesco caught Danny's eyes following Carlo's exit.

Danny tensed, then swallowed hard. "What is going on?"

"Carlo is going to verify those men," Francesco said, eyes fixed on Danny. "He will talk to them."

Danny gave a jerky nod, Adam's apple bobbing. "Okay." His voice came flat.

Francesco narrowed his eyes and let the silence stretch, watching Danny squirm. Then he shifted tactics.

"Did you not sell this shop to Richard Kensington?"

Danny froze. For a moment, confusion flickered across his face. Then he smoothed it over.

"Yes. Got a good price for it too. Today is the last day I am open, you know? After this, I am moving on to a fresh start. You know?"

His tone brought suspicion into Francesco's chest. He took a slow step closer.

"Why sell so suddenly?" His voice dropped lower, as intimate as a lover's whisper. "This shop is your livelihood, your craft."

Danny fidgeted at the nearness. Stems snapped in his trembling hands. Red petals scattered across the counter like drops of blood.

"Been thinking about it a while. You know how it is. Time to try something new. Different chapter."

The words rang false. Floristry was not a hobby. It was a craft built on years of study and practice, shaped by patience and obsession. It was never something a man abandoned overnight for vague dreams of something new. Francesco did not believe any of it.

He slowly pulled a pen from his jacket pocket and wrote two numbers on a scrap of paper, his own and the Randolph's. He slid it across the counter.

"Call either of these numbers if you remember anything else," he said softly. "Anything at all might help us find her." He leaned closer, close enough that Danny had to tilt his head back to meet his eyes. "And I know you want to help her, do you not Danny?"

"Yes, of course I do." Danny's voice cracked slightly. "It is okay. I really do."

Francesco watched him for a long moment, gaze steady and unblinking, black eyes holding the younger man's until Danny shifted, breath shallow and quickening.

Then Francesco straightened and headed for the door with the casual grace of a man who knew his prey would stay put for as long as he needed. Bruno followed him.

Outside, rain threatened in the gray sky above. Francesco lit a cigarette.

"Boss?" Bruno said in a low questioning voice.

"*He's lying.*" Francesco exhaled smoke, watching it curl and dissipate. "*About everything. The sale, the men, and Miss Silvano.*"

His instincts screamed the same truth, a steady surge of certainty. Danny knew something. If he was not involved outright, he still knew more than he let on, and Francesco would find it. He always did.

Francesco looked at the front of the shop again and down the street. Somewhere in this city, something was off. He was not alone.

He was not alone. He was not alone. He was not alone.

Somewhere in this city, Serafina was scared and alone. And every man who helped put her there, knowingly or not, would pay the price. He would personally make sure the lessons were... very thorough.

Serafina shivered in her cell. The cold pressed into her bones. Her teeth chattered so violently that she bit her tongue. Her shaking fingers tore a piece of bread and forced it into her mouth. She swallowed with gulps of bitter coffee that scorched all the way down. Each bite took willpower, but she needed strength and clarity.

She was certain she had heard Francesco's voice earlier. That meant he was hunting, and that thought gave her hope. She had to be ready when rescue came, but she needed to find a way to help herself in the meantime. She knew Francesco would tear this city apart to find her, but she could not simply wait and do nothing like some damsel in a tower.

She examined her prison more carefully, running raw fingertips over brick. She presumed the walls had been reinforced somehow, possibly soundproofed. A drain in the corner made her stomach turn when she thought about what it might have been used for before. Danny had clearly built this prison himself, an so doubted the drain was there for no purpose. How many women had died here in the few years the shop had been open?

Time dragged. Normal life went on outside while she rotted in the faint light of the one dim bulb he'd turned on. At one point she thought of screaming, even if it meant tearing her throat raw. The street was not so far, and maybe someone would hear. But what if no one heard except Danny? She shuddered at the thought of what he might do. No, what he *would* do. Her chance had to come another way.

Then the door opened and the lock of the outer gate opened. Metal screeched. Danny stepped in, the mask of the timid florist left behind. His face was set in stone, his eyes flat and dead. He locked the gate behind him before opening hers, ensuring no chance for her to run.

He collected the bucket that served as her makeshift toilet without comment, then returned with it a couple minutes later. Then he crouched and leaned forward, elbows on his knees, watching her as if he were examining a possession, an object he owned.

"I only asked for a cup of coffee, Serafina," he said softly, as if they were discussing the weather.

Serafina swallowed her fear. "I told you I did not want to give you false hope."

His eyes flickered with irritation. "You must have realized I was attracted to you." His voice sharpened. "All those smiles and conversations—you must have known your feelings would change eventually."

Her pulse pounded in her ears. "That is not how love happens."

Danny's hand snapped up. The slap cracked across her face

with enough force to whip her head sideways. Pain exploded white hot across her cheekbone. Stars burst behind her eyes. Blood filled her mouth.

"Do *not* lecture me about love," he said, voice cold as ice. "You belong to me now. You do what I want, when I want. "He yanked her jaw to force her to look at him. "Please me and you live a little longer. Defy me and I will break you piece by piece until you comply. Or I will take what I want by force."

Her stomach lurched. She tasted bile.

His thumb dragged across her split lip, smearing blood across her mouth like lipstick. "If I do, I cannot promise you will survive it."

"Danny, please. You are better than this."

He laughed. "That is what they all say. Every single one."

A chill rippled through her.

"Who are they?" Her voice shook.

"Oh, there was Cora. She fought like a wild cat and screamed until her voice gave out." He said it the way others might discuss roses. Calm. Fond. Well, almost fond. "Then there was Samantha. She cried endless tears, begging and pleading for me to take it easy on her. Caroline gave in within a week, but she was useless after that. Just a shell. A cold body. There is no fun in that. None of them lasted long enough to be interesting. Want to hear more?"

More? Serafina's throat tightened until she could barely breathe. "Where are they now?"

"Buried at my horse ranch." He examined his nails with bored detachment. "There is good soil there. Rich soil. One of my stallions is running the derby next year, you know. I like to think my girls are contributing something at last."

Serafina's blood turned to ice.

"Your... you ranch?" She fought rising panic. "Your name is not Danny, is it?"

He chuckled. "Edward Whitmore. Remember it. Not that you will live long enough to use it much. But I want you to know who owns you and who will be the last thing you see."

Her lungs seized. She could not breathe. The reality struck like a fist to her chest, driving the air from her body. She knew then he intended to kill her, no matter what she did. Compliance would not save her. Resistance would not save her. She was already dead in his eyes. The only question was how long he would play with his toy before breaking it.

Still, Serafina burned the names into her memory.

Edward Whitmore.

Cora. Samantha. Caroline.

If she survived—no, when she survived, the police might be able to track down families and give them at least some closure.

"If you are a good girl, I will bring you a mattress and maybe a blanket." Edward's voice was almost kind now, mocking in its gentleness. "A bit of comfort for however long you have left. Now get on your knees."

He stood and leaned over her.

For one wild second, Serafina drew in a deep breath with the intention of screaming. But Edward was too close. He could stop her. She could picture his hand clamped over her mouth and his other crushing her windpipe. She would not survive the hour if she tried. And she would not give him the satisfaction of killing her just then. But she also did not want to give him the satisfaction of giving him what he wanted.

"No."

Edward's expression darkened. "Get on your fucking knees."

She met his eyes and refused to look away. "I said no."

His face twisted into something monstrous. He shook the bars hard. Then he slammed the door and stormed out.

The silence pressed in on her. Suffocated her. She pushed herself to her feet, her body shaking, but her will hardening like steel.

She searched the walls again, and this time she found one brick that shifted ever so slightly. It was a cruel tease, but it held a small promise. She scraped at the mortar with her nails, then with a small piece of jagged stone she found on the ground. She ignored the pain as her fingertips split open. The scrape of mortar flaking away gave her purpose, even if only for a moment.

Then she heard the door opening. She dropped to the ground,

trying to look as though she had not moved. He balanced bowls of soup and water as he unlocked the first gate.

"Say my name."

She stayed silent.

"*Say it*," he hissed, crouching close on the other side of the bars. "Say my name."

Her skin crawled, but she forced herself to speak.

"Edward."

His grin widened. "Yeah. That is the name you will be screaming soon, when I am inside you, breaking you."

He reached through the bars, dragging his fingers down her cheek. "I am going to take my time with you, Serafina. Really make it last."

Then he left again, leaving the bowls on his side of the bars.

Serafina had to press her face against the metal to hold the edge of the bowl to her lips. She drank every drop of soup and all the water she could keep down.

When she finished, she looked at the spoon. There had been no reason to bring it when she was able to drink the soup without it. But still... thin metal edges. Worn, but sharp enough to be a weapon. Or a tool. Maybe both.

She gripped it with her bleeding hands and returned to the wall, to that one loose brick.

The edge of the spoon bit into the mortar with a faint scratch. She pressed harder, chipping again.

Scrape.

Scrape.

The mortar crumbled in powdery flakes that stung her raw fingertips. The blood made the spoon slippery, but she tightened her grip until her knuckles blanched, and she kept going. Pain was good. Pain meant she was alive. Pain meant she was still fighting.

Hours bled together. Time lost all meaning again. Her fingers swelled, nails torn back, palms blistered. The spoon cut deeper into the mortar now, leaving grooves. The brick shifted a little more. Only slightly, but it was progress.

She drew back and dug again, welcoming the agony. It kept her sharp. It kept her from thinking about Edward's promises, and about what would happen when he decided talking was over.

But she would not break, and she would not kneel. She would not stop.

Every scrape of metal against mortar was a message to herself.

I am here. And I am still fighting. I will endure this until Francesco comes for me.

And when he did, when he finally tore in with fire and fury, Edward would learn what it meant to touch something precious to Francesco Romano.

She smiled through the blood and the pain, almost gleeful as she imagined it.

CHAPTER 20

Time died in Serafina's prison. The bare bulb glowed dimmer than it had before. Soon it would probably be extinguished entirely. Her body ached from the cold and the terror, wondering if she would expire before it.

The dreaded sound of a key turning in the lock made her heart slam. Then Edward unlocked the second set of bars.

"I have been so patient with you, Serafina," he said softly. "But you keep making me hurt you."

She pressed her back against the cold brick wall. "Please, Edward, do not do this."

"After we're together, you will understand. You will see that you belong to me and you always have."

He stepped closer. She could smell something sweet. Something chemical. Maybe chloroform.

"I have watched you for so long. I have waited. Do you know how long it has been? Watching that *gangster* put his hands on my girl?"

"Danny," she tried desperately, using the name of the gentle man she had once known. "Remember the white lilies you brought me? You were so kind. That man would not—"

"*Danny is dead!*" Edward screamed, lunging forward. "You killed him every time he smiled at that monster, every time he ignored me. You drove another nail into his coffin!"

He grabbed her and forced her to the ground. Adrenaline flooded her system. She kicked and scratched, but he was much stronger than she had realized. He pinned her arms above her head with one hand, and yanked her nightgown up with the other. Then his hand went to his trousers.

Serafina's mind went somewhere else, somewhere far away. She could hear her own breathing, fast and shallow, but it sounded distant. She could feel the cold stone beneath her back, the weight of him, the smell...

This is happening, this is really happening, she thought.

When he shifted his weight slightly, pure survival instinct took over. She brought her knee up with every ounce of strength she had left and drove it straight into his groin.

Edward howled in pain and rolled off her, cursing viciously.

"You little *bitch,*" he spat, his voice contorted in agony.

Serafina scrambled backward, her body shaking so violently she could barely stand. Her nightgown was torn and her lip bled where he had struck her. She steeled herself for what he might do next.

"I am going to fuck you until you bleed and then I am going to cut your throat just like I did to the others." Still bent over and hissing with pain, Edward glared at her. "You are dead in twenty four hours."

He stumbled back out, locking both doors behind him.

Serafina collapsed. For a long time she could not move or even think. Then her stomach heaved and she vomited into the corner of the cell. She wiped her mouth with the back of her hand and tasted her own blood.

Twenty four hours.

She crawled to where she had been working on the brick and grabbed the spoon. She had to get this brick loose. She had to. It was the only chance she had left. The only chance at a real weapon. She had to get out. She had to survive this.

And then the brick shifted. She pulled it free with a gasp of relief and peered through the small hole into darkness. Wood. She was not sure if it was the back of the bookshop wall or if there was more between her and the place she knew.

She pressed her ear to the opening and listened, but she could not get close enough to hear anything.

She knocked once.

The sound was solid and reassuring. If it had been hollow, her heart would have sunk. But it was solid. Hopefully the sound would carry through.

Then she had an idea. She swept the bits of mortar into a small pile and used the back end of the spoon to pulverize it the best she could. She tried to spit, but her mouth was too dry. So she squatted over it and managed to force out just enough urine to make a paste. She scooped it up with the spoon and smashed it into the lock mechanism. It might not keep them out forever, but it might buy her enough extra time.

She went back to the wall and knocked again. Then again.

The rhythm became steady, matching her racing pulse.

Knock, knock, pause.

Knock, knock, pause.

Please, someone please hear me.

She kept knocking.

Knock, pause.

Knock, pause.

A desperate rhythm in the darkness.

Her eyelids grew heavy. Exhaustion pulled at her. She slumped against the wall, still knocking, but her movements grew slower and weaker.

She didn't remember falling asleep.

Edward lay on his bed in his upscale apartment, the pain from the groin kick finally beginning to subside to a dull, throbbing ache.

Each breath had been agony for the past hour, but now he could think clearly again.

He stared at the ceiling, his mind replaying the scene in the cell. Serafina beneath him, finally within his grasp after months of watching and waiting. Her torn nightgown. The terror in her eyes. The way she'd fought him. *That goddamn kick.*

His hand moved to his groin, testing the soreness. Still painful, but bearable now. And beneath the pain, a twisted heat stirred.

As he pulled himself free, he thought about going back tomorrow. About what he'd do differently this time. Earlier that day, he'd considered using the chloroform to keep her docile, compliant. But now? Now that she'd pissed him off with her defiance, the alternative excited him. No chloroform. No easy submission. He'd make her feel every second of fear, every moment of dread as he dragged her onto that cold stone floor and took what she'd denied him. He'd force her to understand that she belonged to him, and always had since the first moment he'd seen her in that bookshop.

He gripped himself despite the residual pain, and began to pump slowly. The friction sent a sharp wince through him as the soreness flared. He gritted his teeth. The sting fueled his anger at her for causing this and for fighting back when she should have surrendered. The pain made him madder, sharper, and hungrier. He continued anyway, stroking harder now, the ache blending with the building pleasure into something raw and vicious.

The image crystallized in his mind: Serafina's face when she realized no one was coming to save her. Her body thrashing beneath him as she fought in vain. The sounds she'd make, the gasps, the whimpers and screams. The way she'd break, her spirit shattering under his weight...

And after... after he'd claimed what was his, thrusting into her with all the fury she'd ignited...he'd wrap his hands around her scrawny throat and watch the light leave her eyes. Just like Cora. Just like Lily. Just like Jessica. Just like Elsie and Mabel and Gretchen...

All women who'd rejected him, who'd laughed at his love, spurned his devotion, chosen other men over him.

Well, they'd all learned their lesson in the end.

His breathing quickened. The pain meant nothing now, overtaken by the fantasy playing out behind his closed eyelids. Serafina, finally his. Serafina, broken and pleading. Serafina, understanding too late what she'd thrown away.

He pumped with increasing speed, wincing again as a fresh wave of soreness hit, but he didn't stop. The violent fantasy and arousal were inseparable now, the throb in his groin a reminder of *her* crime against him, stoking his rage even as it drove him closer to the edge. This was what *she* had driven him to. This was what rejection did. It transformed love into something desperate.

When he finished, he lay there breathing hard, his hand sticky, the release tainted by the lingering ache that only made him hate her more. For a moment, just a brief, flickering moment, Danny's voice whispered in his consciousness: *What have you become?*

Edward crushed it immediately. Danny was weak. Danny had tried patience and kindness and gotten nothing but contempt in return. Edward was what the world had made him.

He cleaned himself slowly as his mind planned. Tomorrow he'd go back without the chloroform. He'd be smarter this time. He wouldn't give her another chance to fight, not until he'd savored her terror.

And when it was over, when she was cold and still and finally *his*, he'd feel that same rush of satisfaction he'd felt with the others and dump her with their bodies. Then maybe he'd go back for Clara after all.

The thought made him hard again.

He touched himself once more, slower this time, savoring the new images... of Clara's fear. Clara's pain. Clara's submission... Each stroke brought a wince, but he embraced it, letting it feed the fire, making him angrier, more determined, eager to see what lay beyond Serafina.

By the time he was done, Danny was gasping his last breaths. No more gentle florist with shy smiles and carefully arranged bouquets.

Just Edward. Just hunger and the need to possess what had been denied him.

I'm sorry, Serafina, Danny's voice whispered in his head, the last he'd ever hear it before Danny died for good. *But you left no choice.* Edward smiled. *No choice at all.*

Mr. Randolph, the younger Mr. Randolph, and Francesco sat in the dimly lit parlor, sipping rum from an illicit bottle Francesco had brought that morning. He had been awake for thirty six hours straight. His eyes burned and his hands would not stay still. He kept reaching for his glass, draining it, then refilling it. The alcohol barely touched the edges of his panic. He was not used to panicking at all, and now he struggled to contain it.

The elder Mr. Randolph broke the heavy silence first. "Thank you for helping with the search for Serafina."

Francesco nodded curtly. He doubted the man's son knew of his debts, but none of that mattered now. Nothing did except finding Serafina.

The Randolphs remained silent for a while. Francesco stayed quiet as well. His men had been combing through every lead, questioning every contact, and pressing every advantage they had in the city, but the trail had gone cold.

"There is something we are missing," Francesco said, more to himself than to the others. His jaw clenched. "Someone does not just vanish."

"What about the florist, Danny?" the younger Mr. Randolph asked.

"The police questioned him," his father replied. "He seemed genuinely concerned about Serafina."

"I questioned him too." Francesco glanced at him, then back down at his glass. For once, he struggled to pinpoint what was off. On the surface everything seemed to check out, but there was still something wrong.

"Why do you care so much?" George asked suddenly. "About finding her. You barely know her."

Francesco's eyes snapped up. The room went still.

"You are Francesco Romano," George continued, clearly uncomfortable but pressing forward anyway. "Why would you personally involve yourself in"

"Because she is mine," Francesco said, his voice low and dangerous.

Mr. Randolph's eyebrows rose. George's mouth fell open slightly. Then he took a deep breath, collecting himself.

Francesco set his glass down.

"Did anyone verify the florist's story about where he was the night Serafina disappeared?"

The elder Mr. Randolph recovered first.

"I do not believe so. The police focused on the more obvious suspects first."

Suddenly something clicked. Danny had not been home during the time Francesco had been watching his apartment. The apartment was small and very sparsely furnished, almost enough that it seemed unlived in. There was no mail in it. No personal effects. Francesco stood abruptly and moved toward the door.

Twenty minutes later, he pushed through the bookshop door hard enough that the bell jingled violently. Mr. Thompson glanced up from behind the counter, his face etched with worry and exhaustion.

"Mr. Romano," he said wearily, "any news about—"

"Danny's address. What address do you have for him?"

Mr. Thompson blinked at the harsh tone.

"I believe he lives on Maple Street. Here, uh..." The man pulled out his index card file and flipped though it. "Yes, forty seven Maple. Top floor."

Francesco was already turning back to the door.

"Mr. Romano, wait. Is Danny a suspect? Should I call the police?"

Francesco did not answer. That was not address the police had.

Not long later, Francesco and Ricci stood outside a rather nice apartment building on Maple Street. Francesco led the way inside, up to the top floor, and pressed his ear to the door. There were no sounds inside. He nodded to Ricci, who picked the lock in a matter of seconds.

"Keep watch," Francesco muttered before slipping inside.

The apartment was surprisingly large and well appointed for someone who was supposed to be just a florist. Francesco moved through it, eyes narrowing, every instinct on high alert. He threw open drawers and rifled through closets. In the bedroom he tore through the desk until he found a stack of documents, including a property tax bill for Sunshine Meadows Horse Ranch, insurance papers for horses, and veterinary bills. Every single one had the owner's name meticulously cut away with scissors.

He found deeds to a couple other properties as well, but it was what he found in the bottom drawer that made his blood run cold.

A woman's handkerchief, delicate, embroidered with small flowers, with the initials SS. He recognized it as Serafina's.

Next to it were newspaper clippings about two missing women from the past year, and a lock of dark hair tied with ribbon.

And photographs. Dozens of photographs of women who looked like Serafina. Similar hair color, slight build, facial features that could have passed for her at a quick glance but were not her.

Francesco pocketed the handkerchief. He wanted to destroy this place and burn it to the ground, but he needed more information. More than he needed catharsis.

He quickly made sure that everything he moved was back in its place, then went back to the door.

"Ricci," he said, his voice tight as they locked the door. "Head back out."

He held up the property tax bill. "Sunshine Meadows Horse Ranch. A few hours north of the city."

"What kind of florist has horses?" Ricci's eyebrows shot up.

"The kind who has Serafina."

330

The drive to Sunshine Meadows took Francesco and Ricci through rolling countryside. Francesco gripped the steering wheel so hard his hands ached, his foot heavy on the accelerator. Every minute that passed was another minute Serafina remained in danger.

If she's even still alive, a voice whispered in his head. He crushed the thought immediately.

"Boss," Ricci said quietly, "*looks like we should reach the ranch within the hour.*"

Francesco pressed harder on the accelerator. The car lurched forward.

The ranch appeared around a bend in the road like something from a magazine. White fencing stretched for acres, enclosing emerald pastures where thoroughbreds grazed in the afternoon sun. The main house was a sprawling colonial with pristine white columns and manicured gardens. Stables and outbuildings dotted the property, all maintained to perfection.

"Jesus," Ricci whistled low.

Francesco parked near the main house, but no one came out to greet them. He strode toward the stables, where he could see several workers tending to the horses. The closest was a young man with nervous eyes who was brushing down a chestnut mare.

Francesco parked and strode toward the stables, where a young stable hand was brushing down a mare.

"You." Francesco's voice made the young man jump. "Where's your boss?"

The worker's eyes widened. "Mr. Whitmore? He doesn't come around much, sir. He's usually working in the city."

"Whitmore?" Francesco exchanged a sharp glance with Ricci.

"Yes, sir. Edward Whitmore. Owns this place but hasn't been by in a month." The young man shifted nervously under Francesco's intense stare. "Is something wrong?"

"What did he do when he was here?"

"Just checked on Thunder. That's his prize stallion. Seemed agitated about something. Left within an hour."

Francesco eyes' narrowed. A wealthy man hiding behind the identity of a poor florist. Someone with resources. With property. With privacy to do whatever he wanted.

"*Get back to the city,*" Francesco ordered Ricci. "*Now.*"

Francesco drove like a madman, barely bothering to slow at intersections and ignoring the speed limits. Every minute that passed brought Serafina closer to danger.

Once they reached the city, Francesco pulled up to a pay telephone outside a drugstore. He dropped coins into the slot and dialed his contact at the police department.

"It's Romano. I need you to check your files for an Edward Whitmore... Yes, I'll hold."

The minutes crawled by while Francesco paced beside the telephone booth, watching pedestrians hurry past. Finally, the voice came back through the receiver.

"Romano?" The voice came back. "Edward Whitmore is wanted for questioning in connection with two murders. Lily Shaw and Gretchen Mills. He's not a suspect, but both young women are known to have turned down his advances. We want to know who else they both my have known. They were both found dead after being held captive. There are a few others. that look similar. Whoever killed Shaw and Mills might have killed them, too."

Francesco's vision tunneled. "Where were they captive?"

"Makeshift cells. Basements, hidden rooms. He keeps them confined for days before..." The officer's voice trailed off.

Francesco hung up without another word.

"*Back to the bookshop,*" he told Ricci, his voice deadly calm. "*Right now.*"

A faint clicking sound jerked Serafina awake. She sat up, disoriented, and saw Edward standing at the door, turning the outer lock.

"Miss me?"

Serafina huddled against the wall, making herself small. Then, desperately: "Danny, remember your horses. The ones you loved. Would they recognize you now? Would they trust the man you've become?"

For just a moment, just one fleeting second, something soft crossed his face. His hands shook slightly.

Then it was gone.

He moved to the inner gate and inserted his key. It wouldn't go in. He jiggled it, trying to force it into the keyhole, but something was blocking it completely.

"What the—" He peered closer, trying to see in the dim light. The keyhole was packed solid with something. He tried scraping at it with his fingernail, but whatever it was had hardened like cement.

Serafina pressed herself against the far wall, her heart pounding. The crushed mortar mixed with urine had dried overnight into a rock-hard plug.

Edward's face darkened with rage. He rattled the gate violently, but it held firm. "You clever little bitch," he snarled. "You think this will stop me?"

He pulled the knife from his belt and began digging at the lock mechanism, scraping and prying. Chunks of the hardened material fell away slowly. Each scrape of metal on metal echoed through the cell.

Serafina's hands closed around the brick she'd hidden behind her back. This was taking him time. Precious seconds. But he was getting through.

"I'm going to make you regret this," Edward muttered, still working at the lock. "Every second you've made me wait, I'm going to make you pay for it.

"More material crumbled away. The knife blade scraped deeper into the mechanism. Edward's breathing was heavy with exertion and fury.

Finally... *click*. Something gave way. He yanked the knife out and shoved his key in. This time it turned.

The gate swung open with a rusty screech.

Edward stepped into the cell, knife still in his hand, his face twisted with rage. "You think you're so smart?"

Serafina grabbed for her brick, but Edward was already on her. He caught her wrist, twisting it viciously until something popped and she screamed, the brick clattering away into the corner.

"You've made this so much harder than it had to be," Edward snarled, shoving her down onto the cold stone floor. His weight crashed down on top of her, knocking the air from her lungs. "But I'm done being patient."

"No! Get off—" Serafina thrashed beneath him, but days of starvation had left her weak. Her fists beat uselessly against his chest.

His hand clamped over her mouth, cutting off her screams. "Shut up. Just *shut up* and accept it."

She bit down hard on his palm. Edward howled and yanked his hand back, blood welling from the teeth marks. He backhanded her viciously, her head snapping to the side. Pain exploded across her face, her cheek splitting open.

"You want to fight?" His hand went to his belt, fumbling with it. "Fine. I'll make this hurt."

Serafina bucked and twisted desperately. Her hand shot out, fingers scrabbling across the stone floor until she found the sharpened spoon she'd hidden. Edward's weight shifted as he struggled with his trousers. That was her chance. She drove the makeshift weapon deep into his thigh with all the strength she had left.

Edward howled, his body jerking. Blood bloomed dark against his pants. He lurched backward off her, grabbing at the spoon protruding from his leg.

Serafina rolled away, scrambling for the brick in the corner. Her fingers closed around it just as Edward yanked the spoon free with a roar of pain.

She swung.

The brick connected with the back of his skull with a sickening thud. Edward staggered, spinning toward her. Blood streamed down his neck, but the blow hadn't dropped him.

"You little *whore!*" He lunged for her, limping badly, blood soaking his pants leg.

She ducked under his grasping hands and swung the brick again, catching him across the face. His nose crunched. More blood.

Edward backhanded her so hard she crashed into the wall. Stars exploded across her vision. But she rolled away as his boot stomped where her head had been seconds before.

"I was going to make this easy for you," Edward snarled, advancing on her. His face was a mask of blood from his head wound, his broken nose, and the gash on his cheek. "But you want to fight? Fine. I'll break every bone in your body, *then* I'll fuck you, *then* I'll kill you."

Serafina scrambled backward, but the cell was too small. Nowhere to run. Nowhere to hide.

"Danny!" she gasped, her voice breaking. "Please! Remember the flowers! Remember how—"

"*Danny is dead!*" Edward roared, spittle and blood flying from his mouth. "You killed him! Every time you smiled at that gangster, every time you let him touch you, you drove another nail into his coffin!"

He grabbed her by the throat with both hands, lifting her partially off the ground. His fingers dug into her windpipe, crushing. No air. No breath.

Serafina clawed at his hands, her vision darkening.

"I should have done this months ago," Edward whispered, his blood-covered face inches from hers. His breath was hot and rank. "Should have taken you the first night I watched you sleep. But I was *kind*. And this is how you repay me?"

The pressure increased. Serafina's lungs screamed for air that wouldn't come.

"But that's all right," Edward continued, almost conversationally. "After you're dead, I'll find another. Someone who appreciates what I have to offer. Someone who doesn't throw my love back in my face like garbage."

Darkness crept in from the edges of her vision. Her struggles were becoming weaker. This was it. She was going to die here.

Francesco, she thought desperately. *Please. Please find me.*

With the very last of her strength, she brought her knee up toward his groin, aiming for the injury she'd given him before.

But Edward was ready this time. He shifted his weight, and her knee glanced uselessly off his hip.

He laughed a horrible, breathless sound. "Already tried that trick, remember? Not falling for it again."

The pressure on her throat increased. Black spots danced across her vision. Her hands fell limply from his wrists. No strength left. Nothing left.

Edward's face swam above her, distorted and monstrous. "That's it. Just let go. It'll be over soon."

Her consciousness was slipping away. The cell faded. Everything faded.

Francesco...

Edward released one hand from her throat. Just enough that she could draw a tiny, gasping breath, and fumbled with his trousers again. "No, can't have you dead yet. Not until I've had what's mine. And you're going to feel every bit of it."

CHAPTER 21

Francesco stood outside the flower shop, staring through the darkened window. The cheerful display of wilted flowers mocked him. He stepped back. The proportions were off.

He walked to the bookshop next door, shoving through the door hard enough that the bell's cheerful chime sounded violent in the quiet space.

"Mr. Romano," Mr. Thompson called from behind the counter, standing quickly. "Any news about Serafina? Please, tell me—"

Francesco ignored him completely. He scanned the shop's dimensions, walked to the back wall with measured strides, then returned to the front. Thirty-two paces from front to back.

He stepped outside again without a word, measuring the distance between the flower shop and bookshop entrances with his stride. The buildings pressed against each other with no gap between them.

Back at the flower shop window, Francesco peered inside more carefully. The space looked shallow, maybe twenty paces deep at most. But the bookshop stretched much deeper, even accounting for the stockroom he'd glimpsed at the back.

The spaces didn't match. There were at least ten feet unaccounted for.

Francesco's heart began to pound. He burst back into the bookshop.

Mr. Thompson opened his mouth to speak, but Francesco raised a hand sharply. "Be quiet."

He moved through the aisles, his eyes fixed on the wall that divided the two buildings. His hands traced along the plaster, feeling for irregularities. Years of breaking into warehouses and safes had taught him how to read a building's secrets.

The plaster felt solid, old. But as he moved along its length, his trained fingers detected something—patches. Repairs. Fresh paint over old work. As if something had been walled up and someone had tried to hide it.

"How deep does this building go?" Francesco demanded.

Mr. Thompson blinked. "Well, there's the main shop, then the stockroom—"

"The flower shop next door. How deep is it?"

"I... I don't know. I've never been inside. Why would—"

Francesco pressed his ear against the wall.

Silence.

He knocked hard. Three sharp raps.

Nothing.

He knocked again, harder, his knuckles cracking against the plaster.

And then—so faint he almost missed it—a shrill scream came from the other side.

Francesco's blood turned to ice. Then fire.

"Serafina?" he called, his voice rough.

The knocking became frantic. Desperate. And then a muffled scream that tore through his chest like a blade.

"*RICCI!*" Francesco bellowed, not caring who heard. "*Get in here! She's behind this wall!*"

Mr. Thompson stumbled backward, his face white. "Behind the wall? But that's impossible—"

"*Get out of my way,*" Francesco snarled.

He looked around frantically for something to break through. His eyes landed on a heavy bookend—solid brass, shaped like a lion. He grabbed it and swung at the wall with all his strength.

Plaster exploded. Dust filled the air. He swung again. And again. Each impact sent pain shooting through his arms and shoulders, but he didn't care. He couldn't feel anything except the desperate need to reach her.

Ricci burst through the door. "Boss—"

"Get a crowbar! An axe! Anything!"

Ricci disappeared and returned seconds later with a tire iron from the car. He joined Francesco, both of them attacking the wall.

More screams from the other side. The sounds of struggle. Of violence.

"Faster!" Francesco roared. Sweat poured down his face. The wall was thick—reinforced.

The bookshop's front door opened. George Randolph stood there, staring. "What in God's name—"

"Call the police!" Mr. Thompson shouted at him. "Tell them we've found her!"

Francesco's tire iron punched through the plaster, finally striking wood. He wedged the tool into the gap and pried with everything he had. Muscles straining. Hands bleeding from splinters and torn skin.

A board cracked. Then another.

Light spilled through the opening—dim, artificial light from somewhere beyond. And with it came sounds that made Francesco's vision go red.

Serafina screaming. A man's voice, guttural and enraged.

Francesco tore at the wall with his bare hands, wood shredding the skin from his palms. Blood made his grip slippery, but he didn't stop. Splinters drove deep under his fingernails. He felt one finger dislocate when he wrenched a board free, but the pain was distant, meaningless. Behind the wall, Serafina was screaming. That was the only thing that mattered.

When he reached the brick, he began punching. The opening widened. Widened more.

And then he saw her.

Serafina lay crumpled on the filthy floor, her nightgown torn open, exposing her skin. Blood covered her face. her lip split, her cheek gashed open. Her wrists were scraped raw. One of her eyes was swelling shut. Her fingers were crimson.

And Edward stood over her with a knife, his pants unbuckled, his intentions clear. He raised the blade high.

"*NO!*"

The bellow came from behind Edward, filled with such primal rage that even Serafina, half-conscious and terrified, felt it in her bones.

Francesco Romano burst through the opening in the wall like an avenging demon. Wood and plaster dust covered him. His hands were bleeding. His eyes were wild.

The knife descended toward Serafina's chest—

She twisted aside at the last second, pure instinct. The blade scraped along the stone wall, throwing sparks.

Francesco crashed into Edward with the force of a freight train, driving him away from Serafina and into the opposite wall. The impact was so violent that the knife flew from Edward's hand, clattering across the floor.

Edward recovered quickly despite his injuries, throwing a wild punch that caught Francesco on the jaw.

Francesco's head snapped back. For a second, stars exploded across his vision. He tasted blood. The sound that came from his throat something that belonged in nightmares. He'd killed men before. Dozens of them. But he'd never wanted to make someone suffer the way he wanted Edward to suffer now.

He retaliated with a devastating uppercut that lifted Edward off his feet. The man crashed down hard, the air rushing from his lungs.

But Edward was desperate now, fueled by the knowledge that he was fighting for his life. He rolled toward the fallen knife. His blood-slicked fingers closed around the handle just as Francesco lunged for him.

Edward turned, blade slashing in a vicious arc.

Steel sliced deep into Francesco's side, grating against his ribs. He felt the blade scrape bone. Blood gushed hot and fast, soaking through his shirt. The pain was white-hot and blinding. His vision grayed at the edges.

But he stayed on his feet. He had to stay on his feet.

Edward swayed on his feet, breathing hard. Blood still poured from his thigh, his face. He'd lost a lot of blood, and it was starting to show. But he raised the knife again, and his eyes held the desperate gleam of a cornered animal.

"You ruined everything," Edward gasped. "She's mine. I claimed her first. I watched her. I waited. *She's mine!*"

"She belongs to no one," Francesco growled, circling carefully despite the pain in his side. Blood soaked through his shirt, warm and wet. "But if she chooses anyone, it's me."

Edward feinted left, then struck right. Francesco barely avoided the blade, but it caught his shoulder, opening another wound. Blood ran down his arm.

The pain was sharp and bright, but Francesco had been cut before. Stabbed. Shot. This was nothing compared to what he'd survived. And nothing—*nothing*—would stop him from protecting Serafina.

"Francesco!" Serafina's voice, thin and desperate. She'd grabbed the brick again, clutching it with shaking hands. Looking for a chance to help.

Francesco glanced toward her for just a second—just long enough to see she was alive, bloodied but alive.

Edward saw his opening. But instead of attacking Francesco, he dove toward Serafina with the last of his strength.

His arm snaked around her waist before she could react, yanking her against his chest. Edward's arm clamped around Serafina. She gave a have scream as the knife bit into her throat hard enough to draw blood that trickled down her neck.

"Stay back!" Edward shrieked, and Francesco could see in his eyes that he meant it. This wasn't a bluff. Edward would kill her just to keep Francesco from having her. "I'll cut her open right in front of you! I swear to God, I'll do it!"

Francesco froze, his hands raised. Blood dripped from his wounds, pattering softly on the floor. "Edward, listen to me. You don't want to do this."

"*Shut up!*" Edward's grip tightened, and Serafina whimpered as the steel bit into her skin, not breaking it, but the threat was clear. "She was supposed to be mine! *Mine*, damn you! I did everything right! I was patient! I was kind! And she threw it all away for a *killer!*"

Ricci appeared in the opening, working his way through carefully. His eyes assessed the situation in an instant.

"Edward," Francesco said, forcing his voice to stay calm despite the terror clawing at his chest. He could see Serafina's eyes—wide with fear, pleading. "Think about what you're doing. Let her go, and we can talk about this."

"*No more talking!*" Edward snarled. His face was deathly pale now from blood loss, his movements becoming uncoordinated. But the knife stayed steady at Serafina's throat. "If I can't have her, then nobody can!"

Ricci caught Francesco's eye and asked in rapid Italian, "*Does he speak Italian?*"

Serafina, even terrified and barely conscious, understood what Ricci was asking. She managed to gasp out, "What are you saying? Please? We don't speak Italian."

The message was received. Edward clearly had no idea what was being said.

Ricci moved slightly closer to Francesco, positioning himself. He caught Serafina's eye and spoke in a quiet, rapid whisper. "*Tre, calcia e cadi.*" Three, kick and drop.

He shifted just enough for her to see the gun in his hand, held low and behind him.

Serafina's eyes widened slightly in understanding. Her fingers tightened around the brick she still clutched. She had to trust that Ricci knew what he was doing.

Francesco kept talking, keeping Edward's attention on him. "You loved her, didn't you? In your own way?"

"*Loved* her?" Edward's laugh was bitter and broken. "I *love* her. Past, present, future. I've loved her since the first moment I saw her. She just never saw me. Never really looked."

"She sees you now," Francesco said quietly.

Ricci began the count with subtle hand signals. One finger.

Two fingers.

On three, everything happened at once.

Serafina slammed the brick hard into Edward's injured thigh—the same spot where the spoon had punctured deep—and let her legs give out, dropping straight down and out of Edward's grip.

Edward howled and staggered, his arm swinging wide as he tried to catch her.

The gunshot was deafening in the enclosed space.

Edward lurched sideways, blood blooming across his shoulder where Ricci's bullet struck. But he didn't fall. Instead, he stumbled, using the wall for support, the knife still in his hand.

Serafina spun on her knees as Edward reached for her again, his face twisted in pain and rage and something that might have been heartbreak.

She swung the brick one final time.

It connected with his temple with a sickening crunch. Edward's eyes rolled back. His knees buckled. He collapsed.

Silence fell over the chamber, broken only by their labored breathing and the ringing echo of the gunshot.

Francesco stared at Edward's motionless form on the ground. Blood pooled beneath him from multiple wounds—the thigh, the shoulder, the head. His chest still rose and fell shallowly.

Then Francesco looked at Serafina.

She knelt on the filthy floor in her torn nightgown, the brick still raised in her shaking hands. Blood covered her She stared at Edward's body, the brick still raised. Her breath came in rapid, shallow pants. Then she started shaking—violent tremors that wracked her entire frame.

Francesco moved to her, dropping to his knees despite the pain screaming through his wounds. He reached for her slowly, giving her the chance to pull away if she needed to. When he touched her shoulder, she flinched violently, scrambling backward before recognition flooded her eyes.

"Francesco," she gasped. "It's you. It's really you."

Serafina pressed her hand against his ribs where blood seeped through his shirt. She pulled it away and stared at the crimson on her palm.

343

"You're hurt," she whimpered, eyes wide with disbelief. "You're hurt. You're... Francesco, you're bleeding—"

"I'm fine," he lied. The wounds hurt like hell, but they weren't fatal. He'd survived worse.

Her hands shook as she touched his face, his shoulders, as if she needed to confirm he was real. "You came. You came, and... you found me, and..."

"*Always*," he said roughly. "*I'll always find you.*"

Ricci knelt beside Edward, checking his pulse. "*Alive*," he reported. "*Barely conscious.*"

Francesco's eyes never left Serafina. She was looking at Edward now, her expression growing blank.

"He's..." she whispered. "He..."

"*Alive*," Francesco confirmed. Something dark crossed his face. Part of him—a large part—wanted Edward dead. Wanted to finish what they'd started. But Serafina was watching, and he couldn't make her see that. Not now. Not after everything she already had.

Ricci pulled rope from his coat and began binding Edward's hands and feet. The man groaned but didn't regain consciousness.

Mr. Thompson appeared in the opening, his face white. Behind him, George Randolph pushed through, taking in the scene with wide eyes.

"Dear God," Mr. Thompson breathed. "Serafina..."

But Serafina couldn't look at them. She kept her face pressed against Francesco's chest, her hands clutching his bloody shirt.

"You're safe," Francesco murmured into her hair, over and over like a prayer. "You're safe now. I've got you."

But even as he held her, his eyes remained fixed on Edward's unconscious form. The man who had terrorized her. Who had touched her. Who had tried to destroy her.

Every instinct Francesco possessed screamed at him to finish it. To wrap his hands around Edward's throat and squeeze until there was nothing left but a corpse.

But Serafina was shaking in his arms, and that was more important than vengeance. For now.

"Boss?" Ricci's voice was carefully neutral, but Francesco heard the question underneath.

Francesco's vision kept tunneling. He'd lost more blood than he realized. The floor seemed to tilt beneath him. But he didn't loosen his hold on Serafina. Couldn't.

"Boss, you need to sit down," Ricci said, more urgently now. "You're going white."

"No." Francesco's voice came from somewhere far away, distant even to his own ears. "Not until she's safe. Not until she's out of here."

He looked at Edward's bound form, then at Serafina trembling against him. He made his decision.

"Call the police," Francesco said, his voice cold as winter despite the weakness creeping through his limbs. "Tell them we've caught their serial killer."

Ricci nodded and moved toward the opening to make the call.

As sirens began to wail in the distance, Francesco held Serafina tighter, fighting to stay conscious. His wounds ached. Blood soaked his shirt, spreading in a warm, wet stain. But none of that mattered.

She was alive. Breathing in his arms. Her heart beating against his chest.

She was safe.

"It's over," he whispered. "It's over now."

But he knew that it wasn't really over. The nightmares would come. The fear would linger. The scars, physical and otherwise, would remain.

But she was alive. And as Francesco held her close in that dark, terrible place, he made a silent vow: no force on earth would ever separate them again.

Whatever it took. Whatever he had to do. Whatever he had to become.

She was his to protect now. And he would burn the whole world down before he let anyone hurt her again.

The police flooded into the bookshop within minutes, their heavy boots echoing on the wooden floors. Francesco could hear them in the main shop, Mr. Thompson's voice raised in explanation, other voices barking orders.

"Through here!" Mr. Thompson called. "Behind the wall!"

Francesco didn't move. He stayed exactly where he was, kneeling on the filthy floor with Serafina in his arms. Let them come to him. He wasn't letting her go.

A police sergeant pushed through the opening, followed by two officers. They stopped short, taking in the makeshift cell, the blood, Edward's bound form, and Francesco Romano holding Serafina Silvano.

"Jesus Christ," the sergeant breathed. His eyes swept the cell—the bucket in the corner, the chain attached to the wall, the blood spatters..."Is she—"

"She's alive," Francesco said flatly. "He's the one you want. Edward Whitmore. Check your files."

One of the officers knelt by Edward, checking his wounds. "This one needs a doctor. Lost a lot of blood."

"So does she," Francesco snapped. "She gets treated first."

The sergeant's eyes narrowed slightly as he looked at Francesco. He clearly recognized him, recognized the name Romano and everything it implied. But whatever he thought about a mobster rescuing a woman from a serial killer, he kept it to himself.

"We'll need to take statements from both of you," the sergeant said carefully. "And we'll need to bring Whitmore in for questioning once he's conscious."

"He confessed," Serafina's voice was barely a whisper against Francesco's chest. "He told me about the others. Cora. Lily. Jessica. He said he killed them because they rejected him."

The sergeant's expression darkened. "Can you repeat that for the record, miss?"

Serafina nodded weakly, but she didn't pull away from Francesco.

More police entered through the opening. Some began entering through the door Edward hard used from his shop, though the

346

locked gate s stopped them. Someone had brought a camera. Flashbulbs began popping as they documented the scene. Each flash made Serafina flinch.

"Stop," Francesco ordered. "No more photographs while she's in here."

"Mr. Romano, we need to document the crime scene—"

"Document it after we leave." Francesco's voice carried enough menace that the photographer lowered his camera.

A medic pushed through the crowd, a bag in his hand. "I need to examine her. Check for injuries."

Francesco finally looked down at Serafina. Her eyes were closed now, her breathing shallow. She'd been running on adrenaline and terror, and now that she was safe, her body was shutting down.

"Serafina," he said softly. "The doctor needs to look at you."

Her eyes fluttered open. "Don't leave me."

"Never." He looked at the medic. "You examine her here. I don't let go."

The medic opened his mouth to argue, saw Francesco's expression, and apparently decided it wasn't worth the fight. "All right. But I need space to work."

Francesco shifted slightly, still holding Serafina but allowing the medic access. The man began checking her injuries, testing her pupils, examining the cuts on her face and hands, gently probing her ribs.

Serafina hissed in pain when he touched her side.

"Possible cracked ribs," the medic said. "Severe lacerations on her hands. Looks like her fingernails were torn off. Split lip, facial contusions. Signs of strangulation on her throat, but no serious damage to the windpipe." He looked up at the sergeant. "She needs to go to the hospital. Full examination."

"We have an ambulance waiting outside."

"I'm taking her," Francesco said.

"Mr. Romano, protocol requires—"

"I'm taking her." Francesco's tone left no room for argument. "You can follow us to the hospital. You can post guards at her door. You can do whatever you need to do. But I'm the one taking her out of here."

The sergeant and Francesco locked eyes. Some silent understanding passed between them, perhaps recognition that trying to separate them right now would cause more problems than it solved.

"Fine," the sergeant said. "But officers will escort you."

Francesco nodded. He tried to stand, but his vision grayed at the edges. The blood loss. The adrenaline crash. His body was finally catching up to what he'd put it through.

"*Boss.*" Ricci was beside him instantly, gripping his arm. "*You can't carry her. Not with those wounds.*"

"*I can—*" Francesco started, but even as he said it, he knew Ricci was right. His legs shook. His side screamed where the knife had gone deep.

"*Let me,*" Ricci said quietly. He looked at Serafina. "Miss Silvano, I need to carry you out. Is that all right?"

Serafina's eyes widened with panic. She reached for Francesco. "No, I need—"

"I'll be right beside you," Francesco said, forcing steadiness into his voice. "Every step. I'm not leaving you. But Ricci's right. I've lost too much blood. I won't make it ten feet carrying you."

He hated needing to make the admission, but it was true.

Serafina looked between them, then nodded reluctantly. Ricci carefully lifted her, and Francesco used the wall to pull himself upright. Pain exploded through his side, but he stayed on his feet through sheer will.

They moved toward the opening, Ricci carrying Serafina with Francesco stumbling alongside them. He kept his hand on her shoulder as much for her comfort as his balance.

As they reached the opening, she suddenly tensed. "Wait."

Ricci stopped immediately. "What is it?"

"Him." She turned her head slightly, looking back at Edward's unconscious form. "Is he... will he..."

"He'll go to prison," Francesco said quietly. "Then he'll meet Sparky. He'll never touch you again. Never."

Serafina stared at Edward for a long moment. Francesco could feel the tremors running through her body.

"I want to see him wake up," she whispered. "I want him to know I survived, and that I won."

Francesco looked at the sergeant, who shifted uncomfortably. "Miss Silvano, I don't think that's advisable. You should get medical attention—"

"Please." Her voice was barely audible, but there was steel underneath. "Just for a moment."

The sergeant hesitated, then nodded to one of his officers. "Wake him up."

The officer grabbed the bucket Serafina had been given as a toilet and dumped it over Edward's face.

Edward sputtered and gasped, his eyes flying open. For a moment, he looked confused, disoriented. Then his gaze focused on Serafina in Ricci's arms.

Something ugly twisted across his face. "Serafina—"

"No," she said, her voice stronger now. "You don't get to say my name anymore. You don't get to speak to me. You don't get anything."

Edward's face crumpled. For just a second, he looked like Danny again, lost and confused and broken. "I loved you. I just wanted you to understand—"

"You didn't love me," Serafina said. "You don't know what love is. Love doesn't hurt or cage or destroy."

She turned her face back to Ricci's shoulder. "I'm ready to go now."

Francesco swayed slightly, his hand pressed to his bleeding side. The brief moment of stillness had made his body realize just how much damage had been done.

As they passed Edward, Francesco paused just long enough to look down at the man who had terrorized the woman he loved.

"If you ever speak her name again," Francesco said, his voice soft and deadly, "I'll find you. I don't care if you're in a cell. I don't care if you're surrounded by guards. I will find you, and I will make you wish you'd died in this room."

Edward's eyes widened in fear. Whatever he saw in Francesco's face made him shrink back against the wall.

"Boss, you need to sit down," Ricci said urgently.

"No. Not until she's out of here." Francesco's voice came from somewhere far away. *"Keep moving."*

Ricci carried Serafina through the hole in the wall and into the bookshop beyond. Francesco had to brace himself against the rough edges, leaving bloody handprints on the wood. Each step sent fresh pain through his wounds, but he forced himself to keep going. The space had grown crowded with police officers, Mr. Thompson, George Randolph, and curiosity seekers who'd heard the commotion. Everyone stopped and stared as they emerged: Ricci carrying a broken Serafina, Francesco barely staying upright, both of them covered in blood.

Mr. Thompson's eyes filled with tears. "Oh, my dear girl."

But Francesco didn't stop. He pushed through the crowd, one hand on Ricci's shoulder for balance, the other on Serafina. They made it through and out into the cool evening air.

The sun was setting, painting the sky in shades of orange and red. Serafina turned her face up to it, feeling real air on her skin for the first time in days.

"The sky," she whispered. "I thought I'd never see it again."

Francesco touched her face with his bloodied hand. He didn't trust himself to speak. He hardly trusted his legs to keep holding him up much longer.

An ambulance waited at the curb with its back doors open. Francesco expected Ricci to head toward his own car, but the police sergeant appeared beside them first.

"You're both going in the ambulance," the sergeant said. "Mr. Romano, you can barely stand. Miss Silvano needs immediate medical attention. This isn't negotiable."

Francesco wanted to argue. But his vision was tunneling again, and he knew the sergeant was right. "Together," he managed. "She doesn't go anywhere without me."

"Together," the sergeant agreed.

But the paramedics had two gurneys ready and tried to separate them, to put Serafina in one ambulance and Francesco in another.

"No," Serafina said, her voice gaining strength despite her injuries. "He stays with me."

"Miss, we need to treat you properly—"

"Then treat us in the same ambulance." Her fingers clutched at Francesco's bloody shirt. "I'm not letting him go."

The paramedics exchanged glances, then nodded. They crammed both gurneys into the ambulance the side of one atop the other. Francesco reached across the tiny space, and Serafina's bandaged hand found his.

"I've got you," Francesco said, though his voice was fading. "Not letting go."

"You better not pass out on me," Serafina whispered, seeing his eyes starting to close. "Francesco? Stay awake. Please stay away. Don't die."

"Trying." His grip on her hand tightened. "Not... not leaving you."

The paramedic pressed a hand to Francesco's forehead, then checked his pulse at his neck, then glanced up at his partner. "He's going into shock. We need to move. Mr. Romano? Stay with us."

The ambulance lurched forward, the driver calling out to clear the way as they navigated the evening streets. Through the back windows, Francesco could see Ricci following in the car, the police sergeant's vehicle behind him.

Serafina squeezed his hand. "You found me," she said again, needing him to hear it. "You saved me."

Francesco's eyes met hers, and despite the pain, despite the blood loss, despite everything, he managed to speak one word: "Always."

His eyes finally closed.

The paramedic tapped Francesco's. cheek. "Mr. Romano, you need to stay with us."

Serafina watched with tears in her eyes. The paramedic pressed clean gauze to Francesco's side, trying to slow the bleeding, but it soaked through almost immediately.

"He'll be okay, won't he? Tell me he'll be okay."

The paramedic was too focused on keeping pressure on Francesco's wounds, his hands working quickly to apply more bandages, to reply.

And as the ambulance raced through the darkening streets toward the hospital, the driver shouting warnings to pedestrians and other vehicles, Serafina held onto Francesco's hand and prayed—to a

God she wasn't sure she believed in anymore—that after surviving her nightmare, she wouldn't lose the man who'd walked through hell to save her.

CHAPTER 22

Francesco sat in the back seat of his own car, Serafina curled against less uninjured side. Ricci drove, his eyes flicking to the rearview mirror every few seconds to check on them.

They'd spent the entire night at the hospital. The doctors had worked on Francesco first. Twenty-three stitches in his side where Edward's knife had carved deep, another twelve in his shoulder. The blade had missed anything vital, but he'd lost enough blood that they'd insisted on keeping him for observation. He'd refused to be admitted until he knew Serafina was safe.

While the doctors examined Serafina in another room, cleaning her wounds and documenting her injuries, asking questions in soft, careful voices, Francesco had sat in a hospital chair and let them stitch him back together. The procaine had worn off hours ago. Now every breath sent sharp pain through his ribs, and his shoulder throbbed with each heartbeat.

Ricci had shown up at the hospital just before dawn with a clean shirt and jacket for Francesco. The hospital had cleaned most of the blood off him, but his clothes had been ruined, torn and soaked through. Francesco had been grateful for the fresh clothes, even if putting them on had made his stitches scream in protest.

But Serafina was pressed against his good side, her bandaged hand clutching his clean shirt, and that mattered ore than his own comfort.

The police had been relentless with their questions. The sergeant wanted Serafina to stay in the hospital, easily available for more questioning. But Mr. Randolph had arrived just after midnight with his lawyer, and between legal threats and Francesco's barely contained violence—even injured, he was dangerous—they'd reached a compromise: Serafina would stay at the Randolph estate, and officers could visit there to take additional statements as needed.

Finally, as dawn broke over the city, the doctors had agreed to discharge them both. Strict instructions for Francesco: rest, no strenuous activity, return immediately if he showed signs of infection or reopened wounds. The nurse had looked pointedly at his bloody knuckles when she'd said it.

He hadn't told them about the dislocated finger Ricci had popped back into place for him. Some things didn't need medical attention.

"*How much further?*" Francesco asked.

"*Twenty minutes, boss.*" Ricci paused. "*You look like hell.*"

"*I feel like hell.*"

"*Should've stayed in the hospital.*"

"*She needed to leave. I wasn't letting her go alone.*" Francesco's jaw tightened. "*Besides, I'll heal. She's the one I'm worried about.*"

"But you really should be resting in a hospital bed," Serafina said quietly, her voice raspy.

"So should you."

"I couldn't stay there, not in a room with a lock on the outside." She pressed closer to him, and he winced as the movement jarred his stitches. She immediately pulled back. "I'm sorry—"

"Don't." He carefully shifted, wrapping his better arm around her. "Come here."

They drove in silence for a few minutes. Francesco kept glancing down at Serafina, needing to confirm she was really there. Really safe.

"Does it hurt so much?" she asked quietly. "This side?"

"Everything hurts. But I'm alive. That's more than I thought I'd be when I saw that knife coming."

Serafina's hand moved to his bandaged ribs, hovering just above the wound without touching. "You could have died. You almost died."

"But I didn't." He caught her hand gently. "Neither of us did."

"He would have killed me," she whispered. "If you'd been even a minute later—"

"But I wasn't." Francesco's voice was firm. "Don't think about what might have happened. We're both here. We're both alive."

She was quiet for a moment. "When I heard you breaking through that wall, I thought that my mind had finally broken from the terror and that I was dreaming it."

"I'm real." He squeezed her hand. "We're real. This is real."

"I know." But her voice shook. "I just keep waiting to wake up back in that cell."

Francesco pressed a careful kiss to the top of her head. "You won't. I promise you won't."

She settled against him more carefully this time, her head on his shoulder. Within minutes, exhaustion overtook her and her breathing deepened into sleep. Through the rearview mirror, Francesco caught Ricci's eyes.

"*She's out,*" Ricci observed quietly.

"*Good. She needs it.*"

Ricci was quiet for a moment, his hands tight on the steering wheel. "*Boss, when we were breaking through that wall... when we heard her screaming...*" He trailed off.

"*What?*"

"*I kept thinking about Angela. She's only three weeks old. Tiny. Perfect.*" Ricci's voice roughened. "*And someday she'll be a young woman. Out in the world. And there are men like Whitmore everywhere.*"

Francesco looked at his friend—this man who'd killed alongside him without hesitation—and saw real fear in his eyes. Fear for his infant daughter.

"Yes," Francesco said honestly. "*There are.*"

"*We're bad men, boss. We know what bad men are capable of because we are bad men.*" Ricci's jaw clenched. "*But Whitmore...*

that's different. What he did to those women. What he tried to do to Miss Silvano. That's—"

"Evil," Francesco finished quietly. "We break bones and kill people who know the risks. Who chose this life. Whitmore hunted innocent women. Caged them. Destroyed them for rejecting him." He paused. "There's a difference between what we do and what he is."

"Is there? To the rest of the world, we're all monsters."

"Maybe. But we have lines we don't cross." Francesco glanced down at Serafina sleeping against him. "He crossed every line there is."

Ricci nodded slowly. "How do I protect Angela from men like him? How do I keep her safe when I can't watch her every second? What if something happens and I'm not there? What if I'm too late?"

Francesco thought of how close he'd come to being too late. "You teach her to be smart. To trust her instincts. And you make sure she knows—absolutely knows—that if anyone ever hurts her, you'll move heaven and earth to get her back." He paused. "The way you helped me last night."

"Last night you tore through a wall with your bare hands," Ricci said quietly. "I watched you break yourself getting to her. I'd do the same for Angela. But what if it's not enough?"

"Then you do what I did. You break yourself anyway. You don't stop until you get her back or you die trying." Francesco's voice was firm. "That's what it means to protect someone you love."

Ricci's jaw tightened. "She's lucky. Miss Silvano. That you found her in time."

"We both are."

They drove in silence for a few more minutes. Francesco kept his eyes on Serafina's face, watching her sleep, grateful beyond words that she could.

Ricci cleared his throat from the front seat. "Well, Boss, we're almost there."

Ricci brought the car to a gentle stop in the circular drive. The front door opened before Ricci could come around to help.

Mrs. Randolph appeared on the steps, Clara close behind her. Both women's faces showed the strain of a sleepless night spent waiting for news.

Francesco carefully shifted, trying not to startle Serafina. "We're here," he said softly.

Her eyes fluttered open, disoriented for a moment before awareness returned. She tensed, then relaxed slightly when she saw where they were.

Ricci opened the car door and helped Serafina out carefully. Francesco climbed out on his own, one hand pressed to his bandaged side, moving stiffly.

"Oh, my dear girl," Mrs. Randolph breathed as she approached. Her eyes took in the fresh bandages, the cuts and bruises on Serafina's face. "Oh, Serafina."

Clara made a small sound. Her hand flew to her mouth.

Mrs. Randolph's gaze shifted to Francesco. "How are you, Mr. Romano?"

"I'm fine," Francesco said, though the lie was obvious. He moved to Serafina's side, and she immediately reached for him. His arm came around her waist, supporting her as they moved toward the house.

"We called Dr. Morrison last night after we heard," Mrs. Randolph said, leading them inside. "He said the hospital would take good care of you both, but he wanted to check on you himself. He's waiting in Serafina's new room, next to Clara's. Can't have her in the same room she was. Dr. Curtis is with him as well."

"That wasn't necessary," Francesco said. "The hospital doctors—"

"It's necessary for our peace of mind," Mrs. Randolph interrupted gently but firmly.

"Who is here?" Serafina's voice was thin.

"Just the doctors, George, and Dad," Clara said quickly, walking beside them. "No one else."

The entry hall was overwhelmingly bright after the darkness of the cell and the harsh fluorescent lights of the hospital. Serafina blinked against the light from the chandelier, swaying slightly.

"Easy," Francesco murmured, tightening his hold on her despite the way it pulled his stitches.

Mr. Randolph appeared from the parlor, his son behind him. Both men stopped short when they saw them.

"Dear God," Mr. Randolph said quietly, though his expression held relief. He looked at Francesco, and some understanding that transcended words passed between them. "Thank you for bringing her home."

Francesco nodded once, curtly.

George stepped forward, his eyes moving between them. "You both look... better than you did last night." His voice was tight. "At the bookshop, when they brought you out—" He stopped, swallowing hard. "I thought... I wasn't sure either of you would survive."

"We're here," Serafina said softly. "We made it."

"I should have been more vigilant," George continued. "Should have paid more attention. If I'd noticed something was wrong with that florist—"

"It's not your fault," Serafina said. "I new him better and never would have imagined."

"Let's get you upstairs," Mrs. Randolph said gently, but firmly, already ushering them toward the grand staircase. "Clara, go ahead and let the doctors know we're coming."

Clara hurried up the stairs while Mrs. Randolph and Francesco guided Serafina up slowly. By the time they reached the landing, she was leaning heavily on Francesco, who was struggling himself not to show how much the climb hurt him.

"Almost there," he murmured. "Just a little further."

Mrs. Randolph took them to a room with pale lavender walls with white furniture, and pristine sprigged linens on the large canopy bed. Serafina stopped in the doorway, her breathing suddenly rapid and shallow.

"The room," she managed. "It's... the door. Is there a lock?"

Mrs. Randolph looked confused. "Well, yes, dear. All the bedrooms have locks."

"On the inside? Can I lock it from the inside only?"

Understanding dawned on Mrs. Randolph's face. "Yes. Yes, of course. The key is right here—" She moved to the door, showing Serafina the key hanging from a ribbon on the inside handle. "See? You can lock it whenever you want. No one can come in unless you let them."

Serafina stared at the key for a long moment, then nodded. "All right. That's... that's good."

Dr. Morrison stood from the chair by the window where he'd been waiting. He was an older man with kind eyes, the same doctor who'd treated Mrs. Thompson's pneumonia, who'd been caring for the Randolph family for decades. Beside him stood Dr. Curtis, his own medical bag in hand.

"Miss Silvano, Mr. Romano," Dr. Morrison said gently. "I'm very glad to see you both home safe. The hospital called with their reports, but I'd like to examine you both myself if you don't mind. Just to ensure everything is healing properly and that you're comfortable."

Serafina looked at Francesco. "Will you stay?"

"If you want me to." He looked at Dr. Morrison. "Is that appropriate?"

The doctor glanced between them. "Under the circumstances, I think Miss Silvano should have whoever she needs present. Though Mrs. Randolph should probably stay as well. For propriety."

Mrs. Randolph nodded. "Clara, dear, why don't you go downstairs with your father and brother? I'll stay here."

Clara hesitated, looking at Serafina.

"It's all right," Serafina said. "I'm not going anywhere. And you mother will be right here."

Clara nodded and slipped out, leaving Mrs. Randolph positioned discreetly near the door.

Francesco helped Serafina to the bed. She sat on the edge, her hands twisting in her lap. The bandages made the gesture awkward, and she looked down at them as if surprised to find them there.

"I can't feel my fingertips," she said suddenly. "Is that normal?"

Dr. Morrison knelt in front of her, gently taking one of her hands. "May I?"

She nodded. He carefully unwrapped the bandage, revealing the torn and bloody nail beds underneath. Serafina looked away.

"The nerve endings are damaged," Dr. Morrison explained. "You'll have some numbness for a while, possibly permanently in a few fingers. But sensation should return to most of them as they heal."

"And if it doesn't?"

He met her eyes. "Then you'll adapt. The human body is remarkably resilient, Miss Silvano. As, I suspect, are you."

He continued his examination by checking the bandages on her ribs, looking at the cuts on her face, and examining her throat where bruises had started to form in the shape of Edward's fingers.

Throughout it all, Serafina remained very still, very quiet. Too quiet. Francesco watched her face, seeing how carefully blank she kept her expression, and his chest ached.

"No signs of serious internal damage," Dr. Morrison finally said, rewrapping her hands with fresh bandages. "The ribs should heal on their own in four to six weeks. The cuts will scar, I'm afraid, but they should fade with time." He paused. "Physically, you'll recover. But, Miss Silvano, I want you to understand that an ordeal of this nature affects more than just the body."

Serafina's jaw tightened. "I'm fine."

"You're not fine. And that's all right. No one expects you to be."

"I just want to sleep," Serafina said, her voice suddenly very small. "I'm so tired."

Dr. Morrison stood. "Then we'll let you rest soon." He turned to Francesco. "Mr. Romano, would you like me to examine your wounds as well? Just to ensure the hospital doctors—"

"That won't be necessary," Francesco said. "I have my own doctor."

"Francesco," Serafina said softly. "Please. Let him check. It would... it would help me feel better, knowing you're all right."

Francesco met her eyes and saw the plea there. After everything she'd been through, this small thing mattered to her.

"All right," he said quietly.

"I should assist as well," Dr. Curtis said, stepping forward. "If Mr. Romano is amenable, that is. Two sets of eyes are better than one for knife wounds."

Francesco nodded curtly.

He carefully removed his jacket, then unbuttoned his shirt. The movements pulled at his stitches, and he couldn't quite suppress a wince.

When he peeled the shirt away, the white bandages wrapped around his torso were already showing spots of fresh blood where he'd strained the wounds during the climb upstairs.

"Twenty-three stitches in your side," Dr. Morrison said, repeated from the hospital report. "Twelve in your shoulder. The blade went deep."

He and Dr. Curtis worked together to unwrap the bandages carefully. Serafina watched with wide eyes.

The wound in his side was angry and red, the black stitches stark against his skin. The knife had carved a path several inches long between his ribs.

"You're fortunate," Dr. Curtis observed, his voice clinical. "Another inch to the left and it would have punctured your lung. As it is, you'll have significant scarring."

"I've had worse," Francesco said flatly.

Dr. Morrison examined both wounds thoroughly, then nodded to Dr. Curtis. Together they rewrapped the injuries with fresh bandages.

"No signs of infection yet, which is good," Dr. Morrison said. "But you need to rest, Mr. Romano. No strenuous activity for at least two weeks. These wounds need time to heal properly."

"I'll rest."

"I mean it. No lifting, no fighting, no—" Dr. Morrison paused delicately. "No activities that might strain the stitches. The wound in your side went quite deep."

"I understand."

"And someone should check these daily." Dr. Curtis aded. "If they start seeping, if you develop a fever, if the area becomes hot or swollen—those are signs of infection. Don't ignore them."

"I won't."

After the doctors finished, Francesco carefully pulled his clean shirt. The simple act of lifting his arms made him grit his teeth, but he managed without complaint.

"Thank you," Serafina said to both doctors. "For checking him, and for everything."

"Of course, Miss Silvano," Dr. Morrison said kindly. He closed his medical bag. "I'll leave laudanum for the pain, for. both of you Just a few drops in water before bed. And if you need me at any time, day or night—you, too, Mr. Romano—Mrs. Randolph knows how to reach me."

After Dr. Morrison and Dr. Curtis left, Mrs. Randolph lingered at the door. "I'll have Clara bring up some tea in a bit. And Mr. Romano..." She met his eyes. "Thank you for bringing her home."

"There's nothing to thank me for," Francesco said.

"I disagree." She smiled softly, closing the door behind her.

Francesco turned to find Serafina staring at the bed like it might bite her.

"What's wrong?" he asked.

"I don't know if I can sleep there. In a bed. It's too soft. Too..." She wrapped her arms around herself. "The cell was hard. Cold stone. If I close my eyes and feel something soft, I might think I'm dreaming. and that I'm still there."

Francesco looked around the room, then moved to gather several thick blankets from the wardrobe. He carried them to the floor beside the bed and knelt carefully.

He started spreading the first blanket, but his movements were stiff, awkward. The wound in his side ached.

"Let me help," Serafina said, lowering herself to her knees beside him.

"You should rest—"

"So should you." She took the edge of the blanket and helped spread it flat, her bandaged hands clumsy. "We can do this together."

They worked in silence, spreading the blankets one by one. Francesco had to pause twice when the movement pulled too sharply, and Serafina moved slowly, her cracked ribs making every breath painful.

When they finished, Francesco used the bedpost to pull himself upright, his face gray with effort. Serafina remained on her knees, staring at the makeshift bed they'd created together. Her eyes filled with tears. "Thank you."

"We made it together," he said quietly. "Do you need help changing?" He gestured to the nightgown Mrs. Randolph had laid out. "Or I can get—"

"I can manage." She paused. "But don't leave. Please?"

Francesco turned his back while she changed, giving her privacy while staying in the room. He heard the soft rustle of fabric and her sharp intake of breath when she hissed in some pain.

"All right," she said finally. "I'm decent."

He turned to find her in a white cotton nightgown, standing uncertainly by the makeshift bed on the floor.

"Do you want the laudanum?" he asked.

She shook her head. "Not yet. I need... I need to feel real for a while longer. The drugs will make everything fuzzy."

She lowered herself carefully to the pallet. Francesco grabbed a pillow from the bed and put it under her head.

"Is that better?"

Yes." She looked up at him. "Will you... can you lay beside me? Just for a while? I need to know you're close."

Francesco hesitated. The chair would be more proper. But propriety seemed meaningless after everything they'd been through.

"All right."

He lowered himself carefully to the makeshift bed beside her, his movements achingly slow. Even so, the wound in his side twinged, and he couldn't quite suppress a sharp intake of breath.

"You're in pain," Serafina said, her eyes widening with concern.

"I'm fine." But he wasn't. The blood loss, the stitches, and the exhaustion all caught up to him at once again. His vision swam slightly as he settled onto his back beside her.

"You're not fine," she whispered. "You're as broken as I am."

"Then we're broken together." He turned his head to look at her, their faces inches apart on the hard floor.

Serafina reached out with one bandaged hand, and Francesco

took it carefully, mindful of her injuries. She shifted slightly closer, resting her head near his shoulder—not quite touching, but close enough to feel his warmth.

"I thought I was going to die," Serafina said into the quiet. "When he had the knife at my throat, when I couldn't breathe—I was certain I'd die in that cell."

"But you didn't." Francesco's voice was rough. "You fought. You survived."

"I survived." She said it like she was testing the words. "I'm alive."

"You're alive."

She closed her eyes, and Francesco thought she might be sleeping. But then she spoke again, so quietly he almost missed it.

"I can still smell it. The cell. The damp. The..." She swallowed hard. "Him."

Francesco's hands clenched into fists. "The doctors said you could bathe tomorrow. That could help wash it all away."

"Will it wash away? Really?" Her eyes opened, fixing on him. "Or will I smell it forever?"

"I don't know," Francesco said honestly. "But I'll be here while you try."

Serafina reached out with one bandaged hand, and Francesco took it carefully.

"Don't leave," she whispered. "Not today. Not tonight. Maybe not for a while."

"I won't," he promised. "Sleep now. I'll be right here."

She closed her eyes again, her breathing gradually evening out. But even in sleep, she didn't let go of his hand.

Francesco lay beside her through the long hours, fighting his own exhaustion. His side ached. His shoulder throbbed. The hard floor did nothing to ease the pain. But Serafina was breathing steadily beside him, alive and safe, and that was all that mattered.

His own eyes grew heavy. The blood loss made everything feel distant, dreamlike. He fought to stay awake, to keep watch over her.

But eventually, despite his best efforts, exhaustion won.

When the nightmares came, when Serafina woke gasping and clawing at invisible bonds, Francesco was there beside her, close

364

enough that she could feel his presence immediately. He whispered that she was safe, that it was over, that he wouldn't let anything hurt her again.

Even if he had to lie to make her believe it.

And when she finally fell back into fitful sleep, Francesco lay awake in, one hand still holding hers, the other pressed to his wounded side, and made a silent vow: no one would ever touch her again. Not while he drew breath.

Francesco must have dozed off beside her sometime. He slightly roused to afternoon light streaming through the lace-curtained windows and Dr. Morrison standing in the doorway with Mrs. Randolph.

"They're both still sleeping?" the doctor asked quietly.

Mrs. Randolph nodded, her eyes on the two figures lying side by side on the ground. "She finally settled a few hours ago. And he... poor man was exhausted."

"Let them both rest as long as they need." Dr. Morrison glanced at Mrs. Randolph. "I'll check on them again this evening. Call me if anything changes."

After the doctor left, Mrs. Randolph quietly set a tray with cups of coffee and sandwiches on the table near the door, then slipped out without waking them.

It was nearly four when Francesco finally fully stirred. His side screamed when he tried to move. After lying in the same position for hours, his stitches had stiffened. He bit back a groan, not wanting to wake Serafina.

But she was already awake, watching him with blue haunted eyes.

"You stayed," she whispered.

"I told you I would." His voice was rough with sleep and pain.

"But you hurt. I should have had you take the bed."

"I was where I needed to be."

She sat up carefully, lips between her teeth and nose scrunched.

"You need to eat something," she said, seeing the tray Mrs. Randolph had left and carefully rising to her feet.

"So do you."

"Then we'll eat together."

They shared the simple food that neither of them tasted. Francesco forced himself to eat despite his stomach turning and not wanting anything. The coffee helped clear his head, at least, though it also reminded him that he did need to call Ricci to take him home soon, to change into clean clothes that weren't bloodstained and check in about business that couldn't wait. The Romano family didn't stop operating just because their boss had gotten himself stabbed.

But not yet. Not until he knew Serafina was settled.

When they finished, Serafina set down her cup. "I need to use the washroom. And maybe... maybe try to clean up properly?"

Francesco made his way to the door and opened it. Mrs. Randolph was just coming down the hall, and he caught her eye.

"Mrs. Randolph, Serafina needs some help cleaning herself."

"Of course. Mr. Randolph would like a word with you downstairs, anyway, if you're feeling up to it."

Within minutes, Clara appeared with fresh water, clean cloths, and gentle hands to help Serafina wash away the worst of the grime and blood that the hospital hadn't managed to remove.

When Serafina occupied with Clara, safe for the moment, Francesco made his way downstairs slowly, one hand on the banister for balance. Mr. Randolph waited in the parlor with his morning paper and a contemplative expression.

"You stayed with her all night, and today," the older man said. It wasn't quite a question.

"She needed me to."

Mr. Randolph folded his paper carefully. "But you were on the floor, beside her. Mrs. Randolph told me."

"She needed to know I was close. After everything she's been through..." Francesco's jaw tightened. "The chair wasn't close enough."

"I understand." Mr. Randolph gestured to a seat. "Please, sit. You look like you're about to fall over."

Francesco sat gratefully, though he tried not to show his relief.

"Mr. Romano, I think we need to discuss your intentions toward Serafina."

Francesco had been expecting this conversation. "My intentions are to protect her and care for her, and to make sure nothing like this ever happens again."

"That sounds like the beginning of something more permanent than a business arrangement."

"It is."

"I see." Mr. Randolph steepled his fingers. "You understand that Serafina has just been through a terrible ordeal. She's vulnerable. Dependent on you, perhaps, because you saved her. That's not a solid foundation for—"

"I love her," Francesco interrupted. "I've loved before any of this happened. And she chose me too, before the kidnapping. This isn't about gratitude or dependence."

Mr. Randolph studied him for a long moment.

"I want to marry her," Francesco said bluntly. "When she's ready. And I'm asking for your blessing to do so."

Mr. Randolph's eyebrows rose slightly. "You're asking. That's... unexpected."

"Why is it unexpected?"

"Because you're Francesco Romano." Mr. Randolph's voice was quiet but direct. "You saved her life. You've protected my family on more than one occasion. The business arrangements we have, the loans, the investments... I'm in your debt. Considerably. You could simply inform me you intend to marry her, and what could I possibly say?"

Francesco leaned forward, adjusting his coat to keep pressure off his ribs. "You could say no. You could refuse to attend the wedding. You could make her choose between you and me." He paused. "I don't want that for her. She's lost enough."

"So you're asking out of... what? Respect?"

"Because she deserves to be honored," Francesco said firmly. "You're the closest thing she has to a father, and I want to do this right. For her." His jaw tightened. "Not because I have to, but because

I *want* to. I can't imagine my life without her in it." His voice turned quiet. "She sees me. Not Francesco Romano the gangster, but *me*, the man underneath."

Mr. Randolph stared out the window for a moment. "And what of the danger?"

"She was already in danger from a man no one suspected. A respectable florist who brought her flowers and smiled. My world didn't put her in that cell. An ordinary monster did."

"But your world has monsters too."

"It does," Francesco acknowledged. "But mine I can control. I can protect her from them. I couldn't protect her from Edward Whitmore because I didn't see him coming. That won't happen again."

"What kind of life can you really offer her?" Mr. Randolph probed. "A life where she jumps at every shadow, wondering if your enemies will use her to get to you? Where she can never truly be safe because of who you are?"

"A life where she's protected," Francesco said firmly. "Where she has everything she needs. Where she can write and dream and be happy." He paused. "I can't change what I am. But I nearly died for her. I would do it again without hesitation."

"I can see that." Mr. Randolph's expression softened slightly. "You do love her."

"More than my own life."

The older man was quiet for a long moment, his fingers drumming on the arm of his chair. "She's been through enough suffering. If you hurt her, if your world touches her in ways that harm her..."

"Then you'll have my permission to kill me yourself," Francesco said quietly.

Mr. Randolph's eyebrows rose at the blunt honesty. Then, slowly, he nodded. "All right. You have my blessing. But you'll marry her properly. Church wedding. Family present. Everything done right."

"Of course." Francesco felt something tight in his chest loosen slightly. "Thank you."

"Don't thank me yet. You still have to convince Serafina. And I suspect that will be the harder task."

Francesco allowed himself a small smile. "If it is, then I'm up for the challenge."

George appeared in the doorway. "Clara says Serafina is asking for Mr. Romano."

Francesco stood immediately, though the movement made his vision swim briefly. Mr. Randolph rose as well, extending his hand.

"Well, son, welcome to the family," he said quietly. "Such as it is."

CHAPTER 23

September 1927

The lilac room had become both haven and prison for Serafina. Francesco visited every day, sometimes twice, bringing her books, flowers, her favorite foods she couldn't bring herself to eat, and little trinkets he thought might make her smile, or even staying over night to sit with her through the nightmares that still came more often than not. He never pushed her, and never made demands. He was just there. for her.

But tonight, Clara kept vigil. Francesco had the kind of business in the city that Serafina didn't ask about and he didn't volunteer.

Clara dozed in the chair by the window, a blanket wrapped around her shoulders. On the floor, Serafina slept on her makeshift bed, still unable to tolerate the softness of the actual mattress.

The nightmare came without warning.

She was back in the cell. Cold stone against her cheek. The smell of dampness and fear. Edward's footsteps overhead, getting closer, closer—

The key in the lock.

The door opening.

His hands on her.

Forcing her down.

The weight, the terror.

This was it.

This was it.

This was—

"No!" Serafina woke with a scream, her hands flailing, striking out at phantoms only she could see. "Get off me! *Get off!*"

Clara jerked awake, nearly falling from her chair. "Serafina! You're safe! You're—"

But Serafina couldn't hearing her. She was still trapped in the nightmare, still feeling Edward's hands on her throat. She scrambled backward, slamming into the wall, her breathing rapid and panicked.

"Don't touch me! Please, please don't—"

"Serafina, it's me! It's Clara!" Clara approached slowly, hands raised. "You're here at home, at the Randolph estate. You're safe. Edward is in prison. He can't hurt you."

The words penetrated slowly. Serafina blinked, her vision clearing. Lilac walls. Clara's worried face. Not the cell. Not Edward.

"Oh God," Serafina gasped, pressing her shaking hands to her face. They were always shaking now. "I'm sorry. I didn't mean to—"

"Hush. It's all right." Clara knelt beside her. "The same dream?"

Serafina nodded, wiping sweat from her forehead. "I can still smell that place, and feel the cold stone against my cheek, and hear his footsteps." Her voice caught. "In some ways, I think I'm still there."

"But you're not. You're safe now." Clara moved to sit on the floor. "And Edward is locked away. He'll never leave prison alive. He can never hurt you or anyone else again."

"I know." Serafina took a shaky breath, trying to slow her racing pulse. "But my mind doesn't seem to understand that yet. The logical part of me knows I'm free, but my body still think I'm trapped."

Clara squeezed her hand gently. "Dr. Morrison says that's normal. That it takes time for the mind to catch up with reality after something like that."

"I wish it didn't take so long." Serafina's voice broke. "It's been three months, Clara. *Three months.* Shouldn't I be better by now?"

"There's no schedule for healing from something like this." Clara's voice was gentle but firm. "You survived something terrible. Give yourself time."

Serafina leaned her head back against the wall, staring at the ceiling. "Francesco has been so patient. But I can see it in his eyes. He's worried. And I..." She swallowed hard. "I don't know if I'll ever be the woman he remembers, the one who could laugh and tease and feel safe in the world."

"You're still that woman. You're just also someone who survived. Those things can exist together."

"Can they?" Serafina looked at her friend. "Because right now, I feel like Edward took that woman and killed her in that cell. And what's left is just... broken."

"You're not broken. You're healing. There's a difference."

Serafina didn't answer. She pulled her knees up to her chest, wrapping her arms around them.

"You know," Clara said quietly, "Mr. Romano's been downstairs since two this morning. He arrived shortly before I fell asleep on the chair."

Serafina's head snapped up. "He's here? Now?"

"Waiting for you to wake." Clara smiled softly. "Would you like me to have him c me up?"

Serafina felt tears prick her eyes. "Please."

"Then maybe you should tell him I'll be down in a moment."

After Clara left, Serafina stood up an caught sight of herself in the mirror over the dresser. She looked terrible with her hair tangled, her nightgown wrinkled, and dark circles under her eyes. The cuts on her face had healed to angry red scars. She didn't look like the woman who'd gone to balls in sapphire silk dresses.

A soft knock came at the door. "Serafina? May I come in?"

"Yes," she called. "Come in."

The door opened, and Francesco stepped inside. He looked tired, but his eyes lit up when he saw her standing, but quickly dimmed.

"Another nightmare?" he asked gently.

"How did you know?"

"I know you." He stayed by the door, not advancing until she invited him closer. "Do you want to talk about it?"

Serafina shook her head. "I want to forget it. All of it." She paused. "Will you sit with me for a while?"

"As long as you need."

He settled into the chair by her makeshift bed, and Serafina sat back down on the blankets, arms around his legs, head against the side of his knee. It was how she found the most comfort.

"Francesco," Serafina said after a moment. "I need to ask you something."

"Anything."

"Why do you keep coming? Day after day, sitting through these nightmares, watching me fall apart?" She met his eyes. "You could have anyone. Someone whole, or at least someone who isn't..." She gestured at herself. "This."

Francesco leaned forward, his elbows on his knees. "Do you want the truth?"

"Always the truth from you."

"When I look at you, I see someone who fought like hell to survive and come back to me." His voice became rough. "I see the woman I love. Nothing that happened in that cell changes that."

"You love me? Still?" She asked as she still often did.

"Still. Always." He reached out slowly, giving her time to pull away. When she didn't, he took her hand, still lightly bandaged to protect the still-tender nail beds. "I loved you before any of this happened. I'll love you after. Nothing changes that."

"Everything has changed," Serafina whispered. "I've changed."

"I love who you are now and who you're becoming." He brought her hand to his lips, pressing a kiss to her fingers. "However long it takes. Whatever you need."

The tears Serafina had been holding back finally spilled over. "I'm so tired of being afraid, and jumping at shadows, and waking up screaming. I don't know how to stop."

"You don't have to stop alone." Francesco's dark eyes held hers. "Let me help carry it."

"You already do."

"Then let me do more." He paused, seeming to gather courage. "Move in with me, to the penthouse. I'll give you your own room, your own space. But I'll be there when the nightmares come, every time. You won't have to face them alone anymore."

Serafina stared at him. "Francesco, I couldn't possibly—the impropriety—"

"*I don't give a damn about propriety.*" His voice was fierce. "I care about you being safe. About you healing. About you not spending another night terrified and alone."

"What would people say?"

"Nothing they don't already say about me." He softened his tone. "Serafina, I'm not asking you to share my bed. I'm asking you to share my home. Let me take care of you the way you deserve."

She wanted to. God, how she wanted to. The thought of Francesco just down the hall, close enough to reach when the nightmares came, was almost unbearably appealing.

But there was something else she needed to know first.

"And after?" she asked quietly. "After I heal—if I heal—what then?"

Francesco held her gaze steadily. "Then I ask you to marry me. Properly. With a ring and a proposal and everything you deserve."

Serafina's heart stuttered. "You want to marry me? Like this?"

"I want to marry you exactly as you are. Scars and nightmares and all." He smiled slightly. "Though I'd prefer to wait until you're ready to say yes. So for now, just move in. Let me prove that you're safe with me and that I'm not going anywhere."

"The Randolphs—"

"Already know I'm asking. Mr. Randolph has given his blessing." Francesco squeezed her hand gently. "So the only question that matters is: what do you want?"

What did she want? Serafina closed her eyes, letting herself imagine it. Waking up in Francesco's penthouse. Writing in a real office. Not being alone with her terror. Having someone who understood the darkness because he lived in it too.

"I want to feel safe again," she finally said. "I want to stop being afraid."

"Then come home with me and let me help you find that safety."

Serafina opened her eyes and looked at this man who'd broken through walls to reach her, who'd bled for her, who sat patiently through her nightmares without complaint.

"All right," she whispered. "I'll go with you."

Francesco smile softly at her. "Thank you."

"For what?"

"For trusting me with you."

He stood and helped her to her feet. And for the first time in three months, Serafina felt something other than fear or panic.

She felt hope for her future.

November 1927

Serafina stood outside the flower shop, her hand tight in Francesco's. The building looked even more derelict than before. The windows were still partially papered over, the "closed" sign faded and crooked. Police tape remnants fluttered from the doorframe.

Five months. Almost six months... since Francesco had broken through that wall.

"Are you sure about this?" Francesco asked, his voice concerned. "We don't have to do this."

Serafina nodded, though her hands trembled. The laudanum-tinged fog that had surrounded her for months, the nightmare-broken nights, and the days that bled together in the blue room had finally started to lift. She could think again. Feel things again. Which meant she could finally do this.

"I know. But I need to see it one last time before it's gone."

Francesco had already arranged for the demolition. The building would come down next week, reduced to rubble and carted away. The lot would be cleared, sold and turned into something else.

He'd asked her once, months ago when she could barely string sentences together, if she wanted it renovated and turned into something bright and cheerful, children's laughter replacing screams. A toy shop, he'd suggested.

She'd looked at him with hollow eyes and said, "*Burn it. I want to watch it burn.*"

They'd compromised on demolition instead.

Francesco pulled out a set of keys to use them one last time. The door opened with a familiar creak that made Serafina's breath catch.

Just a door, she told herself. *Just wood and hinges. It can't hurt you.*

Inside, the front room looked exactly as it had the day of the rescue. Dust coated every surface. Dead flowers rotted in vases. The bookcase that concealed the first gate to her cell stood ajar. She hadn't seen it open before. She walked slowly toward the back, each step feeling like moving through water. When she reached the wall where the cell had been hidden, she walked through it and to the cell.

Someone had patched the hole Francesco had torn through. Fresh plaster, unpainted, marked where he'd broken through to save her, but the broken brick hadn't been replaced. Serafina picked up a chunk of it. Blood...

And suddenly she was back there. Cold stone against her cheek. The metallic taste of fear coating her mouth. Edward's voice echoing through the darkness: "*If I can't have you, no one can.*" The damn smell, her own terror, the weight of hopelessness pressing down until she couldn't breathe, Danny's face, Edward's weight— Her breath came in short, sharp gasps. The room tilted. Her vision darkened at the edges.

"Serafina." Francesco's voice. His hand on her elbow. "You're safe. You're with me. You're not there anymore."

She focused on his voice and the warmth of his palm. *Present. I'm in the present. The cell is gone. Edward is in prison. I'm standing in an empty flower shop with Francesco beside me.*

Her breathing slowed gradually. The flashback receded, leaving her shaking but present.

"I'm okay," she managed. "I'm okay."

Not okay. But alive. That counts for something.

"You don't have to be okay." Francesco's hand moved to her back. "We can leave right now."

"No. I need—" Serafina swallowed hard. "I need to say goodbye to this place and to what happened here."

She looked around the empty shop one more time. This was where Danny had brought her flowers with shy smiles, and where Edward had watched her through the window, a man unknown to her. This was where she'd almost died.

"When they tear it down," she said quietly, "I want to be here so I can watch."

"Are you certain?"

"Yes." She turned to him. "I need to see it gone and to know it can't hurt anyone else ever again."

"Then we'll both watch." He squeezed her hand. "Together."

They left the flower shop, and Francesco locked the door for the last time. As they walked toward the bookshop next door, something loosened in Serafina's chest. I wasn't relief exactly, but a step toward it.

Serafina gripped his hand for dear life and turned toward the door. "Let's go next door. I want to see the bookshop."

The familiar bell chimed as they entered The Purrfect Tale. Whiskers immediately wound around Serafina's legs, purring his welcome. The sound made her smile a small, but genuine smile.

Mr. Thompson looked up from behind the counter. When he saw Serafina, his expression flickered through several emotions... joy, relief, concern, worry... before settling on cautious welcome.

"Serafina," he said carefully. "What a... this is unexpected."

Mrs. Thompson appeared from the back room, moving slowly. She'd recovered from her pneumonia but still looked frailer than before. Her eyes widened when she saw Serafina.

"Oh, my dear," she breathed, but she didn't rush forward. Instead, she stayed where she was.

The awkwardness hung thick and uncomfortable. This wasn't the warm reunion Serafina had imagined during her months of recovery.

"I'm sorry to just show up," Serafina said, her voice smaller than she'd intended. "I should have sent a calling card first."

"No, no, it's not that." Mr. Thompson came around the counter but stopped several feet away. "We're just... we didn't expect to see you. We thought perhaps you'd want to stay away from this place given everything that happened."

"Given that I was kidnapped and kept right next door?" Serafina's attempt at lightness fell flat.

"We wrote to you," Mrs. Thompson said softly. "Several letters. We weren't sure if you received them."

"I got them," she said, guilt knotting in her stomach. "I'm sorry I didn't write back. I wasn't... I couldn't... read past the first few lines before the memories became too much. I meant to respond, but didn't know what to say that would be enough."

"Please, don't apologize," Mr. Thompson said softly. "We only wanted you to know we were thinking of you."

Another uncomfortable silence fell. Whiskers, oblivious to the tension, continued purring and rubbing against Serafina's legs.

Say it. Just say what you came here to say.

Francesco stepped closer to her side in silent support.

"I wanted—" Serafina took a breath. "I wanted to ask if I could come back, to work here, if you'd have me."

Mr. and Mrs. Thompson exchanged a long look. Something passed between them—some wordless conversation that made Serafina's stomach drop.

They're going to say no. They don't want me back.

"Serafina," Mr. Thompson began carefully, "we would love nothing more than to have you back. You know that. But..." He paused, clearly struggling with how to say something difficult. "Are you certain that's wise? Being here, so close to where it happened?"

"I need to," Serafina said, hearing the desperation creep into her voice. She hated how she sounded so pleading and broken. "I need to prove to myself that I can, and that he didn't take this from me too."

Mrs. Thompson moved closer, her expression pained. "Dear girl, no one would blame you for never wanting to set foot in this neighborhood again. What you went through—" Her voice caught. "We can't imagine. And the thought of you being here, having to walk past that place every day..."

Too broken. They think I'm too broken...

"They're tearing it down next week," Francesco interjected quietly. "The flower shop. It won't be there much longer."

"Even so." Mr. Thompson looked at Serafina with such gentle concern it made her want to cry. "We want you to be safe and healthy. We're not certain that working here, where you'd be constantly reminded, would be good for your recovery."

"So you don't want me back." The words came out flat.

"That's not what we're saying." Mr. Thompson held up his hands. "We're saying we want you to be certain. We want you to think about whether this is truly what you need, or if you're trying to prove something that doesn't need proving."

"We love you like a daughter," Mrs. Thompson added, her eyes bright with unshed tears as she slowly walked forward. "We have to put your wellbeing first, even if it's not what you want to hear."

Something crumble inside Serafina. She'd been so focused on returning to normal and reclaiming what Edward had stolen that she hadn't considered they might not want her back and that her presence might make them uncomfortable.

I make everyone uncomfortable now, even the people who love me.

"I understand," she said, though her voice shook. "You're right. It was foolish to think—"

"We're not saying no," Mr. Thompson interrupted gently. "We're saying... take more time. Give yourself space to heal properly. And if, after a few more months, you still want to come back, then we can revisit this conversation."

"How long?" Serafina asked. "How long until you'll consider it?"

Another exchanged glance between the Thompsons.

"Six months," Mrs. Thompson said softly. "Give yourself six more months. Work on your recovery. Write your stories. Find your footing again. And then, if you still want this, come back and we'll talk."

"But your position will be here," Mr. Thompson added quickly. "You'll always have a place here. We're just asking you to be sure."

Serafina nodded, not trusting her voice. Six more months. Half a year more before she could even try to reclaim this piece of her life.

Francesco's hand found the small of her back. "Thank you for being honest with her," he said to the Thompsons. "She needs people who will tell her the truth, even when it's hard."

"We only want what's best for her," Mrs. Thompson said. "We love her, and we do miss having her here."

"I know." Francesco guided Serafina gently toward the door. "Come on. Let's go home."

Home. Francesco's penthouse. When did that become home?

As they left the bookshop, Serafina felt tears finally spill over as she realized just how much Edward had taken from her.

"They don't want me," she sobbed outside.

"They want you healthy," Francesco corrected. "There's a difference."

"It doesn't feel different."

He turned her to face him, his hands on her shoulders. "Serafina, listen to me. They're right. You're not ready yet."

"When will I be ready?" The question came out broken. "When will I stop being the girl who got kidnapped? When do I get to be normal again? When do I get to just be me?"

"I don't know. Maybe never." Francesco said, brutally honest. "Maybe you'll always carry this. But that doesn't mean you can't build a good life anyway."

Serafina leaned against him, exhausted. The fog may have lifted, but what lay beneath it was sharp and painful. "I just want it to be over."

"I know." He held her close. "But healing works on its own time."

They stood like that for a long moment. Finally, Serafina pulled back and wiped her eyes.

Keep moving. One foot in front of the other. That's all I can do.

"We still watch, though?" she asked. "When they tear down the flower shop?"

"We'll watch it come down together. And then we'll leave this place behind and focus on building something new."

"Promise?"

"I promise."

As they walked back to the car, Serafina glanced over her shoulder one last time at the bookshop. Someday, she told herself. Someday she'd be strong enough to walk through that door again without the weight of her ordeal crushing her.

But not today.

Today, she just needed to survive, and to keep putting one foot in front of the other.

That evening, Serafina sat at her desk in Francesco's penthouse, in the office he'd created specifically for her. Floor-to-ceiling bookshelves lined the walls, filled with first editions and her favorite novels, including replacements for the poetry books destroyed in her apartment. A comfortable reading chair upholstered in rose velvet waited by the tall windows with a soft throw draped over its arm. Her writing desk was positioned perfectly to catch the afternoon light.

But it was the typewriter that held her attention now, the same shining black Underwood number five Francesco had repaired.

She'd begin to write here in the evenings while Francesco worked in his own office just down the hall. The arrangement suited them both. He was close enough for her to feel his presence, but separate enough to maintain the boundaries that kept her safe from his darker world.

Sometimes she could hear the low murmur of his voice during telephone calls, speaking in that serious tone he reserved for business she didn't ask about. She'd learned not to inquire. Some doors were better left closed.

Though society would not deem it proper for an unmarried woman to be staying with an unmarried man, it worked. Mr. Randolph had been surprisingly understanding, especially after Francesco had formally asked for Serafina's hand in marriage.

The proposal had come two months ago, quiet and private. No grand gestures. Just Francesco on one knee in this very office, holding a ring and asking if she'd spend her life with him.

She'd said yes without hesitation.

The wedding was planned for spring. It would be a proper church ceremony as Mr. Randolph had insisted. Clara was helping with the arrangements, enthusiastically planning everything from flowers to music while Serafina tried to work up enthusiasm for details that still felt overwhelming.

But the nightmares still came sometimes. Not every night anymore, maybe once or twice a week instead of every time she closed her eyes. Progress, Dr. Morrison called it. Healing.

When the dreams came, when she woke in a panic with her throat closing and Edward's face looming in her memory, there was nowhere she felt safer than in Francesco's arms. He never asked questions about the dreams anymore. He simply held her until the terror passed and her breathing steadied.

Serafina glanced down at the diamond ring on her finger. The large stone caught the lamplight and threw tiny rainbows across her desk. What it represented still surprised her sometimes. It was not so much the promise of marriage, but the promise of a future and the idea that there could be life after darkness, and love after terror.

Tonight, she wanted to write something different from her usual fiction. The manuscript for Sarah's next adventure sat beside her typewriter, but for months she hadn't been able to touch it. The romantic storylines she'd once crafted so easily now felt hollow and dishonest.

She rolled a fresh sheet of paper into the machine and paused, her fingers hovering over the keys.

What do I write now? she wondered. *How do I tell stories about love when I know what monsters look like? When I've seen how easily safety can be stripped away?*

But even as she thought it, she knew the answer. She would write the truth, not the sanitized version she'd penned before Edward. Not the fairy tale where everything ended neatly.

She would write about Sarah, her fictional self, but infuse her with new depth. Sarah would still have adventures, but she'd carry experience and the knowledge that heroism often came with a cost.

She would be a woman who survived and carried scars, both visible and invisible, and learned to live with them, and who found love not in spite of the darkness, but alongside it.

Her fingers found the keys and began to type.

Safety is an illusion. Terror could wear a gentle face in a world that contained more darkness than she'd ever imagined. But she had also learned that she was stronger than she'd known. Survival isn't just about enduring, but about choosing again and again to live.

A soft knock at the door interrupted her typing. "Serafina? May I come in?"

"Of course."

Francesco entered carrying two glasses of wine, offering one to her. "You're writing."

"Trying to." She accepted the glass, taking a small sip. "It's been so long, I wasn't sure I still could."

Francesco glanced at the paper in her typewriter. "May I?"

She nodded, and he leaned over her shoulder to read what she'd written. She felt suddenly vulnerable, exposed in a way she hadn't with her earlier work.

"This is different," he said finally. "Darker than your other stories."

"Is that bad?"

"No." He straightened, his hand coming to rest gently on her shoulder.

Serafina leaned back in her chair, looking up at him. "I can't write fairy tales anymore. I can't pretend the world is simpler than it is."

"Write what you know, even if it's hard."

"What if no one wants to read it? What if it's too dark, too—"

"Then you write it anyway." He moved around to perch on the edge of her desk. "You don't write for them. You write for you, to make sense of everything that happened."

Serafina considered this, turning the wineglass in her hands. "You really think I can?"

"I know you can. You're one of the strongest people I've ever met."

"I don't feel strong. Most days I still feel broken."

"Broken things can be put back together." Francesco's eyes held hers. "They might look different afterward. But sometimes the scars make them stronger than before."

"Is that what you think I am? Stronger?"

"I think you're still becoming stronger."

Serafina set down her wineglass and stood, moving to the window. The city spread out around them. Somewhere out there, Edward sat in a prison cell. His trial had been swift. Between his confession to the police, the physical evidence, and the testimony from the previous victims' families and Serafina herself, he had an execution date.

She should feel relief. Some days she did. But other days, she just felt tired. Tired of being afraid... tired of looking over her shoulder... tired of the way her body still flinched at unexpected sounds...

"Do you ever regret it?" she asked quietly. "Choosing me? This complicated, damaged version of me?"

Francesco came to stand beside her at the window. "Never."

"Not even when I wake you up screaming? Not even when I can't—" She gestured vaguely, unable to finish the thought.

"Especially not then." He turned her to face him, his hands gentle on her shoulders. "Serafina, I didn't fall in love with some perfect, undamaged version of you. I fell in love with *you*. All of you. That includes the parts that are scared and healing. strong.

"I might always have nightmares."

"Then I'll always be there to hold you through them."

"I might never be the carefree girl I was before."

"I don't want that girl back. I want the woman standing in front of me right now."

Serafina felt tears prick her eyes. "How can you be so certain?"

"Because I've seen you at your worst and it only made me love you more." Francesco's voice roughened with his own emotion. "You survived something that should have destroyed you, and you're still standing and fighting and building a life worth living."

384

"I'm going to marry you in the spring," she said against his shirt. "Walk down that aisle and promise to love you forever. But I won't wear white."

"I know."

"And I'm going to have nightmares on our wedding night."

"Probably."

"And you're going to hold me through them."

"Always." He pressed a kiss to the top of her head. "That's what 'for worse' means."

They stood like that for a long moment, wrapped in each other while the city glittered below. Finally, Serafina pulled back slightly.

"I should write some more, while the words are flowing."

Francesco smiled. "Then I'll leave you to it. I have some calls to make anyway."

As he moved toward the door, Serafina called out, "Francesco?"

He turned back. "Yes?"

"Thank you for everything. For finding me, and staying, and not giving up on me even when I'd given up on myself."

"You never have to thank me for loving you. It's the easiest thing I've ever done."

After he left, Serafina returned to her desk. She looked at what she'd written, then continued:

```
     She had found love in the aftermath of darkness, but it wasn't the kind
of love that erased the past or made everything better with a kiss. It was
the kind of love that acknowledged the scars, held endless patience for all the
nightmares, then said "I see all of you, from the strong parts to the
broken parts, and I love you anyway."
     That kind of love didn't fix her. But it gave her a reason to fix
herself.
     And that, she was learning, made all the difference in the world.
```

Contentment bloomed in Serafina's chest. Happiness still resided too far away, but this was a step, and every step renewed her purpose.

She had survived. She was healing. And tomorrow, she would

return to the bookshop and take another step forward.

One day at a time. One word at a time.

And one breath at a time.

May 1928

The church wedding was small and intimate, exactly what Serafina had wanted. No grand cathedral, no crowds of strangers. Just family and close friends gathered in the warm late spring sunlight that streamed through stained glass windows.

Serafina stood in the back room in a simple ivory gown with delicate lace sleeves that covered the faint scars on her arms. She couldn't bring herself to wear white. Clara fussing with her dress and her veil. Serafina only wore one at all for Clara's sake.

"You look beautiful," Mrs. Randolph said, her eyes bright with tears. "Absolutely beautiful."

Serafina stared at herself in the mirror. The scars on her face had faded to thin white lines that were nearly invisible unless you knew where to look. Her hair was pinned up with small orange blossoms woven through. She supposed she looked like a bride, though she felt like she was pretending.

"What if I can't do this?" she whispered. "What if I get to the altar and panic?"

Clara took her hands firmly. "Then Mr. Romano will wait. And if you need to leave, he'll leave with you."

"I just..." Serafina took a shaky breath. "I want to enjoy this. I want to be fully here, not lost in my own fear."

"Then focus on him," Mrs. Randolph suggested gently. "When you walk down that aisle, don't look at anyone else. Just the man who loves you."

Then the music began. Serafina had asked for a simple violin arrangement rather than the traditional wedding march.

Mr. Randolph stepped into the doorway, looking distinguished in his formal coat. "Ready?"

Clara and Mrs. Randolph slipped ahead to take their seats.

Serafina watched them leave, then took a deep breath. "Yes. I think so." She took his offered arm, and they walked toward the sanctuary doors.

"Serafina," Mr. Randolph said quietly, "you know you don't have to do this. If you're not ready—"

"I'm ready. I've never been more certain of anything. I just don't know if I can really be enough."

The doors opened, and Serafina bit her lip.

The church was perfect, filled with flowers Clara had personally arranged. The guests were so few it could hardly be called a crowd. Mrs. Randolph and Clara sat with George in the front pew. Lucia, dabbed at her eyes with a handkerchief. Mr. and Mrs. Thompson smiled warmly. Even Mr. Ricci, stood off to the side in an impeccably tailored suit with his wife and their infant daughter.

But Serafina barely saw any of them because Francesco stood at the altar, and when their eyes met, the rest of the world faded away.

She nearly giggled at how his dark hair had been slightly tousled, as if he'd run his hands through it a few times, perhaps as nervous as she. The intensity of his eyes made her heart race and feel warm.

Mr. Randolph led her down the aisle slowly. Serafina kept her eyes on Francesco, just as Mrs. Randolph had suggested. She watched his expression shift. from control to the fierce tenderness he saved only for her.

When they reached the altar, Mr. Randolph placed her hand in Francesco's.

"Take care of her," he said quietly.

"With my life," Francesco promised.

The priest began the ceremony, but Serafina barely heard the words. She was too focused on Francesco's hands holding hers and her disbelief that any of this was real, that he was truly choosing her.

"Do you, Serafina Maria Silvano, take Francesco Antonio Romano to be your lawfully wedded husband? To have and to hold, in sickness and in health, for richer or poorer, as long as you both shall live?"

Serafina looked into Francesco's dark eyes and thought about everything that had brought them to this moment. The fake courtship that became real. The terror and rescue. The long months of healing. The nightmares and the patience. The scars they both carried...

"I do," she said clearly. "I absolutely do."

The reception was held at the Randolph estate, in the garden where lights had been strung between the trees. It was beautiful in its simplicity, nothing ostentatious, nothing that would draw unwanted attention to Francesco's less-than-legal enterprises. Just good food, good wine, and the people they loved the most.

Serafina sat at the head table. Francesco's hand rested on her knee under the tablecloth. Though she was exhausted, she was also more content than she'd been in ages.

"You're smiling," Francesco observed, his voice warm.

"I am, aren't I?" Serafina looked at him. "Is this what happy feels like? I'd almost forgotten."

He brought her hand to his lips. "Get used to it. I plan to make you smile as often as possible."

Clara approached their table, her own engagement ring catching the light. She and Irving would be married in the fall. "May I steal the bride for a moment?"

Francesco nodded, and Clara pulled Serafina aside to the edge of the garden where they could speak privately.

"How are you doing?" Clara asked. "Really?"

"I'm good." Serafina said it with surprise. "I'm actually good. I'm not having to pretend or force it. I'm just... good."

"I'm so glad." Clara hugged her tightly. "You deserve all of this."

"I still have nightmares sometimes," Serafina admitted quietly. "Last night, I woke up at three in the morning convinced I was back in that cell."

"What did Francesco do?"

"He held me and sat with me until the sun came up as he always does." Serafina smiled softly. "He never makes me feel broken."

"That's because you're not broken." Clara squeezed her hand. "You're brave."

They stood together for a moment, watching the party. Mr. Thompson was deep in conversation with Mr. Randolph. Mrs. Thompson and Mrs. Randolph were comparing notes on something, probably recipes. George was attempting to engage Lucia Romano in conversation, though she seemed far more interested in the wine.

"Did you ever think we'd end up here?" Serafina asked. "You marrying a doctor, me marrying a—" She lowered her voice. "A mobster?"

Clara laughed. "Never in a million years. But life is strange that way, isn't it?"

"Strange," Serafina agreed. "But good. Sometimes good."

Francesco joined them for a moment. "May I steal my wife back?"

My wife. The words sent a thrill through Serafina.

He led her to a quiet corner of the garden, away from the other guests. Music drifted from the strings quartet.

"Dance with me," Francesco said.

"Here? With no dance floor? I still don't know how to dance."

"You don't need to know how. Just follow me." He pulled her close. "I've got you."

Serafina melted in his arms, as they swayed gently to the music.

"Thank you," Francesco said after a moment.

"For what?"

"For spilling wine on me that first night." His voice held quiet amusement. "I might not have thought of you again if you hadn't made such a memorable impression."

"I didn't—" She felt heat rise in her cheeks, then caught the teasing warmth in his eyes. "You're never going to let me forget that, are you?"

"Never." His hand moved gently against her back. "And thank you for saying yes, for marrying me despite everything and trusting me with your heart."

Serafina rested her head against his chest, listening to his heartbeat. "You make it sound like I did you a favor. You're the one who saved me."

"We saved each other." Francesco's arms tightened around her. "You saved me from a life where I thought I'd never feel love again. I'd convinced myself that caring about anyone was weakness. Now I know that caring about you is the strongest thing I've ever done."

They danced until the song ended, then stood there in the gathering dusk, wrapped up in each other.

"We should probably get back," Serafina said reluctantly. "People will talk."

"Let them talk." But Francesco led her back to the party anyway.

The evening wore on. Mr. Randolph gave a touching toast, speaking about family being more than blood. Lucia's was shorter but sincere, welcoming Serafina to the family as a new sister.

Then Francesco stood with his wine glass and looked directly at Serafina. "I'm not good with speeches," he began. "And I'm not going to pretend to be something I'm not. You all know what I am and what I do."

A few people shifted uncomfortably. Mr. Randolph looked concerned.

"But what you might not know," Francesco continued turning to the others, "is that this woman saved my life, not by taking a bullet or pulling me from a fire, but by showing me that I could be more than what the world expects, and that I could protect something instead of destroy. I didn't know I could love without taking."

He looked at Serafina again, his eyes suspiciously bright. "You're the best thing that's ever happened to me. And I promise you, in front of all these witnesses, that I will spend the rest of my life trying to be worthy of you."

Serafina's vision blurred with tears. She stood and threw her arms around him, not caring that everyone was watching. "You already are," she whispered. "You always have been."

As the night drew to a close, Serafina leaned against her husband and sighed.

"Ready to go home?" Francesco asked quietly.

"God, yes."

In the car, Serafina lay her head back against the seat and closed her eyes. Francesco's hand found hers in the darkness as he silently drove.

"You survived your wedding day, Mrs. Romano," he said in a fondly teasing tone.

The name sent a warm flutter through her chest. Mrs. Romano. His wife. She couldn't help the small giggle that bubbled up within her.

"And you were beautiful, as always," he continued, his thumb brushing over her knuckles. He brought her hand to his lips.

When they reached the penthouse, Francesco carried her over the threshold, playing at tradition in a way that made Serafina drop her head back and laugh

"What?" he asked, setting her down.

"You. Being romantic."

"I have my moments." He smiled too, but his eyes were serious. "Serafina, tonight... we don't have to do anything you're not ready for. This marriage isn't about expectations or obligations."

"I know," she said quietly. "And I love you for that. But I want to try. It's been nearly a year, and now... I'm choosing to."

"Only if you're certain."

"I'm certain I want to try. I can't promise I won't panic or that it'll be what either of us hopes." She met his eyes. "But I trust you to stop if I need you to."

"Always."

Francesco touched her face first. His fingers traced the thin scar along her cheekbone. Serafina closed her eyes, focusing on the gentleness of it.

This is Francesco. Not Edward. Francesco, who had broken through walls to save me.

When he kissed her, she pressed closer, her hands fisting in his shirt with a hunger that startled her. An overwhelming need to prove that her body was hers again punched through her.

His hands moved to the buttons of her wedding dress, fumbling slightly. "Tell me if—"

"I will," she promised.

Each button opened slowly. Serafina focused in her breathing. *In. Out. This is Francesco. You're safe. You chose this.*

The dress slipped from her shoulders. Francesco's hands warmed her skin. He kissed her shoulder, her collarbone, the hollow of her throat where Edward's fingers had—

Serafina went rigid. Her breath stopped. The room tilted.

Hands on her throat. Pressure. Darkness closing in. "If I can't have you—"

"Serafina." Francesco's voice cut through the memory. His hands immediately moved away from her neck, settling on her shoulders instead. "Serafina, are you all right?"

She gasped, her eyes flying open. Francesco's face swam into focus.

"I'm sorry," she choked out. "I thought I could—"

"*Shh.*" He pulled her close, wrapping his arms around her. "We can stop. It's okay."

Serafina pressed her face against his chest, feeling his heartbeat.

"I don't want to stop," she said after a moment. "I just need... can you not touch my throat? Or—or hold me down?"

"Of course. Whatever you need."

She pulled back enough to look at him. "Show me where you'll touch me. Let me see your hands."

He held them up, palms out. She took them, one at a time, and placed them where she could handle contact. Her waist. Her hips. Her back. But not her arms. Not her wrists.

"Here is okay," she said, guiding him. "And here. But not—"

"I understand."

They started again, slower this time. Serafina kept her eyes open, watching Francesco's face. He was careful to the point of frustration, stopping to check with her after every new touch.

"I'm not going to break," she said at one point.

"I know. But I won't risk hurting you." His hand cupped her face. "Not even by accident."

When his weight shifting over her brought a flash of Edward pinning her down, she froze. Francesco rolled immediately to his side, giving her space.

"Sorry," Serafina breathed. "I'm so sorry. It's not you. My body just... it remembers things I wish it would forget."

"Then we'll teach it new memories." Francesco kissed her forehead, her cheek, her jaw. "As long as it takes."

She guided his hands again, showing him what she could tolerate. Some touches were fine. A couple she thought were made her flinch instead.

Eventually they found a rhythm, though awkward and frequent starting and stopping, nothing like the passionate encounters of their earlier times. But there was something profound in Francesco's patience and in her own determination to reclaim this part of herself.

When her breathing quickened with panic instead of pleasure, he stopped. When she froze, uncertain, he waited. When she whispered "keep going," he did, but only as far as she could handle.

"I'm sorry this isn't—" she started at one point.

"Stop apologizing." Francesco's voice was firm. "This is exactly what it should be. We're together. That's all that matters now."

Tears slipped down Serafina's temples. Francesco kissed them away.

"I want this to work," she whispered.

"It is working. Maybe not the way you imagined, but it's working." He settled beside her, pulling her close. "And we have the rest of our lives to figure this all out. There's no rush."

She curled into him, exhausted from the day and the emotional weight of trying. Her body ached from tension and from fighting her own instincts.

"Will it always be this hard?" she asked into the darkness.

"I don't know. Maybe it gets easier. But Serafina—" He tilted her face up to his. "Even if it's always hard, I'm here. Whatever this looks like, however long it takes, I'm not going anywhere. *Capisci, amore mia?*"

"*Ti amo,*" she murmured, already drifting toward sleep.

"*I love you, too,*" Francesco replied. "Sleep now. Tomorrow we start building the rest of our life."

And in the safety of his embrace, for the first time in nearly a year, Serafina fell asleep without dreading the dreams that might come.

EPILOGUE

May 1929

Serafina sat at her desk in the penthouse, the afternoon sun streaming through the windows. Her typewriter clacked steadily as she worked on the final chapter of her new novel. Not Sarah's adventures this time, but something new and light.

This time, it was a mystery about a clever socialite who solved crimes at speakeasies while her gangster husband provided the muscle. She'd decided on equal parts danger and wit, with a heroine who wore pearls and carried a derringer, who kissed her husband between car chases and found utter delight in loving such a dangerous man.

The book would be published in the fall. Her publisher—not Kensington Publishing, which had suddenly and mysteriously closed several months ago— had loved her proposal.

Behind her, the door opened. She smiled without turning around.

"How's the book?" Francesco asked, coming to stand behind her chair.

"Almost done. One more chapter and it's finished."

His hands came to rest on her shoulders, and she leaned back into his touch. They'd been married for a year now, and she'd learned his rhythms, learned when his touch meant comfort and when it meant something more.

"The bookshop called," Francesco said. "Mr. Thompson wants to host a reading when it's published."

"That would be lovely." Serafina saved her work and turned to face him. "And I was thinking... maybe we could finally take that trip you've been suggesting, to Sicily to see where I was born."

Francesco's eyebrows rose. "Are you sure?"

"I think I'm ready." She stood, wrapping her arms around his waist. "I want to see the places my grandmother talked about. I want to make new memories in a new land."

"Then we'll go." He kissed her forehead. "Whenever you want."

They stood like that for a moment, wrapped in comfortable silence. Then Serafina pulled back slightly.

"I had a nightmare last night," she said. "Did you notice?"

"I did. But you didn't wake up screaming. You just shifted and reached for me. Then you went back to sleep."

"That's progress, isn't it?" Serafina smiled. "The nightmares are still there, but they don't control me anymore. And do you know what I realized today?"

"What?"

"I'm happy. Actually, genuinely happy. My heart... I'm just happy again."

Francesco's smile was brilliant. "Good. You deserve to be."

"So do you."

"I am." He pulled her close. "Every single day with you."

The nightmares would still come sometimes. Maybe they always would. But when they did, Francesco would be there to hold her through them.

And she carried scars, from the thin white lines on her face to the missing fingernails that had never quite grown back right.

But she also carried joy and dreams and love.

This wasn't the fairy tale ending she'd once imagined when she wrote stories about Sarah and her adventures. This was messier and more complicated, but it was hers. And it was close enough.

No, closer than enough. It was absolutely everything.

ABOUT THE AUTHOR

Noëlle Alexandria discovered her calling early, spinning tales of mermaids and fairy-princesses in childhood notebooks before her stories evolved into romantasy realms and the grittier worlds of mobsters and showgirls. Her journey from whimsical fantasy to noir-tinged fiction is one for a storyteller whose imagination knows no boundaries.

When she's not crafting her next manuscript, Noëlle takes to the skies as a certificated private pilot, finding inspiration in the freedom of flight and the ever-changing landscapes below. Her travels fuel both her wanderlust and her storytelling.

A lifelong student of the arts, Noëlle has dedicated years to developing and refining various artistic skills from painting to drawing, from opera singing those high notes to ballet, and more. Noëlle weaves what she learns from each discipline directly into her stories, but her dedication to authenticity goes even further. When she wants to write about something she doesn't know firsthand, she makes a point to learn it herself, which is exactly how she earned her first concussion. Wanting to write about a figure skater naturally meant taking lessons and learning to spin, and as any skater will tell you, a concussion is practically a rite of passage.

For Noëlle, writing transcends mere passion; it's an essential way of life that weaves itself through everything she does. As long as there are untold stories waiting to be discovered—and there will always be more stories to tell—she'll continue crafting stories and looking for the next grand adventure.

Originally from California, Noëlle now calls Vancouver, Washington home with her family, where she balances the demands of storytelling with the joys of aviation and exploration.

ABOUT THE EDITOR

Thanks to her encyclopedia-salesman father, proof editor and Missouri-native Jennifer Long was fortunate enough to always have an extra set of encyclopedias laying around the house. She craved the knowledge that can be gained from reading non-fiction. She also thirsted for the places, characters, and lives you can live by reading fiction. She fell in love with the action and mystery in the *This Thing of Ours* series, which perfectly weaves her love for both sides of the written word, and in many ways, have become a rock for the author in more ways than she knows.

Content warning:

Resplendent contains themes of abuse of power by a man in a trusted position of power, sexual abuse, attempted rape, physical assault, stalking, and mafia violence, in addition to discussion of a supporting character's prior fiancé who died in a real train car derailment. Some depictions are graphic.

If more detailed information is needed such as page numbers for specific scene, or for a censored ebook with specific scenes whited out with a very brief summary telling what happened, please click **Contact** on **www.NoelleAlexandria.com** (no umlaut) and every attempt will be made to fill your request.

www.ingramcontent.com/pod-product-compliance
Lightning Source LLC
Chambersburg PA
CBHW050916030726
47503CB00007BB/2323